ECHOES OF TOMORROW

Jenny Lykins

JOVE BOOKS, NEW YORK

ECHOES OF TOMORROW

A Jove Book / published by arrangement with
the author

PRINTING HISTORY
Jove edition / June 1997

The Putnam Berkley World Wide Web site address is
http://www.berkley.com

ISBN: 0-515-12079-0

A JOVE BOOK®
Jove Books are published by The Berkley Publishing Group,
200 Madison Avenue, New York, New York 10016.
JOVE and the "J" design are trademarks
belonging to Jove Publications, Inc.

PRINTED IN THE UNITED STATES OF AMERICA

10 9 8 7 6 5 4 3 2 1

For Richie, the *real* Reed
and
For Donna and Loretta

Prologue

HE'D NEVER MET her. He wasn't even sure she existed. But unless she appeared at the proverbial eleventh hour, the woman Reed Blackwell searched for would not be at this gathering.

His eyes missed nothing as his gaze scanned the cream of New Orleans aristocracy, watching dozens of his guests dance or chat in the elegant, glittering ballroom. He suffered a now familiar twinge of frustration.

No new faces looked back at him.

The scent of expensive perfumes swirled around him to mingle with snatches of conversations. Compliments about the "excellent host," flattering, insincere comments on someone's gown, and halfhearted threats to steal away his cook gained no more than a cursory nod from him. His eyes began to glaze over. He allowed himself that luxury for a few moments.

What he wouldn't give for a stimulating conversation with a woman. An intelligent woman.

The right woman.

He had planned this ball in hopes of finding a lady who stood apart from the crowd. A woman who struck him as a true individual with a mind of her own, as interested in all of life as these women seemed in fashion. But, to his disappointment, there seemed to be a complete absence of such a being in his social circle. Oh, most probably such a woman did, indeed, exist. But as the years passed, he despaired of ever finding her.

He blinked, then tried to force himself to refocus with a somewhat interested gaze.

It was no use. He'd had enough.

Summoning up an apologetic grin, he excused himself from the many elaborately clad guests surrounding him. With a sense of disappointment that he'd long ago learned to live with, he discreetly signaled to the orchestra leader for the final waltz.

Nell watched the master of Oak Vista become more and more restless. It was only a matter of time before he called an end to yet another disappointing search.

Drastic steps would have to be taken.

The wiry old housekeeper watched the man she'd raised from an infant swallow the full contents of a glass of champagne in one gulp. That action inspired her next move. An herbal tea would be the best medium for the voodoo spell she hoped would change Reed's life.

She'd watched through hooded eyes all evening while weaving her way among the pampered New Orleans planters, a silver tray of wineglasses balanced in her coffee-colored hands. As a servant she was all but invisible, her presence noted only when an emptied glass needed replacing. It served her purpose well, allowing her every vantage point to view her subject. The more she observed, the more convinced she was of what had to be done.

Four sets of French doors at the far end of the ballroom led to the garden. She melted into the shadows through one of them, into the dark, fragrant night on a mission to find the ingredients she would use in her spell.

Angeline Simon's heart fluttered while Reed made his way toward her. His head rose several inches above all others in the room, and the golden streaks of sun in his chestnut hair glistened in the candlelight. Even this far away she could see the brilliant blue eyes that seemed to have the disconcerting ability to look right into a person's soul. The width of his shoulders bespoke power, but she'd seen this man hold a slave's newborn babe as if it were his heir.

He was too good to let slip through her fingers.

She knew she was a perfectly gowned, perfectly coiffed china doll of a woman. Hadn't dozens of men just tonight declared her so? And Reed, to her delight, had claimed several dances on her dance card.

She took mental inventory as she waited. Her angelic expression was in place, with only a slightly helpless air about it. The fan of carved ivory swayed in languorous motion. She prepared to step into his arms with a practiced grace that should both impress him and make him feel protective toward her fragility.

Give a man what he wants and he'll give you everything he's got. That was Angeline's motto. And the man she wanted was Reed Blackwell. Rich, prosperous, and extremely handsome, Reed had everything a woman like Angeline could want.

Of course, she was willing to overlook the little eccentricities of his lifestyle. Not every woman would be

willing to accept the fact that he had systematically freed
all of his slaves—some nonsense about allowing them to
buy their freedom. Then not one of them had left Oak
Vista to stand on his own two feet. And the very thought
of Reed going to his darkies, even field hands, for advice
on how to better the crops and working conditions! He
should be grateful for her tolerance. After all, she was
the undisputed belle of New Orleans society.

Reed swept Angeline onto the ballroom floor, but the
fragile, angelic face she so expertly turned to him failed
to move him. He concentrated on making polite conversation until this dance was over, until he could bid his
guests farewell and climb the spiral, cantilevered staircase to his bedchamber. At least there he could sleep and
perhaps lose his disappointment over the evening. If he
had to wear this mask of a smile much longer, he believed his face would crack.

He wore his smile longer than anticipated. When he
informed Angeline that they were dancing the final
dance, she threw herself into a snit and began pouting in
earnest. This tactic was an age-old game played by the
women of his social circle, and normally he refused to
cooperate. But the absolute last thing he wanted was a
scene, only because it would prolong the evening. If he
didn't pacify her, he knew she would cause one, and in
such a way as to leave herself completely blameless.

"My dear Angeline, I shan't be budged in my resolve
to end this interminable evening, whether you intend to
carry on with your sulking or not." When Angeline's
sullen look turned into one of deepest hurt, Reed blew
out a long, exasperated breath and continued. "But I will
promise to collect you tomorrow and take you for a ride
along the bluffs."

She immediately bestowed upon him a brilliant smile

and reached up to peck his cheek, her golden ringlets bouncing with the movement. He'd known that offer would placate her. There seemed to be a status attached to riding along the bluffs with certain gentlemen. For reasons he could not fathom, he was one of them.

Ah, well. It would not hurt to exercise his horse tomorrow, and Angeline could be a charming companion when she wasn't scheming to get her way.

The last carriage crunched slowly down the drive before Reed turned and walked through the huge, mahogany front door. His heart took a stab of defeat as he mounted the sweeping stairs. Thirty-six years old, and all he asked was to have a woman to love and a family to care for. Why, when every other man around seemed to accomplish that feat with no effort at all, did he find it so difficult?

Who taught these women to be so all-fired frivolous? Try as he might, he could not develop even a hint of interest in one. Was he being overly critical? Was he expecting too much in wanting to see at least a modicum of intelligence shine through all that lace and frippery?

Not for the first time, he thought he may as well give up and accept the possibility of following in his Uncle Ian's bachelor footsteps.

Reed's shoulders slumped more with each step upward. When he rounded the top of the staircase, he dragged his arms from the sleeves of his meticulously tailored coat and headed straight for his suite of rooms.

As he slid off his waistcoat and removed his cravat, a gentle tap sounded at the door. "Come in," he mumbled, then began removing the gold and pearl studs from his shirt.

Nell bustled in with a small pot of tea and placed it on the bedside table. She rounded on Reed, put both hands on his back and propelled him to it, just as she had done hundreds of times in his youth.

"I's thinkin' you be wantin' some of my special tea afore you turns in," she said. Sympathy etched even deeper lines into her weathered face when she looked at him. It galled him to think he was the subject of anyone's pity, but he knew Nell thought only of him. "It'll help my poor baby sleep better," she said quietly as she patted his shoulder. She poured him a full cup of her brew and stood back, apparently waiting for him to sip the steaming tea and share any thoughts he might have on the evening.

He chose not to burden Nell with his depressing thoughts but grimaced at the vile smell of the tea, tossing it down in one gulp. The taste was never as bad as the smell, and he'd had to remind himself of that ever since he'd been a boy. He watched Nell move around the room, straightening his discarded jacket, opening the windows wider for a better breeze, lowering the mosquito netting. He poured a second cup and sat down on the counterpane as the tea cooled on the table. The bed felt heavenly, and he grinned at Nell.

"Your tea always does the trick, Nellie, my love," he teased. "I vow, I am ready to roll over here and sleep for a month!"

He flopped onto his side and feigned a loud snore, which only gained a snort from Nell. A quilt dropped unceremoniously atop his head—retaliation for his teasing. Just to antagonize her he stayed in that same position while she finished putting his room in order. At the muffled sound of the door opening and closing, he realized he was so tired he could barely raise his head from the pillow. After only one feeble attempt to rise, he gave up and succumbed to the weariness sweeping over him.

Chapter 1

ELISE GERARD'S BLOOD roared in her ears, but she concentrated on what had to be a hallucination going on in front of her.

It wasn't really a mist. She could see through it. But it became more dense, and the outline of a human shape began to form.

She'd stopped struggling with the last two buttons on the back of the antebellum gown and watched, wide-eyed with disbelief, at the transformation taking place on her bed.

A leather-clad calf materialized and dangled over the side of the bed. It seemed to be attached to the body-shaped mound of covers. A tanned, muscular, definitely masculine hand solidified on the pink paisley sheets and protruded from beneath the bed linens.

Elbows skyward, unable even to remove her fingers from the buttons at the back of her neck, she stood frozen. Blinking her eyes didn't clear the apparition from her vision. Neither did squinting or shaking her head.

Good grief! It looked for all the world like a man had just appeared under the covers of her unmade bed!

He heard the birds first. The chirping invaded his sleeping mind and prodded him gently awake. Then came the awareness of daylight beyond his closed eyelids and the fact that the quilt Nell had thrown over him the night before still covered his head. He must have been more exhausted than he'd realized. Had he ever slept through the night without so much as rolling over?

After grabbing the quilt and pulling it away from his face, he rolled to his back and released a huge yawn. He pried his eyes open and stretched mightily.

He stopped in midstretch.

Frozen at the foot of his bed stood a complete and total stranger. And a very beautiful one at that. With her arms stretched over and behind her head, she appeared to be in the final stages of buttoning her morning gown. The stranger stared at him with the oddest shade of green eyes he'd ever encountered.

Her eyes locked with his, eyes filled with shock and a considerable amount of terror. Several seconds elapsed while disbelief joined the terror, and then the stranger made a dive for a satchel on the dresser behind her. She whirled back around, holding a small leather canister with strange keys dangling from it. She held it at arm's length, pointed in his direction.

"Move one muscle and I'll hose you down," she

threatened, her strange, moss-colored eyes narrowed, her extended arm unwavering.

Up to this point Reed had not moved from sheer shock of waking to find a strange woman dressing in his bedchamber. But enough was enough, and he meant to get to the bottom of this. Beautiful or not, he refused to be ordered about. What did she think he was going to do, cower in a corner while she shook odd-looking keys in his face?

He flung the quilt aside, swung his legs over the side of the bed and prepared to escort the uninvited guest from his chambers. Before his feet hit the floor, a thin stream of liquid shot from the leather case and struck him directly in the face.

Pain such as he had never experienced in his life seared across his face. His eyes slammed shut and burned with the intensity of a flame on his flesh. He fell onto the Aubusson carpet, gasping for a breath that wouldn't come. His throat constricted, and he writhed in helpless agony. All that existed for him was the pain, the difficulty in breathing, the lack of control in his limbs.

An eternity passed; then, blessedly, an icy wet object fell across his face and hands. After several moments the smallest degree of control began to slip back into his body. With slow, jerking movements he pressed the wonderful, soothing cloth against his face. When he tried to remove the towel, the burning increased tenfold. Another towel fell onto his hands, and he scrambled to grab it and scrub the fire from his skin. Somewhere in his mind a small voice told him he must look like a groveling fool, but at that moment a cold cloth seemed like the most important thing in the world.

In gradual, almost imperceptible stages, the pain began to subside, and he regained control of his breathing. He drew the last cloth from his face and looked up to see the stranger standing a safe distance away, that damnable leather case still pointed at him.

"Who the hell are you, and how did you do that?" she yelled, her arm still unwavering.

Reed could not believe his ears.

"Who am *I*? And what do you mean, how did I do that? You are the one who did it, Madam! Or are you saying you did not try to blind me with that . . . that thing in your hands?"

The stranger's look darkened. She pushed the case closer, her voice menacing. "How did you appear on my bed while I stood there and watched it happen? And don't tell me you're David Copperfield."

Leather case or no leather case, Reed shot her a look that said she was mad.

"*Your* bed? Madam, this is my bed, and I'm not David anyone. My name is Reed Blackwell, and I own this plantation. Now suppose you tell me who you are and why you are in my bedroom half-clothed."

The stranger's eyebrows shot up with a surely-you-jest look in her eyes.

"Look, jerk," she stated, "this is my plantation. I'm Elise Gerard and my name is on all the papers, including the deed. I own everything on Oak Vista, lock, stock and barrel."

"I said my name is Reed, not Jerk, and if this is another practical joke instituted by the McNeely brothers, then you have all carried it to a very tiresome extreme. I would be more than pleased to pay you to go away. Name your price."

The strange woman stood there, anger and indecision warring on her face, the only sound in the room the metallic *ching* of keys dangling in her shaking hand.

"Get up," she ordered after several seconds. "You can

explain it to the police." She waved the leather case toward the bedchamber door.

Reed slowly got to his feet, deciding to play along. Arguing might get him another dose of that liquid fire in his face. Besides, all he need do was catch her off guard and disarm her.

He glanced around the room, looking for something with which to bind her hands, if need be, when he realized with a start that some things were very different. How had she changed the heavy draperies on all the windows? And the bed hangings and counterpane? Even some of the furniture had been rearranged. Where was his mother's hope chest?

Before he could look closer at the bedroom, his eyes fell on the open door to his dressing room. He stopped dead in his tracks.

What, in the name of all that was holy, had happened? There in his dressing room sat a strange, beige, porcelain-looking seat, with a rounded bottom on a pedestal. Along one wall sat a huge, oblong tub, big enough for two people to sit in, with gold knobs on one end. If he didn't know better, he'd think it was a bathing tub, but that monstrosity could never be taken out and emptied. Indeed, the thing looked to be a permanent fixture. A shelf made of marble ran along another wall. A bowl had been formed into it with the same kind of hole in the bottom and the same gold knobs on top. Around the mirror above the shelf were small, round globes, glowing like lanterns, but no flame lit them.

As he stared, rooted to the spot, the woman made a wide berth around him, reached past the door and hit a small knob on the wall. Every one of the glowing globes went out at exactly the same time.

Reed's gaze left the now dark globes and slid to the woman. He clenched his fists while his heart banged in his chest. Little hairs at the back of his neck rose to rasp against his shirt collar. He swallowed in a vain attempt to moisten his throat.

"What has happened to my home?"

The woman stared at him, a bewildered look mingling with the wariness in her eyes. Through his baffling haze of disbelief he thought for a moment her guard had slipped, but then she spoke.

"We're going downstairs, and we'll talk it over while we wait for the police. If you try anything I'll give you another face full of tear gas."

Was her threat tinged with confusion?

Reed fought jolts of alarm at all the changes as he and the woman walked the corridors of the home they both claimed. Most of his furniture remained there, but in different places. New paintings hung on the walls, and every now and then he passed an unidentifiable contraption.

The first was a small white panel on a wall with colored blinking lights and numbered buttons. The woman stopped and punched a few of the buttons. Reed had time only to make out one of the words on the panel: *Alarm*. She motioned for him to move on ahead of her, and he walked past more of those glowing globes and buttons on the walls.

He almost caressed the familiar staircase with relief until his eyes fell on yet another contraption sitting on a small table at the bottom of the stairs. This one was a small, black box with red, glowing numbers on the front that read 9:15. As he watched, the numbers changed to 9:16. While he wondered at the workings of this amazing contraption, his gaze drifted across the table and he again stopped dead in his tracks. For the first time in his life, his head spun and the room swirled around him.

There on the table next to the box sat an open appointment book. At the very top in bold, black letters was printed: *March 19, 1994*.

The woman, unprepared for his sudden stop, collided into him. She immediately jumped back up two steps and aimed the canister at Reed's face. Her posture relaxed when he failed to move.

"Why does this book say March 19, 1994?" he asked in a barely audible voice.

Only a heartbeat of silence elapsed before she answered.

"Because, Mr. Copperfield, I haven't had a chance this morning to change the page to the twentieth."

Reed turned his head toward her but his gaze remained on the calendar. In a shaky voice he asked, "Can you prove that it is 1994?"

For some reason, a gut feeling maybe, Elise believed this man truly needed proof. She was reasonably sure she wasn't dreaming all of this, but she had no other explanation for this morning's strange occurrences.

She couldn't deny what she'd seen. This man, this gorgeous man with the double-take face, had materialized on her bed like an eerie vapor while she'd struggled to button this ridiculous dress. At first she'd thought it was a trick of the morning light. The lumpy quilt that covered him looked like part of her unmade bed. But the translucent vapor solidified, and the lump rolled over and stretched. No, there had to be a logical explanation. She'd seen too many magic shows not to know the most astounding illusion was a fairly simple trick. But when he'd questioned the date, the hairs on the back of her neck stood on end. Her mind snapped back to the present situation.

"Proof? Proof. Yeah, sure. Proof. Let's see . . ." Elise's mind scanned possibilities. How much more proof do you need than a calendar? She snapped her fingers when an idea popped into her head. She darted the few feet to the front door, keeping the tear gas on him at all times, and scooped up a huge, rolled newspaper from the porch. With a triumphant smile she flicked the paper open. There, in bold print above the headlines detailing the latest presidential problems, was printed: *Sunday, March 20, 1994.*

While Reed absorbed this piece of evidence, Elise yanked out the drawer in the table beside them. She rummaged through it for a second, then fished out several coins.

"Let's see, 1965, '81, '77," she read aloud as she scanned the spare change she always threw in the drawer. "Wait. Wait. Here's a penny minted in 1993. Is that good enough? You know we're barely three months into '94, and this money's been here a while. If you need more proof I can get my billfold and see if I have . . ."

Her last word trailed off, and she snapped her mouth shut. This was insane. It was bad enough trying to prove what year it was. What was she doing, offering to get her billfold for a total stranger? One who'd dropped into her home uninvited and unexplained.

Reed just stared at her while long, silent seconds ticked by. His eyes never left hers when he reached into a pocket of his slacks and pulled something out of it.

He offered his hand to Elise, and when she opened her palm, he laid the object in it. His fingers were icy against her skin, but the warmth of his body lingered on the metal in her hand.

She tore her eyes from his. A twenty-dollar gold piece shone up at her from the center of her palm.

Elise's father had been an amateur coin collector. Without having to examine the coin much closer, she knew it had to have been minted in the late 1830s.

When she looked into Reed's face, her confusion and fear were mirrored in his eyes. But when she allowed a certain degree of skepticism to taint her features, his sky-blue eyes took on a sort of helpless look. He reached into his other pocket and pulled out a small piece of paper.

She hesitated before taking the folded scrap of paper and opening it. When she read the words, her skin crawled and chill bumps formed on her arms. The tear gas canister fell unheeded to clatter on the table.

In her hand she held a clipping from a financial page of an old New Orleans newspaper, dated March 18, 1844. The problem was, the paper didn't look old; no yellowing or dry, cracked edges. It looked as if it had been freshly printed. But Elise knew by instinct that this wasn't one of those novelty papers that can be printed at the mall for five dollars.

"That was given to me last night," Reed stated quietly, "by a friend who wanted to interest me in investing in one of the companies in that article." He pointed to one that gave details of several "up and coming businesses."

She continued to stare at the paper. She walked blindly into the parlor and dropped like a rock into the nearest chair.

The ridiculous gown she'd been struggling to get into earlier immediately flew up and whacked her in the face. She knocked the stupid hoopskirt back down and re-arranged her position to accommodate the skirt.

Thank God, she'd slipped on a pair of jogging shorts under her skirts. Embarrassed at her clumsiness, she shrugged and tried to act nonchalant.

"This is Azalea Festival time, and since my home is on the tour, the Chamber suggested we wear period costumes. I'm not used to wearing a birdcage."

Reed took a breath to reply when a loud knock jarred the front door.

"Damn." Elise catapulted out of the chair and rushed to the door.

At least fifteen people of all ages and sizes filtered into the foyer. Most of them came in gawking at the staircase and furniture.

"Hey, he really looks authentic." A rotund woman in shorts batted her eyes at Reed. "This is the first house we've come to that has a man dressed in costume. All he needs is a silver mint julep cup in his hand."

Elise chanced a glance at Reed. He stood there, looking thunderstruck, then turned on his heel and strode into the drawing room and out of sight.

Dear heavens, the woman was right. He looked as if he'd just stepped out of the nineteenth century.

"Excuse me, everyone. Excuse me," Elise shouted. "I'm sorry, but this house will have to be taken off the tour for today. We have a problem, you see. A, uh . . . an illness that needs to be quarantined. The measles. And I'm sure none of you wants to be exposed. I assure you your money for the tour of this home will be refunded. Just see your tour guide. Thank you." Elise herded everyone out the door and apologized again as they left. She stuck her head out for a few words with the tour guide, then shut and locked the door.

When she turned to dash back to Reed in the drawing room, she was brought up short. The day was getting worse by the minute.

At the foot of the staircase, leaning against the polished banister, stood someone she had hoped she'd never see again.

Her first instinct was to kill him.

"Jeffrey, get out." Her calm voice belied what she really felt inside.

The trim, blond, unwanted visitor stared at her with cocky gray eyes while he made himself more comfortable against the newel post.

"I said get out."

"Now, Elise, you don't really mean that. I think you and I should talk. I've always said we could work things out." Jeffrey pushed himself away from the banister and took a step toward her.

Rage and hate swelled inside her chest as she watched the tall, arrogant man swagger in her direction. She knew if he came any closer, she would claw the carefully groomed stubble from his cheeks.

"We have nothing to talk about. There is nothing to work out. You make me sick, and if you don't get the hell out of here, I'm calling the police."

When Elise picked up the phone on the entry table, Jeffrey grabbed it out of her hand.

"You're not calling anyone, and I'm not going anywhere until we've had a chance to talk. Besides," he said, obviously thinking he was witty, "I paid good money to get in here." He waved a pink pilgrimage ticket in her face.

Just as Elise swung her arm away and broke Jeffrey's hold, there was a tap on his shoulder from behind. When he whirled around at this unexpected intrusion, he was faced with a glaring Reed towering several inches over him.

"I believe the lady has sufficiently expressed her displeasure at your presence." Reed maintained an air of civility while managing to be threatening at the same time.

"Who the hell are you?" Jeffrey shouted, looking around, as if expecting people to jump from behind the furniture.

"I am your escort to the front door," Reed said with a deceptive smile. He grabbed Jeff's shirt collar and propelled him to the door. Unlocking it and swinging it wide, he sent Jeff shooting onto the veranda to stumble down several steps. Without waiting to make sure he would leave, Reed turned and shut the door.

"I hope I did the correct thing in showing your friend out," he said with a quirked eyebrow.

Elise forced her insides to calm and took several deep breaths.

"Yes. Yes, and thank you. He's not a friend, but I can't seem to make him understand that. He shows up in my life every now and then, but this is the first time he's ever come back here to my home."

She couldn't believe her sense of gratitude to this man. He had stepped in and handled Jeff for her, definitely not what she'd expected. Actually, she'd come to never expect chivalry from any man.

Elise could see through the window that Jeffrey had gotten into his cherry red Corvette, the latest toy in a long string of them, and was tearing down the avenue of oaks. She tried to push his intrusion from her mind. She had more important things to think about right now.

She turned a curious eye to Reed.

"Why did you storm out of here when the tourists arrived? You looked ready to swallow your tongue."

To her relief, Reed seemed to dismiss the incident with Jeffrey.

"What kind of a place is this 1994? Do people make a habit of visiting in a state of undress?"

Elise started to ask him who he'd seen undressed when realization struck her. All of the men in that group had been wearing shorts and sleeveless or short-sleeved shirts. Most of the women had on similar attire. She recalled one woman in particular who had been wearing a cropped top that exposed her torso, and shorts so tight she nearly exposed her derriere—a very flabby torso and derriere.

She couldn't explain why, but her belief in his story just bumped up a notch. She didn't even question her reaction.

"I'm sorry, Mr. . . . Blackwell, is it? Not everyone dresses like those people, but most of us do here in the South during the summer. You have to admit, their attire has to be a lot more comfortable than this ridiculous getup I'm wearing. Geez, no wonder women fainted right and left back then. And I'm not even wearing a corset." Elise shook the folds of her dress to illustrate the yards of heat-creating fabric.

"But you are not dressed in such a fashion," Reed pointed out to her, his look a mixture of outrage and bewilderment.

"Of course. That's what I was telling you when they knocked. The Chamber of Commerce asked us to dress as they did in the 1800s. You know, antebellum, pre–Civil War. It makes for a lot more atmosphere."

"Pre–Civil War? What Civil War?"

Suddenly Elise remembered the date of the newspaper clipping. 1844. Lord, he had no idea what his country was going to go through. More men would die in that war than all the other wars the United States fought combined. This was a can of worms she didn't want to open right now.

Am I crazy? she wondered. *I'm already assuming this man is from the past.* She really did have to get a grip. Cutting him off before he could ask more questions, she jumped up and headed for the kitchen.

"We have a lot to talk about, and we both have a lot of questions. Why don't we go sit down, and I'll fix us a drink."

"You've decided not to send for the constable?"

Elise realized she felt no threat from this man. Strange, but she wasn't afraid of having him here in her home with no one else around to protect her. Under normal circumstances she would be extremely cautious, a woman alone, knowing the threats and dangers that face women every day in the nineties. But against all training, all common sense, and all logic, she let her guard down around this stranger.

Chapter 2

REED TRIED DESPERATELY to collect his thoughts
and calm his emotions as he watched the clumsy woman
bang her way around a very strange room she called the
kitchen. Not like any kitchen he had ever seen, it was
filled with objects whose function he couldn't begin to
guess. A clear pitcher sitting on a pedestal with buttons,
a silver box with two slots on top, a large metal box with
a door on the front and several buttons beside the door.
The people of the future must have a fetish for buttons.

Elise shocked him again with her language when she
let out another "Damn!" She had turned and gotten her
hoopskirt tangled between a chair and the cabinet.

Doing a little side step to catch her balance, she
grabbed a handful of fabric and yanked the dress free.
The hoopskirt clanged back and forth against her legs

like a giant bell. Reed stifled a chuckle. She looked like a complete idiot, and a graceless one at that.

She started to giggle, and as she caught Reed's look of amused disbelief, she giggled harder. When he muffled a snicker with his fist, she exploded in laughter, doubling over and laughing until she had to wipe her eyes. Reed finally gave over to impulse and joined in, their mingled laughter resounding through the kitchen. She seemed to be making a valiant effort to bring herself under control, and after a thorough wiping of eyes, she managed to present a straight face.

"Oh! Oh my!" she breathed between giggles. "I've got to get out of this thing before I destroy something. I'll be right back."

She grabbed the skirt, scrunched it into her body and made a dash out the door toward the stairway. He stared at her retreating figure and caught a healthy glimpse of bare calf, but he hardly noticed. On her feet were the ugliest shoes he'd ever seen. Huge, white leather things with bright pink strings and the word REEBOK printed on the side.

Once upstairs, Elise took the time to try and make sense of the morning's events. She would have liked to believe this was all a very strange dream, but she knew there wouldn't be any waking up from this one.

There seemed to be no rational explanation and no arguing with the only irrational explanation she had. She'd stood at the foot of her bed and watched the man who now sat downstairs in her kitchen materialize on her bed. He had handed her an old, gold coin, and he'd shown her a fresh newspaper clipping from one hundred and fifty years ago. Neither of those, of course, proved anything, but she kept remembering his reactions to everything that was modern: her bathroom, the telephone, the calendar's date, the way the tourists were dressed, and his awe and confusion as he looked around the kitchen. These were all either totally genuine, or this guy deserved an Academy Award.

His clothes were also convincing. They were the real thing unless he had access to a great costume department. His trousers were skintight, with no zipper, but a buckle at the back of his waistband. His shirt was a starched, snowy linen with a winged collar. There were no pockets on the shirt, and it was definitely not the fitted look all the yuppies went for. His boots came to the knee and were made of fine, soft leather, polished to a high sheen.

Even his speech patterns were convincing. His accent was as thick as New Orleans air in July, and she couldn't remember even one of her college professors speaking so formally.

She took advantage of the moments she had alone. She rushed over to the bed and threw back the covers, searched the sheets, climbed onto the mattress and felt along the canopy and hangings, looking for . . . what? She didn't know. She just knew she needed to look for something that could explain her seeing a man appear in her bed.

As she'd suspected, she found nothing. But her security alarm had been on. How could he have gotten in without setting it off? She kept the alarm on at all times. The only reason she'd turned it off this morning after he appeared was because she thought the police would be coming.

Knowing she had no real proof that this man was from the past, she found herself unable to accept any other explanation for his presence. Besides, several times in her career as a pilot she had seen unexplainable "things" sharing the sky with her. She knew there were things

constantly happening out there beyond man's compre-
hension. Time travel or UFOs—which was more unbelievable?

While Elise changed her clothing, Reed tried to make
sense of what was happening to him. The last sane thing
he remembered was going to his room, wanting nothing
more than to go to sleep, then Nell bringing him a cup of
her herbal tea.

He couldn't logically believe that he had just fallen
asleep to wake in the year 1994, but he also knew he was
wide awake now, and this was definitely not the day
after his ball.

With all the evidence around him, he knew he was in
the future, but why and how he got there was something
his mind couldn't begin to explain. Could Elise, or
someone else in the future, have brought him here? And
if they did, could they send him back? The first pangs of
panic started to rise in him and he forced himself to remain calm. Panic would serve no purpose.

Several minutes of mulling over the facts, roaming
around and looking at all the evidence got him nowhere
in his mental investigations. Anything his gaze fell upon
that looked even remotely familiar—the grandfather
clock, the dining room table, his mother's tea caddy—
also had a patina of age that he couldn't explain.

The sound of Elise bounding down the stairs interrupted his thoughts. She appeared in the doorway, her
shoulder-length, golden-brown hair bouncing as she
strode into the dining room. Her apology for taking so
long sounded halfhearted to his ears.

Reed took one look at her and immediately fixed his
eyes somewhere above her head.

"I see you meant it when you said everyone dresses in

that manner here." He stared at the carved molding along the ceiling above her.

His reaction to her state of undress wasn't all outrage. He hoped fervently that the side effect wasn't apparent, but he casually stepped behind a chair, just in case.

"Yeah. Hey! You might as well get used to it because this is almost a summer uniform down here. Come on, you're allowed to look at me. There's nothing wrong with the way I'm dressed. Walking shorts and a T-shirt are hardly shocking. Actually this is pretty conservative."

Reed pulled his eyes toward her, but had trouble getting them to actually land on her. He looked at everything around before finally looking her straight in the eyes.

He was no prude; one could even say he was well acquainted with women. But he was having a problem now. He'd never come across a woman who showed so much flesh, acted as if it was perfectly natural, and wasn't doing it for money. The occasional flash of leg he'd seen belonging to a respectable woman was always followed by a hasty settling of the skirts and a becoming blush. Whether the glimpse and blush were innocent or contrived, it was never blatant.

And the fact that all this exposed flesh belonged to an extremely attractive creature was unnerving, to say the very least.

"There. See? Not so bad, huh? You should see what I wear at the beach."

Good heavens, could it possibly be less?

Ignoring Reed's confused look, Elise spun around and started running water into the squat glass pitcher from the pedestal.

"Would you like tea or coffee?" She turned to catch his answer and almost bumped noses with him.

He had moved so close, his head hovered near her shoulders, his gaze glued to the sink. He forced out the word "tea," then reached over and pushed up the silver lever. Water gushed forth into the sink and disappeared down a drain.

His hopes of returning home disappeared with it.

Elise found herself mesmerized with his reactions to everything new. All the things in her life, necessities to her, were luxuries beyond his imagination. His genuine awe made her see things in a whole new way. Excitement pulsed through her as she realized she could be the one to show this man what his world would turn into.

While the tea brewed, she emptied the refrigerator of anything resembling breakfast—Danish and croissants, butter, jelly, and honey—and set them on the table. When she glanced up she saw him investigating the refrigerator, opening and closing the door. He stuck his hand in the freezer side, then the refrigerator side. She smiled to herself and wondered how he would react to airplanes . . . and the fact that she flew them for a living.

The two of them sat together at the table, buttering croissants and feeling uncomfortable. The *ching* of the silverware against their china sounded loud in the awkward silence.

"So. Reed. Tell me about yourself. Maybe we can find a clue as to how you got here."

"You believe I am not from this time?" he asked, sounding shocked. "I must tell you I am having difficulty myself coming to terms with the events of this morning."

"I don't know what to believe," Elise answered with a confused shake of her head. "There's no other logical explanation to what I saw and why you're here, not that saying you're from the past is a logical explanation. But

I know I saw you materialize out of nowhere on my bed. If nothing else, that goes a long way in convincing me."

Reed breathed a long sigh and relaxed his body for a moment. He took a deep breath before starting his story. As he spoke, Elise listened in awe. She settled back in her chair and got comfortable, propping her ankle on the opposite knee. She let her foot bob up and down and draped one arm over the back of the chair. Reed's eyes widened, then he glanced away from her as he hesitated with his story. He rambled for a moment as if trying to collect himself.

He virtually started at the beginning, with the death of his parents from an outbreak of yellow fever when he was three years old. His two older sisters had also died during the outbreak, and he credited Nell, his housekeeper who was then his mammy, with saving his life. She'd locked herself in the sickroom with him and stayed up several days and nights in a row until the worst had passed.

"The family solicitors tracked down a distant cousin of my father's and requested that he come and run the plantation until I came of age. Uncle Ian, as I called him, was a fair man, but he had never been married and never had children. He did not cherish the prospect of raising a child but came out of a sense of duty. From sheer lack of his attention I learned early on to find the affection I craved with Nell and the other household staff. Shortly before my eighteenth birthday, Uncle Ian and I had a serious argument. He decided it was best he return to England. He confided to me before he left that he had been extremely homesick for several years. He had put enough money back to buy himself a farm and live quietly on it, which was all he had ever wanted in life."

Reed ended with telling about the ball, his disappointment at not finding a woman who could hold his interest, and going to bed with a cup of herbal tea to sleep and forget his troubles.

"The next thing I remember, I was watching you dress."

Elise uncrossed her legs and propped her forearms on the edge of the table. She went over the information, mentally scanning it for any hint of an answer.

"So you're not married, and you don't have a girl-friend back home that might be wondering where you are?"

Reed shook his head. Elise was inordinately pleased about that answer. After all, the man across the table from her was not hard to look at. The sun-kissed brown hair, soul-searching blue eyes, dark complexion and chiseled jaw all added up to one devastating picture. His hair was a shade long and had never seen the fifty-dollar haircut so many of the men she went out with sported; yet it still seemed to have a style of its own. Just a touch of natural curl gave it life, and as he nervously ran his fingers through it from forehead to crown, it sprang back and fell into place flawlessly.

She wanted to reach over and touch it.

"No," he answered with resignation. "I have never found a woman who could capture my interest, and if I am going to spend my life with someone, we should at least find each other interesting. Do you not agree?"

"I couldn't agree more." Elise leaned back again, enjoying the view from across the table. "From everything you've told me about yourself, Reed, there must be some clue as to your presence here. We just have to put our heads together and see if we can ferret it out."

They spent the rest of the morning and a big part of the afternoon going over and over the facts. As the hours slipped by, Elise made herself comfortable in various ways, from propping her feet on the table edge and tilting back on two legs of the chair to flipping the chair around and straddling it. Each time she settled into a new position, Reed seemed to lose his train of thought.

Elise delved into every aspect of his life. She asked about his business associates, his servants, and his daily routine. She questioned him about the house, what it looked like and how it was run. She even asked about the furniture and outbuildings.

When the grandfather clock in the hallway chimed three o'clock, she dropped her feet from the edge of the table and her chair came to rest on all fours. Propelled out of her seat, she patted her midsection and stated that she was starving to death.

She snatched up her purse and keys. "How about we go grab some lunch? My last trip was eight days to Europe, so there's not much left in the house that's edible."

This statement made no sense whatsoever to Reed, but just as he opened his mouth to question her she swung around and gave him a thorough once-over.

"Yeah, you'll do," she said with a nod, punched a few buttons on a panel on the wall, then headed out the kitchen door.

His previous question forgotten, Reed froze, stunned, over this latest announcement.

"Do? I'll do?"

His confidence slipped a notch or two. He tried to bolster it by reminding himself that every other woman he'd ever met thought he would do better than just "do." Why, he could even say . . .

"Oh. I meant your clothes will do. They won't draw attention to us. It just looks like a riding outfit." Elise's head disappeared again out the back door and he heard a faint "Geez, you gotta stroke those egos no matter what time they live in."

He didn't stop to figure out where they were going to "grab lunch" outside, or what an "ego" was. He just pushed his way out the back door and pulled it shut behind him with only a little irritation when Elise shouted back that order. It occurred to him she would make a wonderful overseer. She certainly had the gift of giving orders.

"I will be with you . . . momentarily," Reed called as his eyes scanned the immediate vicinity.

His steps slowed, and he turned in a circle just as Elise swung around to wait for him.

"Is there a problem?"

"Uh, no," he said. "Just tell me where you've moved the privy."

"Oh. Yeah." Elise whacked her forehead with the heel of her hand. She motioned for him to follow, then headed back to the house.

Still deep in thought about his latest modern experience, Reed caught up with her at the corner of the house and followed her to a rather elaborate storage shed. He was just telling himself that he should make the best of his situation when he was brought up short by the most unusual thing he'd seen thus far.

There, in the middle of the shed, surrounded by countless, nameless objects and machines, sat a big, silvery gray "thing." It resembled nothing he had ever seen. He stood there and stared at it—something that was becoming altogether too common for him. Elise walked over and actually opened a door on it.

This "thing" seemed to have a door on the other side as well. Windows surrounded it, and a silver cat at the front end was frozen in a leaping pose. He walked around the thing. Words and letters . . . Jaguar, XJS, V12, and a metal plate on the back that said FLYGIRL with "Louisiana" printed in small letters held no meaning for him.

Elise dropped into a leather seat, reached across and pushed the opposite door open.

"Hop in," she said, while she adjusted a small mirror on the glass in front of her.

He hesitantly folded himself into the opening and tried to settle himself so his head didn't hit the roof. "What in the world is this thing?" he choked out.

"Oh, this is a car, or automobile. It's replaced the horse and carriage. There are hundreds of different kinds now, but of course, this one's my favorite. I think you'll find this mode of transportation much more convenient than what you're used to." He could have sworn he heard a hint of a smile in her voice.

Reed took in the interior of the thing, tried but failed to figure out a single feature.

Elise reached over him and pulled a strap across his lap as another slid around the window and crossed his chest. A heady fragrance engulfed him as she leaned nearer, and he wasn't sure if his sudden discomfort was from her enticing scent or from being physically restrained.

"Er, excuse me, Miss Gerard, but . . ."

"Elise."

"Er, Elise. I beg your pardon, but is it necessary for these . . . straps . . . that is, they are rather confining."

"They're supposed to be. Nothing to worry about, though. See? They come loose whenever you want them to."

Elise demonstrated how to release the straps for him, then clicked them back into place. "Besides, it's the law."

Before the question left his lips, she turned a strange key in a slit and the "thing" roared to life. She touched yet another button affixed to a flap over the window and chuckled when Reed jumped as the door of the shed rose in front of them. Throat dry with apprehension, he watched her reach down and grab a T-shaped stick between them. She yanked it back. Her foot pushed a lever on the floor at the same time. Reed was thrown back against his seat, and butterflies took flight in his stomach as the "thing" shot forward like a bullet from a gun.

Elise smiled, thoroughly enjoying his reaction and pleased beyond reason that he hadn't disappointed her. She was looking forward to this little ride, maybe more than she'd ever looked forward to anything, including her first ride in a T-38.

She watched the road while they cruised at a mild forty miles an hour and took a few minutes to explain what little she knew about how a car runs. After a few seconds of silence she stole a glance at her passenger. His hands clasped his thighs, white knuckles glared up at her, and his face held a look of impending doom.

Unable to resist the long, empty stretch of road in front of her, Elise floored the Jag. She felt the immediate acceleration to a smooth, unbelievable speed.

After a few seconds, she took pity on her guest from the past and slowed down to her original pace. She suffered a little remorse at seeing him deathly white, sweat rolling from his temples, his fingers embedded in his thighs.

"Oh, Reed, I'm sorry." Her voice quivered on the edge of a giggle.

Reed looked at her as if she'd sprouted horns. He couldn't seem to make his mouth move. He just sat there, looking half bewildered, half horrified.

His expression finally sobered her. She reassured him that she was, indeed, sorry for not warning him of what to expect. She swore that, all except for a few seconds, the speed at which they'd traveled was completely normal and safe for this time period.

Several seconds of silence ticked by after she stopped talking. Concern replaced her amusement when he failed to react. She eased the car off the road and turned in her seat to face him.

Reed peeled his right hand off of his thigh and with slow deliberation, reached out and grabbed the steering wheel.

She flinched but stopped herself from backing away. She stared at him, trying to gauge what his next reaction would be. A tongue lashing wouldn't surprise her.

"That was the most . . ." Reed started out in a low, controlled voice, "the most . . . unbelievably. . . . exhilarating experience I have ever had!"

He rushed on. In his excitement, he had trouble finishing a complete sentence, but he had no trouble asking if they could do it again.

Her concern fell away, and she beamed at him. How amazing that this man from the past had been terrified and shown it. Instead of being furious with her, as his counterparts of the present would be, he had found the experience exhilarating and was thanking her for it.

She threw the car into drive. With a stab to the controls, the windows and sunroof opened, and she hit the road with the wind whipping around them as they went, gravel spraying behind them.

When the car sped away, his excited voice could be heard above the roar of the engine. "Can you teach me to do this?"

Chapter 3

Elise decided during the drive that it would be wise to keep Reed away from modern-day restaurants until he had more time to adapt. She figured he'd had enough to digest for the day, but without thinking she pulled her cellular phone out of her purse and ordered a large pizza to go. By the time she tucked the phone away, Reed had that now familiar stare on his face.

She sighed and slumped in her seat at her own stupidity. The concept of telephones as sort of "telegraphs with voices" didn't go over too well, so she promised a demonstration when they got home.

By the time they reached the restaurant, the pizza was hot and ready to go. She pulled to the drive-up window, gave her name, and asked for a cold six-pack of Diet Coke and a bag of chips. Reed held the huge flat box while she stacked the Cokes and chips on top. In seconds they were back on the highway.

They cruised along the river road for a while. Elise chose a small park that was usually deserted as the site for their lunch.

Tires crunched on the gravel as they eased into the parking lot and came to a stop several yards from a picnic table situated under a huge live oak. Spanish moss dripped from the branches, and dappled sunlight fell in patches all around.

She climbed out of the car and ran around to the other side to help Reed unfold his body. A slight tug-of-war with the pizza box ensued when he insisted he could manage. But with one leg out of the car, the other with his knee nearly to his chin, and doing a balancing act with the pizza, he finally gave in and handed the food over so he could grab the roof of the car and pull himself out. He stood in the wedge of the door and studied the area he had just vacated, as if trying to figure out how he had gotten his entire body in there to begin with.

Elise opened the pizza box and pulled two cans of soda from the six-pack. She settled herself on the top of a table overlooking the river and patted the area next to her. Reed gave a considering eye to her choice of seats, then lowered his body to straddle the bench instead.

The masculine position shot little jolts of electricity through her as she admired her lunch partner. She could picture him astride a spirited horse, planter's hat pulled low over his eyes to shield him from the sun, while he roamed the fields of his plantation. His leather boots would stretch over those powerful calves to his knees and the billowing shirt would be open at the collar . . .

"This smells wonderful. What type of food is it?" Reed's face was the picture of ecstasy.

She jerked herself back to the present and shook her head. "It's called pizza. It's sort of an Italian meat, vegetable and cheese pie. It's probably the most popular food in America."

She pulled off a slice, stringing out the cheese until it snapped, then offered it to him. He held the wedge in the palms of his hands, his brows dipped into a questioning *V.*

"Oh. You eat it like this." She grinned and strung out a slice for herself. "It's very important now," she instructed with a straight face, "you always eat the pointed end first. Otherwise it doesn't taste the same."

Reed took a bite with one eyebrow quirked, as if trying to figure out how that could possibly make it taste different.

His face changed to a look of pleasant surprise. "This is absolutely delicious," he declared. "What did you say the ingredients are?"

Elise popped the tops of two sodas and handed him one. "Oh, pepperoni, onions, tomatoes, olives, green peppers." She stopped and took a long drink from her Coke and went on. "Of course, you can put anything you want . . ."

Reed had eyed the opening in his Coke can, then imitated Elise by tipping it up and taking several long swallows. A mist of soda came spraying out of his mouth in a strangled cough. He jumped to his feet, gasping for breath.

Elise sat frozen.

Reed croaked, "What in the name of God is this? For God's sake, Elise, the stuff came out my nose!"

Oh no! She felt those giggles rising up again, and she knew she couldn't control them. She bit the inside of her mouth and bowed her head, biting harder as the urge grew. Her shoulders started to shake, and the harder she bit, the harder she wanted to giggle. She gave up the effort and let it out, lying back on the table and holding her side, laughing until it was out of her system.

"Oh, Reed!" she gasped, "I never dreamed! I guess it may take some getting used to, at that. It's a carbonated drink. They use carbonated water. That's what caused the . . . well, didn't you drink champagne back in your time?"

Reed had never been so embarrassed in his life.

"Of course I have had champagne, but not in a series of large gulps!" He didn't bother to consider his downing a full glass the night before. He looked down at Elise, still reclining on the tabletop. One foot dangled over the side from her fit of laughter. He was struck, not for the first time, by how attractive she was. She smiled up at him, her golden-brown hair tousled, half of it swaying off the table. Velvety green eyes danced with mischief, and he felt even more embarrassed by his coughing fit.

"Besides, you cannot convince me that you compare this beverage to champagne!"

"Oh, no! No way. Just that they're both carbonated, or bubbly. I've never thought about it, but I guess there *is* sort of a knack to drinking soda without having that happen." This last comment ended with a suspicious quiver in her voice as Elise elbowed her way to a sitting position.

"The only other time I've had a reaction like that was when I downed my first shot of whiskey," Reed grumbled, trying to reestablish a semblance of masculinity instead of village idiocy.

"You know," she began, clearly attempting to placate him, "I'm really amazed at how well you've dealt with your situation. I can't begin to imagine what I'd do if I found myself even a few years in the future, not to mention one that doesn't resemble what I came from. I'd probably be a basket case, pinging off the walls. But you're . . . well, you're handling it really well." She shook her head and gazed up at him with a look of wonder.

Reed was glad to know he wasn't "pinging," whatever that was. He felt a little better and reached over to snap off another slice of pizza, which was easier to do now that it had cooled a bit. He took a few bites before speaking.

"From what I have witnessed of you, Elise, you would arrive at any place in time and settle in without help from anyone. I am just thankful I have you to help me through this, and most importantly, that you believe me. I am trying desperately to believe it myself."

The two sat quietly for a while and watched the river as they finished off the pizza. Elise tore bits of crust and tossed them to some cardinals nearby. He'd never before been with a woman who was so dominant and in control, and the whole concept made him uncomfortable. Yet he also realized that he felt an admiration and attraction for this woman he'd known only a few hours—an admiration he'd never felt for any other woman. He was surprised that the independence she exhibited made her more attractive to him, not less. Yes, he thought, the independence, the green eyes, the sense of humor and . . . those long, smooth legs. He felt as though something had just clicked into place in his life.

A dull roar started down river and built. Reed rose with a look of concern.

Elise groaned and mumbled that there was just no getting away from exposing him to the modern world.

She yanked on his sleeve for attention and managed to say, "It's okay," just as a strange boat came roaring around a bend, pulling behind it a man standing on what appeared to be boards. As the boat drew even with the park, the driver cut the engine and the man went down. He swam to the boat and handed up the boards, then hoisted himself up a ladder.

Elise and Reed watched the boat chug its way to the park. When it stopped at the edge of the river, two couples came out from beneath the canopy of the boat and pulled out a picnic basket.

"GOOD LORD!" Reed exploded. Elise grabbed his arm, snatched up the sodas and chips, and threw the pizza box into a trash can.

"Let's go, Reed. I'll tell you about it on the way to the car. Those are called string bikinis. It's what women wear when they want to get a tan."

The drive back to the plantation was relatively uneventful, considering all the possibilities. Elise was amused at how Reed took great interest in the different types of cars they encountered. He nearly broke his neck at one point when he jerked around to watch a motorcycle speed past them in the opposite direction. This was followed by a flood of questions—how does it stay upright, why did the driver have a huge, round helmet over his head, when was it invented?

After a while the conversation lulled and Elise slid a tape into the tape deck. Strains of the "Emperor's Waltz" filtered through the car. Reed leaned his head back onto the pale leather seat and let out a long sigh.

"Finally, something familiar." He sighed again, and Elise watched him relax for the first time. "It's nice to know that at least the music hasn't changed."

She opened her mouth to tell him that music had indeed changed but decided he could wait a while for the shock of rock music, blues, and jazz. She wouldn't even try to explain rap. He'd had enough to absorb for one day.

She noticed in her musings that Reed had taken the tape deck and music in stride, without the look of incredulity so many other things had garnered. He really was very resilient.

As the music moved into her favorite part of the waltz she scrunched down into the seat and leaned her head against the headrest. She indulged in the same daydream she always did at this point.

"Do you know what I've always wanted to do?" she questioned wistfully, almost to herself. "I've always dreamed of being in a huge ballroom, wearing a long, flowing gown and waltzing around and around with a Patrick Swayze type, intoxicated by the music, my partner, the moment . . ."

Reed remained quiet, and Elise continued to enjoy the little scenario playing out in her mind. She ached a little for what would be, to her, the perfect romantic evening. It didn't even cross her mind that she had opened up more of herself to this man than to any other man in her life. She had never before shared a fantasy.

Reed wondered at her wistful look. He couldn't believe she'd never experienced a ball. After all, Oak Vista boasted a wonderful ballroom. But he was more curious about what this Patrick person meant to her. Would he prevent her from assisting him? Was he someone special to her?

The Jag, as Elise called it, rolled through the avenue of oaks and slipped under the rising shed door at the back of the house.

As they climbed out of the car and headed for the house, he wondered at why her simple statement had stirred such foreign feelings in him. He didn't have time to explore the cause, though. As they approached the back door, a strange, intermittent ringing sounded from within. Elise broke into a run, fumbling for house keys along the way. Alarmed, Reed ran behind her. She rammed the key into the lock, turned the knob, and they both stumbled into the kitchen just as the ringing blasted again.

Elise ran to one of those strange boxes and picked up the top half, put it to her ear and said "Hello." A choppy conversation with it followed while she dropped her keys into her reticule and sank to the kitchen chair.

"Oh, no. How did you do that?" She paused. "Yeah, that'll do it everytime." Another pause. "Don't worry, Lettie. I certainly don't expect you to clean a house with a broken arm. You just . . . yes . . . uh-huh . . . well, you take as long as you need. I don't create so much clutter that I can't handle it myself for a few weeks. Okay . . . you take care. Let me know if you need anything. Okay. Bye-bye."

No sooner had she fit the box together than the thing let out another ring. Another disjointed speech ensued. After a few minutes she seemed to decline some kind of offer, then replaced the top of the box back in position.

When she turned back to Reed, she bestowed a hesitant smile. First, she explained that the phone was similar to what she'd used to call in the pizza. Then she said, "That was a friend of mine, wanting to get together for dinner, but I told him I had a houseguest and we'd have to make it another time."

Him? She told "him?" Was it this Patrick person?

He felt a stab of . . . what? Jealousy? Fear at her leaving? He wasn't sure. He'd never had occasion to experience either of those emotions before, and he wasn't comfortable with how they made him feel. Indeed, he was surprised at himself for feeling them at all.

An awkward silence descended between them, then Elise did a little drumroll on the counter with her hands.

"Hey, I bet you'd like to freshen up. Would you like a shower or bath, maybe a shave? I've got extra razors, and I think I've got some clothes here that might fit."

"If it would not inconvenience you too much," he said. Anything to get this awkward moment over with.

Elise showed Reed to the guest bath. She explained the use of each facility, except those she'd given a red-faced explanation to earlier, then showed him how to turn on both the shower and bath and adjust the temperature. She pulled out huge fluffy mauve towels and a disposable razor and shaving cream, both of which called for a brief lesson in their uses. She even found a new toothbrush and toothpaste, prompting more instructions with the toothpaste pump.

"I'll see if I can round up those clothes while you're in here. They'll be on the bed outside the door."

Reed nodded. He looked anxious to try out these new gadgets, so Elise backed out the door and closed it behind her.

While Reed enjoyed his very first steaming shower, Elise dug through a seldom used drawer and came up with an old pair of jeans, oxford shirt, socks, and underwear. She was sure Don wouldn't mind Reed using them. Her close friends, Don and Jan Sevier, kept a change of clothes at her house. One or both of them would come over and exercise her horses if she was out of town for any length of time. They also made sure Alan, a neighborhood kid, kept the horses fed and watered.

She waited for Reed across the hall in her favorite room. Her den was the only completely modern room in the house, aside from the kitchen and the upstairs bath.

She had tried to maintain the integrity of the antebellum home throughout the rest of the house. Her den was where she came to get away from the nineteenth century.

She'd chosen creamy, wall-to-wall carpet. The walls were forest green, the furniture and accents shades of cream and green. Her decorator had said she'd had nightmares over this room, but it was exactly as Elise wanted it.

Deep in thought, she didn't hear Reed step out of the bedroom and into the doorway of the den. She was unprepared for the jolt of pure, scorching lust that flashed through her when she looked up to see him watching her. Lord, it'd been a long time since a man had had *that* affect on her. Taking a deep breath, she schooled her features to something besides those of a drooling idiot.

There he stood, framed in the doorway. The clean smell of shaving cream and soap drifted to her. His damp hair had been given a token combing but curled with a mind of its own. Don's jeans fit him as though tailormade, but the oxford shirt pulled across his shoulders, so the top few buttons had to be left open. The *V* created there exposed dark curls against a tanned chest and a collarbone so well-defined Elise had to fight the urge to trace the outline with her fingertips. She continued to stare, not caring if she looked like a starving woman within reach of a banquet.

Reed braced both hands on the frame of the door and leaned forward. The shirt stretched tight across his broad chest and taut stomach. He smiled with a look of ecstasy.

"That," he declared with enthusiasm, "was one of the most relaxing experiences I have ever enjoyed. Folding myself into a hip bath never felt nearly so wonderful."

He let go of the door frame and ambled into the room. The blood raced through her veins when he looked at her, a soft smile on his lips.

He began to roam around the room, taking in all the modern conveniences. Elise hopped up from the couch and followed him as he circled the room. She began to explain what she could about all these "newfangled inventions," breathing deeply of his clean, masculine scent. Lord, her soap had never smelled so good.

She explained the light switches and wall sockets and pointed out a cordless telephone. She dialed the time and temperature number and let him listen. Of course, he had to try it himself after that. She opened the wet bar and showed him the bar-sized refrigerator. She flipped on the stereo and filled the room with music, then switched it off and opened the cabinet that held the TV. When she reached for the "on" button she positioned herself so she had a perfect view of Reed's face.

He didn't disappoint her.

When the picture expanded onto the screen, his head jerked back several inches. Bewilderment captured and held his features. He turned to Elise, then back to the TV, then back to Elise.

The movie on the television was an old black-and-white Errol Flynn swashbuckler that had been colorized. Reed watched a ship pull alongside another. Errol Flynn swung across the ocean onto the other ship and began one of his infamous sword battles. Reed turned once again to Elise and shook his head. He managed to utter "How . . . ?"

She didn't even try to pretend she knew the workings of a television set. She described how most of the things were shows, like a play only filmed with cameras—descendents of the daguerreotype—that took moving pictures. She didn't get into the concepts of commercials, talk shows, news broadcasts, or any other kind of show. Even if she knew the intricate workings of a television, Reed would never be able to understand the technology.

After he recovered from the biggest part of his shock,

he continued around the room. He stopped at the book-shelves, glanced over the titles of several books, and commented that none of them were familiar to him. Moving on and finishing the circuit of the room, he ended up in front of the cold fireplace.

Elise sank to the carpet, then curled up her legs and patted the floor for him to do the same.

He looked self-conscious but lowered himself to the floor—apparently not an area of the house he was used to occupying. It took several attempts at repositioning to make himself comfortable.

"Why don't you kick off your boots? I'm not a real formal person, as you've probably noticed." Elise shoved the back of one Reebok with her toe, then re-peated the action on the other shoe. She wiggled her toes for a minute, then jumped up and grabbed the heel of Reed's boot.

"Here. I'll help you. I know you guys wouldn't even take off your jacket, let alone boots, in front of a woman."

"Here, now!" Reed yelped, but the first boot was al-ready off and she had the other in her hands. She won-dered if he felt the same surge of heat at their touch as she did.

It wasn't long before he began to relax. Even though he'd managed to retain an outward calm during the day, inside he had to feel every nerve in his body screaming. At least that's the way she would feel, and his next words confirmed it.

"My mind feels as though it is tearing in two, both from denying even the most remote possibility of my being catapulted into the future and knowing without a doubt that I am unarguably not in my own time."

Elise nodded with sympathy and tossed him a couple

of throw pillows. He followed her lead. Propped in a semireclining position, he tried to get comfortable.

"Tell me about yourself, Elise. Maybe *your* story will shed some light on my being here."

Elise was hesitant to talk about herself, but she could see Reed's point. Perhaps their paths had been destined to cross.

She focused on a spot on the wall and began her story, explaining that she was an only child and that her parents, Philip and Anne Gerard, were both deceased.

"My mother died of breast cancer when I was fifteen, and Dad never got over the grief. He really tried to be the father he had been before Mom's death, but grief nearly consumed him. Three years after Mom died, Dad was found dead in his office. A heart attack was the official cause. I believe he willed himself to die.

"Being eighteen and the only living relative of my parents, I inherited everything. It wasn't a lot, but it was enough to get me through college." Afterward, she'd gone straight into her chosen field. She skimmed over this area, unprepared to explain Air Force pilot training and all that came after it.

She moved on and mentioned how she'd come to buy this house.

"It was rumored the original family was ready to sell. There were several heirs, and none of them lived in New Orleans. Most of the furniture was still here, in the exact same places their ancestors had chosen. It spoke so vividly of the respect for their heritage that I decided then and there to buy everything and leave it as it was." With the money she'd stockpiled while in the service and her job with the airline, she was more than able to qualify for any loan.

"I immediately contacted the family, confirmed the rumor, and negotiated a deal we were all happy with.

"The antebellum period has always held a fascination for me. Sometimes I think I must have been a Southern belle in a previous life. I tried to leave the house as close to the mid-1800s as I could, but I had to have a few modern touches."

She realized as she spoke that the original family whose heirs had scattered over the country must have been some of Reed's descendents. Since he failed to question her about this, she moved swiftly ahead and continued to direct her narrative to the spot on the wall.

As she talked, she touched on the fact that she'd never been married but had been engaged once. She'd broken off the engagement but didn't elaborate on that or any other relationship.

When she got around to confessing that she was thirty-one, she rolled her head sideways to gauge Reed's reaction to this little tidbit of news.

She didn't know whether to laugh or sigh at the sight that confronted her.

Reed had been unusually quiet during most of her monologue. Now he reclined, half-buried in the pillows, his right arm thrown behind his head, and at the moment enjoyed a very deep sleep.

"My, my, Gerard. Aren't we the fascinating conversationalist?"

Smiling, she turned on her side. The rise and fall of his chest and the clean line of his jaw held her rapt attention. She took her time examining his face. She could look at those devastating features all night. The classic, chiseled lines looked so boyish in sleep.

Her body began to relax, so she closed her eyes for a few moments to relieve the burning. *Just a few minutes, then I'll wake him up and we'll go to our beds. Geez, I must be nuts.*

Chapter 4

A GLARING LIGHT forced Elise out of her sleep.

Her first thought was that she'd forgotten to close the room-darkening shades again. But before the thought was complete, she realized she wasn't scrunched in her cozy bed. This had to be the hardest hotel bed she'd ever slept on, and with her job, she had a lot to compare it with.

As reality crept into her mind, her eyes flew open. She held her breath and blinked away the remaining vestiges of sleep. Sure enough, lying comfortably across from her, one arm flung across his eyes and the other resting on his very taut stomach, slept the impossible visitor of the day before.

Now, in the light of a new day, the whole story seemed insane. Elise panicked. She had to get to her tear gas again, as quickly and quietly as possible. But as she inched herself up onto her elbows, the stranger across from her lifted his arm from his face, stretched, and opened his electric blue eyes.

Bewilderment clouded those eyes, then as he caught her movement and turned his head to gaze at her, he let out a long, frustrated sigh.

"So, it is true. It was not a dream."

Elise tried to keep the nervousness out of her voice. "No, I guess it wasn't."

They stared at each other as the seconds dragged by. A clock ticking somewhere in the house seemed to boom in the silence. Elise got to her feet and made her way to the door, picking up a few cushions along the way and tossing them back onto the couch.

"I, uh, I guess I'll go make some coffee," she said as she finally reached the door. She made a beeline for her purse and clipped the canister of tear gas to the inside of her pocket. Reason told her he had been a perfect gentleman the day before, and she obviously survived the night without getting her throat slit. But caution told her that if she was dealing with a nut she couldn't rely on past behavior.

In the kitchen she slid the coffee holder into the Mr. Coffee and wondered whether or not to call the police. How could she explain that she'd let him spend the night? She felt, rather than heard him come into the room. When she whirled around, he jumped back just in time to keep from bumping noses with her.

"Do you have to hover?" Elise snapped, unnerved and irritated by his unexpected, close proximity.

"Elise, I must offer you my apologies. What I did was unforgivable, but I can only hope that you will take into account the circumstances and somehow find it in your heart to make allowances." Reed's face was both stoic and repentant.

A chill snaked up her spine, and she slowly moved her hand to cover her tear gas.

"What circumstances? What are you talking about?" She couldn't begin to explain away the strange emptiness his apology created. What kind of trick had he played on her, and why?

Reed glanced into her narrowed eyes, then studied the floor. As he spoke, he looked up at her every now and then, as if to gauge her reaction.

"I fell asleep last night on the floor of your study, and as God is my witness, I did not realize you were asleep, too. I have never compromised a woman in my life, and I can only try to excuse my behavior by saying that I was exhausted. Had I not been in that physical state, I never would have allowed myself to spend the night in there beside you."

It took several seconds for the meaning of his words to seep into her twentieth-century brain. When it did, she went limp with relief.

"You've got to be kidding. Good grief, I thought you'd actually done something. Believe me, in this day and age, falling asleep on the same floor with a woman several feet away is definitely not going to compromise her. Now that I think about it, there's not much of anything that compromises a woman today."

With a skeptical look, Reed stared at her as though he couldn't believe such unacceptable behavior was viewed with so cavalier an attitude. It took Elise several attempts to reassure him that she was neither offended nor compromised, and even then she felt certain he still didn't believe her.

"Well, I am sorry, also, that I hovered. But I am so overwhelmed by all of these . . . devices. It has become somewhat of a game to try and figure out the purpose of each one." He flung his arms wide to encompass the entire room. The gesture made the already-too-small shirt stretch tightly across his chest, exposing a generous amount of well-developed muscle. Through the taut shirt she could see the ripples of his stomach muscles. A sudden zing shot through her chest, and her heart thudded against her rib cage.

Lust. Simple lust. He's too good-looking for his own good. Her body didn't want to respond when she willed her heartbeat into a slower cadence.

His story of the day before settled more comfortably around Elise when she watched Reed pick up an electric can opener and jump a foot when he accidentally pushed on the lever. When she turned on the oven to bake some biscuits and he had to open the door and gingerly check the heat with his hand, she forgot all about calling the police.

She cracked open a can of biscuits by slamming it on the edge of the counter. Reed watched her with undisguised curiosity as she doled them out onto a cookie sheet. She also noted he was trying desperately not to "hover."

She shot him a sheepish grin and said, "I'm sorry I snapped at you earlier. I guess I'm not a morning person today. Hover all you want."

Reed beamed and stepped closer, so close she could feel the heat of his body. She had to fight the urge to lean back into him—to lean against the length of him and have him wrap his arms around her while she snuggled the back of her head against his chest.

Get a grip, Gerard, she admonished herself when she realized how close she'd come to giving in to the urge. She'd been too long without a man, and it was making her weird.

During breakfast Elise watched Reed's discreet attempts to adjust and readjust his snug-fitting shirt. She realized

he needed some clothes that fit him better, since he
didn't appear to be going anywhere. From the look of
what he'd "arrived" in, he was accustomed to tailored
clothing with a precision fit. When she brought the subject of a shopping trip up, she was sure she noticed a
look of relief, even though he insisted that he was fine
and could make do with Don's wardrobe.

"Nonsense." Elise grabbed her plate and cup and slid
them into the dishwasher. "We don't know how long
you'll be here, and you need more than one change of
clothes. We can leave right after I clean up."

"Elise, the only currency I possess is the twenty-dollar
gold piece I showed you, and I hesitate to give that up. It
is one of the few links I have to my past."

"Oh, is that what you're worried about?" Elise gave
herself another mental shake and tried to concoct a story
on the spot. She wasn't a convincing liar, so she tried
evasion. "You don't need any money, Reed. I'll buy you
a few things, and you can find a way to pay me back
later, okay?"

"Well . . . it is true this attire is cursed uncomfortable,
but I insist on paying you back some way. Perhaps I
could work off the debt by overseeing some of the work
here, or doing some bookkeeping for you." Reed's face
was so earnest Elise almost laughed.

"Yeah. Sure. You bet."

Reed walked through what Elise called the mall, making
a conscious effort to keep his mouth from falling open in
awe or craning his neck like a country bumpkin. The trip
into town had become more and more amazing as they
got into the heavily populated areas, and everything
from what he now knew to be traffic lights to billboards
elicited an explosion of questions.

When a 727 glided across the sky, Elise seemed to

read his mind. Before he had the chance to choke out, "What in the name of God . . . ?" she pulled the car to the side of the road and gave him a brief and simple description of an airplane. She mentioned a couple of brothers named Wright; then she launched into an explanation of why, even though it seems impossible to the average person, air flight is not at all amazing, and once the fundamentals are understood, it's quite simple. Then she smiled great big and told him that that particular plane was a Boeing 727 and to remember that.

He was astonished, then disbelieving. He waited for a punch line. Elise just nodded and eased the car back into the traffic. He filed away a dozen questions to ask her when he had less to absorb.

Now he could see he had more to cope with than he'd bargained for. He did not want to embarrass Elise or make a fool of himself, so as they strolled through the mall he fixed a blasé look on his face and tried to give the impression that he had been there hundreds of times.

Elise busily explained malls and how all large cities had them. While he tried to keep his face expressionless, she grinned and knocked her shoulder into his arm, making him sidestep awkwardly. With a delighted giggle, she said, "That's better. I was beginning to think you were taking your new surroundings for granted."

Reed readjusted his blasé expression. "I was trying not to embarrass you," he said, but she just continued to grin at him. He hooked his thumbs into his pockets, as he had seen other men do, and continued strolling along.

They swung into what Elise called a department store and headed toward the men's department.

Reed spent the next hour or so accepting or rejecting each selection, then trying on what was left. He self-consciously suffered through choosing small clothes with Elise in attendance. He adamantly refused, though, to even try on, let alone purchase, any style of short trousers.

Their next trip was to the shoe department, where Elise waved away his first selections and ordered him to try on a pair of well-padded Reeboks.

He slipped his feet into the shoes and took a few tentative steps. Never had he worn anything so comfortable. He felt as if he walked on pillows, and proceeded to tell Elise until she jabbed him in the ribs, indicating with a tilt of her head the young salesman who peered up at him through squinted eyes.

Elise was obviously enjoying herself immensely, and she picked out a pair of dress shoes for him as well. He grumbled a bit that they weren't as comfortable as the other ones, but she nodded to the sales clerk and whipped out what she called a "charge card."

She led him out of the store in a different direction, but before they got too far, he was brought up short by another amazing sight.

What appeared to be a staircase stood, or rather moved, in front of him. Elise called the stairs an escalator, and he insisted on stepping on and trying it out. It took him several seconds to decide when to step, and then only because Elise shoved him in the back. His arms flailed, and he grabbed for the rail. Several people turned to stare. Elise just smiled sweetly and said something about him being off his medication.

The trip back down proved much less daunting. He turned and smiled at her with smug triumph.

On their way home from the mall, Elise made a quick trip to the courthouse. Her search for some kind of records of Reed's existence in the past met with a dead end. The young man who helped her made a thorough search but returned from his task shaking his head.

"It seems, Ms. Gerard, that most records from any-where near that time have been destroyed."

"When were they destroyed? During the Civ . . . 1800s?"

"Actually, it's hard to say when the damage was done. Our biggest enemy in the records department has been the Mississippi River. It's flooded this area so many times that I couldn't even tell you when the records you're looking for might have been destroyed. There's a good seventy-five-year window of opportunity here be-tween the time of the records you're looking for and when the levees were built to hold back the floodwaters. Sorry."

Elise studied the clerk thoughtfully.

"That's okay. Thanks, anyway, for all your help."

She turned and gave Reed an apologetic look. He wondered if the misery he felt showed in his face. He got his answer when she took his hand in hers and squeezed.

Each morning Reed would wake and immediately scan his surroundings. When he found himself still in the guest bedroom, his emotions were torn between relief that he hadn't left Elise and agony at being separated from a life and time that was his. He wondered, more than he liked to admit, how he would feel if he woke in his own time to discover he had left Elise behind. He wondered, also, about Nell, his staff, and his friends that were back in 1844 while he was here. Was he dead? Was he even gone from there, or was there a part of him that had been left behind? It was not something he could begin to answer, so he tried to put it from his mind.

Elise was in much the same predicament. Each morning she would wake and go immediately to look for Reed, to assure herself he was still there. With each passing day she grew closer to him, leaned on him, and she was becoming more and more worried that one morning soon she'd wake up and he'd be gone, with only the imprint of his body on his bed to prove he'd ever been there at all.

After nearly three weeks she knew she had to have a talk with him. She'd been on a two-week vacation, and that, added to her scheduled days off for that month, had amounted to three weeks. In two days she would have to fly her first trip since Reed's arrival, and she was in a quandary as to how to explain to him that she was an airline pilot. How could she explain to him that her job was to fly those huge planes he'd been staring at, open-mouthed? She would have to leave him soon to fly a four-day trip.

That evening at dinner they sat across from each other, finishing off a dessert of old-fashioned bread pudding. Reed looked up from his plate with quirked eyebrows.

"You've been awfully quiet this evening."

Elise cleared her throat. It was now or never.

"Reed . . . I, uh . . . well, I mentioned my job once and . . . and you were rude enough to fall asleep." This produced an apologetic, little-boy grin. Her heartstrings tugged. "Anyway, my job is . . . that is to say . . . I fly those airplanes you've been running outside to look at for three weeks. Only I fly cargo and not passengers, and I'm out of vacation time, and I'm due to go back to work in two days, and I have a four-day trip, and I'm going to have to leave you here while I'm gone!" Elise sucked in her breath and held it when she finished, an apprehensive stare locked onto Reed.

His face was priceless! *Oh Lord, where's a camera when you need one?*

"You . . . fly . . . airplanes?" Reed said it as if he had to think very hard between the words to grasp the reality of it. Several minutes elapsed as he absorbed this piece of news.

"I hadn't given the topic of your income any thought at all. The women of my time did not work unless absolutely necessary, and you seemed so . . . well, to be vulgar, well-off that I assumed you had an income from the plantation and an overseer to run it. I realize now that my assumption was foolish, considering all the changes I've witnessed in the last three weeks."

"I know it's hard for you to fathom, but you know, we have talked about the differences in the role of women today. And flying is something I love. Anyway, I have this trip, and I hate it more than I can say, but I'll be gone for four days. I should be back here before the weekend, and then I'll have a few days off before my next trip. Do you think you'll be okay until I get back . . . I mean with all the 'devices' to deal with?" He still referred to everything as a device.

He waved his hand as if batting at flies.

"Give it no more thought, little one. I feel I've mastered your machines and can fend for myself. I have plenty to fill my days. I'll keep busy and," this he said with a grin, "keep out of trouble. You go on and don't give a second thought to me. Just know that I will be more than ready to see you at the end of your trip."

Elise had only half listened after he'd called her "little one," but the comment about seeing her at the end of her trip doused the glow and brought her reeling back to reality. A wave of nausea flowed through her, and she knew she'd never forgive herself if she came home to find that he'd somehow been transported back to his own time. Maybe she shouldn't go. Maybe she should call in sick. Dozens of ideas raced through her mind, but she forced them away. She couldn't live her life around a possibility.

How in the world had this man come to mean so much to her in such a short period of time?

The next two days were like a fairy tale for Elise. They spent every waking moment together, horseback riding, stopping for picnics, renting movies. As Reed watched the screen, awestruck, Elise watched Reed with a soft ache building in her chest. They stayed up until all hours of the night talking, delving into each other's personalities or looking for a clue to his being there. Elise had dozens of questions about the house and what it was like when Reed owned it. He promised to take her on his own type of tour of "their" plantation when she got back.

Finally, the night before Elise's trip came, and she begged off early. She needed a few hours sleep before her one-thirty A.M. show time.

After dozing and tossing in a restless sleep, she finally gave up and got out of bed a little after midnight. She shuffled to the shower and stepped into a lukewarm blast of water.

The shower revived her enough to get her into her captain's uniform, finish her makeup and blow-dry her hair. She had a quick bite to tide her over until morning, then she found herself standing with uncertainty at the bottom of the cantilevered staircase. An indecisive right foot rested lightly on the bottom step. She made her decision, lowered her head, and quietly climbed the stairs.

Her footsteps were soft as she walked to Reed's bedroom door, eased it open, and peered around the edge. Alarm shot through her. She searched the rumpled sheets for Reed's body, and the same nausea she'd experienced a few days earlier overwhelmed her. She forced herself to take several deep breaths to regulate her breathing, then walked with hesitant and hopeful steps down the hall to the den.

She stood in the doorway and waited for her eyes to adjust to the darkness of the room. A silhouette rose from the chair by the window and moved toward her.

Each step was indecisive, uncertain, and as Reed's dear face formed in the darkness Elise realized her heart had been lodged in her throat.

He was in front of her now, towering over her. When she raised her face to look into his eyes, he slipped his arms around her and gently pulled her to him. She laid her head on his chest, and her arms encircled his waist as she made contact with his body. She thought if she tried, she could melt right into him. Long seconds passed as she rubbed her cheek on his chest in a slow, sensual motion, savoring his clean scent and the foreign feeling of complete contentment.

She raised her chin to smile at him, her cheek still on his chest. Reed's head dipped until his lips brushed hers, brushed them again, and came back to rest for a long, gentle kiss, full of warmth and tenderness. Elise felt her resolve as well as her knees weaken. She also felt an undercurrent of something; was it pain? She wasn't even certain if the pain was hers, from all of her past disappointments, or if she was feeling a level of pain from Reed. He held her as if he didn't want to, yet kissed her as if he never wanted to stop.

Her warm hands moved over his back, and she gave in to the ache at the center of her chest. Reed pulled away and gazed down at her with a tender, unrepentant look on his face.

"I'm not sorry for that. I have held that in for days, and as I sat here thinking of you leaving, I realized I wanted to kiss you more than I wanted to breathe."

Elise blinked when she felt the first burning of tears, then forced a flirtatious grin and whispered, "I'm not sorry, either. I was beginning to think I'd have to take matters into my own hands and molest you."

Reed's shock was only partially feigned. These weeks with Elise had taught him that she was outrageously unconventional and that she was forever doing the unexpected. He realized with amusement that she probably meant what she'd said about molesting him. Now *there* was a pleasant thought.

The moment had been lightened, and Elise told him that she needed to get moving or she just might not go.

He watched her gallop down the stairs in the manner he was finally getting used to. As she pulled open the front door, she turned and blew him a kiss, her eyes sparkling; then the door shut behind her. Days ago he had learned that she didn't need or want an escort every time she stepped out of the house.

He watched from the upstairs window in the den when Elise honked and waved as she tore out of the driveway. He'd never felt so alone in his life.

It was quite possible that driving the Jag down the driveway was the hardest thing Elise had ever forced herself to do. Before she even got into the car, she'd felt an emptiness well up inside her that was physically painful.

She forced herself to drive to the airport, file a flight plan, get on the plane, and take off. She knew if she let the copilot take control, she'd entertain ideas about coming down with a sudden, debilitating illness. A captain on standby at the airport would have to be called in. No, she needed to function at full capacity so her mind would be filled with the flight and not of Reed.

To make matters worse, when she'd gotten to work

there had been a message from Jeffrey in her E-mail. The message half begged, half threatened Elise to meet him. Her skin crawled. Jeffrey didn't have access to the company computers. How in the world had he gotten into the system? She'd attempted to trace the message to the terminal of origination but hit a blank wall. She didn't have time for this. She'd logged off, balanced her pubs bag on her rolling suitcase, and left for the crew bus.

The four days passed. Elise called once, but only after the machine picked it up and Reed heard her voice did he answer. She told him she was moping whenever she ran out of things to occupy her mind. She was so preoccupied that her crew gave up all attempts at conversation and socializing with her after the first two days.

Reed found himself moping, too. This was only after he had read books, ridden horses, and walked the entire width and breadth of the plantation. He'd practiced with the toaster, coffeemaker, microwave, and telephone. When he'd gotten several "Hellos" on the other end, and once even a monologue in a foreign language, he'd decided to stop practicing with the latter.

He then gave in and turned his thoughts fully to Elise. He relived all of their conversations and outings, especially dwelling on the last few moments they'd spent together.

As he sat in the chair and stared at the sunset, he felt the last vestiges of energy drain from his body, as if someone had turned on a tap and drained him. His last thought, as his head sank back comfortably onto the soft headrest, was that this time tomorrow night Elise would be home.

Chapter 5

THE JAG ROARED into the driveway at two in the morning. Elise threw the car into park and jumped out. She ran up the steps, tried the door and found it locked, then wasted precious seconds fumbling for the right key. Every second wasted was an eternity. It already seemed like she'd been separated from Reed for a month.

Once the door was unlocked, she threw it open and yelled, "Reed! Reed, I'm home!"

She stood poised, ready for his reply, but only a chilling silence greeted her. She burst into the foyer and took the stairs two at a time as she called Reed's name. Her heart pounded against her rib cage, and desperation caused her voice to crack.

His room was empty. She raced to her own and performed the ritual of the desperate by opening closet doors and looking in every corner. She even checked in the shower, though the water wasn't on, and she knew he wasn't there.

With exaggerated gentleness she closed the shower door, as if pushing too hard would cause it to shatter.

A film of sweat collected on her skin. As she turned toward the hallway, she didn't even realize she was talking to herself.

"He's in the den. Yeah. He'd wait for me there." She forced herself to walk calmly down the huge hallway. "He's in the den. He's asleep in the den. Let him be in the den. Please, God, let him be in the den."

Empty.

She stood in the doorway and scanned every inch of the room, her breathing so shallow it was almost nonexistent. The hair on her neck dampened, and she swallowed convulsively. A trickle of sweat ran between her breasts.

"Oh God, oh God, oh God, nooooo! He's not gone! Please!" She flattened herself against the door and begged for this not to be true. Her body slowly slid down the wall, and she slumped to her knees.

She felt as if her body had become a vacuum. A totally empty shell. She took her fist and pressed it hard against the center of her chest to try to ease the pain.

As she knelt there, her head shaking back and forth in futile, agonized denial, she became aware of music filtering into her consciousness. She slowly raised her head and turned, unable to pinpoint its origin.

With the dread of someone in mourning, she rose from her kneeling position and slowly, resentfully made her way back down the hallway. Whatever this was, she couldn't deal with it right now. If Jeffrey was in the house again, she would kill him.

When she approached the top of the stairs, the music became clear enough for her to identify. It was "The Emperor's Waltz."

Totally confused, and not a little hesitant, she held tight to the banister and made her way down to the first floor. The music drifted from the ballroom.

Could it be Reed? It couldn't be. There was no stereo equipment in the ballroom, and even if there was, he wouldn't know how to work it. He would have answered her call when she entered the house.

She stopped in the foyer and picked up her tear gas, then walked the length of the hall. Confusion and fear muddled her thoughts. Pushing one of the white, gilt-trimmed double doors open to arm's length, she hesitated, then peeked into the enormous, mirrored room.

She expected to see Jeffrey. It was just like him to come into her house again and commandeer it. Her adrenaline pumping, she was ready for a fight. Her heartbeat roared in her ears.

What she saw made her heart stop.

At the far end of the room, leaning against a white, marble mantel, a lazy fire glowing behind him, stood Reed. He was dressed in the clothes he'd arrived in, gazing at her with a nonchalant, sensual smile.

As she watched, he pushed himself away from the mantel, clicked his heels once and bowed. In the most seductive voice she'd ever heard he asked huskily, "Would you honor me with this dance?"

For the first time in her life, she fainted.

Her first awareness was a coolness on her forehead, then a gentle, yet persistent, tapping on her cheeks. She took a deep breath and forced her eyes open. The sight she encountered was that of a nearly hysterical Reed. He frantically patted her cheeks, then rubbed her hands between his.

"Thank God, Elise! You're awake! I thought I'd killed you! I never meant to scare you. I'd never . . ."

Elise threw her arms around his neck and cut off any

further apologies. She hugged him so hard he coughed. When she loosened her grip slightly, his arms encompassed her and returned her hug with an urgency of his own.

She buried her face in his neck and chanted, "Thank you, God! Thank you, God! Thank you, God!" She laughed and cried at the same time.

His fingers splayed across the base of her skull, massaging and kneading as he rubbed his cheek across the top of her head.

"My sentiments exactly," he whispered hoarsely. He gave her a final squeeze, then drew away.

"I'm sorry, little one," he moaned as his thumb wiped away a tear from her cheek. "I've spoiled everything. I remembered you saying one of your dreams was to dance to a waltz, and I only wanted to fulfill that dream. I didn't answer you when you came in because I was having trouble working this damnable music machine I'd moved in here. I didn't want you to find me out until I had the stage set, so to speak. I never imagined I'd frighten you into a faint."

Elise could only stare at Reed. Never, ever, in all her experience with men, had a man ever done anything so sweet, so thoughtful, as to try to fulfill even her smallest dream. According to them, all her wildest fantasies would be fulfilled if she'd only fall into bed with them. She'd opted not to fulfill those fantasies in all but two cases. And those two times when she had given in had been major disappointments.

She continued to stare, and when all of Reed's words sank in, her aching heart transformed into a glowing smile.

"Wait right there," she ordered. "Don't move!"

She uncurled her arms from around his neck, then flew down the hallway and thundered up the stairs.

He was worried. He'd made Elise swoon, and when he'd explained himself, she'd looked at him as if he'd sprouted horns. Granted, she had smiled at him before she'd run away, but he couldn't shake the feeling that he'd done something wrong. Maybe she was disappointed that he wasn't this Patrick Swayze person. Well, whoever Patrick was, he was a damn fool for not trying harder to please Elise.

It seemed an eternity passed before Reed heard her footsteps in the hallway. As he stopped pacing, he experienced a sense of dread. Her steps were slow and deliberate, not the usual quick-stepped clatter she was wont to create.

A shadow fell across the floor in front of him. He raised his head slowly, expecting the worst.

His gaze, however, did not encounter Elise. At least not the Elise he knew. The person he stared at was an ethereal creature, bathed in a golden light from the fire, and garbed in an exquisite gown of delicate peach silk. The skirt still rippled around her calves from her sudden stop in the doorway. A multitude of dangling beads on the bodice shimmered with each quick, excited breath she took.

His eyes raked her hungrily, from the top of her golden-brown hair, piled in artless curls at her crown, to the tips of her satin-clad slippers.

While the music still played in the background, he took a few steps forward, enclosed the tips of her fingers in his, and bent to kiss the back of her hand. As he peered up at her through thick, black lashes, he turned her hand to kiss her palm and then placed it against his cheek.

"May I . . . have the pleasure of this dance?"

A bolt of electricity seared a fiery trail from Elise's fingers to her heart. Before it exploded, she slipped into his arms, as if she'd been doing it for years.

She glowed with inner happiness. Reed sucked in his breath, and she knew his heartbeat had quickened.

They stood poised, seemingly captured in time. Then Reed stepped and began the fulfillment of Elise's dream.

With just a few movements she absorbed Reed's rhythm and they moved as one. She knew instinctively what he would do. As the music swelled, their dancing intensified into more complicated steps. Elise never missed a beat. She turned, spun, followed every move Reed led her through.

They circled the dance floor. She relaxed and gazed around her. She caught the shimmering rainbows that glistened from the chandelier. She saw the out-of-season fire burning cozily in its grate. Best of all, with each turn she could see herself and Reed reflected in the many mirrors lining the walls. Reed moved her about the room with an assurance that came from complete self-confidence, and she saw herself swirling, snug in his arms, her generous silk skirts flowing and belling out around her with a gracefulness that belied her ability.

It was everything she had dreamed it would be, and more.

There were many more dances after the first one, and the more she danced, the more playful she became. After they'd exhausted Elise's meager supply of classical CDs, she picked a selection of her own.

"Now I'll teach you a few steps," she said mischievously. "You've never seen these where you come from."

When the chords from an organ, sounding amazingly like a hymn, filled the room, Reed turned a quizzical look toward Elise. Just at that moment the tempo changed. It became quick and upbeat, and the male singer sang about "faith." Elise began to move in a very seductive, unusual manner. She stood alone, swaying, moving her arms and legs. To Reed this was very similar to the voodoo dances he'd witnessed as a boy while safely hidden behind thick bushes. She threw her head back. A look of pure sensuality flowed into her face and translated into her movements.

She seemed to be in a world of her own. "This is an old one, but it's one of my favorite songs," she whispered, her eyes closed.

Her movements became more suggestive by the minute. If she kept this up, he just might take some of those suggestions seriously. Finally she seemed to focus on him again and grabbed his hand.

"C'mon. You try. It's easy!" She backed away and motioned for him to mimic her.

Reed self-consciously began to move, ever so slightly. There was no way he could duplicate some of the things she was doing. But when he looked at Elise, her eyebrow quirked with a "you can do better than that" look on her face, and the competitor in him rose. Before long he felt more than adequate, and Elise was lavish in her praise. It was ironic that she praised him for doing something that, in his time, would have gotten him banned from every drawing room in New Orleans.

During a slower song she grabbed his hands and led him into a waltz. She openly enjoyed his look of shock as she took the lead. He decided to humor her and followed with only a slight amount of effort. She began to incorporate some of her own steps into the dance, and all went well for several minutes. Before long, however, she started to giggle, and he had trouble keeping his own laughter in check. Elise missed a step, and their feet tangled hopelessly. They found themselves sidestepping quickly to regain their balance, but before they knew what happened they both pitched forward to the floor. Reed managed to throw himself around to cushion Elise's fall.

This only produced more laughter, which bounced off

the mirrored walls and echoed throughout the ballroom. The longer they lay there, the harder they laughed.

As the last giggle worked its way up Elise's throat, she raised her head to smile at Reed. With a jolt that penetrated every nerve of her body she became acutely aware of her position atop Reed, as well as his . . . condition . . . beneath her. The look on his face was so intense, a look of wonder, of pain, and of longing, that Elise was completely at a loss.

Just as she looked away uncomfortably and started to roll off of him, Reed wrapped an arm around her and gently lifted her chin.

"Don't go," he whispered and raised his head to softly kiss her. The softness gave way to a long-denied hunger, and the pair slowly rolled over until Elise was beneath him.

She found herself on the receiving end of his unleashed passion. It swept over her like a tidal wave, merging his emotions with her own, then rushing to engulf them both like an oncoming tide of heat.

She totally surrendered to his kiss, and as the moments stretched on, she gave as much as Reed.

She was amazed at her reaction. She had discovered years ago that giving too much equaled pain and a battered ego, among other things. She had become an expert at pulling away and suppressing her natural inclination to open up her heart. Too many men had used her feelings to wipe their feet on and inflate their egos.

She shoved those thoughts from her mind and concentrated on the fiery sensations Reed created. She was rewarded with a rumbling groan as he pulled her closer to him, so close she could actually feel his heart beating against her chest.

As their kisses continued, the tension drained from her body only to be replaced with a warm languor so intense she felt drugged. An almost forgotten ache spiraled through her. An ache that seemed to penetrate her very soul. She welcomed it back joyously, for she had despaired of ever feeling it again. Oh, dear Lord, it had been so long.

From her past experiences, Elise expected the usual kisses to graduate to a more frenzied pace. Next the hands would begin to roam and grope. She was surprised, and this time disappointed, when Reed slowed his kisses and gently pulled away. She moaned as his lips left hers, and when she finally opened her eyes, she found him smiling gently down at her.

When he moved to rise, she stayed his progress by cupping her hands tenderly behind his head.

"Please don't stop," she whispered, swallowing her pride and hoping she didn't sound desperate.

He continued to rise until he stood over her. As he straightened, he grinned down at her with a look that melted her bones.

"I have no intention of stopping, little one." He bent and swept her into his arms, her skirts trailing beneath her. When he spoke in a low, gentle voice her heart missed a beat. "I also have no intention of making love to you for the first time on a hard, wooden floor. First times are made for memories. And believe me, I want you to remember this."

The memory was better than any fantasy ever hoped to be.

. Elise's mind came slowly awake, and she snuggled closer to Reed, backing herself tighter against his chest. In his sleep his hand tightened across her stomach and pulled her closer still. His arm scooted down to form a pillow for her head.

In the half-conscious state that sometimes precedes wakefulness, Elise's mind was a fuzzy blur. At first she sleepily savored the lingering effects of the dream she'd had, hoping that it would become a recurring one. But as the fog of sleep lifted, she realized the dream had been a reality. A reality beyond anything that she had ever hoped for.

Her mind relived the hours spent after Reed had carried her upstairs, lingering over moments that even now caused her heart to pound. She was filled with wonder at the thought of his gentleness, his infinite patience, his . . . slow hands. She smiled. All men could take a lesson from the one beside her.

He had devastated her with sensations. There were times she'd nearly cried from his overwhelming passion. Yet the mechanics had not been all that different from times with the two men who had come before—men who had left her with an emptiness that had never been filled. Until now.

The difference, Elise realized with wonder, was not what was done, but in the attitude in which it was done. Reed made her feel cherished. She'd felt as if she were priceless, something he'd searched for his entire life, prepared to pay any price for. And when he'd found her, he'd treated her as one treats anything that is totally and preciously unique. He conveyed without words that no one in the world had ever made him feel the way she made him feel.

He had taken his time with her and made each touch and every movement seem original. Though all their actions had been as ancient as time itself, Reed had reinvented them especially for her.

As she savored her memories and watched the light of dawn creep through the gap in the draperies, Reed's lips nuzzled softly along her neck. Smiling, she rolled over into his embrace and let him prove to her that her waking thoughts were not mere remnants of a dream.

*   *   *

Reed had lain awake for some time, cherishing the warm body nestled close to his. He couldn't believe this woman had given herself to him so completely. If she had held anything back, then God help him when she gave her all, for she would surely kill him.

He felt a moment of red-hot jealousy when he thought of the other two men who had already known Elise in this way. During the night she had spoken of her experiences with men only briefly, and even then with little enthusiasm. This attitude was an enigma to him, for she certainly hadn't reacted with indifference last night or this morning.

At first he'd refused to accept the moral standards that would allow a decent, unmarried woman to take two separate men into her bed. But he was forced to reevaluate his opinion the longer he lived in the twentieth century. It would be next to impossible to remain celibate in a society that bombarded one with sex, be it on television, in movies, or in every aspect of advertising. But he remained steadfast in the belief of his own morals.

He wasn't proud of his lack of control last night. He had broken his own moral code, and his only defense was that he had been overcome by the moment. When Elise had pierced him with that heated, sea green gaze and asked him not to stop, he knew he was like the drowning man going down for the third time. It didn't make it right, but he could have flown her plane easier than he could have resisted her body.

Chapter 6

"OKAY, DARLIN', I'VE been thinking. We need to get you out and expose you to the world." Elise slid their plates into the dishwasher, then wrung out a cloth to wipe the table. "You've adjusted remarkably well to all the things around the house and the few ventures we've made outside. Okay, I admit you'll never adjust to some of the TV shows. You have to believe me when I say not everyone takes what they see on television seriously. I mean, soap operas are about as far from reality as you can get, and those talk shows during the day . . . well, intelligent people just don't watch them. People with lives don't find the sex lives of gay, transvestite hookers who marry their brothers interesting. And that pretty much speaks for all the talk show topics."

Reed shook his head in disgust. He'd never discussed even the most innocent aspects of nature with the opposite sex, and to have seen and heard more graphic conversations than he'd had with his male friends shocked him to the core. He'd wanted to smash the television into a million pieces.

"Let's not discuss that, little one, it only infuriates me anew. I just hope you plan to expose me to something more appealing than television." This last he said with a teasing grin.

"Oh, I think it will be." A mysterious smile curved Elise's lips. "First, I want to take you on a tour of the plane I fly. Unfortunately, I can't take you for a ride in it, but I can rent a Cessna and take you up."

Reed lowered his eyebrows. She couldn't be serious. He had no idea what a Cessna was, and he wasn't at all sure he wanted to go "up."

"C'mon. It'll be fun. Just imagine . . . doing what men have dreamed of doing for centuries, soaring through the sky with the birds, and bursting through a cloud! Flying above a storm, with the sun above you and endless clouds below you is an experience too beautiful to describe."

The glow on Elise's face and her enticing description were too much for Reed to resist. He'd always had an adventurous spirit, but he'd never had a chance to indulge it to any degree. And he couldn't imagine another adventure that would begin to compare to soaring above the clouds.

"When do we go?" He slapped both hands onto the breakfast table in challenge.

"How about this afternoon? There'll be a Boeing available at the airport, and I'll call and reserve the Cessna."

One o'clock found them pulling into Moisant International. Elise hustled Reed into the security area where she flashed her ID and acquired a visitor's badge for him. In no time they were on the tarmac, headed for a 727 that had just seen the clean-up crew.

The size of the plane astounded Reed, since he'd only seen them from a distance in the air. Elise launched into statistics about the weight, length and how many tons of cargo and fuel it could carry.

As he entered the plane he tried to digest this information as well as the running commentary she gave in the cargo hold about cargo igloos and loading pallets. He couldn't get a word in edgewise, so he made mental notes of questions to ask later.

All of those questions vanished from his mind when he entered the cockpit.

Elise dropped into the left seat and gestured for him to take the right. He maneuvered his way around the throttle and yoke, then sat back stiffly and stared at the hundreds of dials, buttons, levers and gauges. Elise picked a few large instruments to point out. He could tell she made her descriptions of their purpose as simple as possible.

A new and intimidating respect for this remarkable woman surged through him. Good Lord, the woman was amazing. He couldn't begin to comprehend the vastness of her knowledge, her abilities, her courage. Up until now, to him she had been an extremely intelligent woman with a wonderful sense of humor and a generous gift for helping him adjust to his new life. He had thought of her as a free spirit. But now . . . now she was on a level Reed could not relate to with a woman. He felt ignorant as he sat there, worse than a country bumpkin.

The tour of the airplane finally came to an end. Reed, miserable now and feeling totally inadequate, followed Elise to a hangar and waited while she excitedly filled out the paperwork to rent the plane.

"All set!" she chirped. He followed her to the plane, but without the self-assured stride he had before. She opened the cockpit door with a flourish and made a low bow. "Climb in."

Plastering what he hoped was a smile of anticipation on his face, he settled into his seat.

Elise strapped them each in, ran through the checklist and started up the engines. Then she picked up a thing she called a "mike," had a conversation with "the tower," and started "taxiing" out to the runway.

So far this was not so different from riding in the Jag, plus there weren't nearly as many controls as in the large plane. Reed began to relax and feel a little better.

As Elise increased the speed, he noticed she kept a close watch on him from the corner of her eye. When the plane lifted off the runway and soared upward, his stomach did a dangerous flip. She laughed, obviously delighted by his reaction.

They climbed for several seconds before leveling off high enough to see the world and low enough to make out houses, backyard swimming pools and boats on Lake Ponchartrain. Good lord, he could not believe a bridge had been built that spanned the lake!

Reed's knuckles turned white. This was worse than the first time in a car. His mind could not accept what he was seeing. As he gazed about he sat very still and tried hard not to move. He was sure if he leaned over too far to look below him he'd cause the plane to tip like a rowboat.

Elise seemed to sense what he was thinking and reached her hand out to cover his.

"It's okay," she said with a smile. "Moving won't affect the plane. See?" She swayed to and fro in her seat with exaggerated movements and ended with a couple of bounces for good measure. Sure enough, the plane remained steady.

Reed moved a little to test the theory, then forgot his fear of tipping over as he watched a huge, thick cloud loom ahead of them. He flinched as they entered the cloud, expecting to feel an impact. The next thing he knew they were in the midst of it, and just as he was likening it to no more than a dense fog they burst through into sunlight. He could not believe his eyes.

As far as the eye could see there were mounds upon mounds of whipped cream clouds below them. He'd never seen anything so beautiful. He had an overwhelming urge to fall back into them and see if he would float. Ridiculous, he knew, but he enjoyed the fantasy. He could picture himself and Elise wading through them together.

They soared above the clouds for several minutes before Elise picked up the mike and spoke into it again.

"Houston Center, this is November Zero One Echo Gulf. What are the bases of the clouds in the area?"

"Roger, November Zero One Echo Gulf, cloud base is reported at six thousand feet MSL."

"Roger. I'd like clearance to descend to five thousand feet."

"Roger, November Zero One Echo Gulf, descend and maintain five thousand."

"Roger. Departing nine thousand for five thousand."

Reed listened to this exchange between Elise and the disembodied voice with only a little less awe than what he was experiencing over this plane ride. He wanted to ask Elise who Roger was but knew it would be a stupid question. Not that he hadn't asked his share of them.

The plane's nose dipped forward when Elise started her descent into the clouds. The white mist engulfed them again, and for several seconds Reed was disoriented when his vision failed to penetrate the clouds. Just as the feeling was becoming uncomfortable, the mist started to break up. Tiny houses and ribbons of roads materialized through the fog.

When the plane had slipped completely out of the cloud bank Elise keyed the mike again.

"Houston Center, this is November Zero One Echo Gulf. Cancel IFR."

"Roger. Cancellation approved. Squawk VFR. Have a nice day."

Elise replaced the mike and explained that she was setting the transponder to one two zero zero. He had no idea what a transponder was or why she had to set it, but that was the least of his questions.

Elise turned to him, gave him an impish grin and wiggled both eyebrows.

"Now we can really have some fun!"

"Ohhhhhhh," was all Reed managed to croak before the left wing dipped low, and he had a bird's-eye view of the ground out the left window. His head floated several inches above his body, and an invisible force pressed him into his seat. The sensation disappeared when the horizon leveled off before him and he could again see from the windshield.

They dipped low enough to fly over the house, and Reed recognized Oak Vista. To the north the world looked like a patchwork quilt in shades of light and dark green, and the river snaked along the landscape, a brown ribbon dividing towns and farms. While Reed's head still spun from the sights, Elise began their descent into Moisant and requested permission to land.

He watched with horror as the runway came up to meet them at an incredible speed, and he was sure his heart stopped when the landing gear bounced onto the runway. They settled into a smooth roll, slowing as Elise taxied to her parking position. Only after he realized they were safely on the ground again did he start to breathe and allow some blood to return to his clenched fists.

"It was the most . . . the most . . . I can't find words to describe it! Waking up and finding myself one hundred

and fifty years into the future was almost easier to describe than flying."

Elise had to agree with him. The flight had been absolutely perfect, and so was Reed's reaction.

They were now ensconced in a comfortable corner
booth at the back of the bar. Elise listened while Reed
desperately tried to verbalize his feelings without attract-
ing the attention of any of the other patrons.

His eyes sparkled with animation as he searched for
words to describe his adventure. She watched his hands
as he used them to talk, admired the smooth line of his
jaw. She leaned toward him over the table, one leg
tucked under her as she moved forward. His speech faltered and then stopped as the top half of her body
reached his.

"Volant," she whispered against his lips, breathing in
his breath and brushing his lips with hers. When he
moved forward to meet her kiss, warmth rippled over
her like waves against the shore. Her hand found its way
to outline the jaw she had just been admiring. His fingers
sifted through her hair and cupped the back of her head.
Every nerve tingled, alive with want for him to hold her.

"Hey, anybody got a bucket of water we can throw on
these two?"

They jumped apart so quickly Reed banged his head
on the back of the seat and Elise knocked her glass over,
dumping ice into her lap and sending frigid water across
the table into Reed's. They bumped heads as they
jumped up to empty their laps, and after a few futile
brushes at their damp clothing Elise looked around for
the owner of the voice.

The culprit was draped across the back of a booth, one
leg on the seat, his face buried in the crook of his arm.
He emitted strange croaking sounds, and his shoulders
and head virtually vibrated. After a couple of gasps for

air he raised his elbow and peered out from under it. The whole process started again.

Elise cuffed him hard on the back of the head.

"Damn you, Don!"

Don ducked his head and raised a deflecting arm before she could attack again. He danced backward away from her, making a "time out" sign and dragging his sleeve across his watery eyes. His lower legs made contact with the opposite booth, and he fell back into a sitting position. As Elise bore down on him, she saw his female accomplice in much the same position across the table from him.

"Hey, we didn't mean it about the water, but thanks for accommodating." The feminine version wheezed, then snorted and fell backward onto the seat, holding her sides.

"Oh, ha, ha, ha," Elise said with a forced sneer. She brushed at her lap again and tried to squelch the smile tugging at her lips. She looked around for a weapon to bash a couple of skulls.

Reed sat on the edge of the booth, alternately rubbing the back of his head and his temple and looking as if he were trying to decide the protocol for this situation.

Elise gave a huge sigh and said, "Reed, I'd like you to meet a couple of friends, and I use that term loosely. This is Don and Janice Sevier." The two people in question began to struggle up and forward from their reclining positions at the table. Don was the first to reach Reed.

"Don Sevier," he said with a huge smile as he pumped Reed's hand. "Sorry about that," he nodded toward Reed's other hand that still massaged his head. "But that was just too priceless to pass u—"

He staggered sideways from the shove Elise gave him.

Jan appeared before Reed, looking somewhat contrite but enjoying herself immensely all the same.

"It's nice to meet you, Reed. We're usually better behaved than this, but Elise brings out the worst in us."

"She has the same effect on me. Reed Blackwell, at your service."

Jan's jaw fell open when Reed stood and bent over her hand. With a raised eyebrow she slid a look at Elise.

Elise just smirked at her and wiggled her eyebrows. She had to try hard not to give in to the urge to grab Reed's collar and pull him away from Jan's hand.

After a waitress mopped up the table and brought their order, Reed slid in beside Elise, and Don and Jan took the other side of the booth.

Reed had come to the conclusion that these people really were friends of Elise's and that apparently it was perfectly normal for Elise to slap and shove her male friends. She had even blatantly tried once to kick Don under the table, but because she'd taken too long to locate the correct set of shins, he'd tiptoed them out of her reach.

Just when I think I have it all figured out, he thought, then realized he was being stared at.

"I was asking how you two met," Jan repeated, that look of amusement still on her face.

"Oh, well, we met at . . ." How could he explain how they met?

"He came to my house during the pilgrimage," Elise said smoothly.

"Oh. Are you interested in antebellum homes, Reed?"

"Ante . . ."

"Reed's into architecture as a hobby, so he's interested in all types of homes. He's especially into prerevolutionary homes."

Reed knew Elise was concocting this story to avoid questions they couldn't answer, but all the same, he was having a hard time keeping his face straight. He decided to join in.

"Yes. Virginia, especially Williamsburg, is my favorite area to explore. Though I'm not familiar enough with the area to know if there are any antebellum— WHOOF!"

Elise removed her elbow from between his ribs.

"Now, darlin', they'll take you seriously if you keep such a straight face." She smiled at him with a sugary smile.

Reed picked up his hamburger and took a huge bite to keep from having to answer any more questions. He managed to maintain a mouthful of food throughout the rest of the meal. He didn't allow himself to swallow without taking an immediate bite until after Janice and Don rose to leave.

"Well, it was great meeting you, Reed," Don said as he pumped his hand again. "Sorry again for the way we met. Hey, Jan, have you mailed the invitations yet?"

Jan fished around in her purse, producing an envelope and a tube of lipstick. She handed the envelope to Elise but looked at Reed.

"This has Elise's name on it, but please consider yourself invited. We're having a party for our tenth anniversary, and we'd like you *both* to come."

Her voice trailed off when Reed took her hand again.

Elise slapped her arm around Jan's shoulder and gave her a hearty hug. "Of course. We'd love to. Just let me check my schedule and make sure I'm in town. I'll get back with you."

Jan started toward the door but turned around to give Elise a peck on the cheek.

"Don't let him get away, kiddo," she mumbled against

Elise's ear. "It'll take more than a lap full of ice water to cool this one off."

When she walked away she gave Elise a lascivious smile, applying her lipstick in a most obscene manner.

On the way home Elise filled Reed in on her two friends. They were probably her best friends, she said, but they had drifted a little apart. She was still single, and after Jan had given birth to twins five years ago it had created a gap in their relationship.

"I don't seem to have much input in a conversation about diaper rash and baby food."

As they strolled to the back door of the house, he draped his arm over her shoulders and tucked her up against him.

"Too bad they happened by when they did," he murmured into her hair, his breath causing it to stir slightly.

She stopped on the step and turned her face up to his with a grin.

"I rather liked the conversation we were having when they so rudely interrupted us," he whispered against her neck. "Volant. Why did you say volant right before you kissed me? What does it mean?" His warm breath on her neck caused shivers along her spine. Elise nuzzled her face against his and brushed his lips with hers.

"You were . . . trying . . . to . . . describe . . . flying." One long, mind-numbing kiss followed. Her bones melted, and that welcome ache that had begun earlier in the day grew with every passing second.

"Oh, hell. Look it up!" She grabbed a handful of shirt-front and dragged Reed through the back door.

Chapter 7

REED PACED THE floor like a caged lion. The dark evening sky created a mirror on the den window, and after several passes he caught a glimpse of himself. He paced in the opposite direction. Elise was on another flight and had only been gone since two o'clock that morning, but he was totally lost without her. How could anyone take over his mind and his life in less than a month's time?

He looked at the clock again. A quarter past ten. It had only been three minutes since the last time he'd looked at it.

He picked up the remote and flipped on the TV. The control still felt foreign in his hand, but according to Elise he'd begun to use it like every other man in this day and age. Watch ten seconds, flip to another channel; another ten seconds, another channel; finally get interested and a commercial prompts more flipping. Once she'd finally grabbed it out of his hand and aimed it toward him. He'd half expected the darned thing to actually do something to him!

He sank to the couch, rested his forearms on his thighs, and after one last flip, dropped the remote between his feet. He settled back and decided to leave it on one channel in some kind of silly tribute to Elise.

At two A.M. he woke up and staggered to bed, wondering what Elise was doing, where she was, if she was thinking about him.

The jangling finally penetrated Reed's sleeping brain. He jumped out of bed and banged the alarm clock with a fist. He would never get used to that obnoxious, relentless sound.

The jangling stopped for a second, then started up again. He banged the clock again then shoved it under the closest pillow. As he came fully awake he realized the sound was coming from the phone. Hesitantly he reached for the receiver and slowly put it up to his ear. He'd only answered the phone once before. He always just let it ring until that machine answered it for him.

"Reed? Reed? It's me, darlin'. Are you there?"

"Elise?"

"Oh, I hope I didn't wake you. Did I?"

Reed stared at the receiver, then placed it back against his ear.

"Why would you imagine I was asleep? Why, it's . . ." he dug under the pillow to find the clock, "four-thirty in the morning. My day's half over. I was just about to go make some lunch."

"Oh, I'm sorry. It's just two-thirty here." Just two-thirty. Reed smiled and shook his head. "I've tried for hours to go to sleep, and I thought maybe if I could talk to you I'd be able to sleep better."

He grinned to himself and reassured her that he didn't mind. "There's only a couple of better ways I can think of to be woken up," he mumbled, then smiled when Elise groaned.

They talked quietly for a few more minutes, mostly trying to find new ways to say "I miss you," then Elise said she'd better try again to get some sleep. Her last words before hanging up were a sleepy, "I'll see you tomorrow night, my volant lover."

Reed hung up the phone, grinning at Elise's reference to their day at the restaurant. "Look it up," she'd said when she grabbed his shirt and dragged him into the kitchen. He hadn't given it another thought until now.

Look it up. Very well. A quick trip to the bookshelves in the den should satisfy his curiosity.

After locating a dictionary among the eclectic array of books, he flipped it open and glanced at a guide word: *antebellum*.

"Oh, there's another one I meant to look for," he said to himself as he glanced down to the bottom of the page.

He read the definition, then squinted with concentration and read it again.

> *antebellum—before the war. Usually*
> *in reference to the American Civil War.*

American Civil War? Could they be referring to the Revolutionary War? He'd never heard it described as a civil war.

He laid the dictionary to the side and scanned the bookshelves again. Somewhere there was an encyclopedia Elise had shown him earlier.

Not sure exactly how to find his topic he pulled out the A and C volumes. He found it under C.

"Ah, here it is," he said, and settled back to get comfortable.

He was back on the edge of his seat in an instant. A cold sweat dampened his shirt and a knot suddenly formed in his throat.

The very first piece of information was:

Civil War (1861–1865)

He readjusted his precarious seat on the edge of the couch and read on. He read about how more lives were lost in that war than all the other wars in American history combined.

My God! How many wars had there been?

He read about the slavery issue and the differing attitudes between North and South. This was no news to him. He'd long debated the morality and legality of slavery and had heard a few radical suggestions of a southern nation.

He visualized the first shots at Fort Sumter, the raid on Harper's Ferry, the southern states seceding from the Union. He saw the pictures of dead soldiers in trenches, some missing parts of their bodies. There were pictures of a man named Lincoln in one of the camp tents; of the most famous generals of both sides. There were black men in Northern uniform, and the caption said twenty-three of them had been given the highest honor for bravery.

He read about two ironclad ships battling with no apparent victor; the battles of Bull Run, Antietam, Shiloh and Gettysburg. He read about the Emancipation Proclamation, Sherman's march to the sea, and every other word written in the book about it, ending with the South's surrender and the president named Lincoln's assassination.

He felt like he was going to throw up. Sweat drenched his shirt, and he couldn't swallow past the constriction in his throat. He got up and numbly walked to the bathroom, turned on the cold water and stuck his head under it.

Dear God Almighty. He stood and raised his eyes to heaven. Water ran unheeded down his back and chest. *This is going to happen in twenty years. Just twenty years. No. Not twenty years. It's already happened. These men are already dead. One hundred and thirty years ago. No one is left alive from when it happened. Except me. I'm alive. I'm alive, and some of my friends died in a war one hundred and thirty years ago.*

For the first time since waking in this time, he felt a wave of depression settle over him like a heavy, suffocating blanket. He plunged his head back under the cold water. After several seconds he calmly dried off and walked back into the den, picked up the book, and turned to the last page that was titled "related topics."

Elise roared into the driveway, not bothering to call out as she stormed into the house. She'd seen the den light on and knew where to find Reed this time.

Bless his heart, he waited up for me, she thought as she clattered up the sweeping staircase and down the hall. She jumped the last couple of feet to land squarely in the middle of the doorway, arms flung wide and a huge, stupid smile on her face. When her gaze took in the room, her head jerked back and she blinked.

Books, most of them open, were scattered on every possible surface. Three or four lay on cushions and the arms of the couch. Reed, looking like hell with a day's growth of beard and dark circles under his eyes, sat in the middle of them with one open on each leg. As she forged a slow path through the room, she glanced down at the open pages. All of them had one thing in common.

The Civil War.

Her eyes flew to Reed's, and as he saw the look of sympathy on her face, he rose in stages, like an old man. The books fell to the floor unnoticed. He took a few hesitant steps in her direction; then she had her arms around him, his face buried in her shoulder. He leaned against her as if it hurt for him to stand on his own.

He held her tight, almost squeezing the breath from her, and her knees started to buckle. They both sank to the floor and knelt against each other. Finally she guided Reed's weight over to lean against the couch, his face still buried in her neck.

She smoothed his hair and rocked him back and forth, trying to find soothing words. His head shook in denial.

After several minutes he finally took a deep breath and blew out slowly. Stiffly, he started moving away from Elise. He sat up straight and flopped his back against the couch, his knees pulled up in front of him. Plunging his fingers through his hair, he held on to his head with his palms cupped at the back.

"Now I know why you evaded the word 'antebellum.'" His voice wasn't much more than a whisper. Elise looked at him, sitting there, with forearm dangling on one knee and shoulders slumped.

She opened her mouth to speak but could find no words to comfort him. Finally she simply let her heart do her speaking for her. She gathered him into her arms and held him tight, waiting until he was ready to talk.

Chapter 8

THE COFFEE HAD just finished brewing when Elise thought she heard Reed moving around upstairs.

What a hellish night. It had been one-thirty in the morning when she'd walked into the scene in the den, and four-thirty or later before, exhausted and numb, they had finally gone to bed. That was only after Reed had barraged her with questions, some of which she could answer, and some which no one could. After three hours of talking, Reed had still asked questions, trying to fathom the devastation of the war. But he'd seen that Elise was nearly asleep on her feet, and he'd had to admit he was, too. They'd both fallen into bed with their clothes on.

She turned toward the refrigerator to pull out a couple of eggs to scramble when she saw Reed standing in the doorway. With palms on the door frame he leaned into the kitchen, studying her. The night had taken its toll on him.

Closing the space between them, Elise slid her arms around his waist and laid her head on his chest. It only took him a second to wrap his arms around her and rest his head on top of hers.

"How's my best guy this morning?" she whispered as she snuggled up closer.

He was quiet for several seconds before he shrugged.

"I feel better, I suppose." He released her, scooped up two mugs and poured each of them a cup of coffee. After tipping a few drops of milk into one he handed it to Elise then leaned against the counter. He crossed his ankles with misleading nonchalance.

"I've had time to think about it. I woke up a couple hours ago and just lay there, trying to sort out my feelings. The news about the war was devastating, and I believe it will haunt me for the rest of my life. But I realized this morning that up until last night I've never really come to grips with or accepted the fact that I'm here, in this time, seemingly for good. With all the things to see and learn, and with you here to help me, I guess I've always felt this was more like a dream than reality. Last night the reality came crashing home. I'm here. I don't know why; I don't know how. All I know is that if it weren't for you, I'd be insane right now."

Elise warmed at his words yet struggled with this type of a declaration. She was always uncomfortable with ambiguous statements from men. Did he mean he was merely grateful for her help or that she meant so much to him, she could make an impossible situation livable?

"I know what you're feeling. Sometimes when I'm on trips I think I must be losing it. I can't make myself believe that I have a man from the mid-nineteenth century living in my home. You know, I never really reacted to your being here like a rational human being. I'll make up my mind to come home and quiz you until I get to the bottom of all of this, but when I walk in the door and you slide your arms around my waist, all my doubts melt away. My resolve disappears. You make everything feel right. In fact, I don't care where you came from, as long as you don't go back there."

Reed grinned, a tender look in his eyes, and moved forward to slip his arms around her waist.

"You have a similar effect on me." He growled deep in his throat as he nuzzled her neck. Chill bumps danced across her shoulders and down her spine.

This was one of the many times she wished Reed wasn't so honorable. After their first memorable night together, when he had waltzed her around the ballroom and then swept her upstairs to his bedroom, he had remained a perfect gentleman. Oh, there had been lots of kisses, and more, and a few times she thought they would have a repeat of that night. But Reed always pulled away before they were both carried to the limits. Elise wondered if his behavior was his way of telling her he'd carried things as far as he cared to. It couldn't be the "honorable thing" he'd been insisting it was all along.

"Reed," she said, pulling away from him and looking into his eyes, "do you find me unattractive?"

Reed stared at her for several seconds, his eyebrows raised nearly to his hairline. "Unattractive! What in the world makes you think I find you unattractive?"

"What am I supposed to think? Every time we're together and things start to heat up, you pull away and find something else to do. You know, it doesn't do a lot for a girl's ego."

She wished now she'd never brought the subject up,

but she couldn't rid her mind of that night with Reed. She had assumed he felt the same.

Reed remained silent. The longer the silence stretched on, the more she wished she'd kept her mouth shut.

You just had to open your mouth, didn't you? she thought, picking up a dish towel and wiping her already clean hands. *When are you going to learn to just—*

Reed's mouth covered hers as he took the dish towel from her hands and tossed it into the air. Slowly, his lips never leaving hers, he pulled her to the floor, until she found herself on her back, the cool of the tile creeping through her clothes and the heat of Reed's arms wrapped around her. His long, languorous kisses drugged her, set butterflies free in her stomach. A trail of nibbling kisses along the sensitive tendon of her neck ignited a ribbon of fire that rippled through her blood.

Eyes closed, Elise moved her head to make her neck more accessible as his lips began the tingling journey back to hers. After literally kissing the breath from her, he slowly raised his head and gazed at her.

He continued to stare, the corners of his mouth curved upward in a mischievous grin. He shifted position slightly, and those blue eyes looked into her soul. He shifted again, and then again, and as his eyes rolled upward he moaned in a choked whisper, "Do you honestly think this means I'm not attracted to you?"

It was obvious, in the physical sense and more, that he was.

"But then why . . . ?"

"Elise, how can I explain this to you? I was raised by Nell, a wonderful woman, and surrounded by women throughout my childhood. Maybe because of that I have more respect for your gender than what you've come to expect. Uncle Ian, as well as Nell, taught me that making love was reserved for a husband and wife.

"I realize things today are totally different from what they were in my time, and I've tried to adapt, honestly, right down to trying to speak like people today. But as much as I'd like to, this is one aspect of the twentieth century I won't adapt to.

"Don't think I'm trying to tell you that I was as pure as the driven snow before you came along. I had . . . indulged . . . the 'raging hormones,' as you quaintly put it so many times, but never with a woman whose life would be affected by my actions."

By this time Reed had rolled onto his back and pulled Elise against his side. Her right leg nestled over his and her arm draped across his chest. The top of her head rested against his cheek, and he nuzzled it thoughtfully.

"If you want to know the truth, little one," he said softly, sounding as if he wasn't sure he wanted to continue, "I'm more than attracted to you. I love you."

Elise tensed and she studied him, waiting for the "but." It didn't come. With more conviction he said, "I've loved you since that first day, when you sprayed me with tear gas and then clanged around the kitchen in that ridiculous, cheap gown. The first time you galloped up the stairs after flashing a view of those ugly Reeboks was the clincher. But I don't think I admitted it to myself until after you left on your first trip. I was barely maintaining a firm grip on my sanity to begin with, but when you left I felt you'd taken the sun with you. All I could think of was doing something special to show you how I feel."

With this last comment Elise propped herself onto her elbows and stared at Reed, afraid to believe what she was hearing.

"Special! Do you realize that no one, *no one*, has ever gone out of their way to please me like that? Geez, making one of my daydreams come true! You overwhelmed me, darlin'. I felt like a bystander watching it all happen to someone else."

Reed covered her face with little, nibbling kisses and pulled her closer. She felt that if she tried hard enough, she could actually climb right into his skin.

"You know, I've tried to fight it, but I think I fell in love with you when I took you for that first ride in the Jag, and you got so excited you wanted me to teach you how to drive. I was half afraid you were going to back-hand me for scaring you."

Reed jerked his head back several inches, a deep crease etched between his brows. He gently cradled Elise's head in his hands, studying her face, shaking his head slowly back and forth in denial.

"Elise, have I ever done anything to make you think I would react in such a manner?" The concern in his voice made her uncomfortable. Self-conscious now, she pulled her head out of his grasp and refused to meet his gaze.

"No. No, you've never done anything to cause me to feel that way."

"Someone else, then. Has someone else threatened to hurt you?"

She slid out of his embrace and slowly pushed herself into a sitting position. Pain, indecision, and embarrass-ment warred inside her.

Resting her chin on her knees, she stared off into space for several seconds. Now was as good a time as any.

"No. I was never 'threatened,' so to speak." She had never told this part of her life to anyone, even a friend. Swallowing her pride and taking a deep breath, she went on.

"I had a fiancé once." At Reed's inquiring look she clarified. "Betrothed. We were going to be married. He was very attentive, but also very controlling. He hated it when I teased him or had my own life. One night when I decided to spend the evening with a few girlfriends, he demanded that I stay home. And that," she said with a grin directed toward her feet, "is the quickest way to insure that I do exactly what I want to do."

Elise continued to stare at a spot on the floor.

"Anyway, I went with my friends, and when I came home, he was here waiting for me. He accused me of being with someone else, and when I tried to laugh off his accusation, he grabbed me and backhanded me. He got several blows in before the shock passed and I managed to get away. Before it was over, though, he'd slung me against the wall, then yanked me off the floor by a handful of hair."

Reed closed his eyes, trying to calm himself, to erase the picture of Elise being beaten. He'd never felt such an overwhelming urge to kill someone. Tenderly, he cupped Elise's chin and turned her face until their eyes met.

"You ended the betrothal then, of course," he stated matter-of-factly.

Elise chewed on her lower lip and slid her gaze to study the pattern of the brickwork on the kitchen floor.

"No . . . not exactly. Jeff had been drinking that night, and the next morning he came to me with flowers and apologies and tears in his eyes. He swore he didn't know what had come over him and that he'd never do it again. I think I was still in shock, but he convinced me to give him a second chance."

A long, silent pause seemed to stretch on forever before she continued. He let her take her time to tell the story.

"A few weeks later a fellow pilot called—a guy I work with—and Jeff answered the phone. Allen just wanted to trade a trip with me, but Jeff read his own story into it. When I hung up he started giving me the third degree, even after I'd explained. When I got disgusted and tried to walk away, he grabbed my hair and threw me to the floor. He cracked a rib when he kicked me on his way out the door.

"The next night, when he arrived with the flowers and the tears, I told him we were through and to get out. When he tried to force his 'apologies' on me, I ignored the pain in my ribs and drove a well-placed knee clear up to his tonsils. I haven't heard much from him since he crawled out of here that night, except for his visit here the day you arrived."

During her monologue, Elise had flicked a few glances in Reed's direction, but now she turned and looked him straight in the eye.

"Maybe it's because his voice is a few octaves higher." Her attempt at humor fell flat.

Reed felt as if he might burst something in his brain as he jumped to his feet and began to pace, slamming a fist into his palm.

"Good God! I'll call the blackguard out! NO! No, a quick death is too good for him. I'll do to him what he's done to you, then I'll call him out!"

When he swung back to Elise, fury distorted his vision. He watched with alarm as her body involuntarily flinched and dodged an anticipated blow.

In a split second he was on his knees beside her. He gathered her into his arms to comfort her, much as she had done with him the night before.

"It's okay," she insisted. "I'm all right now. All this happened a long time ago. Besides, the only time he ever bothers me is if I'm seeing someone. I guess if he can't have me, he doesn't want anyone else to." Elise pulled far enough away from Reed to give him a reassuring look. "He's ancient history as far as I'm concerned. I will tell you this, though. I've made certain that no man will ever be able to physically abuse me again. At least not without crawling away in a great deal of pain."

As he pulled Elise to her feet he commented with typical nineteenth-century mentality, "How do you plan to manage that? Not all men leave that area of their bodies vulnerable, especially the second time around."

He should have known better than to be skeptical.

One minute he was standing there holding Elise's hand. The next thing he knew, she'd grabbed his hand, stepped to his right as she swung his arm down and behind him, forcing him to bend at the waist. Her left hand shoved his upper arm toward the floor and her right hand held the back of his. All the while she applied a gentle, yet very effective pressure in the direction of his elbow.

"Well, this is one of the ways I had in mind," Elise said casually as she maintained her hold on her victim. "If I showed you the most effective way, we'd be calling 911."

Reed had a close-up view of the floor but didn't see it. All he was aware of was that this slip of a woman had managed to put a man twice her size in a position of total submission. If he moved she could easily break his wrist or dislocate his shoulder.

"I think you've made your point," he conceded to the floor, "and I'm really not interested in a demonstration of the most effective technique."

He shook his arm when she released it. She grinned and batted her eyes with an overdone sense of innocence. A whole new respect for this woman swept over him.

"It's called Akido. It's very effective self-defense, but it can also be very dangerous. That's why part of the training is learning when to use it and how much force to use when you do. If I ever have to use it for real, I'll put every ounce of energy I have into it."

Elise smiled up at him.

Dear God, he thought, *the woman I love flies airplanes and can have men twice her size on their knees in pain, begging for mercy. What have I gotten myself into?*

Slowly, pride at her abilities began to mingle with his awe, and a hesitant grin tugged at his mouth.

"Since I've known you, you've sprayed me with chemicals, taken ten years off my life in automobiles and airplanes, and nearly broken my arm. No wonder I love you."

Chapter 9

THE CLOUD OF depression that had hovered over Reed since his learning of the War refused to go away entirely. However, he was a man of logic and common sense, and he told himself there was nothing he could do, especially one hundred and thirty years after the fact. He even admitted to himself that, had he been forewarned about the impending disaster in 1844, there would have been very little, if anything, he could have done to alter the path of history.

He also did some serious thinking about his present situation. Adapting had been a way of life for him. He'd adapted to losing his family; to being raised by a distant cousin. His everyday life on the plantation had always been a series of situations that one could not control and had to adapt to. If disease or weather ruined the cane before it could be harvested, he salvaged what he could and prepared for the next planting. If a hurricane hit, he got everyone into a storm cellar and came out with hammer in hand to repair the damage after the storm had passed. When a drought hit, he irrigated, hauling water side by side with his workers.

He'd dealt with being thrown into the twentieth century in the same manner he dealt with everything else in his life. He'd accepted the situation and done his best to live with it. Brooding and moping wouldn't get him back to 1844, and now he wasn't sure he even wanted to go. What he'd found here, in 1994, was the thing he'd wanted most in his own time.

And there was the problem. The mere thought of living without Elise caused an unbearable ache in the center of his chest. Yet every passing day made him more and more aware of how totally unsuited he was to live in the twentieth century. He would have to go to school to learn some sort of skill, but how could he explain the huge gaps in present-day knowledge that were sure to surface if he did?

He hashed these things over in his mind while he worked at shaving some wood off the bottom of a door that had been sticking. Doing some repair work on his . . . no, Elise's . . . home had kept him busy while she flew her trips. He felt as though he was paying her back in some small way for all the money she'd had to spend on him.

His mind drifted back to Elise as he hefted the solid cypress door and maneuvered it back onto its hinges.

She hadn't been happy when he continued to treat her as he'd been taught to treat a lady. He chuckled deep in his throat and shook his head at the thought. Only Elise. But she never once asked him to put his morals aside, and heaven knows it probably wouldn't take much to persuade him to. The night of their "private dance" had haunted him like a melody, playing itself over and over in his head no matter how hard he tried to change the tune.

Elise was his friend, as well as the woman he loved, and the next time he made love to her he wanted her to be his wife. Nevertheless, he couldn't ask her to marry him. He couldn't ask her to live with the constant fear of him vanishing looming over their heads like a huge, black cloud.

That thought surfaced from the back of his mind every time he held her in his arms. At these times he felt as if he held her with one arm and pushed her away with the other. If only he knew for certain that he would spend his future in the twentieth century.

"Penny for your thoughts." Elise shoved herself off the door frame and ambled into the room. Concentrating on his task, he apparently hadn't heard her barreling up the staircase, so she'd taken the opportunity to study the man who'd become the most important part of her life. Her career, her home—nothing in her life even began to measure up to what Reed had grown to mean to her.

He swung around with a welcoming smile and automatically reached for the shirt he'd discarded earlier.

"Here, let me help you with that." Elise closed the gap between them and held his shirtfront as if to button it, then slid her fingertips down the center of his chest instead. She lightly massaged the bare skin of his sides before encircling his waist with her arms, reveling in the warmth of his body. She gave him an impish grin when she looked up at him. "Well, what were you thinking?"

Reed stared at her with the corners of his mouth curved in a sad little smile.

"I'm afraid my thoughts would cost you more than a penny."

"Try me."

He continued to stare for a few more seconds, then sucked in a deep breath and held it, as if struggling with a decision. He released it with an air of resignation.

"I was thinking about us."

"Oh?"

"I was thinking about how much I love you . . . how I want to spend the rest of my life with you."

When she perched on the edge of the bed of the spare room they were in, he took a seat in the rocker. Butterflies launched in her stomach at his words, but after he paused for several seconds, she quirked a questioning eyebrow at him.

"You want to spend the rest of your life with me *but . . .*"

"But how can I ask you to marry me, never mind plan for the future or a family, if we don't know how long I'll be here? I'd marry you this minute, if you'd have me, if I could be sure I'd be here for you tomorrow."

Elise came off the bed and dropped to her knees in front of Reed. Her sundress billowing around her. With a gentle touch she reached up and placed her hands on both sides of his face. Her thumb softly traced a path across his lips.

"Do you know what I think? I think that we were meant to be together. I feel like you're the missing piece to the puzzle of my life—the biggest piece—and when you fit so perfectly into that huge, empty space I had, you filled my life up and made it perfect. We will be together, darlin'. Other pieces of the puzzle can be removed, but yours is the only one that makes the picture of my life complete."

He took her hand, pressed a kiss to her ring finger.

"You've described my feelings exactly, little one. But I could never have found the words. I believe we were meant to be together. I feel in my heart that someday all our fears will be dealt with, and we'll be free to plan our lives together forever. I want you to know that even though I can't put a ring on your finger this minute . . . it's the ring around my heart that holds me to you. It's more permanent than any wedding ring."

If Elise had harbored even the slightest doubt about her love for this man, it was wiped away with his words. Her heart melted as she repeated them in her mind and stored them away as a keepsake.

She rose from her knees and brought Reed with her, then pressed her body against the warm, solid length of his. Her head snuggled lightly against his chest. She could hear his quickened heartbeat and felt the evidence that their declarations to each other had affected him as much as they had her. The warmth of his hands seeped through her clothes as they slid down both sides of her body. With one hand she smoothed his mussed hair back over one ear. She kissed the hollow at the base of his neck, heard his intake of breath. He made a move toward the inviting bed just a few feet away, then stopped. With a frustrated sigh, he wrapped his strong arms around her, squeezed several times in rapid succession and growled playfully into her neck before releasing her and grabbing up some of the tools he'd been using.

Elise stood still for several seconds, attempting to slow the heated blood Reed had sent rushing through her veins. She knew the frustration he was feeling. She felt it herself. She also knew this abstinence was a matter of honor to him. If she pressed him into giving in to their desires, she would be the cause of the guilt he would suffer later.

Elise would never, for any reason, coerce Reed into doing anything that would cause him to think less of himself. Personal honor was not something high on most twentieth-century priority lists, and she felt immense pride at Reed's stand. Even if it did cause her to toss for hours in a lonely bed at night.

She clapped her hands together and rubbed them in an attempt to release some of her pent-up energy. The last of the tools were laying on the bed, so she snatched them up and tagged along behind Reed as he made his way to his next project.

"Hey, I didn't come up here to get all mushy. I came up here to see if you want to go with me to Janice and Don's party."

She bumped into his back when he came to an abrupt stop in front of a loose towel rack in her bathroom. He eyeballed the towel rack with a great deal of concentration, chose a screwdriver and applied it to the wobbly screw.

"Of course. When did they say it was going to be?"

She watched the muscles in his arm flex as he concentrated on tightening each screw.

He glanced up and quirked an eyebrow at her.

"Oh, the party's this weekend. Saturday night at eight."

He straightened and twisted a few kinks out of his back, giving her a dazzling smile and displaying a row of straight, white teeth.

As he swiveled around in the opposite direction he said, "Do you think we could celebrate my birthday while we're at it?"

"Really? Your birthday's May 7th? You're kidding. How old will you be?"

"One hundred and eighty-seven."

Elise punched him in the arm for managing such a straight face. She had to dance out of his reach while she did some quick subtraction. His retaliation for her physical abuse of him was usually a healthy dose of tickling.

"So you'll be an old man of thirty-seven. I'm not sure I want to be seen with you."

"Oh, so if you're such a babe in the woods, when were you born?" Reed was stalking her now, his arms outstretched to block her escape. Elise retreated toward the shower.

"I'll be thirty-two on June 22nd. Considerably younger than your advanced years." She now had one arm in front of her to ward off his attack and the other behind her in a frantic search for the handle to the shower door. Just as she found it, Reed lunged. She threw the door open and jumped into the shower, realizing her mistake too late.

A smug, victorious smile spread across Reed's face as he swaggered the last couple of steps to the shower door. He pulled it open, then began inspecting his fingernails as he leaned against the metal frame.

Elise knew he was watching her out of the corner of his eye, but she wasn't ready to give up yet. She waited patiently while he savored his victory.

"I know you're planning something, little one." Reed took a step into the shower. "You can forget it, though. There's no way around—" An icy blast of water hit him full in the face. His arm shot out just as Elise darted past him, and he pulled her under the frigid downpour with him.

"I've heard of taking cold showers," she yelled above the rushing water, "but I always thought the point was to take them alone."

Reed stood in front of his bathroom mirror, peeling the sodden T-shirt away from his stomach and over his dripping head. It was a good thing the shower had been a cold one. He wasn't sure if his resolve would have survived a moist, steamy encounter with Elise. Things got steamy enough under the cold water.

It was getting harder for him to live up to his pledge to have Elise as his wife before making love to her again, especially since she made it clear she would be so willing.

Reed's mind wandered over the conversations they'd had this morning. He warmed at the memory of her touching declaration of her feelings and the sincerity she'd conveyed with her eyes. He had exercised every ounce of willpower to merely hug her and walk away instead of lowering her to the bed and allowing them the release they both craved. He knew if he ever gave in to the ache that had taken up permanent residence in the center of his chest, he would never again be able to hold it under control. The need was not just physical. He knew no matter how many times he and Elise made love, he would still feel this way. He wanted to show Elise how much he loved her. His feelings were so strong he couldn't put them into words, even in his thoughts. All he could do was *feel* them. He had realized this the night he had carried her to his bed. It was as if an unknown force had guided his every touch and translated his feelings into the most ancient language.

"Hey, I'm getting hungry out here!" Elise banged once on the door, then moved on down the hall. He heard the distant jingle of car keys as she galloped down the stairs.

"Be right there," he called as he swung the door open, giving his left pant leg a couple of tugs. A quick glance in the mirror told him it was safe to leave the room without having to limp.

As he grabbed a polo shirt and drew it over his head, Elise reappeared at his door.

"Aren't you ready yet? Geez, I had to re-do my hair and makeup and still beat you to the punch. And they say women are vain."

Reed raised an eyebrow at Elise's insulting little grin and shrugged with a knowing smile.

"I guess I'd better not tell you then that . . . I'm worth the wait."

As he walked away, the warmth of her hand burned through his jeans as it trailed its way from the back of his waist to his left thigh.

"Oh, darlin', I already know that."

The day dawned with a shimmering blue sky. Occasional feathery clouds passed across the sun, doing little to dilute its brilliance. At breakfast Reed offered to take Elise on the long-promised tour of "his" plantation as seen through 1844 eyes.

She tried to answer through a mouthful of croissant but only managed a muffled "Mmph." Nodding her head instead, she stood and gulped her coffee.

"It's a perfect day for one. What a great idea. The only thing is, I have a trip that leaves at five o'clock, but it's just to Indianapolis, and I'll be back by one. So when do we start?"

They both pulled on old jeans and T-shirts for their explorations. Sliding her hand into Reed's, Elise all but dragged him out the back door. She'd been looking forward to this for weeks.

Their first stop was the solitary slave cabin still standing. It had been kept up and maintained over the years as a storage shed. Reed had even used it after he'd freed his slaves. But the shack now held scant resemblance to its original state. His vivid descriptions, however, had Elise's imagination cranking at full tilt.

"There was a huge, flat rock here, used as a doorstep. And there were two windows instead of one. See? Someone boarded the west side up. A small fireplace burned over here, in the center of the longest wall. A rope bed stood against the south wall, and a homemade table and two chairs sat close to the fire."

The clutter of the cabin melted away, and she could almost smell dinner cooking on the fire as Reed spoke.

Next he led her to where an apple orchard had existed in his time. Only a few scattered trees remained, and the place bore no resemblance to an orchard at all. Reed speculated that one of the trees was the one he'd fallen from and broken his left arm when he had been eight years old.

None of the fields remained of the original property. They'd been sold generations ago, perhaps even after the Civil War to pay taxes.

His shoulders slumped a little as he scanned the horizon. Elise wasn't sure if his reaction was from the failure to find anything familiar or from homesickness brought on by his reminiscing.

As they swung around to return to the house, he again pointed out where the family cemetery had been. They'd gone in search of this place after his arrival, only to find that all traces of a cemetery had disappeared. There were no headstones or markers of any type. Elise assumed the war had been responsible for that. The house and grounds had fallen on hard times during the 1930s. She wasn't sure when one of Reed's descendants had found the capital to restore the home, but apparently the cemetery had been forgotten.

All in all, this little adventure wasn't going as she'd expected. To distract him, Elise grabbed his hand and pulled him into a run, challenging him to a race she knew she would lose. Of course, he let her win, and when he caught up with her at the back door, he offered to describe the house the way it had been in his time. It was as if he needed to go through this—to finish the tour and put it to rest in his mind.

He walked through the downstairs rooms, pointing out all the things that hadn't changed and describing those that had.

"The white ballroom was white even in my time. The chandelier would have been filled with candles of beeswax whenever the room was being used. Elise, I wish you could have seen it. Flowers and garlands covered every surface, filling the air with their perfume. Ladies sparkled in their finery . . ."

Elise could see it—could almost hear the music and murmuring voices of a genteel past.

In a voice barely above a whisper she said, "I wish I could see it, too."

They shook off their whimsy and moved on to the dining room, which had originally been blue. Blue paint had been extremely expensive because of the pigment used in making it and therefore was saved for the rooms where people were to be entertained and impressed. The epergne in the center of the table was not familiar to Reed, but had it been his, he informed her, it would have been filled with lemons. Again, the fruit was extremely rare and expensive and was used to symbolize wealth during social functions.

Elise already knew all of these little tidbits of information, but she enjoyed his look of pleasure while he related them. His version of blue paint and lemons was the twentieth century's version of expensive art and status cars.

He continued walking her through the downstairs, gave details of the ventilation system in the summer and pointed out a renovation that had been made in the area she used for a kitchen.

"My kitchen was separate from the house. This had been a work area for the servants and held the stairs to the cellar. C'mon, I'll show you."

A little more enthusiastic now, he opened the door to the cellar and motioned with his head for her to follow.

The two prowled around the dingy basement for a while. Reed seemed to be looking for something. After a few minutes he spoke.

"This was my favorite place to come and hide as a child. Nell would let a couple of the plantation children play hide-and-seek with me, and I always headed straight for the cellar. I bet you don't even know this is here."

He walked over to one of the rough-hewn planks covering the wall and gave it a shove. A whole panel of planks popped open and with a loud, rusty creak the door swung outward, revealing a small, closet-sized room.

Elise's heart jumped at the discovery. Her house had a secret room!

"Wow! This is great. What was it used for? Hiding runaways?"

"My father died when I was so young, I never knew why he had this built here. But it was great for hide-and-seek."

The two of them crowded into the tiny room. Dusty plank shelves decorated with lacy cobwebs lined the walls, and several old brown crocks were scattered randomly on the shelves. There was not enough light in the room to see well, so Elise squeezed back out. Reed brought a couple of the crocks with him.

After she knocked the dust from her jeans and pulled a few cobwebs from Reed's hair, she hefted one of the crocks and started upstairs with it.

"These'll look great in the kitchen. It can use a little 1844 ambiance."

When she plunked the stoneware down on the counter, her eyes fell on the clock.

"Oh, my gosh! Look at the time. I've got to get ready for work, and I definitely need a shower before I go."

She started to run out of the room but turned and skipped back to Reed. Shouldering up to him, she smoothed her hands across his dirt-smudged, T-shirt-clad chest and nuzzled his neck.

"Care to help me get cleaned up?" she questioned. Her voice lowered to a sexy huskiness.

Reed gazed down at her with a "what am I going to do with you" look.

"Little one, you have to be at the airport in less than two hours. If I helped you get cleaned up, you'd be lucky to get there by next week."

The heat in his voice left her with no question that he meant what he said.

Chapter 10

SHE WAS SO happy, it scared her. She spent half her time walking on a cloud and the other half waiting for a disaster. No one could be this happy and not have the rug yanked out from under her.

Right now she'd been swept off her feet. Literally. Reed had waited up for her again, in the ballroom, and they'd relived that glorious night, right down to their clothes.

He'd waited for her there on other nights when she'd come in from a trip. They'd always gone to their separate rooms and spent frustrating, lonely nights alone. But she could tell tonight would be different. She could feel it. And when he'd scooped her into his arms with a low, animal growl, all remaining doubt vanished.

She felt like a delicate flower in his arms. With her hands clasped behind his neck, she snuggled closer while his long strides ate up the length of the hall to the foyer.

Was he as excited as she? She had a feeling his staccato heartbeat was not from taking the stairs two at a time.

Elise's fantasy was on its way to the perfect ending when it stopped with jarring abruptness halfway up the staircase.

The front door flew open so hard it banged against the wall, slammed shut, and was kicked open again.

Reed spun to face the door. Elise's trailing gown fluttered out around them.

Every muscle in her body tensed. She was going to jail for homicide, if she didn't kill herself first for leaving the door unlocked.

"My, my, what a touching scene." Jeffrey's eyes looked as if it was all he could do to keep them open. Even from this distance she could see his dilated pupils. "What? D'ya have to get dressed up to get laid around here now?"

His words hadn't had time to register before Elise found herself standing on the stairs alone, watching Reed throw a nasty right into Jeff's jaw. The door took more abuse when Jeff bounced against it.

Amazingly, he didn't fall but sprang back, swinging at the air inches from Reed's face. He didn't seem to realize none of his punches hit their target. Reed hadn't moved a muscle to dodge them.

"You sonofabitch. I'll teach you to move in on my territory. I marked her long ago!"

That did it! Elise kicked off first one high heel and then the other. She stomped down the stairs with murder on her mind.

"You pompous piece of slime. I am not your territory. You may have made me feel like you'd stepped on me

more than once, but you, you underendowed, under-
achiever, have no claim on me whatsoever.

"I hate your guts! Do you hear me? I . . . hate . . . your . . .
guts!" She poked his chest with her index finger. "So get
out of my house and out of my life! GET OUT!"

She punctuated her last words with a mighty shove.
He staggered backward, but not far enough for her to
slam the door.

He grabbed the doorknob and pushed his face right up
into Elise's. The sour smell of scotch urged her back, but
she refused to budge.

"Don't think this is over, Elise. We're not through yet."

Reed grabbed a handful of Jeffrey's eighty-dollar tie
and lifted him up to meet him nose to nose.

"I'm afraid it is over, my disgusting friend. You see,
Elise and I are to be married."

Elise's eyes flew to Reed, and she fought to keep her
heart from exploding.

Reed seemed as surprised at his words as she. His
head shot back, and he turned and searched her face for
her reaction. Her huge, brilliant smile and barely percep-
tible nod gave him all the answer he needed.

"The next time you see her, she will be Mrs. Reed
Blackwell. And unless you are somewhat masochistic,
when next we meet I suggest you turn and go in the opposite direction. In fact, that advice applies now." Reed
spun Jeff by the shoulders and gave him a shove right
between the shoulder blades.

This time he not only shot through the door, but he
landed with a close-up view of the veranda floor.

Before she closed the door, Elise leaned her head
against the edge of it and sighed dramatically.

"You know, Jeff, shoving you out this front door is beginning to get tiresome. What say we don't do it anymore?"

With a flick of the wrist, she left the door to close it-self. He wasn't worth the energy of a slam.

Jeff was out of her thoughts the minute he was out of her sight.

Did Reed mean what he said about marriage, or was it just something he'd blurted out in the heat of his anger? When she turned from the door, she looked up into his soul-searching eyes. His face was impossible to read, but she felt his gaze delve deep into her heart.

Finally, he reached out and took her left hand in his. His movements were so slow and deliberate, it might have been happening in slow motion.

He brought her hand up to cradle his cheek as he sank to one knee and stared up at her through thick, black lashes. His other hand caressed the fingers of her free hand.

"Yes, I meant it," he said, and she wondered if she'd spoken her earlier thoughts aloud. "I love you, little one. I want to spend the rest of my life with you, in whatever century that might be." Elise fought the shiver that jolted through her body. "Will you do me the great honor of becoming my wife?"

Her heart melted. It literally melted and trickled like warm honey into every pore of her body. Reed stared up at her with those electric blue eyes. He still held her hand to his cheek, and her fingers rasped against a trace of stubble.

The tears came totally unexpected and hovered on her lower lashes. She'd never expected a proposal from Reed, and now that he'd asked, she couldn't even choke a "yes" past the huge lump in her throat. Instead she blinked hard and nodded and tried like crazy to stop her chin from quivering.

A gentle tug on her hand brought her down to perch

on his knee. Her face nuzzled against his neck, and he sifted his fingers through the back of her hair.

"Can I take that to mean a 'yes'?"

She giggled and raised her head to look at him.

"Just try backing out now, darlin'."

"Why does he need a fake ID, Elise? This isn't good. And here I'd decided he's the perfect man for you." Jan fired a couple more questions in Elise's direction, but Elise held up her hand in the time-out sign until all questioning stopped.

"He *is* perfect for me, Jan. You have to trust me on this one. I could lie to you and say he lost his birth certificate and we don't want to go through the hassle and wait of getting another one. But you're my friend. The truth is, he just flat out doesn't have one, or any other form of ID, and we want to get married right now."

Jan's voice had long since lost all the bleary traces of sleep. It was three A.M. when Elise had shown up on her doorstep. She'd known Jan would be able to help.

"Why are you in such a hurry? You're not pregnant, are you?" Jan's eyes dropped to Elise's midsection.

Elise laughed.

"No, Jan. I can definitely tell you that I am not pregnant."

"Then why? Why are you in such a hurry? How can this guy exist without any kind of identification? Elise, take your time with this. Don't do anything stupid."

She was too happy to take offense at anything Jan might say. Besides, she knew it was all said with her best interests at heart.

"Jan, I know I've always marched to the beat of a different drummer. I've been accused of being eccentric. But, think about it. Have I ever done anything really stupid?"

A long stretch of silence followed the question. Elise watched Jan search her mind for an act that qualified as stupid.

"No, I guess not," she said slowly. "But there's always the first time."

Elise laughed and hugged her friend. "I know this sounds crazy, but trust me. I know all about Reed. He's not a criminal or an illegal alien. I know why he doesn't have any ID, and someday I'll explain it all to you. But right now I want to get married!" She wiggled her eyebrows at Jan in a conspiratorial way. "Are you in?"

Jan groaned, long and loud, but she finally dragged herself to her feet and headed for her office at the back of the house.

"This is what I get for telling you what a computer graphics artist can do. Little did I know you would engage me in illegal activity. Now give me your damn birth certificate."

Elise watched, fascinated, while Jan took the document and managed to create a duplicate with all of Reed's information on it. She did a quick calculation in her head when Jan asked for Reed's year of birth, but that was the worst of the procedure.

Actually, the worst part was waiting for Jan to get through. By the time Jan handed over the finished product, Elise held it to her breast like a precious artifact and forced Jan to dance around the room with her.

They both fell into a sprawl on the wicker sofa in the office. Jan arched a cynical brow at her.

"So when is this wedding going to take place?"

Elise flopped into the corner of the couch and slid the birth certificate between thumb and forefinger.

"As soon as we can get a marriage license and find someone to marry us. Hopefully this afternoon, 'cause I gotta tell you, if it doesn't happen soon I'm going to ex-

plode. Can you imagine? Reed insists on having the
wedding night after the wedding."

Jan's eyes widened, and a new look of respect for
Reed lit them from within. Then she frowned.

"Well, what are you wearing to get married in? Not
that, I hope." She eyed the jeans and T-shirt Elise had
thrown on as if she believed she might actually wear
them. "Never mind." Jan cut Elise off before she had a
chance to answer. "If you're going to do this, you're
going to do it right. Have you changed your security
code at the house?"

"No, but . . ."

"Good. Go get your marriage license, then be back at
your house around, oh, noon."

"But what if . . ."

"Noon. If you can fly a plane, you can be at your
house at noon. And, oh! You might want to pick up a
ring."

The paperwork involved in obtaining a marriage license
was tedious. Reed let Elise take charge of all the forms,
and she grumbled over some of the blanks which asked
for numbers. He didn't know what a Social Security
number was, but she'd decided to make one up.

After their trip to the courthouse, they stopped by a
jeweler's to pick out a wedding ring. He agreed with
Elise to have a special set of matching rings made. Nothing the jeweler had in stock did justice to their feelings
for each other. The man promised the custom-made rings
would be ready in four weeks. Elise said she could wear
her mother's birthstone ring at the ceremony.

Now that those details were taken care of, all Reed
wanted to do was find a justice of the peace and get himself married to this woman. His morals wouldn't allow
him to sleep with her again before marriage. He'd

slipped up once in the heat of the moment, and the experience made it nearly impossible to stick to his beliefs. It would have happened again last night if not for Jeffrey's questionably timed appearance. His resolve slipped more by the moment, and it was only a matter of time before Elise's appeal canceled all his best intentions. The fact that he loved her was the driving force behind his desire to get married, but he'd be lying if he said it was uppermost on his mind right now.

"I want to get married, too, darlin'." Elise massaged his knee while she drove. Her hand worked its way up his thigh, and he slid a little lower on the seat to make his leg more accessible. "But Jan's taken charge here, and we've been given orders to be back at the house at noon. And if I know her," she said with a smile, "we'll be married just as quickly, but with a lot more style."

Her hand left his leg and returned to the wheel. Reed gave a sigh of relief. Even though he'd enjoyed the impromptu massage, his mouth had gone dry, and the car had become entirely too small to get comfortable in.

The Seviers' car sat at the end of the avenue of oaks. Elise parked beside it and leaned across the console to plant a long, promise-filled kiss on Reed's lips. When she drew away, she gave him a look so provocative it had every nerve in his body standing at attention. Then she bounced back into her seat and threw open the door.

"So! Let's go get married!"

A groan rumbled in his throat at this unpredictable woman. One thing was certain. He would never worry about boredom.

Elise grabbed his hand after he'd unfurled himself from the interior of the car. She slid her arm around his waist, and he draped one arm across her shoulders on the walk to the house.

The front door swung inward before they ever reached it. Jan stood there, beaming.

"It's about time."

Jan's digital watch beeped the noon hour as she spoke.

When they stepped through the door Elise inhaled a deep, appreciative breath at the sight before them.

Ropes of fragrant, green wisteria vines spiraled up the banister of the cantilevered staircase and decorated the archways above the doors leading off the foyer. Purple blossoms dripped from the vines, and white roses with delicate, lacy bows dotted the greenery. Milky tapers stood clustered together in every available candleholder, ready to be lighted. The windows flanking the front door had been opened, and the white sheers rippled inward on a gentle breeze.

Elise spun in a circle, murmuring a soft "Ohhhhhhh." Her gaze took in every detail. She cried out with delight at the sight of the dining room. Reed tagged along behind her when she ran in to get a better look.

The table was draped with an antique, Battenberg lace tablecloth. Two bottles of Dom Perignon nestled amid a mountain of ice cubes in sterling silver buckets, and several pieces of Baccarat crystal waited to be filled. In the very center, surrounded by a ring of waxy magnolia blossoms, stood a three-tiered wedding cake.

"How did you . . . where did you ever . . . ?"

Jan smiled and shrugged. "Let's just say I owe Fouchard's Bakery a *big* favor."

Elise hurled herself into Jan's arms and hugged her friend. She thanked her in a voice thick with tears. Reed was surprised to find a lump forming in his own throat. He knew this gesture of friendship would forever leave a warm spot in his heart for the Seviers.

Jan allowed herself to be hugged only a few seconds

before she pulled Elise toward the stairway and looked pointedly at Don.

"Take Reed up and get him into your mess dress, honey. Just leave off the shoulder boards and fruit salad, and he'll look fine. And you," she turned to Elise, "we have a wedding gown to get you into."

Don looked at Reed and mumbled, "Bossy, isn't she?" but the two men nevertheless set off to do as they were told.

Reed freshened up and donned the black, formal military uniform that would be his wedding garb. The short-waisted jacket and satin-striped trousers fit him as though tailor-made. Even the shoes were close enough in size to make do.

Without the shoulder ranks on the epaulettes and the clusters of medals and ribbons on the chest, the uniform looked very civilian.

Reed was surprised to discover a vain streak in his nature. As he studied his trim, powerful reflection in the mirror, he acknowledged the term "mess dress" was a misnomer. Indeed, upon looking at his reflection, he concluded he'd never felt less of a mess in his life.

"I always hated that uniform," Don said. He sat back in the antique saber chair and crossed an ankle over a knee. "I always felt like I should drape a towel over my arm and go take somebody's dinner order. But women love the thing." He cast a rakish leer in Reed's direction and laughed the universal male laugh. "If you know what I mean."

Reed nodded with a chuckle and adjusted his cuffs. It wouldn't do to dwell on Don's meaning until after the ceremony. It could prove embarrassing otherwise.

"How did the two of you manage all this in such a short time?" He deemed it best to change the subject.

Don snorted and scrunched lower in the two-sided

seat. He had already changed into a black, double-breasted suit.

"Never underestimate the powers of Jan Sevier. The woman dragged me out of bed around four-thirty this morning with a list of honey-do's a mile long. When she gets an idea, I've learned to obey orders and go with the flow."

The sound of the front door knocker echoed through the house. Don was already on his feet when Jan's disembodied voice asked him to get the door.

"Probably the minister. No JP for you guys."

Reed followed Don down the hallway. He was in the process of running a nervous finger around the collar of his shirt when Jan's head popped out of Elise's doorway.

"If that's Reverend Mitchell, tell him we'll be . . ." she stopped in midsentence and blocked his view of the room with her body. "Hey," she drew the word out in flattering appreciation, "you clean up pretty well."

Reed grinned. It was obvious why she and Elise got along so well.

"Anyway, if that's the minister, we should only be another fifteen minutes or so." The door shut in his face.

Don made the introductions between Reed and the man who would perform the ceremony. The minister exuded a warmth and fatherly aura. Reed took a liking to him right away.

"I have to tell you, Reed, you're getting a wonderful, unique woman. She's been coming to our little church for years, and I've been tempted to play matchmaker for her several times, but my wife wouldn't allow it." His laughter boomed against the ceiling. "That's a switch, isn't it?

"Don, I assume you and your lovely wife will be the official witnesses."

Don nodded. "In fact, we'll probably be the only witnesses. We didn't catch anyone home when we started calling friends. We left messages on machines, but I'll be surprised if anyone shows up in time for the ceremony."

Jan appeared for a moment at the top of the stairs, cleared her throat dramatically, then was gone again.

"Oh, that's my cue."

Don lit the many candles, then disappeared into the ballroom. Seconds later the soft strains of the wedding march filtered into the foyer.

This is it! All the blood drained from Reed's extremities and left his hands icy cold and his knees trembling. He was only vaguely aware of Don guiding him into position at the bottom of the staircase.

He watched Jan appear again and begin to slowly descend the stairs. She wore an orchid suit that accented her tan and made her look more feminine than ever. She carried a single white rose atop a Bible that Reed recognized as Elise's.

Then all coherent thought stopped.

His bride gazed down at him from the top of the stairs. He hadn't thought she could be more beautiful, but she surpassed anything he could ever dream.

The gown was the color of rich, heavy cream and embroidered heavily with seed pearls. The skirts hugged her tiny waist, only to flare out gently, and the pearl-encrusted hem dusted the floor when she moved. Long sleeves fell from just off her shoulders and encased her arms all the way into points on the back of her hands.

The point was repeated in the center of her forehead, where a diadem of pearls and baby's breath encircled her head. The frothy, diaphanous veil haloed the curls in her hair, then fell to mingle with the embroidery at her feet.

Reed forgot to breathe. Blood roared in his ears and his heart pounded, but it wasn't until Elise took her first step toward him that he inhaled. He drew a shaky breath of the wisteria-scented air and fought to slow his heartbeat.

He unconsciously swiped the palms of his hands against his trousers before reaching out to take Elise's fingers. At his icy touch, she glanced up and smiled empathetically. Her own hands were none too warm. She pulled his fingers up and warmed them against her cheek before they turned to face the minister.

Reed was only vaguely aware of Jan and Don stepping to each side of them. He heard Reverend Mitchell's voice and responded when he should, but he couldn't take his eyes from Elise's face.

She glowed with love. It was a tangible thing. He absorbed it into his soul, and it filled the empty space that had plagued him his entire life. Suddenly warmth flooded back into his fingers, his knees stopped trembling, and he felt as though he now basked in the rays of a summer sun.

"The ring, please."

Jan snapped to attention and handed a ring to Don, who handed it to Reverend Mitchell. The older man spoke about the symbol of eternity, and before Reed knew it, he was slipping the birthstone ring onto Elise's left hand and murmuring, "With this ring, I thee wed."

The ceremony was over in the blink of an eye. He leaned down to kiss Elise Gerard Blackwell, and the innocent nibble he'd intended turned into a full body press. The kiss dissolved into laughter, though, when Jan mentioned something about the ice buckets in the dining room.

He smiled down at Elise and just studied her face.

"What are you thinking?" she asked in a voice no more than a whisper.

"I'm thinking, little one, that I don't feel any different. What does 'married' feel like?"

She narrowed her eyes and flashed him a wicked grin. The warmth of her hand branded through his clothing in a most disconcerting area.

"It feels . . . like this."

The weakness came back to his knees. His eyebrows shot to his hairline, and he glanced around to see who had witnessed this little interchange. To his relief, the others were entering the dining room, so he took the opportunity to enjoy feeling "married," and made Elise feel a little "married" herself.

"Oh, geez, get a room." Don's face, etched with feigned disgust, hovered at the dining room door. Once he got their attention, he waved a bottle of champagne in their direction, as if to lure them to him.

Reed spent several seconds fluffing and readjusting Elise's veil while he waited for his body to return to a state fit for mixed company. Just when he'd completely recovered, he had to catch his wife's errant hand in an ironclad grip.

"Little one!" Her grin made her eyes sparkle even more. He let out a long, happy sigh. "Don't ever change."

Jan snapped pictures as the handsome couple fed cake to each other, and Don videoed the proceedings. Toasts ranged from the sincere to the outrageous among the small group.

More pictures were taken by the staircase. For the benefit of the camera, Reed swept Elise into his arms halfway up the steps, as if on their way to their rooms. The whole party even trooped outside and posed under a moss-hung live oak.

Finally, Jan came over and gave Elise a sisterly hug.

"Don't worry about getting my gown and the suit back. I'll pick them up next time . . ." Her eyes fell on the gold filigree locket that hung from a choker around Elise's neck. "That's beautiful. Is it new?"

Elise's hand came up and toyed with the locket, then she reached around and removed it for closer inspection.

"No, actually it's an antique. It's my 'something old.' I found it ages ago, pinned on one of the old dresses in the trunks in the attic. See? It doubles as a brooch."

Jan admired the piece of jewelry a moment longer, then fastened it back around Elise's throat.

"It really sets the dress off. The perfect touch. Well," she waggled her eyebrows, "I guess we won't be seeing you two at the anniversary party tonight."

Elise gasped, then slammed the palm of her hand to her forehead.

"Oh, Jan, I completely forgot. And . . . oh no! This is Reed's birthday. I didn't even get him a gift!" She turned to her new husband and looked so unhappy he wanted to kiss her.

Reed gave her a crestfallen look, then leaned close to her ear and whispered dramatically, "We'll make it to the party. But as for my gift, well, I guess you'll have to find some way to make it up to me."

"Here's to a most extraordinary life with a most extraordinary woman." Reed chinked his champagne glass against hers, and they entwined their arms in a lovers' toast.

Elise stared into Reed's penetrating eyes, and her stomach did flip-flops even after she looked away.

They lay nestled in the bed in her room. They'd dived into it the minute the guests were gone and their wedding attire was off. But once there, things slowed down to an agonizing pace.

Now here he was, making romantic toasts to her, with most of his body either draped, entwined, or pressed against hers.

The scorch of her gaze reflected what her body was feeling.

Okay, darlin'. Two can play at this game.

A glistening drop of champagne slid from the gold-rimmed edge of Reed's goblet where his lips had been only moments before. She watched it cut a lazy path through the condensation and allowed it to slide down the stem of the crystal before she reached out and stopped its progress with her index finger.

She retraced the path, upward this time. Her finger slid in torturous languor up the stem and over the cut-glass bowl. When she reached the gold rim, she raised her eyes and, with one look, promised him every fantasy he could ever conceive.

He swallowed, hard, and her finger continued on to circle the rim once. She held his gaze as she brought her champagne-moist finger seductively to her mouth. Her lips closed over her finger as her eyes fluttered closed.

The sound of the growl deep in his throat was her last coherent thought for hours.

Chapter 11

THE AIR WAS balmy with a tropical breeze as the silver Jag shot down the avenue of oaks. Stars glittered like diamonds in a cloudless sky.

Elise glittered, too, as beautiful as the stars, in the tiny, black-beaded cocktail dress she'd bought for the occasion. She leaned her head back against the leather seat and let the wind whip through her hair.

Reed glanced over at her and was struck again at her two transformations of the day. He was used to admiring her beauty; Elise always looked wonderful. But today she'd been a breathtaking bride, and tonight . . . tonight she had stepped out of her daily persona and had become a totally different woman. Her shoulder-length hair was full and wind tossed, her lips a moist, inviting red. But her eyes . . . she'd made up her eyes in shades of brown and gray, and when she turned them on him he felt as if an exotic, green-eyed cat were piercing him with its gaze. That feline quality extended itself into her mannerisms as she moved with the grace of a panther.

He jerked his eyes back to the road and readjusted his grip on the steering wheel. Even though he and Elise had spent a lot of time practicing on back roads, he still didn't feel altogether comfortable behind the wheel of a car. He did, however, feel exhilarated.

Elise gave directions as they came to a stop at a traffic light. He turned his head to check the left lane before pulling out and met two pairs of eyes, both very feminine and very admiring. The blond in the passenger seat of the car next to him leaned toward her window.

"Nice car," she said, her voice low and throaty.

From beside him, Reed could feel his new wife moving about.

"Thank you," Elise returned in a husky voice of her own. She leaned her head onto Reed's shoulder and gave the girls in the next car a brilliant smile.

Reed's admirers looked at each other with disappointment. The neighboring car sped away when the light turned green, but not without one final glance of approval in Reed's direction from its occupants.

Elise didn't mention the little encounter. Instead she turned her attention to giving him directions and praising his driving skills. She gave him a verbal pat on the back as he pulled up to a space close to their friends' house.

Reed impressed himself with what he had accomplished in driving them to the party. His first attempt at driving had left them both with seat belt burns on their necks when he'd applied the brake.

Elise jumped from the car and waited for him on the curb as he unfolded himself from the interior. She threaded her fingers through his, and they strolled up the gaslit walk to the front door.

Before they stepped inside, Elise squeezed Reed's hand and gave him a questioning look. He bent over and kissed her forehead.

"Don't worry, little one. If I can conquer microwaves, VCRs, automobiles and you," he said with a teasing grin, "a room full of twentieth-century people should be a walk in the park."

It was unlike any social function Reed had ever been to. They walked right into the house, unannounced and without knocking, and into the midst of a throng of people. He was only mildly surprised at the absence of a receiving line. Within seconds Jan was upon them, hugging Reed with as much warmth as she did Elise. Don was only moments behind, a glass of champagne in each hand for the new arrivals.

"You realize you guys have just cost me fifty bucks. I bet Jan you two wouldn't see the outside of your bedroom for a week, let alone make it to this party."

"Elise, we need to talk," Jan whispered as she hugged her again.

"Sure. What's up?"

Looking around, Jan seemed to be searching for someone. "Well, Cathy brought a date."

"Is that so?" Elise widened her eyes in obviously feigned shock.

"Yes. I just want you to know I didn't invite him."

Reed watched Elise as her gaze fell upon the person in question. She let out a snort of disgust and squeezed her eyes shut. Jeffrey was still there when she opened them.

As if he felt her stare, he turned and saw her looking in his direction. With a smirk on his stubbled face he excused himself from his date and moved with an arrogant strut toward their little group.

Reed felt her stiffen when Jeff started toward them.

She took no notice when Reed released her hand and stepped away.

It was all Reed could do to keep himself from smashing his fist into the man's conceited face. Instead, he stepped into Jeff's path.

Jeffrey bestowed an indignant stare and tried to step around him. Reed moved with him. He ignored Jeffrey's threatening look and spoke in a very low, yet audible voice.

"You seem to have a very poor memory, sir. Elise is now my wife." He enjoyed the disbelief that jerked Jeffrey's body. "If you have no desire to attract unpleasant attention, you will remain a respectful distance from her. Do not try to approach her. Do not try to talk to her. If you choose not to heed my warning, you will be fortunate if you are able to crawl to your automobile afterward."

Reed turned his back and walked away, that very action an insult to the cretin who had dared to lay a violent hand on his wife.

Jeffrey glared at Reed's retreating back. A dull, brick red color suffused his face and neck. He looked as though he might launch himself into Reed, but he merely grabbed a drink from a passing waiter and stomped off in the opposite direction.

"What did you say to him?" Elise grabbed Reed's arm. Her worried look turned into a dazzling smile that made her exotic eyes twinkle when he smiled at her.

"I simply refreshed his memory and pointed out the inadvisability of his approaching you." Reed shrugged off the encounter as if it were nothing.

"Well, whatever you said, it was definitely effective. I've never seen Jeff so ready to explode."

Elise felt as if a heavy weight had been lifted from her when she realized she would never again have to endure

a verbal sparring match with Jeff. And that's exactly
what she would have had to do this evening. That or
spend the night dodging him.

She stretched upward and nuzzled Reed's neck, murmuring a thank-you.

The few drops of cologne he'd splashed on after his
shower wreaked havoc on her senses. He had been so
sparing with it she was forced to cuddle up close just to
catch the scent. Deciding it was masochistic to torture
herself in that way, she moved away to mingle and regain her self-control. Every time she inhaled, she had to
fight the urge to show Reed the way to the master bedroom. She would love to give him a tour of Jan and
Don's king-sized bed. After all, they were legal now.

Her daydreaming stopped when she felt a warm hand
encircle her elbow. As she turned with a smile and aimed
her sense of smell toward Reed's neck, she was brought
up short with annoying abruptness.

She stiffened when she realized the hand on her arm
was not Reed's. The grip tightened.

"Don't cause a scene, Elise. Your husband is otherwise occupied. I just want to talk."

Jeffrey attempted to guide Elise out of the room, but
she dug in her heels in the hallway and refused to budge
further. He threw a nervous glance over his shoulder.

"I have no qualms in causing a scene, Jeff, if you
don't let go of my arm and leave me alone."

"Elise, this bozo who's appointed himself your
guardian angel won't be around forever, once he finds
out you married him on the rebound. You may as well
talk to me now, while I'm willing to be patient. I may
not be so understanding when you come crawling to me
after he splits."

Elise glared at him for several seconds, then released
a deep breath, in the hopes he would think she was re-

considering. The nerve of this maggot, to suggest she married Reed on the rebound from him. The only rebound he caused was bouncing her off the walls.

She peered up at him through her lashes, striving for the picture of innocence. He released her arm as she slid her hands up to cradle his face, a tender caress that left the index and middle fingers of both hands in the hollow beneath his ears, directly behind his jaw.

"Let me put this to you in a language you'll understand, Jeffrey." Her fingers began a pressure inward that increased in intensity. He tried to jerk back at the first twinge of pain, which only increased the pressure.

"I want you to leave me alone. I hate you. There will never be a time when I come crawling back to you or even look in your direction. Do you understand? LEAVE ME ALONE!" With this final statement hissed through clinched teeth she released the pressure and shoved his face out of her hands. She took the opportunity to slip back into the crowd while he was still rubbing the pain from his jaws and catching his balance.

What would it take to get this jerk off her back? If she didn't think he'd fight dirty, she'd let Reed deal with him and put him in his place. She never, in her wildest dreams, ever expected to find herself embroiled in an abusive situation, one she had almost no control of, no matter what she did to stop it. She knew Reed would handle it. There wasn't a doubt in her mind he would lay down his life for her.

"Hello . . . earth to Elise. Anybody home?"

Her attention snapped back to the party. She focused on Jan's waving hand in front of her face.

"Huh? Oh, what were you saying?"

Without moving her head, Jan sliced her eyes to the left, indicating two very chic women by the wet bar. She lowered her voice to a conspiratorial whisper.

"Do you know those two? They've spent the last five minutes sending looks to your husband that must be scorching his clothes." Elise followed Jan's gaze and studied the sultry pair while her friend continued. "I don't know them well. They work with Don, so we had to invite them. They have a reputation for jumping anyone with facial hair."

Recognition lit in Elise. She watched the women in question slink across the living room and flank an unsuspecting Reed. Each of them clung to a muscular arm.

"Oh, yes. They were admiring my car earlier." Elise's voice was saccharin sweet. "Would you excuse me, Jan? I feel the need to make sure Reed is clean shaven."

Jan's face glowed with delight, and she followed close on Elise's heels.

Elise pulled her cellular phone from her clutch bag while she elbowed her last few feet to Reed. With the phone held to her ear, she touched Reed's chest to interrupt the conversation.

"Excuse me, darlin', but this is the hospital lab on the phone. The test results are back and they're . . . well, they're positive." Then, with a grimace on her face she said in a dramatic whisper, "They want to know if that rash is still oozing."

The hands jerked away from Reed's arms as if they'd touched hot coals. Burning, sensual gazes dulled into blank looks of total disinterest, and the pair of sequin-clad bodies slithered back into the crowd.

She could hear Jan's trademark laugh bubbling over her shoulder. When Elise put her hand behind her back, palm up, Jan slapped it with her own before strolling away.

Reed stared at Elise with a quirked eyebrow. He failed to hide a smile behind his long-suffering look.

"Madam, you are incorrigible," he said, unable to mask his amusement. "I should be annoyed with you for placing my health in question, but I fear if those ladies had had their way, I may have truly ended up with the phantom rash you spoke of . . . or worse."

"Don't mention it, suh. You know we Southan gals ahn't as delicate as we appeah. And I was just protectin' mah interests." Elise batted her eyes and fluttered an imaginary fan, her face the picture of innocence. In reality, her heart was doing flip-flops. She fought down the flame that rose through her body when she looked into her husband's laughing blue eyes. It had only been a few hours, but she wanted this man—in the worst way. The need for him built inside her like a well-stoked fire. It was just a matter of time before the fire engulfed her, and when it did she planned to take him with her.

Reed couldn't help staring at Elise. If she'd had on a ruffled ballgown, he could have believed himself to be back home, so true was her nineteenth-century accent and mannerisms. Unexpected homesickness mingled with his love for her, and he felt himself being pulled in two different directions. It was the first time this pairing of emotions had been this strong. He didn't cherish the feeling.

He knocked back the remains of his champagne and attempted to refocus his thoughts.

Don walked up to the couple, sliding his arm around Elise's shoulders as he gave her an affectionate squeeze. He gestured to Reed with his chin and smiled. "So, how's the first few hours of married life?"

Without missing a beat, Elise narrowed her eyes to a torrid, feline gaze, and stared at Don for several seconds. The barest hint of a smile curved her lips when she slowly reached up and moistened her finger with her tongue. Throwing her head back in a pose of ecstasy and making a soft hissing sound, like that of raindrops hitting a flame, her finger trailed down her neck to come to rest on her collarbone. She looked through her lashes, piercing Reed with an emerald stare.

"Ohhhh, woman," Don groaned. "You know all the right buttons to push. If you two feel the need to duck out of here early, I think I'll know who to blame."

By the time Elise had concluded her little "simulation," Reed's mind had gone blank. For several seconds no coherent thought penetrated the burning that threatened to incinerate his body. His first returning thought was that he was in danger of being reduced to a pile of smoking ashes right there in the middle of the Seviers' living room floor. The next thought was the need to counteract the immediate physical condition his mischievous imp of a wife had generated.

He made a monumental effort toward that goal, but after Don sauntered off to join another group, Elise shot Reed a considering look before speaking.

"That's not a bad idea Don had." Then, in her best Shakespearean voice, "What say you we slip the bonds of this common gathering and gather alone 'neath a starlit sky?"

Reed chuckled at Elise as she waxed poetic. She had warned him champagne always had an unpredictable effect on her.

The Jag was a blur on the silvery landscape as it rocketed along the river road to Oak Vista.

Reed was again driving. Elise leaned back in her seat, eyes closed, allowing the warm, muggy air to swirl around her in an attempt to cool her body and mind. It only made things worse.

She opened her eyes and turned her gaze to the heartwrenching profile of the man she loved. Her husband.

Her hand, of its own volition, rose to caress his cheek, then trace the outline of his jaw.

She leaned closer. Her fingers followed the tendon in his neck until she encountered a starched, linen collar. She dipped a finger into the collar and ran it along the edge. My, but his tie was entirely too tight.

"Here, why don't we loosen your tie and get you more comfortable?" she murmured as she slid her fingers to the formal black bow.

With agonizing slowness she found one of the ends and drew out the knot. The silk dropped to his chest, and she freed the top onyx stud with a flick of her wrist. The black, silk strip held the warmth from his body, exuding his special scent when Elise pulled it free from the confines of his collar and encircled her neck with it.

Heated longing coiled in her stomach when she watched Reed's Adam's apple convulse with a forced swallow.

The war was over. The conflagration had begun, and there was no controlling it. Reed was the only one who could extinguish this fire now.

She leaned closer still and laid a warm hand on his thigh. Another flick of the wrist freed a second stud. She heard Reed's breathing catch, then stop for a moment.

Careful to stay out of his line of vision, she eased her lips onto his, using them to tease him with promises of better things to come.

She felt the car swerve onto their property and blaze a bumpy new trail to the river.

He pulled to a stop beneath an ancient live oak, and his arms encircled her like steel bands. His lips forced the promised kisses from hers, and the moan building deep in his throat mingled with her own.

She was nearly in his lap now, her body draped across his, her hands cupping each side of his face. Their kisses became more frantic, switching from deep, languid passion to heated, frenzied urgency.

Suddenly, Reed jerked the handle and kicked the door open. Cradling her in his arms, he rose from the car and sought a grassy spot in which to lay her.

With exquisite gentleness he lowered her to a soft patch of grass, his lips still on hers, fanning the flames instead of extinguishing them. His body pressed her back into the soft cushion of grass. Her fingers flew down the studs of his shirt, yanking them apart when they proved too stubborn.

Her searching hands slid beneath his shirt, encircled his waist, kneaded the smooth, hard muscles of his back. Her patience at an end, Elise grabbed the linen and drew it over his shoulders, turning the sleeves inside-out in her impatient endeavor.

Reed released her only long enough to free his arms, then reached again, this time to lower the straps of her beaded dress.

Elise stilled his hands. She held up one finger in a gesture to wait. She wasn't through giving him his birthday gift.

She backed away, never taking her eyes from his, and rose to her feet. In slow motion she turned her back to him. Reaching behind her, she found the zipper and drew it down one agonizing inch at a time. She took an eternity to reach the bottom.

Her head turned back to Reed first, then her body. She teased him with a knowing, confident smile that barely curved the corners of her mouth.

She moved one shoulder in a tiny rotation. A sparkling strap hovering at the edge of her shoulder fell to her arm. Still holding Reed with her gaze she reached up and hooked the other strap with her thumb, sending it over her shoulder. The form-fitting dress fell into a shimmering black pool at her feet.

Her eyes glowed bright with reflected moonlight. A come-hither look invited him to finish what she'd started.

She narrowed her eyes and blinked, fear slamming into her chest.

"No!" she screamed. "Oh my God! No!"

Reed jumped to his feet in alarm as Elise lunged at him. His face was a mask of confusion, and though his mouth formed a question, he made no sound.

"Grab my hand!" she screamed. "Hold my hand!"

Elise grabbed for Reed, desperate to hold a part of him. To her horror, her hands reached for his and passed right through them, as his body became more and more translucent. She clawed at the air in a mindless attempt to find something solid to grasp.

"I love you, Reed! I love you! Stay with me!" she sobbed, her spirit fading with him as she watched the outline of his body become more and more faint.

All she could see was his face, etched with indescribable pain and sorrow. His pleading eyes seared her soul with a blue flame, he mouthed the words "I love you."

And then he was gone.

Chapter 12

THE WAILING SHRIEK that rent the night air sounded like that of a wounded animal. Elise dropped to her knees, screaming Reed's name into her hands, rocking back and forth, denying what had just happened.

Suddenly her head jerked up and she scrambled on her hands and knees, weeping, to the place where Reed had disappeared. She hoped with all her heart to be caught up in the same force that had taken him. But all she felt was a void spreading through her body, permeating her every cell. The pain was almost too intense to bear.

With a gentle caress she smoothed the grass around her, still bent from the weight of Reed's body. Wracked with sobs so violent they hurt her ribs, she inched her face to the grass and laid her cheek on the spot where Reed's head had lain.

After what seemed like hours her crying subsided and a numbness set in. She lay there, her body covering the last place Reed had touched. She never wanted to leave.

The inky blackness of the heavens gave way to an opalescent pink dawn. Elise's unblinking eyes continued to stare blindly, but her mind at last began to function.

A cold, fat raindrop on her cheek caused a slight stir within her numbness. When a steady stream began to beat down on her, she forced herself to rise to her knees and crawl to where she had dropped her dress with such tantalizing joy only hours before.

With immense effort, she stood and slipped the dress over her rain-drenched teddy. She lacked the will to bother zipping it up.

Pushing her dripping hair from her eyes, she staggered to the Jag. Her eyes closed in dismay and a sob tore at her raw throat when she saw the car. The driver's door stood wide open, and not even a glimmer of an interior light shone. She knew without checking that the head-lights and radio had not been turned off either.

Sighing in tortured resignation, tears she thought had dried up hours ago burned the backs of her eyelids. The pouring rain washed away any that may have spilled over onto her cheeks. She dragged her purse from the floor of the Jag and turned in a lifeless walk toward her home.

It was no more than a quarter of a mile, but it might as well have been a marathon. The effort she spent to put one foot in front of the next drained her of what little re-serve of energy she had. She wished she'd just die.

Why did he leave me? Our love should have been strong enough to keep him here.

She'd just begun to gather a modicum of control when she let herself in the back door of the home they'd shared and her gaze fell on a pair of men's Reeboks by the door. Tears welled up and hovered on her lower lashes, and her chin quivered in suppressed pain. Her insides began to crumple again. She slammed the door with a ferocious kick. Biting the inside of her jaw and staring at the ceiling to keep the tears at bay, Elise shoved her wet, matted hair out of her eyes and ran up the stairs.

Her room felt cold and empty now, even though she'd never shared it with Reed. Their one afternoon as a married couple had been spent in his room. She looked around, expecting to see something changed or missing to account for the emptiness. Everything was exactly as she'd left it the night before.

A rage welled up inside her chest. The unfairness nearly overwhelmed her. In one swift move, she yanked the heavy beaded dress up and over her head. She tried to rip it down the middle. When the wet fabric refused to give, she wadded the dress up and hurled it against the wall. It hit with a sharp *clack* before thudding to the polished wood floor. A wet stain darkened the ivory moiré wall, and a puddle formed on the floor around the sodden dress.

"Damn you! Damn you, damn you, damn you!"

Elise dropped to the chaise and dragged her fingers through tangled hair, then pressed the heels of her hands to her eyes. She wasn't sure who she was damning—herself for falling in love or Reed for leaving her. She thought she might be sick.

Pulling herself to her feet, she walked the few steps to her bed, dragged back the covers, and fell limply onto the sheets. She curled into the fetal position, yanked the quilt up to her chin and remained motionless until a deep, dreamless sleep overtook her.

*　　*　　*

Elise fought to pry her swollen, puffy lids open to mere slits. Without moving her head, she searched for the red beacon of her digital clock. Ten twenty-seven P.M.

"Ohhhhhh." Pain throbbed against her temples like a sledgehammer on bass drums. She reached a shaky hand into the darkness and turned on a bedside lamp, then rolled off the bed and stood. The only lucid thought in her mind was to make it into the bathroom and down a bottle of aspirin. As she passed by the vanity mirror on her way to the medicine cabinet, she almost didn't recognize herself. Stringy, matted hair clung to her head, the swollen skin around her eyes was so red that she looked like an accident victim.

She watched her eyes glisten with tears as the memories flooded her mind. A hairbrush lay on the counter, and she felt her fingers wrap around the smooth wooden handle just before she flung it into the reflection of her face.

As she watched her image distort into five jagged sections she gave a feeble nod of satisfaction and wearily moved on.

"Now . . . I look like I feel."

The following morning Elise sat at her kitchen table, a pitiful, solitary figure. The silence of the room was worse than that of a tomb. There was no companionable *clink* of silver against china, no scooting chair drawing nearer, no teasing witticisms tossed in her direction. Only silence.

Even the smells were different. The very air seemed to be heavy with the absence of shaving cream and soap.

Two empty cups sat at her elbow. In a ridiculous attempt to outfox fate, she had decided to set the table for Reed. He would have to come downstairs then, to eat the breakfast she would prepare, wouldn't he? Common sense took over before she had gotten far with her plan, and she sank to the chair in misery. She had no desire for coffee or breakfast. She wondered with distraction if she would ever want to eat again.

Her head slowly lowered to the table until she felt the coolness of the wood on her forehead. Fresh tears clung to her lashes before dropping, creating tiny puddles so close to her face they were nothing more than shimmering blurs.

She had tried to keep her mind blank and had managed for the most part. But now images raced across her mind's eye: split seconds of time being revisited, until she found herself watching Reed smiling at her while she spoke to him in the guest bedroom.

"Do you know what I think? I think we were meant to be together. I feel like you held the missing piece to the puzzle of my life . . . We will be together, darlin'."

Her own words whirled through her brain, sweeping out the self-pity, inspiring her to get off her butt and do something. Anything.

Elise jumped from her chair, knocking it backward into a cabinet. Why had she wasted so much time? Grieving would get her nowhere.

"I told you we were meant to be together, darlin'," she said aloud. "All I have to do is find a way."

First things first. Her mind flew across the possibilities. She knew it was useless to look for official records. They'd found that out when they'd attempted to track Reed's life immediately after he'd arrived.

Unofficial records, then. *I'll tear this place inside out until I find something.*

Elise stampeded up the stairs and pulled on the first clothes she could find—purple sweat pants and a blue T-shirt. She grabbed a rubber band and gathered the mass of golden-brown curls into a haphazard ponytail. She ignored the disastrous condition of her room and left it at a run, hitting the stairs to the third floor two at a time.

Breathing hard with excitement and exertion, she finished the third flight of stairs and found herself in the middle of the sweltering, humid attic. She had explored the area when she moved into the house and later when some furniture had been stored. She'd thought everything had been thoroughly investigated, but now she realized numerous possibilities had been overlooked.

The original family had left quite a few boxes and trunks. Elise had assumed they weren't worth taking. Now she intended to go through every inch of the attic, trunks and all.

The first box was filled with schoolbooks and papers from the 1950s. Another box held stacks of magazines from the '70s and '80s. She gave up on boxes for the moment and tried a trunk.

Picking out the oldest-looking one she could find, she held her breath and lifted the lid.

Empty.

So was the next one.

Minutes turned into hours as Elise ripped into boxes and broke clasps on trunks, only to find caches of canceled checks, love letters from lonely soldiers, old clothes and myriad other useless items.

The sun sat low in the sky when she rose stiffly to her feet to break for dinner. A dusty, dying ray of light pierced the dimness through a small western window, illuminating a darkened alcove she'd forgotten about. There in the dim light stood a battered, water-stained steamer trunk.

Elise's heart jumped to her throat as she shoved boxes and furniture out of the way to clear a path. She could feel her pulse racing. Her hands left moist fingerprints on the latch as she opened the lock.

The lid fell back with a thud, causing swirls of dust to rise like miniature explosions. The dust settled, and Elise sneezed several times before she dragged her sleeve across her eyes and approached the container again.

Dismay tainted her hope when her eyes fell upon the contents. The interior was filled with what appeared to be ledgers or logs of some sort. They were, indeed, very old, but the water stains on the exterior had done their damage inside as well.

The first book she picked up fell to pieces when she tried to open it. In fact, all the books lining the top layer fell apart. The second layer was in much the same condition, but the third layer proved to have two books that stayed in one piece. Unfortunately, the black ink was so blurred with water stains it had turned a very pale brown. Unreadable.

Elise dug to the very bottom and pulled three books out of the center that seemed to be in better shape than the rest.

Nervous fingers brushed across the covers, wiping off years of mildew. She said a little prayer that one of these would hold an answer.

The binding on the first book crackled as the stiffness of the cover gave under her insistent fingers. Pages stuck together, but with gentle patience she soon separated them.

Elise's breath caught when the flyleaf fell open to her. She felt dizzy for a moment and had to force herself to quiet her hammering heart.

Journal of J. Reed Blackwell was inscribed in elaborate script across the top of the flyleaf.

She released an involuntary sob and had to still her fingers to keep from ripping the pages. With deliberate slowness she eased the page over and looked heavenward before looking back to the book.

Accounts Paid—Oak Vista Plantation—1840
"Damn!"

Heedless of possible damage now, she rifled through the pages, looking for a new account year.

That book was soon discarded in favor of the next. This one held the accounts for 1842.

"Come on, come on, come one," she pleaded as she picked up the final book and opened it without hesitation. It was a book of poems, and she wondered what it was doing in with the household ledgers.

Her breathing stopped completely, her heartbeat a loud roar in her ears. She couldn't believe her eyes.

"He's not coming back," she whispered to herself. Disbelief muddled her thoughts, and she looked again at the writing.

Tears flooded her eyes and fell to her cheeks. Her voice was husky with emotion when she spoke.

"I'm going to him!"

Joyous wonder lit her face as she watched a fat tear fall upon the inscription written by her own hand:

> *To the most wonderful man in the world.*
> *I love you, darlin'. All my love, Elise.*

Suddenly the world seemed brighter; her heart grew lighter as she hugged the book to her breast. Surely she could float above the earth if she tried right now.

The nightmare was over, almost before it had begun. She knew beyond a shadow of a doubt that she would go to Reed. Now her job was to find the portal to his world and enter it. This would not be an easy task—she hadn't the first clue where to look or what to look for. But she would continue to search until she found the means to get back to the one man in all of time that was perfect for her.

*   *   *

The nightmare was *not* over. For two weeks Elise
combed the house and grounds for any viable explanation to Reed's jumping back and forth in time. She went
to the library and spent hours upon hours researching
even the tiniest article on time travel, so she'd have at
least a hint as to what to look for in her search of the
grounds. There were as many theories on the subject as
there were authors of the articles. She came to the conclusion that if she could fly faster than the speed of light,
she could get back there on her own. If. If, if, IF!

Elise could find nothing whatsoever that indicated
special powers or a potential to move someone through
time. She was painfully aware that the most mundane
item or action, one that she might already have dis-
missed, could be the key to her transportation to Reed.

She had reached a point where the more she searched,
the more distraught she became. Hopelessness threatened to engulf her. She had to keep reminding herself
that she *would* go back in time. The inscription in the
book proved that to her. But she also realized the note
could have been written the day she got back there or
years later. Was she doomed to search for years before
finding the answer?

Chapter 13

THE JANGLING RING of the telephone jerked her from her depressing reverie. She gently laid aside the book of poems she'd been reassuring herself with and stretched across the length of the couch to snare the phone with thumb and forefinger. She had to clear her throat twice before she could speak.

"Hello?"

"Hello, babe. Did you get my messages?"

Elise restored the receiver to its cradle in a manner she hoped would do damage to Jeffrey's eardrum.

"That sonofabitch."

He'd been harassing her by phone all week. Somehow he must have gotten wind that Reed was gone. After the first couple of calls, she'd begun to screen them with her answering machine. If only she hadn't been caught off guard with her musings and made the mistake of picking this one up.

It rang again. After the third ring the machine got it.

"Elise, I know you're there. I also know you've taken a leave of absence from your job. What's the problem, Elise? I told you Romeo would split. You know we can work this out if you'd stop being so damn stubborn. Just pick up the phone, baby. . . . Pick up the damn phone, Elise! You're going to . . ."

The long beep of the machine disconnected the increasingly irate voice on the other end. Elise felt the hot flush of anger and fear on her skin. Jeffrey was becoming more insistent in his pursuit of her, and the quicksilver change of his temper brought back feelings she preferred to stay buried. She was going to have to check with an attorney to see what it would take to keep him away from her.

Her anger at Jeffrey started the adrenaline pumping. She jumped up and began pacing, trying to clear her mind of the phone call and focus on the problem at hand.

For the thousandth time she went over her last day with Reed, dissecting every movement and analyzing it.

Her mind scanned back to the couple of hours before the party.

The pair had finally come up for air and decided they were starved. Elise searched the cabinets for a snack while Reed toyed with the crocks from the basement and reminisced. She thought back to their conversation and watched it run like a movie in her mind.

"No one knew why my father had the closet built in there, but Nell used it to dry some of her herbs and store a lot of the remedies she kept mixed up. Oh, look." Reed popped a wax top off of the small crock. "It looks like . . ." he took a sniff, "it is! It's Nell's herbal tea! She use to brew this for me all the time as a child to help me sleep."

An idea lit up his eyes. "I wonder if it would taste the same."

Elise screwed up her face with a dubious look, but Reed was already at the sink, running some water.

"C'mon. Let's try it."

The dull *thunk* of the door knocker sounded before she could answer.

"Hold on, while I get that."

Reed was mumbling to himself when she re-entered the kitchen after paying the paperboy.

"How does one go about brewing tea? ELISE!" he bellowed, then grinned and shrugged when he discovered her behind him.

"Well, darlin', I don't know how Nell did it, but being the modern woman that I am, the only way I know how to brew tea is in my Mr. Coffee."

She stuffed a filter into the coffee holder, then gingerly shook some of the questionable tea into it.

Looks like mulch, she thought as she tried to guess the correct amount to use. *Smells like it, too.*

Reed paced in front of the coffeemaker like a little boy in front of an oven full of cookies. It struck Elise, like a blow to the center of her chest, how homesick he must feel to be this anxious to taste tea that was a century and a half old. Their tour had dredged up memories that, in his mind, were only six weeks old; not all that long by today's standards, but for a nineteenth-century man catapulted into an alien time, it must seem like an eternity.

The last drop hadn't fallen into the pot before Reed scooped it up and poured a cup. He offered it to Elise, but she shook her head, and with a wrinkled nose handed it back to him.

"I think I'll pass this time, darlin'. You enjoy, while I make us a snack."

He sipped the tea as if sipping a magic elixir. A dreamy look of pure enjoyment suffused his face. He'd drained the coffeepot of every drop, checking periodically to make sure Elise hadn't changed her mind about joining him.

After their snack the pair curled up in a hammock in the backyard like a pair of lazy cats in the sun, their bodies entwined. With a sigh of contentment, she'd scrunched in closer and allowed her body to relax.

He'd awakened her in the best possible way she could imagine, with more than enough time to get ready for the party.

Elise stopped her pacing and came to the decision that she had to do something more constructive than just relive old memories. They shed no light on her problem, and they were becoming more painful instead of less.

A glance at the clock told her it was only late afternoon. She had plenty of daylight left to search around the outbuildings again. She trotted down the stairway and through the kitchen. The storm door slammed behind her on her way out.

Several hours later, the only things Elise had uncovered were more dirt, cobwebs and rusty junk. She was so tired she could barely put one foot in front of the other, but with single-mindedness she plodded toward her Jacuzzi bathtub. A long, hot soak was what she needed. The stairs felt like Mt. Everest, but she finally made it to her bedroom door.

Her exhausted mind was beginning to play tricks on her. In the fading light she thought she saw a body stirring on her bed.

"REED!" Her heart flew to her throat, and she scrambled to switch on the light to be sure she wasn't hallucinating.

There was, indeed, a body on the bed, and for a moment her joy knew no bounds. But the joy quickly turned into a coil of fear, paralyzing her limbs, when she recognized Jeffrey's oily smile.

"Hello, sweetheart. I hope you don't mind that I made myself comfortable. You left the back door unlocked, so I decided to wait for you inside."

Elise's paralysis didn't last long. She jumped for her tear gas but realized she'd left it with her purse downstairs.

Jeffrey sprang from the bed at the same time. He grabbed her arms and pinned them at her sides.

"Elise, let's just talk this through. I know we can work things out if you give me half a chance."

She struggled to free herself and realized his stance prevented a direct knee to his groin. She relaxed for a minute and pierced him with a look that could kill.

"Yes, Jeff, I'm sure we could work things out. We could pick up where we left off, couldn't we? You could try to control my life, and when I don't bow to your wishes, you could beat me senseless. I could be stupid enough to hang around and let you do that until you finally beat the life right out of me, either physically or emotionally. You pompous maggot, you're more conceited than I ever dreamed if you think I'm going to allow you to dictate one movement I make or lay another finger on me. Now get your filthy hands off me."

"Who's going to make me, Elise? Your beloved husband has disappeared." A lightning bolt of pain stabbed her heart, but she'd die before she'd let him see it. "So unless you have another knight in shining armor tucked away somewhere, I say we're going to do this my way."

His hand came around to roam roughly across her body, violating her and making her gag. He started pressing her toward the bed.

She knew she had to act fast. She let her body go limp for a second, and when he tightened his hold to catch her, she reared her head back and brought it crashing forward into his temple. She saw stars, but she heard him wail and his grip loosened. She was out of his hold in a flash and managed to put the bed between them before he recovered.

"You little bitch, you're going to pay for that." He held one hand to his temple while he ripped at the covers of the bed.

When he vaulted onto the mattress, Elise ran around and out the door. She threw a small table into his path behind her and knocked a floor lamp over as she raced down the stairway. Grabbing the phone in the foyer, she punched in 911 a split second before he yanked the cord from the wall.

"You've had it now, bitch," he rasped as he stalked her, an evil smile of victory on his face.

Her mind ticked off every self-defense tactic she'd ever learned. She knew whatever she did had better be right. She might not have a second chance. She could hear her instructor's voice repeating, "Keep them off guard."

Instead of continuing to retreat, she stopped dead in her tracks. His brow furrowed in puzzlement; then he became enraged at this show of defiance. His hand came up for a blow to her cheek. It never made contact.

And he never knew what hit him. Instead of retreating, Elise threw herself at him. Her right hand went unerringly to his groin, grabbing a handful of Jeffrey's precious "family jewels" and twisting with all her strength. His shriek of pain was music to her ears. He doubled over, and the moment his face was within reach, she rammed her knee into it with all her might. He dropped like a rock.

"Oh my God, it worked!" she said in wonder, then ran for her purse and grabbed the cellular phone and pepper spray.

The police were already on their way. The call had registered her address a moment before it had been disconnected. Even as she spoke to the 911 operator, she could hear sirens coming from the other end of the avenue of oaks.

She opened the heavy front door and stepped out onto the veranda. In the distance she could see spinning red and blue lights appearing and disappearing behind the huge old trees of the avenue.

Just as Elise moved to step off the veranda, pain shot from the roots of her hair, and she felt herself yanked backward. Jeffrey released the fistful of hair and spun her around, leaving bruises on her arm as he screamed at her.

"You're not running anywhere, bitch. You couldn't run far enough to get away from me." He stood, bent over, with one hand still protecting his groin.

She could hear the pounding footsteps of the sheriff and his men coming closer. Elise raked her nails across Jeffrey's cheek.

He screamed in pain and locked both hands around her throat.

"I'll kill you for that, you filthy whore!" His thumbs increased the pressure, and Elise fought panic and an encroaching blackness as she tried desperately to stomp on his instep. Suddenly the air came whooshing into her lungs, and her assailant's tight grip vanished.

The sheriff and his deputy held Jeffrey with his arms pinioned behind him. He looked around wildly, surprised at this show of force. Rage distorted his features when his gaze fell upon Elise, and he yanked free of his captors, lunging for her neck again.

"You think you've won! You're never going to win! I'll kill you first!"

Those last words were uttered a split second before the sheriff's nightstick came down with a loud *crack* on Jeffrey's head. For the second time in only minutes, Jeff hit the floor like a rock.

A shaken Elise gave the sheriff all the details she could and handed over her answering machine tape with all of Jeff's calls recorded. A deputy asked if she wanted to go in with them and fill out the paperwork to press formal charges. She assured him she would take care of it first thing in the morning.

She watched in grim satisfaction as the paramedics carried Jeffrey out. He still hadn't regained consciousness. She didn't care if he ever did.

The steamy, swirling bath did much to revive Elise's strength but very little for her spirits. Scrubbing herself dry with a huge, thirsty towel, she tried to rub away the dirty feeling Jeffrey's hands had left.

In an attempt to lift her spirits, she slipped into a lacy, peach camisole set. It didn't work.

Oh, Reed, if you were here, you could put your arms around me and make everything all right.

She didn't even realize that she'd wandered into Reed's room. When she became aware of her surroundings, she automatically started searching the room again for a clue.

The drawers yielded nothing new, and the only things under the bed were a few dust bunnies.

When she pulled the closet door open Reed's subtle fragrance engulfed her. Emotions swamped her as his essence filled her senses. She feared she would drown in them but, curiously, enjoyed the feeling. She felt closer to Reed at that moment than she had since she'd watched him fade into the night.

The shirt he'd been wearing the morning he arrived hung in front of her. She pulled it off the hanger and buried her face in the fabric, breathing deeply and cherishing the feel of the softness against her cheek. On impulse, she pulled her camisole off and slipped her arms into the sleeves of the oversized shirt, pulling the edges together and hugging herself.

"Oh, darlin', you've gotta give me a sign. I'm sure you've left me one. If I only knew where to look."

Unable to sit still a moment longer, Elise leapt to her feet and slapped her forehead with the heel of her hand.

"Think. Think, Gerard." A nagging feeling haunted her, like a child tugging on its mother's skirts.

"I know I got back there. There must be a clue for me somewhere. Where would it be? Where would he have put it? THINK!"

Her first instinct was the trunk. That's where she'd discovered the proof that she would go back. At least it was a start.

All traces of tiredness were gone as she took the stairs two at a time. The trunk stood just where she'd left it in the dark alcove. Rather than waste time going back for a flashlight, she dragged it under a bare light bulb and began systematically checking every book.

She was nearing the bottom when her mother's birthstone ring clinked against something metal. She scrambled blindly, her hands searching until her fingers encircled a tin box. Held up to the light, she thought it must be an antique tinderbox.

Hope surged anew at this foreign object in a trunk of

ledgers. She opened it with great care and pulled out a lone piece of folded paper.

"YES!" she shouted as she read the brief contents and recognized her own handwriting, not Reed's.

Four words shone up at her, offering hope and guidance like a lighthouse in the mist: *It's the tea, stupid.*

Books, papers and tinderbox went airborne as Elise made a dash for the stairs.

On her way to the kitchen she put what pieces she had of the puzzle together. The note had said "the tea." Reed had had some earlier in the day before disappearing. She recalled him telling her that Nell had brought him some the night before he arrived here. *It's been in my kitchen all along!* She chastised herself for not realizing that she would have left herself a clue.

She skidded across the kitchen floor, Tom Cruise–style, and came to a stop in front of the coffeemaker. Calming herself, she gently retrieved the old crock and removed the wax lid.

How did I do that, now? I need to brew this just like I did for Reed. Will it make a difference if I don't get it exactly right?

Elise filled the clear, glass pitcher and poured the water into the receptacle. She placed a filter in the coffee holder and sprinkled the rest of the precious tea in. She crossed her fingers and hoped it was enough.

While it brewed, she paced as impatiently as Reed had. The water at last stopped gurgling in the machine, and she poured herself a full cup. Her face screwed up at the disgusting smell, but she shrugged and toasted the air with her cup.

"Here's to you, darlin'. I'm on my way."

Amazingly enough, it didn't taste as nasty as it smelled. She could see how someone could develop a taste for it. She forced another swallow.

She drained that cup and poured another. Reed had consumed the entire pot. So would she.

Not knowing whether she should feel different or not, Elise sat at the table. Nothing so far. How long would it take?

After several minutes she realized that Reed had spent the entire day with her, and the biggest part of the night, before anything happened to him. How would she fill all that time?

Her first instinct was to call her friends and say good-bye, but it was the middle of the night. Besides, what would she say? "Hi, I'm leaving on a long trip. It'll take a hundred and fifty years to get there. Take care." She didn't think so.

She decided to leave them a note. Before she finished the thought, she realized there was something that needed to be done.

She pulled a yellow legal pad and her Waterman pen from the antique desk in the study and sat down to compose her thoughts.

When she finished writing, she reread the holographic will. She'd left the house and antiques to the historical society, with a trust fund from her savings to be formed for the upkeep. The rest of her money and belongings were distributed among charities and friends. She'd named Janice Sevier executrix of her estate. The will was in the event of her death or her disappearance for a period of one year or longer. She hoped it was legal. Somewhere she'd read holographic wills would stand up in court. She stacked the will on several papers that had her signature notarized, for comparisons if need be.

Then she wrote a letter to Jan. In it she explained everything. She promised to try and somehow leave something behind so Jan could believe Elise had truly gone to the past. She told her not to worry, that this was the only way she could ever be truly happy. Then she sealed it in an envelope and wrote on the outside: To be opened May 22, 1995, one year from now.

That done, she rose from the desk and made her way around the house, switching off lights after a long perusal of each room. She ended in her bedroom, the lamp on the nightstand casting a dim, pinkish glow over the bed.

She was exhausted, whether from the day's events or the tea, she wasn't sure.

After crawling into bed, she curled up and hugged one of her pillows to her chest. As she lay there, her mind finally began to accept the magnitude of what she'd done. If this brew sent her into the past, she would be leaving her life, as she knew it, behind. Her career, her independence, her home, friends . . . everything. Fear sliced through her like a sharp knife, setting all her nerves on end and causing her heart to pound with such violence she could hear it in her ears. But at the same time, that heart leapt with joy at the thought of being reunited with Reed. She admitted to herself that there was nothing in her life now. Not even her dear friends could fill the gaping space in her soul that Reed had left. It was as though there was one thing he'd managed to grasp and hold on to as he'd disappeared from her life, and that was the very best part of her.

Her exhaustion intensified, and she felt her muscles relaxing for the first time in weeks. She summoned the energy to reach out to her bedside lamp. When her hand felt for the switch and missed, she pried open one eye to locate it. A frisson of amazement jolted her upright as she stared at the lamp—right through her hand! Equal parts of jubilance and anxiety ricocheted throughout her body; then she watched with dismay as the vapory quality of her hand solidified once more. *Was it even real?*

Am I so exhausted I only imagined I saw through my hand?

That last burst of energy cost her. She had none in reserve, and now her body and mind both ceased to cooperate. As her thought processes shut down and she gave in to overwhelming lethargy, her last conscious thought was, I'm sorry, Reed. I tried.

Chapter 14

THE CROWING OF a rooster sifted into her dreams. Awake instantly, she sat up and scanned the room for changes, having to squint until her eyes adjusted to the gloominess. Even before she could focus, she felt the very atmosphere was different. Bustling sounds of busy people, the clang of metal, and an occasional burst of laughter filtered through heavy draperies on the windows. And she was sitting on a perfectly made bed. The heavy, satin brocade counterpane held no resemblance to her cheerful comforter, and a mass of white gauze hung above her. In her state of euphoria she didn't notice the shadowy outline of the housekeeper standing quietly in a dark corner of the bedroom.

I've done it! Oh, thank you, God! I've done it!

"REED! Reed, I'm here!" she screamed as she hit the floor at a run. She charged into the hallway, throwing open doors and calling his name into each room. She nearly knocked a young black girl down when the servant emerged from a room down the hall.

"Where is he? Where's Reed?" she questioned. She grabbed the girl's shoulders and gave her a little shake.

A great deal of white surrounded the dark brown irises of the girl's eyes. It took another shake from Elise to elicit a response; even then it was only a slow-motion movement pointing in the general vicinity of the stairway. Elise clapped the poor girl in a quick bear hug, then disappeared down the stairs, leaving the open-mouthed maid behind.

She continued to chant Reed's name in a voice that echoed throughout the house, ignoring more shocked black faces as she scouted the downstairs.

The thick cypress door to the study swung open just as Elise grabbed for the doorknob.

In the early morning light, he looked endearingly rugged. Shirt sleeves were rolled up to his elbows, and his collar stood open with a healthy expanse of tanned skin waiting to be caressed.

A sob broke from her throat, and she launched herself into his arms, covering his face with kisses. Her fingers alternated between a frantic sifting through his hair and tracing the outline of the rigid muscles in his back, reassuring herself that he was real.

She felt his arms tighten around her. She rained kisses on his face until her lips settled onto his, the kiss building to incendiary proportions, until they both had to stop and gasp for breath.

"Oh, darlin'! I can't believe I'm here! I've missed you so much!" She nuzzled her face into his chest, then gazed up at her husband with adoring eyes.

A deep furrow appeared on Reed's brow, and he

squinted down at her, a question in his eyes. Elise felt her heart stop when he spoke.

"Do we know each other, madam?"

Reed was completely taken aback.

What in the name of glory is this woman doing . . . Good heavens! All she has on is a man's shirt! My shirt, if I'm not mistaken.

Though he would swear he had never laid eyes on her, he'd felt he'd known her an eternity when her lips had come to rest on his in such an earth-shattering manner. There was a familiar feel to her enticing body pressed against his, but he was forced to write it off as *déjà vu.* He had no doubt in his mind that he would remember if this woman had ever crossed his path before.

He became aware of her staring at him, her face aghast. He put an arm's length between them and repeated his question.

"But Reed, darlin', you must remember me! Elise? Oh, Reed, don't tease me like this! It's cruel!"

Her attire, or lack of it, coupled with the blood-boiling kiss she had bestowed, had muddled his brain. Was she claiming an acquaintance with him? He turned on his heel and marched into the study. After sweeping his jacket from a nearby chair, he settled it around her shoulders. It did little to cover her exposed appendages, but he'd had to try.

"Please forgive me, madam, but I do not believe we've . . ."

His statement was cut off by a gentle rap at the door. Nell slipped inside without waiting for admittance, then came to stand beside Elise. She wrung her hands for a moment before laying them on Elise's shoulders when she spoke.

"Mistah Reed, I couldn't help but hear this poor child.

Mayhap she gots some kinda brain fever. Why don't I takes her up to a room and gives her a tisane? Mayhap she feel better in a bit and we can make some sense of all this."

Reed stared at the wild-eyed woman in front of him. He felt certain she was a demented relative someone had been keeping under lock and key. A very beautiful relative. With her golden-brown hair swirling about her shoulders she looked as if she'd just awakened. But he couldn't have it. The very idea, gallivanting around, invading one's home clad in nothing more than a . . .

"Nell, is that not my shirt she is wearing? The one that was missing along with my trousers and boots, after that disastrous ball?" He didn't mention that he'd awakened after that ball to find himself in a field dressed only in strange trousers and shoes, with even stranger small-clothes beneath.

Nell scrutinized the girl and gave a noncommittal answer, but Reed was positive it was the shirt in question.

"Perhaps you are right, Nell. Take her upstairs and see if you can find her some . . . er . . . clothing. Someone is bound to come looking for her soon."

"Would you guys not talk about me like I'm deaf?" The woman jerked her shoulders out of Nell's grasp as she voiced this strangely worded request.

"My apologies. Please allow Nell, my housekeeper, to show you to a room. I will see that you have time to collect yourself; then perhaps we can talk."

He saw a protest forming on her lips, but Nell leaned over and whispered something in her ear. She jerked her head back and stared at the housekeeper but followed her willingly enough out of the room.

Elise's euphoria evaporated.

This is a bad dream! I haven't woken up yet, and that

damn tea is causing nightmares. Wake up, stupid! Roll over and start a new dream!

Even as the thoughts ricocheted through her mind, she knew she was wide awake. She only wished she was asleep.

She failed again, on her second journey through the house, to notice her surroundings. She was intent on getting Nell alone and finding out what her cryptic statement meant when she'd whispered, "This be my fault, Miz 'Lise."

Nell led Elise into the same bedroom Reed had used in 1994. The irony didn't escape her, but she ignored it and grabbed the old woman's arm as soon as the door shut behind them.

"Nell! What are you talking about? What've you got to do with this?"

The whites of Nell's eyes had yellowed with age, and she turned a rheumy gaze of sympathy to Elise.

"Child, I be the one what sent Mistah Reed to you."

"What?" Elise virtually squeaked.

"That boy be eatin' his heart out for a body to love, but he cain't abide none of the women he meets. I watched him look for years and years. I tells myself he ain't never going to find hisself a wife what'll make him happy."

"Nell," Elise interrupted, "how did you send him one hundred and fifty years into the future?"

"One hundred and . . . Lordy, Lordy."

The housekeeper straightened her bowed spine and threw back her shoulders in a proud stance.

"I is a voodoo priestess." Elise could not believe her ears. "I puts a spell on his tea to send that boy to his true love. I didn't know where he be endin' up. I knew he be gone because I watch him go. Then he no sooner fade away than he come back that same day. Why he come back, Miz 'Lise?"

Elise wanted to scream.

"You mean he came back on the same day he left? He was in 1994 for seven weeks."

Nell's eyes widened.

"Sure 'nough?" she whispered. "Then why he come back?"

"He found some of your tea in the basement—I mean the cellar. In a hidden closet. He was so homesick, he fixed some and drank it. I didn't drink any. It was only after . . . well, it took me a couple of weeks to figure it out. That's how *I* got here. I drank the tea.

"Why doesn't he remember me? He loves me. I love him." Elise paced the floor, wringing her hands and trying to make sense of the situation. "Why didn't I come back on the same day he did? What day is this, anyway?"

Nell shook her head in ignorance.

"I not be knowin' the answers to them questions, Miz 'Lise, 'cept the brew work two ways. Drink it once and it send you to your true love, drink it twiced and it send you home again. All I know is it be nigh on two months since that party here in the big house. Mayhap more."

Elise felt the hope rush from her body like a deflating balloon. *Two months. And he doesn't even remember me.*

"Miz 'Lise?" Nell broke into her thoughts with reluctance in her voice.

"Yes, Nell?"

"There be some bad news."

Elise moaned to herself. *Oh, dear Lord, I can't take this. No more bad news. Please.*

"What is it?"

"Mistah Reed . . . he be going to marry somebody else."

"WHAT?" Elise's shriek caused the servant to jump back several inches. "He told me he wasn't engaged! He said there was no one special here. He can't be getting married! He's married to me!"

Nell's mouth fell open.

"I don't know what in-gaged is, but they ain't nothin' special about this girl. She meaner than a snake when she got a mind to be. And that be most of the time when Mistah Reed ain't lookin'. And he weren't gettin' married afore, but after that night of the ball, he wake up all sad. He say he feel a big, empty hole in his life, and he gots to fill it somehow. Miz Angeline, she be chasing that boy even when she still wearin' her hair in braids. He figure she give him babies good as anybody else. They's going to announce the nuptials at a party here in ten days. I hear Mistah Reed say it be on the first of June. Lordy, Miz 'Lise, he cain't marry her if he be married to you. But he don't even remember you. What we gonna do?"

Elise sank to a lifeless lump onto the bed. Her feet dangled limply over the side of the high tester, her shoulders so slumped she was nearly doubled over. Tears burned the backs of her eyes, but she blinked them away. No time for tears now. She had to think—and think with a clear head.

She threw herself off of the bed and did some furious pacing.

"I've got ten days, Nell. He fell in love with me once. I've got to make him fall in love with me again. Or somehow make him remember me."

Telling him she was from the future was out of the question. She'd had a hard enough time dealing with his story, and she was a century and a half ahead of Reed in open-mindedness.

"What you going to do, child? Ten days ain't much time."

A slow smile spread across Elise's face.

"It'll take some work, Nell, but I think I have a plan."

Chapter 15

NELL AND ELISE set to work immediately. Elise had to play the part of gentle bully when Nell balked at one request.

"No self-respectin' lady be caught dead in a gown like you describin'. It too plain. Let me have Sukie put a frill or two on it. Maybe some bows here and there."

Elise remained adamant. She'd described the gown she'd worn when Reed had arrived down to the last, plain detail. Nell was appalled, but it had to be an exact duplicate. So much for the authentic period gowns of the pilgrimage.

In the meantime, a service gown had to be borrowed from Verda, the little housemaid Elise had nearly knocked down. The only women's clothes in the house belonged to the help.

Nell had taken the gown to have it pressed, so Elise was expecting the soft knock on the bedroom door.

"Come in," Elise said, more than ready to get dressed and get her plans under way.

Reed pushed the door open and strode in, then turned on his heel to leave. Did the woman have no modesty?

"I beg your pardon, madam. I thought I heard you say 'come in.'"

"No! Wait," Elise yelped and grabbed the counterpane from the bed. She looked like an overdressed Grecian goddess by the time she finished wrapping it around herself. Her shiny brown hair glinted with gold in the streaming sunlight, and she'd pinned it up at the sides, creating a mass of curls at the back. The only incongruity was the sleeves of his shirt—he was sure it was his—peeking from beneath the pink brocade.

He felt his heart jump in response to the vision she created. How very beautiful she is, he thought. Where have I seen eyes that shade of green before?

He snapped his mind back to the matter at hand and made certain the bedroom door was still open.

"I trust you are feeling somewhat better?"

Elise turned a most endearing smile on him.

"Oh, yes. Somewhat. However, I'm very confused."

"Perhaps you could tell me how you came to be here, and why you seem to be . . . er . . . wearing my clothing."

She reached up to rub her temples but had to grab to catch the slipping counterpane.

"You know, I can't seem to remember that. All I know is I woke up like this. Maybe it'll come to me if you'll be kind enough to give me a little more time." The innocent look in her eyes wasn't completely convincing.

"Do you not even remember your surname? I believe you called yourself Elise when you . . . when we met."

"Oh sure. I remember that much. My name's Elise Gerard." The last two words were enunciated slowly and precisely, as if she were talking to a very slow-witted child who had forgotten her name.

She stepped forward and offered her hand, her head cocked as if in anticipation of his reaction to her name. Reed stared at her hand for a moment. She had offered it, not as a lady, but as one gentleman to another. He finally took her fingers gently in his and turned them to present the back of her hand to his lips. Another sense of *déjà vu* struck him.

"You are not from these parts," he said more to himself than to her after releasing her fingers. He had never heard a speech pattern such as hers before, and he had certainly never had a woman attempt to shake his hand. In fact, everything about her was foreign.

"That poor gal don't know nothin' but her name, Mistah Reed. Her name and yours. She say it be like she woke up screamin' yo name and then there you be standin' in front of her."

The master of Oak Vista stared across the desk at his longtime housekeeper. He had an eerie feeling that all was not as it appeared. Nell was not a good liar, but he couldn't decide if she was prevaricating or if she was merely uncomfortable about the strange arrival of an even stranger visitor.

The crunch of carriage wheels alerted the household that yet another visitor had arrived. Reed was dismally aware of the probable identity of that person. Knuckling his eyes and shaking his head in denial, he rose from behind the desk and made his reluctant journey to the door. No sense in putting this off.

A veritable cloud of ruffles floated on the breeze in the open door as Angeline sashayed into the foyer. A fleeting thought struck Reed that he much preferred his shirt as feminine attire over this abundance of frippery.

"Reed, sugar, aren't you ready to go visiting?" The pouty look of reproach on Angeline's face had the stamp of being well rehearsed.

Reed had forgotten. The morning's bizarre events had wiped the scheduled activities completely from his mind. He smacked his forehead with the heel of his hand, and after a mental note to never repeat that painful gesture, he wondered where on earth he had ever picked up such a thing.

"I am sorry, my dear. I will be ready in a moment. Business, you know."

He almost—but not quite—cringed at the sound of several elephants galloping down his staircase. For some reason he couldn't quite pinpoint, he wasn't surprised when he turned and found only one small woman creating all the ruckus. Strangely enough, he'd known it was her before ever looking.

"Is this the business you spoke of?" Angeline's voice dripped with such ice, he half expected to see her breath plume in a mist when she spoke. He sent up a prayer of thanks that Elise no longer wore his shirt.

"Angeline, may I present Miss Elise Gerard. Miss Gerard, Angeline Simon."

Elise marched up to Angeline and stuck out her hand, exactly as she had done earlier to him.

Reed groaned.

"Miss Simon, how do you do?"

Angeline turned her frosty stare of disbelief to Elise's outstretched hand.

"I am fine, thank you." She ignored Elise's gesture and gave her an almost imperceptible nod of her head.

Elise withdrew her hand and knocked some imaginary lint from her skirts.

Silence reigned as the trio stood; one bristling, one itching to remove himself, and one seeming to be happily unaware of the tension vibrating the air.

Reed interrupted the silence by clearing his throat.

"It seems Miss Gerard has met with some sort of accident or illness. She . . . appeared at Oak Vista this morning, knowing only her name."

"And yours." Elise volunteered this useful piece of information in a much too cheerful fashion. When two sets of eyes turned to her, she immediately lowered her eyebrows into a look of studied confusion.

"She knew your name? Are you and Miss Gerard acquainted?"

"Not to my knowledge, my dear. I don't recall us ever having met, but Miss Gerard, indeed, knew my name."

"There you guys go again. You know, I'm not deaf, or mute, for that matter. If you'd like to include me in this conversation about myself, I'd be more than happy to participate."

Angeline's face again took on that look of horror. Every time Elise opened her mouth, Angeline reacted in that same manner.

"Miss Gerard, are you someone's servant?" The petite blond's eyes scanned the length of Elise's slim, soberly garbed figure.

"I'm sure she is not," Reed jumped in and cut off Elise's answer. "When she arrived, her clothing was somewhat . . . somewhat . . ."

"Inappropriate?" Angeline offered.

"Oh, no. Not precisely. Perhaps ill-advised for this climate is a better way of stating it. However, Nell located a frock that would do until we can . . ."

"We?" she interrupted again, her toe tapping a violent tattoo on the floor.

"Yes, confound it. I do feel somewhat responsible for her. Until we find out who she is and return her . . ."

Elise's gaze bounced back and forth, as if following a ball being tossed between Reed and Angeline. After several passes, she shrugged, rolled her eyes, and turned on her heel to walk the length of the hallway and out the rear doors.

Reed noticed Elise's departure, but he hesitated to end his conversation with Angeline until he had it resolved. He wanted her to know in no uncertain terms that he was master of his life, and she was not.

"Reed Blackwell, you absolutely cannot have that woman stay here. Why, it isn't done. You are still a single man, and heaven knows what she is."

Reed felt an unaccountable anger rise at this veiled slur against his houseguest, uninvited though she was.

"She will stay here, Angeline. I will hire someone from town, if I must, to stay here as chaperone. I feel it is imperative she remain if her family is to find her. This subject is no longer open for debate."

It was no easier to explain his reaction to himself than to the irate blond who drummed the toe of her tiny leather boot against the floor.

When Reed's expression made it clear he would brook no argument, Angeline released her outrage with a huff and switched on a sugary smile.

"I suppose you know best, darlin'. Just please do find the poor creature's family and return her to them as quickly as possible. Promise me?"

Reed hadn't heard her request past the first sentence. For some strange, inexplicable reason, when Angeline had called him "darlin'," he'd been struck with an overwhelming urge to seek out Elise.

What kind of spell does this woman have over me? I have not had a rational thought since the moment she vaulted into my arms.

He interrupted Angeline's interminable speech, which at the moment droned on about her reputation and what people would think.

"Angeline, you will have to excuse me, but I must beg off of our little excursion today. I think it wise to send a few messengers out to make discreet inquiries about Miss Gerard. Someone must be very worried."

He didn't notice his betrothed's mouth drop open as he held her elbow and escorted her out the door and down the steps of the veranda. He waved away the coachman and nearly threw her into the carriage himself. She plopped onto the seat with a thud, golden ringlets dancing wildly around her shoulders.

"Reed!"

"Oh, terribly sorry, Angeline. Very clumsy of me." Reed tried to restore his manners and fought down an urge to slap the carriage horse on the rump and send it barreling back down the road.

"I will try to make this up to you, my dear. Perhaps you will allow me to call on you tomorrow."

"Why, certainly, darlin'."

As soon as she spoke that last word, Reed bowed stiffly and turned on his heel, the need to see Elise overpowering. He cut across any further speech on her part by mumbling "Good day" and trotting back up the veranda steps. He didn't notice Angeline craning her neck, or her mouth forming a silent, disgusted "Oh" as he closed the huge mahogany door.

Elise wandered the paths of his garden, wrapped in total enjoyment. She had often tried to picture her home as it would have been in its glory. Even her most elaborate daydreams had failed to concoct the beauty of the house and grounds. The garden sprawled out in a natural setting, with trees, shrubs and flowers all interspersed to give one the feel of walking through a beautiful forest. Meandering trails wound through the foliage, and Elise wasn't quite sure where she would come out. What a pity the garden didn't still exist in her time.

So lost in her thoughts, she didn't hear Reed approaching until he was upon her. When she glanced up, she saw the same look of anticipation he'd worn most of his waking hours in 1994. Her heart did a somersault, and it was all she could do not to run to him and drag him down to the soft, feathery grass with her. Instead, she just folded her arms and smiled up at him.

"Hi," she said, trying to sound nonchalant.

A question flickered in Reed's eyes before he spoke.

"Miss Gerard, I must apologize for my rudeness earlier, and that of my guest. Angeline is a rather intolerant woman, and somewhat possessive. I fear she misconstrued your presence here. However, that does not excuse our excluding you from a conversation concerning yourself. Please forgive us."

"No problem." Elise waved away any further apologies. "I've been guilty of the same crime on occasion." She wanted to say, "Besides, I have your full attention now," but she smothered that comment.

Reed took a deep breath and searched her eyes. That same questioning look was back.

"Miss Gerard . . ."

"Elise."

"I beg your pardon?"

"Call me Elise. Please."

"Er, very well, Elise . . ." He seemed to have lost his train of thought. She was enjoying his look of discomfiture.

He stared at her, and she immersed herself in his liquid pools of blue. Her hand started to reach up and trace the line of his jaw, but she caught herself just in time. "You were saying?"

"Uhmmm. Oh yes. Miss Ge . . . Elise, I feel certain you are not from this area."

"You mentioned that before. Why do you feel that way?" She hoped her inquisitive look was convincing.

"Your speech is not at all familiar," he stated uncomfortably, "and you have a somewhat, shall we say, carefree manner about you. That is not to imply, of course, that there is any fault to be found with being carefree," he hastened to clarify.

Elise smiled to herself. She'd forgotten how much Reed had loosened up while he'd been with her. It was going to be fun, loosening him up all over again.

"You know, I agree with you, about not being from here. I don't know why, but I'm sure I traveled a long way to get here."

"If that is the case, then surely you must have relatives looking for you. A lady such as yourself would not travel such a distance alone."

"Ummmm, I guess that's possible. For some reason, though, I have a feeling that any relatives I might have here are very distant, and I probably wouldn't know them." Elise stayed as close to the truth as she could. There was a fine line between lying and equivocating. She hated the thought of deceiving Reed, the one man she respected above all others for his morals and personal convictions. But in this case, it couldn't be helped.

Reed seemed to have nothing to add to that comment, and as long, silent seconds ticked by, he began to act like a confirmed bachelor who had just had a baby plunked into his arms. He stood there, not knowing what to do with the unexpected person, but trying his best not to fumble the situation. Finally, he seemed to have an idea.

"Shall I show you around the grounds? Perhaps, since you knew my name and made your way here, something will jog your memory."

Reed walked beside Elise, strolling at her leisure. She paused every now and then to admire or sniff a blossom, creating a charming picture.

He was struck by how comfortable he felt with this strange, vibrant woman. Comfortable and excited. It was almost as if he'd known her for years; yet the heated attraction he felt for her had intensified rather than cooled. He had never, ever experienced any of these reactions toward another woman. The fact that he now felt them break over him in waves disconcerted him no end. However, since these reactions seemed to be as uncontrollable as certain other reactions he could name, he decided to relax and savor them, without qualifying them in his mind.

The normally mundane trip through the profusion of trees and flowers proved to be most enjoyable. Elise's interest in the garden seemed to be more than passing. Her questions about the various plants were intelligent; some even surprised him with the fact that he failed to know the answer. The best he could do was refer her questions to Digger, the plantation gardener.

Circling back to the house, Reed caught a glimpse of one of his servants, the white, woolly head bobbing along behind a tall hedge.

"We are over here, Obiah," Reed called out when he realized his butler cum valet was searching for them.

They worked their way in the direction of the fuzzy beacon, winding through the paths that had been created in this natural setting.

Obiah finally emerged from a break in the foliage. His stately bearing betrayed no curiosity toward the young woman who had stormed through the house that morning in an indecent state of dishabille.

"Tessa done sent me to fetch you all, Mistah Reed. She say the food be turned to ice if you ain't at the table soon." Obiah's grievous look of impending doom was his own subtle way of poking fun at the cook and her dramatic declarations. Tessa, short for Contessa, ruled her kitchen, the food and the people who ate it with an iron fist. She grumbled constantly over her lack of appreciation, but as soon as one word of compliment was spoken over a meal, she turned into a pussycat.

Reed grinned at the butler's mournful countenance.

"Convey to Tessa that Miss Gerard and I are on our way, Obiah," he said, his degree of solemnity equal to the black man's. It was a little game they played.

Elise picked up the pace on their return trip to the house, and he realized that in all probability she had not eaten for quite some time. How could he have been so inhospitable?

As they passed the kitchen, delicious smells wafted through the open windows, and two servants emerged bearing covered trays.

Elise raised her head and breathed deeply of the wonderful aromas, a heavenly look on her face, her eyes closed. When she opened her eyes, she studied the kitchen with a mystical expression, as if she were awed by it.

"I always wondered where the kitchen was."

Her words caused a prickle along Reed's spine, as if a cold hand slid over his back.

"You always wondered . . . ?" he questioned and then reached up to smooth down the hairs on the back of his neck.

Something akin to alarm registered in Elise's widened eyes, but it quickly changed to wonder.

"Did I say 'always?' Hmmm. I meant that I wasn't sure exactly which building the kitchen was. I must be so tired I'm not thinking straight."

You idiot! You're going to blow it before you ever get a chance! THINK! *Don't open your mouth, Gerard, until you've thought about what you're saying.*

Elise was still berating herself when Reed seated her at the table. The very same table, albeit a shade or two darker, that still sat in her dining room. She stifled the urge to run her hands across the smooth patina of the surface.

The meal was a great deal more elaborate than Elise's normal lunch, and apparently, the same could be said for Reed. He chuckled, shaking his head at the amount of food being paraded through the servant's door.

"You must have made a favorable impression on Tessa. She has a most regrettable habit of making snap judgments on our guests via the servant's grapevine. She always manages to show her approval of someone through her culinary endeavors, even before she meets them. Judging from this display, I'd say you have her unconditional favor."

"And what kind of meal is Angeline served?" The moment the words were out of her mouth Elise kicked herself.

You're going to blow this yet, stupid.

Reed's quizzical look at her comment confirmed her thoughts, but then he just gave her a self-deprecating smile and shook his head.

"I fear Angeline is the recipient of cold food, and a repetitive array of it. Tessa is a woman with a long mem-

ory, and Angeline has little patience with servants. Very
often those two characteristics do not mix."

The remainder of the meal felt like a tap dance
through a minefield for Elise. Reed kept asking probing
questions in the mistaken belief he would jar her memory. Elise was stricken with several coughing fits to
allow herself time to formulate an answer. She refused to
tell him outright lies, but sidestepping the absolute truth
was difficult.

Supper wasn't much better. Reed had spent the afternoon sending out servants to search for her "relatives."
Now he was back, armed with more questions, though
he did seem to be running out of them. Elise never
dreamed she'd be glad to lock herself away in the bedroom upstairs, but by the end of the day she was exhausted from being on her guard.

As she pulled the borrowed dress away from her
moist, sticky skin, she felt as though she were peeling
away several pounds of weights. She never dreamed a
dress could feel so heavy. And her twentieth-century
body rebelled at the absence of air-conditioning. When
she fell onto the bed, completely nude, the cool breeze
that stirred the draperies felt like a breath from heaven.

Chapter 16

Reed raised his head and listened. He thought he'd heard his name being called from the recesses of the house. All was quiet. Shrugging, he returned his attention to the ledger on his desk.

He had to pause again to squeeze his weary eyes shut for a moment. He rubbed his stubbled chin, then plowed shaky fingers through his hair before stopping his palms at his temples and squeezing.

There it was again, the calling of his name. It was getting closer now, and this time the occasional slam of a door accompanied it.

Alarmed, he jumped from his chair and vaulted across his desk, yanking the study door open just as he heard his name screamed from the other side.

"Elise!" *Oh my God! She's here!*

There she stood, wild-eyed and beautiful, her hair in

abandoned disarray and her face a radiant glow when she gazed up at him.

"Oh, thank God! Elise!" was all he managed to get out before she propelled herself into his arms, kissing him with knee-weakening passion.

He tightened his grasp, lifting her off the floor and returning her kisses with fervor. When they stopped to catch their breaths, Reed put her down and held her face in both hands, his eyes searching, his fingers sifting through her hair. His thumbs came to rest on her cheeks, then smoothed across them to trace the outline of her lips.

"Oh, little one!" He hugged her to his chest and squeezed. "It's really you! You're not some vision that will fade in the sunlight! Oh, dear God, how I've missed you."

He whirled her around in a circle, her bare legs belling away from him, the dangling tail of the man's shirt she wore revealing tantalizing glimpses of lean, tanned thighs.

Elise laughed aloud and buried her face joyously in the bend of his neck. When he set her back on her feet, she held his hand and backed into the study, the look in her eye leaving no doubt as to her intentions.

"How did you get here, Elise? How did you discover the secret? I've missed you so much!"

Reed babbled on as Elise guided him to the rug and pulled him down to it. A seductive smile played across her lips as she stood and began to slowly unbutton the studs on the shirt she was wearing—his shirt.

The babbling stopped and speechlessness set in. He felt his eyes roll upward as the second stud popped free, and a glimpse of golden skin was revealed.

His mouth went dry when her fingers slid to the third gold and pearl stud. He was on his knees, reaching up to finish her task with one sweeping movement, when he jumped up in alarm.

Elise's face had turned to a mask of horror. She was screaming, but he couldn't hear her.

She clawed for his hand, grasping at it as a drowning person grasps for a lifeline. With dizzying shock, he watched her hand pass right through his, and then her body began to dissolve into thin air.

Reed jerked bolt upright, throwing the covers onto the floor and wishing he could discard the dream as easily. His heart drummed in his chest and a trickle of perspiration rolled from his temples. He swung his legs around and planted his feet on the solid floor, trying to reassure himself that he was awake.

The dream had shaken him to his very core. Even as he sat there trying to wipe the last vestiges of it from his mind, he knew he would never be able to forget it.

The emotions he'd felt in the dream had been so real he still ached with them. The joy he'd felt at seeing Elise was so forceful; even now he could feel his heart swell. And the horror as he'd watched her disappear caused his stomach to knot up as he relived it.

What in heaven's name could inspire such intense feelings? He'd only known the woman a matter of hours, and here she was, invading his sleep and causing heart palpitations and strange nightmares.

Reed stood and walked to the window. Everything looked completely normal out there. A full moon shone down upon him and illuminated the landscape.

A full moon. That explains it. I'm joining the ranks of the lunatics.

The extremes of emotions in the dream lingered, and Reed turned and paced the length of the room several times, the red and gold Aubusson carpet cushioning his steps. Finally, he stopped in front of his shaving stand and picked up the water pitcher. Without stopping to think, he bent over the matching bowl and dumped the entire pitcher over his head. Slumped over the bowl, the heels of his hands bore the weight of his body as he leaned on the stand and tried to make sense of his dream. He had no luck—he couldn't even categorize what it was, a dream or a nightmare. The unbounded joy he'd felt had been almost celestial, but the absolute horror had been a product of Hell.

In one fluid motion he straightened and slung his dripping head around, spraying droplets of water around the room.

As he reached for a crisp, linen towel to catch the rivulets of water zigzagging down his chest, he heard a clock somewhere in the house chiming four o'clock.

"Well, my night is over," he muttered under his breath, realizing he would never get to sleep again. It would soon be daybreak, at any rate.

A thorough circuit of his fields and a hell-bent ride along the river seemed to have somewhat alleviated the after-effects of his dream. That is, until he stepped into the dining room.

He was almost startled to see an obviously flesh and blood Elise sitting at the breakfast table. A ghost of the nightmare sprang back to haunt him, and he swallowed hard as an echo of the joy and pain resounded through him once more. He could almost feel that sensuous body in his arms.

Reed was less than pleased with this confusing array of emotions attacking his senses. He was a man accustomed to being in control, and these emotions were proving to be uncontrollable.

Sweeping his linen-banded planter's hat from his

head, he slapped it against his leg and walked into the dining room. He displaced the ring left by the hat when he ran nervous fingers through his hair.

Elise had been watching him from the moment he had appeared at the door. A forkful of buttered grits hovered, seemingly forgotten, halfway between her plate and her mouth.

What very attractive lips she had. They'd certainly tasted wonderful yesterday, and he had to admit she seemed to know how to put them to good use. But he hadn't noticed how inviting they . . .

"Good morning." Elise was the first to snap out of the mutual trance. Unlike most of the women Reed knew who would have been pink-faced and uncomfortable after his ill-mannered perusal, Elise was beaming.

"Good morning," he returned, "I trust you slept well."

"Oh, yes, I feel great this morning. How was your night?"

The strange, polite question was innocent enough, but her eyes searched his face, and he could almost believe she looked for something that had nothing to do with her question. Uncomfortable with his answer, he seated himself and concentrated on filling his plate. When he said, "I had a very restful night, thank you," he kept his eyes on the slice of ham he'd just speared.

As he reached for a bowl, his mind was not on food. He absentmindedly selected a serving spoon and began placing scrambled eggs on his plate. His thoughts turned to the woman in the dream.

"You're certainly getting your egg group in today," the dream woman said, a perky note in her voice.

Reed stopped the egg-laden spoon in its journey toward his plate and noticed for the first time what he'd done. With a shrug, he dropped the spoonful onto the already heaping yellow and white mound, completely burying the lonely slice of ham.

Good lord, was all Reed could think when his glassy gaze focused on the ridiculous mountain of food.

He peered across the table at Elise and quirked a brow.

"What, pray tell, is an egg group?" He enunciated the last two words precisely.

The woman who had invaded his home and his dreams and who now sat across the table wearing a drab servant's gown and a huge, beautiful smile, actually laughed in his face.

"I'd say what you have on your plate there pretty much describes one."

The corners of his mouth threatened to turn up, and when he looked back at his plate, they both burst into laughter.

He shook his head and managed a sheepish grin as he shrugged. He didn't offer an explanation for his apparent egg fetish, and she didn't seem to need one.

Elise's heart swelled with hope for the second time that morning. The first had been the moment his gaze had fallen on her. A shock of recognition had registered in his eyes for a split second, and she had prayed that his memory of her had returned. Though she was certain now that it hadn't, she did know that something was going on in his mind. She recognized that look of concentration he'd used to spoon scrambled eggs onto his plate. He was definitely grappling with some inner turmoil, and she knew instinctively that she was in the center of it.

Reed was in the process of demolishing the Mt. Everest of eggs he'd created. In between bites he would ask her a new question or fill her in on the daily routine.

"Feel free to roam wherever you please, Elise. Perhaps you'll come across something that jogs your memory."

It's not my *memory that needs jogging.*

"I am expecting Lillianna Dubose to arrive from New Orleans around noon. It was, uh, brought to my attention yesterday that it could be very damaging to your reputation to remain under my roof without a chaperone, so I sent for the widowed aunt of a dear friend of mine. I think you will find Aunt Lil to be a treasure."

"I'm sure I will," Elise managed to say, she hoped with less dread than she felt. That's all she needed. A nosy old woman interfering with their lives. Damn Angeline.

The rest of the meal went downhill from there. Reed informed her that he would be present for dinner so she and Lillianna could get acquainted, but he would in all probability be having a late supper with Angeline at her home. He was confident that Aunt Lil would do an admirable job of entertaining her.

After breakfast Elise went searching for Nell and found her inspecting the linens. She had just pulled out those that needed mending and was placing fresh potpourri sachets between the remaining ones.

"Nell." Elise rushed forward and grabbed the old woman's gnarled hands. "We have to get busy. He's going to her house for dinner . . . I mean supper. Whatever. I need that dress as soon as possible. When do you think Sukie will finish it?"

Nell's smile was warm and patient. She took Elise's hand and led her to a third-floor room that had been set aside for the seamstress.

"I be fixin' to come and fetch you soon as I was through with them linens. Sukie done worked up that gown, and all she be needin' is to fit it on you. There weren't much to it, Miz 'Lise. I still says you should let her put a ruffle or two . . ."

Elise interrupted Nell with a wave of her hand. "It's all part of the plan, Nell. It can't have a ruffle."

Sukie lowered the frock over Elise's head, and as it billowed into place she sighed with satisfaction. The mint green taffeta was almost the color of her other gown. The little dressmaker had been a wizard with her needle and had stitched up an exact replica of Elise's costume.

The wide straps fell slightly off her shoulders, and the neckline dipped to create a *V*—not too low, but low enough to be seductive. The *V* was repeated at the waistline, making her twentieth-century waist look a bit smaller above the bell-shaped skirt. Just one thing missing. She spoke to Nell's reflection in the mirror.

"Where can I get my hands on a hoopskirt?"

"A hoopskirt?" Nell's questioning look sparked alarm in Elise, who envisioned one of her plans going down the tubes.

"Yes. You know . . . a crinoline. It makes the dress stand out. A stiff petticoat with a hoop in it."

Nell pondered on her description for a few moments, then her eyes lit up.

"I be right back," she said as she disappeared through the doorway. Within seconds she was back carrying an enormous crinoline. It was covered with lace ruffles and ribbons and tiny silk bows, with graduated tiers of hoops under all that fluff.

"I sees why they calls this a hoopskirt," Nell commented, eyeing the thing as though she suspected it of something. "A while back Mistah Reed entertain a man and his wife what come from some other country . . . France, I believe Mistah Reed say. Anyways, they talks funny. After they left, Sukie done found this stored under the bed. They must've forgot it. Ain't never seed one like this, but the lady wore them and said they was all the rage where she come from.

"She sent a message before they got on their ship in New Orleans and told Mistah Reed not to bother sending it back. To just give it to the lady lucky enough to become Mrs. Blackwell."

Nell dropped the petticoat onto the floor and helped Elise step into it. She smiled a grandmotherly smile as she tied the tapes at Elise's waist. "Guess that lucky lady be you."

Elise refused to let Angeline's face form in her thoughts.

"Only if we can make him remember me. I know that boy of yours, Nell. He can be too damned honorable for his own good."

Nell snorted. "Don't I know it, baby. He a good boy, but it 'bout time he has a woman to buy these pretties for. And I ain't talkin' 'bout that Angeline. Ain't nothin' can make that gal pretty on the inside."

Elise's mind focused on how she would appear before Reed in this dress. Once the crinoline was in place, she shook the skirts of her gown back down and turned to view herself in the cheval glass. It was almost perfect. The skirt was not quite as wide as the one she'd worn in the future, but the change was so slight it would make no difference. The biggest difference Elise could see was the richness of the fabric and the meticulous perfection of the seamstress.

Sukie calculated what alterations would have to be made, then mumbled under her breath to Nell while Elise dropped the gown and crinoline and stepped out of them. The housekeeper nodded and mumbled back, then ducked her head, hesitating, when she turned back to Elise.

"Miz 'Lise, Sukie say she cain't do the final fittin' until you puts on your corset."

Elise stared at the two women for several seconds while the meaning of what they said sank in. She threw her head back and laughed out loud at the thought.

"No way. I'm not strapping on one of those torture chambers. I wore a girdle once, and that was enough to kill me. Just fit the dress to me, Sukie, and don't worry about an eighteen-inch waist."

Sukie seemed a bit at odds by this strange attitude and language, but she was accustomed to following orders and not asking questions. Before long Elise was back in her room, slipping the gown over her head again, with Nell trying her best to do something with Elise's hair. Elise stopped her by gently taking the arthritic brown hands in hers.

"Don't worry about the hair, Nell. This is the way I need to look. Everything's perfect. All I need to do now is set the stage."

She could hardly wait to see Reed. She'd give anything to be able to recreate the scene of their first meeting in his bedroom, but she knew that would be impossible.

As if the very thought of him conjured him up, she heard his footsteps coming down the hallway. Before she had a chance to move, there he was, filling up the open doorway with his broad shoulders and larger-than-life presence. Nell hesitated between the two for a moment, then slid from the room in silence.

This was not the way Elise would have chosen to present herself to Reed in her new gown. Oh well, she thought, make the best of it. She realized she was staring at him. Reed was, in turn, staring back at her, and it struck her that this little scenario wasn't altogether different from their first meeting.

*   *   *

Reed stood transfixed. Another wave of *déjà vu* crashed over him. His eyes narrowed, and he cocked his head in wonder at an inexplicable burning on his face. He was certain he was not blushing. The burn was more intense than that. Almost painful.

The sensation vanished when Elise moved toward him. She did a little spin and dropped a curtsy to show off her incredibly plain gown. Funny though, somehow it suited her. Suited her too well, in fact. A man could lose himself in the activity of just looking at her.

"How do you like it?" she questioned as she fanned the skirts out between thumb and forefinger.

She seemed so proud of it Reed decided not to question the lack of feminine gewgaws. And he definitely could not tell her how very much he did like it.

"Very becoming, Elise. I am pleased Sukie managed so quickly." She was looking at him so expectantly. What did she want him to say? The truth? He chose the coward's way out and changed the subject. "I believe Aunt Lil's carriage is coming up the road. May I escort you down the stairs?"

Elise looked a little deflated when she took his proffered arm. Perhaps he should have been more effusive with his compliments. He made a mental note to make certain he didn't repeat that mistake with the next gown. It didn't occur to him until later that he was assuming Elise would be there long enough to require another gown. He just hoped that not all her gowns would have the same effect on him.

The couple reached the bottom of the staircase just as Obiah opened the front door.

Reed coughed to cover a chuckle when his eyes fell upon his newly arrived guest.

Aunt Lil was always a treat to behold. One never knew exactly what manner of dress she would appear in,

from the most severe black mourning to something resembling a military uniform. Today her fat, black
sausage curls, shot through with generous amounts of
gray, framed a pudgy, childlike face. The pink in her
cheeks came as much from the exertion she expended in
her attempt to mount the veranda steps as it did from a
certain robust health. Yes, robust she was, and obviously
with an appetite to match. A surplus of juvenile pink ruffles in today's costume not only matched the pink of her
cheeks but created the illusion of an overstuffed doll.

Reed knew this dear lady was as lovable to be around
as she was ridiculous to look at. She was also a hopeless
romantic. Her husband had been the light of her life, and
she had been his. When he died, she had taken to living
vicarious romances through her nieces and nephews. She
was responsible for stopping more than one arranged
marriage for the sake of love.

"Reed Blackwell, stop grinning like a fool and help
Obiah get me up these steps." Lil teetered on the first
step, peering up at him through a feather that hung from
her bonnet. A well-aimed puff of breath blew the rather
limp appendage back to its original position.

Reed snapped to attention and trotted down the steps,
volunteering to sweep her into his arms and carry her inside. She rewarded him for his efforts with a swat on the
arm with her pink lace fan.

After he and Obiah hefted the dear lady onto the
safety of the porch, she unfurled the fan and made little
hummingbird motions with it in front of her face, puff-
ing once more at the errant feather. Flicking her skirts
and ruffles into voluminous proportions, she turned to
Elise and smiled warmly.

"My dear child, where on earth is your corset?"

"Lil!" Reed exploded.

Elise stood stock-still, her wide eyes blinking and her

eyebrows at her hairline. Before his voice had died away
Elise's giggles rose to sound like wind chimes in the
summer breeze. Reed turned a flabbergasted look on her.
Any other woman would have left their presence in an
irate huff.

As he watched, Elise glided over, actually put an arm
around Lillianna's shoulders, and squeezed. She became
even more of an enigma to him when she spoke.

"You and I are going to get along just fine, Aunt Lil,"
she told the older woman, a look of pure delight and a
touch of mischief written on her features.

Elise had tried not to laugh, but she couldn't help herself. She'd bitten the inside of her cheek from the moment the door opened and she'd caught a glimpse of this
endearing character. But when Lil had asked the question about the corset with such wide-eyed sincerity and
warmth, all was lost.

She guided Aunt Lil through the door and made her
comfortable in the front parlor. Verda scurried off to
fetch refreshments, and Reed made his way to a Waterford decanter of brandy. He splashed a healthy amount
into a matching glass and downed it, all in one fluid
movement.

"Reed Blackwell, what have you done to find this
dear girl's family? Have you had Doctor Freeport look at
her? Have you sent out messengers? Speak up, boy.
Don't just stand there imbibing."

Reed looked as if he would choke on that last sip of
cordial, then admitted that he hadn't sent for the doctor.
Elise was surprised that it hadn't occurred to her that he
might. She certainly didn't want to be a victim of nineteenth century medicine unless absolutely necessary.

"Oh, I really don't feel a doctor is necessary at this
point. It's obvious I'm not sick. I don't have a fever, no

broken bones. Just a little memory lapse." She tried to give them her healthiest smile since they were staring at her looking unconvinced.

"You do have a point, I suppose," Reed conceded, but eyed her with a dubious gaze. "But you must promise that if you feel at all out of sorts, you will allow me to contact the doctor."

"Yes, sir!" she barked with an expertly executed salute. She saw their raised eyebrows and tried to turn the movement into a hair-patting maneuver.

As the afternoon passed and Elise became better acquainted with Aunt Lil, her fears of a meddling old lady vanished. Not only was the rotund woman best described as "one taco short of a combo plate," she had also commandeered the back parlor and was at the moment giving orders to have it turned into a temporary bedroom.

"The devil himself in pursuit," she said, "would not entice me to climb that staircase. What are you thinking, Reed Blackwell, to even suggest such a thing?"

Elise tried to keep her mind off Reed and the fact that he had left to spend the evening with Angeline. What was he doing now? Would he even remember he had a houseguest once Angeline got her sweaty palms on him? Would he kiss Angeline? Would he hold her head against his chest and assure her that the crazy woman would be gone as soon as possible?

Elise had no appetite at supper, and no desire to do anything except sit and stare into the night, willing her husband to come home. After a halfhearted attempt to learn to play whist, she excused herself from Aunt Lil and went to bed early.

She'd never felt so tired. The constant humidity and heat were taking a toll on her body. Even now a trickle of sweat inched its way between her breasts. When she entered her room she found that some well-meaning servant had closed her windows against the "bad" air from the distant swamps. She threw them open and blessed Verda when she found her bed turned down and a cool pitcher of fresh water on the stand in the corner.

Every inch of her gown, camisole and petticoat was damp. Fabric clung to her body like a wet T-shirt contestant's. She had to peel away the stifling layers, and when she finally stepped out of the last vestiges of clothing, she felt as if she'd just removed fifty pounds of excess weight. She draped the multitude of garments across every available piece of furniture to dry before staggering to the washstand.

She wasn't sure whether it was exhaustion or depression that weighed her down. She found her thoughts drifting and returning to her time. She and Reed had been so happy, and now he didn't even know her. Could he forget her so completely if he had truly loved her? Had she traveled one hundred and fifty years to watch her husband marry another woman?

With automatic movements she filled the porcelain bowl and began sponging the cool water over her body. Wringing out the washcloth for the third time, she pretended it was Angeline's neck.

Could this woman really come between her and Reed? With a nauseating feeling in the pit of her stomach, she realized the inscription in the book of poems was signed by her, but it had not actually referred to Reed. Was it possible she hadn't come here to be with Reed? That she would end up with someone else? She knew, viscerally, that it was possible. All it would take would be to remove one stepping-stone in time. To interrupt the domino effect in the chain of events of their lives. Their paths could cross in opposite directions instead of running along, side by side.

She couldn't allow that to happen.

The inviting bed called to her. She finished the futile attempts to cool her body and padded over to it. The night rail stuck to her skin when she tried to pull it on, so she discarded it and decided to sleep in the nude again tonight. If a wayward breeze found its way into the room, she stood a better chance of reaping its benefits.

Reed strode into the parlor, glanced around quickly and found only Lil. She sat at a card table, cheating at a game of solitaire. He stood quietly for a moment, wondering at the feeling of emptiness the room evoked.

"Reed Blackwell, don't stand there gawking. She retired not ten minutes ago. Now sit down here and let me trounce you in a game of whist."

To deny that he was looking for Elise would only confirm that he had been. Instead, he seated himself across from Lil and tried to catch her sleight of hand with the cards.

"How was your evening with Angeline, dear boy?" Aunt Lil never took her eyes from the cards.

"Very enjoyable, thank you. Supper was delicious, as usual."

Reed started to mention the after-dinner activities but decided against it. Angeline's activities had proven to be decidedly different from those her parents had arranged.

She had requested he escort her on a stroll through the gardens, but once they'd walked into the shadows, she had halted their progress and pulled him down to a bench. She then proceeded to behave in a totally alien manner, scooting up close, daring to touch his leg on occasion. When he had taken her in his arms to kiss her, she had moved his hand from her waist and guided it upward.

Reed jumped from his chair and began pacing.

"Reed Blackwell, you've displaced the cards. Well, the game is over now," Lil sighed dramatically. "I may as well retire." She shoved her chair backward, and the furniture groaned as she lifted her weight. She assessed her host with a knowing eye on her way out the door. "And I believe you should do the same."

Reed muttered a distracted "good-night," then stalked to the bell pull and rang for the butler.

"Lock up the house, Obiah. We won't be needing you anymore tonight."

"Yessir, Mistah Reed. You goes on up to bed. You looks plumb done in."

Reed's thoughts matched those of his servant. *Done in. That's exactly how I feel. I just wish I knew why.*

As he walked quietly down the darkened hallway he saw a dim strip of light along the floor. A door opened downstairs and a gust of wind rushed past him, blowing Elise's door open several inches. He brightened. The door stood slightly ajar, and he wondered if she was still awake for a little chat. It couldn't have been more than fifteen minutes since she'd left Aunt Lil.

He poked his head into the narrow opening of the doorway and raised his hand to knock. He stopped before his knuckles ever met wood. A groan threatened to rise from his chest, and he forced himself to swallow in a desperate attempt to moisten his suddenly parched throat. A furious heat began in his face and burned a trail to the very core of his being.

In the shadows of the canopy Elise settled herself into bed. A single flickering candle on the nightstand caused faded beams of light to dance across her gleaming skin. Her hair pooled upon the pillow as she fell backward. A creamy thigh glowed as it moved into the light, then disappeared into shadows. He glimpsed the fullness of a breast before the sheet rose with agonizing slowness, partially covering it, only to reveal the smooth skin of a rounded hip.

Every muscle in his body was paralyzed. Yet there was a part of him that was most definitely not suffering from paralysis. His mind was blank, and his body started toward her of its own volition. At that moment he heard a gentle *whish,* and the room was plunged into darkness.

His head snapped out of the doorway as the darkness brought him to his senses. Moisture returned to his throat, but the other effects of seeing her naked remained. The image of Elise, her body glistening in the heat as she lay atop the sheets, would burn forever in his mind.

His thoughts returned as he limped down the hallway and readjusted his trousers.

Done in. That's exactly what I feel like. But now I know why.

Chapter 17

THE FOLLOWING THREE days were an exercise in patience for Elise. Reed was gone by the time she rose, either to the fields or into town with various errands. He usually returned only in time for a quick, late supper. He would then drag himself upstairs to bed before everyone else retired.

He was avoiding her.

She worried that something had happened the night he was with Angeline—something that threatened to destroy her future . . . or was it her past?

The few moments she'd managed to spend in his presence, he avoided looking at her. Conversation was stilted. How in the world would she be able to jog his memory of her if he continued to remain so indifferent and aloof?

The front door slammed, and she heard Reed's familiar steps approach the parlor. She was alone at the moment. This was perfect timing.

He stopped in the doorway. Predictably, upon seeing Elise he mumbled an excuse and started to back out the door.

"Reed, wait. I want to talk to you."

He strolled into the parlor, inspecting the ceiling, woodwork, furniture—anything and everything but her. When he got to the center of the room he stopped, feet planted wide apart, hands clasped at the small of his back.

She drank in the sight of him and reveled in the intoxication only he could produce. Black riding boots hugged his strong calves. Above the boots, buff-colored breeches accentuated the muscle definition of his massive thighs. The white lawn shirt lay open at his neck, and Elise's fingers tingled to trace the tanned collarbone that was so enticingly revealed. He looked so very much as he had the day they'd met.

He stood motionless, then finally turned his gaze toward her. When she failed to speak, he inclined his head in query.

Time for action. What she hoped for was a subtle jar to his memory. She moved to a love seat as if settling in for a long conversation and executed a much practiced drop onto the brocade cushion. As planned, the underlying hoopskirt immediately flew to her face and hovered there several seconds. Elise knocked it back down and delivered what she hoped to be an excellent act of surprise and embarrassment.

"Oh, goodness. I'm such a klutz."

She made a big display of smoothing her skirts and re-situating herself. When she finally peeked coyly up at Reed, she could have cried.

He stood with his back to her, pouring a measured

amount of brandy into a snifter. When he swung back around, his face showed no indication he'd witnessed her display. He gestured to her with his snifter-filled hand.

"Would you care for a refreshment?" he questioned.

Elise stared at him disgustedly and shook her head "no." She decided the time for beating around the bush was over.

"Reed, have I done something to make you angry?"

He blinked once, but his questioning look didn't falter.

"No. Have I done something to give you the impression that you have?"

The days of his ignoring her, the hours of boredom and tension all came to a head. A sigh of frustration exploded from her lungs.

"No, Reed. I'm just not well-versed in Southern hospitality. I realize I'm an uninvited guest, and I've taken advantage of your kindness." She jumped to her feet and threw her shoulders back. "I'm sorry for the inconvenience. I'll take one of the gowns Sukie made and leave the rest. She made several. You'll be reimbursed when I'm able. I do appreciate you taking me in, but now it's time I move on."

She started to march out the door, but Reed's hand shot out and grabbed her arm. She yanked it away from him but remained where she was.

"Elise, I am terribly sorry. I was not aware of the extent of my rudeness, and I realize now that I have, indeed, been rude. I can only hope you believe me when I say I do not want you to leave. I heartily apologize for any misconceptions I may have created."

She began to feel her heart melt, and her insides flowed with warm honey when his face changed from serious apology to charming smile.

They stared at each other for several seconds. Elise's heart pounded as she welcomed back the wonderful smile she had grown to love, a smile she'd seen far too little of lately.

"I'm sorry I blew up. I guess my situation is getting to me."

"I was entirely at fault and deserved a more severe tongue-lashing than you delivered. I am certainly the one who owes the apology."

Reed gestured for her to seat herself again, then took a place on a Chippendale chair across from her.

"I had intended to speak to you today, anyway. To date, none of the inquiries I have made have produced any information on you or your family. I feel certain it is just a matter of time. In the meantime, there is to be a ball here at Oak Vista in six days. I apologize for failing to mention this sooner, but I want to assure you that your presence at the ball is desired. I realize your wardrobe is limited; therefore I have instructed Sukie to fetch whatever you need. She is at your disposal and is very capable of producing appropriate attire for the function."

Elise saw her chance to spend some time with him.

"Oh, dear."

"Is there a problem?"

"Well, it's just that . . . it's a ball, you say?" Reed nodded. "I'm just not quite sure I know how to dance. That seems to be one of the things I've forgotten."

She wore an apologetic mask when she looked up into his eyes. After a disappointed sigh she shook her head.

"I'm afraid I'll have to take a rain check."

"Rain check?" Reed's eyebrows lowered, his eyes squinted as he questioned this phrase.

"Decline. I wouldn't want to go and embarrass you. I already seem to stand out like a sore thumb." She shrugged and strolled away from him, playing her disappointment to the hilt.

"Er . . . quite." Reed scratched his temple as if he were waging an inner struggle.

He had spent every waking moment finding ways to avoid this woman. Each time he saw her, all he could think of were the flashes of bare, golden skin he'd glimpsed—and still saw vividly each night in his dreams. His thoughts of her were becoming a threat to his relationship with Angeline. And now here she was, being charming and pitiful, obviously wanting to attend the ball—the ball where he would announce his intentions to marry Angeline.

The last thing I need is to spend time with this woman.

"Perhaps I could spare some time each day to instruct you. I am sure you will remember the steps once your memory is refreshed."

Elise perked up at once.

"You would do that for me?" Her smile really was endearing. "How about now?"

"Well . . . I . . ."

"Are you busy?" Her bright-eyed look of anticipation was so sweet.

"Well, no, but . . . I . . . well, okay." *Okay? Good Heavens, now I'm picking up her language.*

"Great! So where do we do it?"

Reed groaned internally as double meanings and second thoughts ran rampant.

"Right here will be fine. We have sufficient room to maneuver. Let's see, where shall we begin . . ."

"The waltz. I want to learn the waltz first."

Her enthusiasm made it difficult to deny her. After squeezing his eyes shut and pinching the bridge of his nose, he dropped his shoulders in defeat and nodded. He had hoped she would at least remember that one.

What ensued was a comedy of errors. Elise's first step treaded lightly on his toes. She apologized and they began again. This time she stepped on his other foot. When they finally managed a few steps without mishap, Reed's hold on her became featherlight. He tried to hold her at arm's length without actually touching her. Just as he seemed to be getting the hang of it, she tripped and barreled into his chest. His hand tightened around her waist, but as she slid downward he found himself cupping her breast instead. Her right hand grabbed the front of his shirt, while the left one slid roughly down the back of his trousers to grab a handful of fabric at his thigh. When they got their balance, the two stood motionless through several heartbeats, then jumped apart as if they'd touched their hands to a flame. Elise laughed.

"Oh, geez, I'm such a klutz! I'm really sorry . . ."

That did it!

"Elise!" he roared, "Where in the name of God do you come from? What is a klutz? What is a rain check? Why do you say 'Hi' instead of 'Hello'?" He paced the floor while he plowed his fingers through his hair. "Why do you speak the way you do? Why do you dress the way you do?" His voice escalated to a bellow.

Verda was passing the doorway, and when his voice crescendoed she skittered, wide-eyed, up the stairs and out of sight. Obiah calmly strolled past the scene, visibly forcing himself not to look.

Reed's diatribe ran out of steam quickly as he watched Elise back away from him, her wide eyes filling with tears and turning pink. She backed away until her hip met the escritoire. She didn't try to speak but simply shook her head slowly in denial, tears shimmering on her lower lashes.

"Elise, I am sorry. I did not mean . . ."

As Reed took a step toward her, his hand outstretched, she turned to run from the room. Her hoopskirt caught between the love seat and table, and when she yanked it free, it clanged back and forth against her legs like a huge bell. He heard her sob "Damn" under her breath, then she ran to the foyer and clattered up the staircase.

"Elise, stop! I didn't mean it, little one!"

He rushed to the newel post, hoping to catch her, but she'd already disappeared.

Elise slammed her bedroom door and fell back against it in a dejected slump. Her eyes burned with tears, but she was too stubborn to allow them to fall.

What had gone wrong? Reed had fallen in love with her so easily in the twentieth century. They were the same people, but now he held himself so distant. She refused to admit the lifestyle they were living now might influence his feelings toward her.

A lone tear found its way onto her cheek, with the threat of more to follow. She swiped at it angrily, then tilted her head back, opened her eyes wide, and blinked until the threat had passed.

While she stood there she strained to hear any sounds from downstairs. She prayed she would hear the familiar thud of boots come down the hall and stop in front of her door. But all she heard was the muffled ticking of the grandfather clock in the foyer.

The flood of tears no longer imminent, Elise walked with stooped shoulders to the window seat overlooking the back gardens.

I really screwed up this time, she thought as she hugged her legs to her chest and propped her chin on her knees.

She had seized the opportunity to coax some dance lessons from Reed just so she would have a reason to touch him and spend more than five minutes in his presence. She had been deliberately clumsy in order to inspire him to continue the lessons until the ball. The flaw in her plan was that she kept expecting him to react like the semiliberated, twentieth-century Reed. The answer was simple. She could either loosen him up all over again, or she could regress a century and a half to being a true Southern belle. She opted to aim for somewhere in the middle.

She had no idea how long she sat there, staring into space, before a gentle rap sounded at the door.

Elise called out "come in" and jumped up to straighten her gown, in hopes her caller was Reed. Her right leg was totally numb, and she was in the middle of flailing her arms to catch her balance when the door swung inward. Aunt Lil entered, taking quick little baby steps, her fat ringlets bouncing up and down like miniature springs. Today she wore yellow from head to toe, resembling a somewhat overfed canary.

Elise stomped the floor with her right foot to encourage circulation and groaned at the thought of a conversation with Lil. Normally the old dear was entertaining, but this afternoon she had no desire to learn a cure for dropsy or how she should massage her eyeballs to maintain perfect vision. She did have to admit, though, that Lil's recipe of borax, burnt alum, French chalk, starch, and oils of bergamot and lemon for a "perspiration powder" was not half bad as a deodorant. It beat the heck out of everything else she'd tried.

"What is the matter with you, child? If your foot is asleep, hold your breath and pinch your left earlobe. Now, I'm not one to mince words," Lil continued without stopping to catch her breath, "so I'll get right to the point. You have to learn the rules of the game, my dear girl. You learn the rules, and learn them well, and then you will know which rules can be broken, and when to break them. Do you understand what I am saying?"

Elise was concentrating more on the needles that were now prickling her right leg. She did, however, nod an affirmation as she limped around the room massaging her leg and pinching her earlobe.

Lil stepped into Elise's path and cupped her face with gentle hands. When she spoke, Elise saw that her eyes were clear and her face sympathetic.

"You give credence to my words, dear girl. They will stand you in good stead."

Elise blinked and murmured, "Yes, ma'am," as the meaning of Lil's words sank in with clarity.

"Now then. Nell!" Lil trilled the name as she bobbed out the door, "Let us plan the demise of that pesky mouse I saw in the pantry last night."

Reed swung himself from his horse before it came to a halt outside the barn. Tossing the reins to a wiry stable boy, he swept his hat from his head and knocked it against his thigh. A tiny cloud of dust erupted and swirled in his wake.

The ride had done little to alleviate his ill humor. The confrontation with Elise kept replaying in his mind, and each time he reviewed it he came away blaming himself for hurting her feelings. After all, she was his guest, and she had suffered . . . something. Exactly what, he did not know.

He grabbed the pump handle and jacked it ferociously. The water spewed forth with unexpected pressure, hitting the side of the trough, splashing onto Reed's breeches in a most embarrassing area. He leapt backward, out of the path of the oncoming water.

He studied the offending dark splotch with disgust. His annoyance grew when he became aware of a carriage careening toward the house. When he recognized it as Angeline's, he hung his head in defeat.

"I am being punished for something. That is it. I am being punished."

He took a moment and sluiced water that was still cascading from the pump over his face and neck. He hoped to make his way unseen to the back of the house so he could slip upstairs and change.

On his way, he caught a glimpse of movement on the upper veranda. His steps slowed, then stopped while he watched with interest the scene being played out.

Elise stepped onto the upper veranda just as the coachman helped Angeline alight from her carriage. Elise walked with her back straight and her head held high, a regal picture as she approached the railing.

Angeline flounced down from the carriage step and spun daintily around to stare upward at Elise.

The two women stood thus, both with challenging stances. Reed was positive, as if they had been men, that a gauntlet had been flung down between them. But he was not sure who had done the flinging.

Chapter 18

HE COULD NOT recall ever having been so uncomfortable. Angeline flitted possessively around the parlor. She ordered around his servants and rearranged his knickknacks. Her forced giggles were becoming tedious in the extreme.

Elise strolled in shortly after his own arrival, her nature subdued and her behavior calm and unsmiling. He could not imagine how she had made her way down the staircase. She had not created her usual clatter, and he had never witnessed her descending the stairs in any other manner. He could only suppose that he was responsible for this subdued character. He wondered at the pang of regret he felt.

"I do hope you are planning to come to the ball, Miss Gerard. It is being looked forward to as the social event of the season." Angeline's smile was almost feline. "But of course we would understand if you are not well enough to attend, considering your poor health. You do look a little peaked."

"I will be there, Miss Simon. I wouldn't want to miss such an occasion."

"But do you have the proper attire? Perhaps I could help you pick something out. I have excellent taste in such . . ."

Elise interrupted with an amused look.

"Thank you, no. I have already taken care of it, thanks to Re . . . Mr. Blackwell. Besides," Elise flicked a telling glance at Angeline's ruffles, "I prefer my own taste."

Reed was positive the two women would soon begin spitting and hissing at each other. His mind raced across topics to introduce that would prove safe for conversation, but he was saved by the sound of a horse and rider approaching.

"Oh!" Angeline lost interest in Elise. "That must be my cousin. I asked him to meet me here after he settled in at Mon Coeur. I wanted him to meet you right away, sugar."

Angeline had jumped to Reed's side and now hung on his arm, smiling up at him adoringly. He had forgotten her cousin was coming in from Baton Rouge for the ball.

Obiah entered the parlor and announced the newest visitor.

"Mistah Vancoeur."

Angeline pranced over to her cousin and pecked him on the cheek as the two men moved together to shake hands.

"Have we met before, sir?" Reed questioned. An eerie sense of familiarity sparked at his memory. He heard Elise gasp behind him.

"Not to my knowledge. Have you spent much time in Baton Rouge?"

Reed answered in the negative, then turned to introduce Elise. He stammered at the introduction when Elise stood, white-faced, and backed away.

"Jeffrey?" she whispered.

"Why, yes, Ma'am. Jeffrey Vancoeur, at your service. Have I already had the pleasure of making your acquaintance?" He waited for Elise to respond and extend her fingers, but when she failed to do so he merely inclined his head.

Elise's left hand toyed with the neckline of her gown. She continued to back away, but her hand came up to her temple, and she stopped and looked at Reed.

"I seem to have developed a terrible headache. Please excuse me."

She didn't even wait for a comment. She was halfway up the stairs before Reed could utter his first word.

He turned back to the others, bemused.

Angeline looked unconcerned and was obviously satisfied to have the two men all to herself.

Jeffrey's face was sardonic when he said, "I do hope it was not me. She seemed stricken so suddenly."

Reed poured himself and Vancouer a brandy as Verda entered with the tea tray.

"I am sure it has nothing to do with you, Mr. Vancoeur. Elise has suffered some illness that still affects her at times."

"That woman is rude in the extreme," Angeline said, clearly seeing an opportunity to berate Elise in the eyes of the men. "Why you do not send her on her way I do not know."

She dropped that tactic at Reed's hard gaze but picked up another.

"And the very idea of her attending our betrothal ball. Why, she is a veritable Amazon. And the gentlemen will have their own trouble attempting to dance with her. I vow they shall be unable to get their arms around her, her waist is so big. I would not be surprised if it were twenty-four inches. And what do we know about this woman? Why, she could be a soiled dove."

"Angeline," Reed said through gritted teeth, "Miss Gerard is my guest here. You will refrain from speaking of her unless you can manage to be pleasant about it."

Angeline feigned a wounded look and retracted her claws.

"Very well, sugar. I shall endeavor to find something pleasant about the woman." She smiled, then glided to the tea tray and poured.

Reed looked to the other man for a little male sympathy, but Jeffrey's attention was elsewhere. The man stood gazing at the second floor landing. A frown lined his brow.

Elise paced the floor of her bedroom. She alternated between wringing her hands and kicking the idiotic hoopskirt out of her way.

Jeffrey! The man downstairs is Jeffrey! How in the world did he follow me here? Was he so vigilant in watching me that he somehow saw me find the tea and drink it? Did the police release him so quickly?

Elise had been so shocked at seeing her nemesis standing there, her only thought was to get away from him.

She forced herself to slow her pacing and calm down. Being emotional would get her nowhere.

Carriage wheels crunched on the drive as it was brought around to the front of the house. She sped across the landing to the upper veranda to try and catch another glimpse of Jeff. She stood inside the door within the shadows and watched as the trio approached the carriage. A surge of jealousy ripped through her as she watched Reed bend stiffly to accept Ángeline's kiss on the cheek.

Jeffrey handed his "cousin" up into the carriage, exchanged a few comments with Reed, then swung up onto his horse. Reed disappeared onto the veranda below her, and the carriage jerked forward. Jeffrey walked his horse a few steps and stopped. He stood in his saddle and looked directly toward Elise. Then he bowed and tipped his hat.

She forced herself to stand there and not dart out of sight. Their eyes met, unblinking. Jeffrey's lips curved into a triumphant smile that exposed two rows of perfect, white teeth.

Elise watched as he kicked his horse into a canter. He looked like Jeffrey; yet he didn't. There was no deliberate stubble on his face, and his hair had been combed straight back with some sort of pomade.

She shook herself.

By now her sense of reasoning had begun to return, and she told herself that this man could not be Jeffrey. The odds of him finding more tea and knowing what to do with it and how to brew it were just too slim.

The two men had the same name and looked enough alike to be twins. This man must be one of Jeffrey's ancestors. Their mannerisms were the same, as well as their cocky attitudes. Elise shivered. Whether this was Jeffrey or one of his ancestors, she intended to stay out of his way.

Staying out of his way was easier said than done. The next several days seemed to throw them together constantly. Angeline was forever showing up on Reed's doorstep with Jeffrey in tow. It occurred to Elise more than once that she'd seen few women in the twentieth century as forward as Angeline.

Even though she had come to the conclusion that this Jeffrey was not her ex-fiancé, she felt every bit as uncomfortable in his presence as she had in his descendant's. And she was convinced that these two were related. Their looks and mannerisms were the same—eerily so.

She had tried to remove herself from the situation and stay as far away from Jeffrey as possible. But today proved to be an occasion when she decided not to.

Reed had invited her to go riding with him and the Bobbsey twins, as Elise had taken to calling them in her mind. Her first impulse was to decline, but she knew she needed to spend more time with Reed. Angeline had made a pest of herself, which left very little time for any one-on-one with Reed.

The dance lessons had resumed after Reed made them both uncomfortable with an apology for his outburst. But it just wasn't the same now. Elise felt truly awkward and had no need to fake her clumsiness. She was even toying with the idea of showing improvement so Reed would feel safe in ending the lessons.

She buttoned the double-breasted riding jacket while she swayed to some internal music in front of the cheval glass. She curtsied to her reflection, as if ending the dance, and reached for the silly little riding hat that matched her violet habit. The hat pin had little to anchor it, since her hair fell loose around her shoulders. It looked okay, she guessed, but the hat was designed to compliment the intricate, upswept coiffures of the 1840s. She had tried her hand at creating one of those styles, but the only thing she'd achieved was a pair of aching arms and a lot of singed hair. And since Oak Vista was sadly lacking in females who needed a lady's maid, there were no servants there with any more ability than Elise. Besides, her hair was the least of her worries right now.

The horses were already at the front of the house when she stepped onto the veranda. Angeline's perfect blond curls gleamed under her perfect riding hat while Reed helped her to mount a sleek Arabian. Elise fantasized about ripping those curls from her head, until she noticed how Angeline was mounted.

Oh, damn. I forgot about sidesaddles.

Another torture device for women designed for appearances rather than health.

Jeffrey gave a tug to the cinch, then led a beautiful, chocolate-brown filly to the mounting block. Elise took her time stepping onto the block, trying desperately to calculate exactly how to go about getting into the saddle.

When she could delay no longer, she took the reins from Jeffrey and lowered herself onto the leather. A split second after her leg wrapped around the pommel and her full weight was on the saddle, the horse whinnied with pain and bucked violently.

Elise tightened her leg and sawed at the reins, but there was no way to grip the horse. After struggling for what seemed like forever, she found herself flying over its head. Seconds later the hard-packed ground knocked the wind from her when she landed flat on her back. Pain shot up her spine and into her shoulders. A cool breeze danced across her thighs while the world was treated to a lengthy view of suntanned legs and the lacy French-cut panties she'd arrived in.

"My Heavens! She's naked under . . . Someone settle her skirts, for pity's sake." Angeline mustered up an adequate amount of outrage, but apparently not enough to stir herself into action.

Elise lay very still for several seconds and waited for the pain to subside and her breath to return to her lungs. Someone alternately rubbed her hands and gently tapped

her cheeks. When she opened her eyes, it was to gaze
into Reed's worried countenance.

When their eyes met, Reed froze, his hand just a whisper on Elise's cheek. His eyebrows lowered in question,
as if Elise held the answer to a memory he was searching
for.

Think, Reed! Remember! Just open your mind!

She stared up at him, willing him to remember. Her
arms slid around his neck, and she moistened her lips for
the kiss she could feel was coming. His face inched its
way toward hers. Their eyes never wavered from each
other. His warm breath caressed her face, and she could
see herself reflected in the blue of his eyes, could almost
taste his lips on hers.

"Reed, sugar, is poor little Elise all right?"

The pair on the ground jerked as if they'd been shot.
Reed was the first to react. He muttered a heartfelt
"Damn" under his breath, then scooped Elise into his
arms and swept her onto the veranda. Gently, he sat her
in a wicker rocker.

"She seems to be," he said, teeth clinched. "Elise, how
do you feel? Do you hurt anywhere?"

She looked into her lap and mumbled, "If I did would
you kiss it and make it better?"

She knew he heard her, but he gave no reaction at all
to her words.

She was so disgusted at the interruption she wouldn't
have felt pain if her back had been broken. She shoved
Reed and the now-hovering Jeffrey out of her way and
jumped from the chair.

"Nothing hurt but my pride," she said as she shot a
few daggers at Angeline and clomped down the steps.
She noticed the twit hadn't bothered to dismount. She
was too busy studying her fingernails.

Angeline's eyes widened when she looked up and saw Elise walk back to her horse and grab the reins.

"Surely you do not mean to ride after all. Why, you should remain here and rest. And perhaps a little more experience before . . ."

Angeline's voice trailed off when Elise grabbed the cinch strap and tugged it free.

Both hands slid under each end of the saddle. Elise swore when something pierced her right thumb. She slid the saddle from the mare's back and dropped it into the dirt. A thorn-studded twig still clung to her upraised hand when she peered over it at Jeffrey. He was the last person to check her horse.

"Gee, I wonder where this came from." Her voice dripped with sarcasm when she held her thumb up, a crimson bead around the thorn. Jeffrey's only reaction was a look of concern.

Reed's gaze flicked toward Angeline before he took the steps in one stride to stand beside Elise.

"I am sorry, Elise. Sometimes these burrs stick to the saddle blankets. I'll have a word with Big John to be more careful." He pulled the thorn from her skin and pressed a snowy white handkerchief against the wound.

"Don't bother. No harm done," was all she said. She handed back the blood-speckled square of linen and sucked the pad of her thumb. She continued to glare at Jeffrey.

"Elise, sugar, we insist you go straight up to bed and rest. I will have Nell bring you a tisane to ease any pain and . . ."

"Get real, Angeline. All I did was fall off a horse. And by the way . . . sugar . . . my name is Elise Amalie, not Elise sugar. See if you can remember that, okay?"

Elise rolled her eyes when she peered over the back of the animal and saw Reed watching her. His mouth was suffering a series of spasms which looked suspiciously like those of a man trying not to laugh.

Angeline huffed and her eyes narrowed as she watched Elise.

"Well, if you intend to ride, why are you pulling off the saddle blanket?"

Elise tossed the blanket onto the ground beside the saddle and dusted off her hands. With a devilish smile, she hitched up her skirts to a scandalous height, stepped onto the mounting block and swung astride the horse's bare back.

"Does this answer your question?"

Elise felt a warm sense of satisfaction spring from within when she looked at Angeline's stunned, speechless expression. She made a token gesture of flicking her skirts down when she saw matching looks of shock and admiration from the two men. Angeline whirled around to glare at both of them.

A sense of freedom coursed through Elise's bloodstream. She yanked the hat from her head and flung it behind her as she wheeled her horse toward the road. Her body leaned low over the mare's neck, and the three stricken observers were left standing in a cloud of dust.

Reed was still speechless over Elise's now famous horseback ride two days earlier. And thanks to the servants' grapevine and Angeline's efforts, the whole countryside now knew of it.

Fortunately he'd heard no murmurings of the display—or lack—of undergarments they'd all been witness to. His blood still stirred every time he thought of that lacy scrap of fabric. He'd never seen the likes of it. Where did one come from who wore that apparel? Not even the girls in the "houses" wore that manner of garment. And the very thought of Vancoeur's expression when he looked his fill . . . By God, he'd been tempted to call him out.

More and more disquieting thoughts had focused on Elise, even before the riding incident. Now, try as he might, he could not get her out of his mind.

He grinned and shook his head as he pinched the bridge of his nose to rest his eyes. Even as he found her actions outrageous and totally unpredictable, he'd felt a glow of admiration when she'd yanked off that saddle and mounted her mare astride. Unexplainable pride had swelled in his chest when he'd watched her race down the avenue of oaks and leave the rest of the party standing there, gawking. He'd had to resist again, however, the overwhelming urge to call Jeffrey out when the man had blatantly admired the expanse of leg dangling beneath her skirts.

The woman could certainly handle a horse, as she seemed to handle everything else, including Angeline. Most women balked at coming head to head with his betrothed. She was known to have a double-edged tongue and could slice a person into shreds without ever actually saying anything opprobrious—all the while wearing an angelic expression. Elise had neither cowed from nor taken any of Angeline's veiled setdowns and had been in the enviable position of leaving his future wife speechless. Angeline seemed to have been born with an opinion, and except for the confrontations with Elise, she had yet to cease expressing them.

Strange, these traits in Angeline had never bothered him before, but now he found them most irritating.

He decided to give up his attempts at working on his accounts. The numbers were beginning to blur, but his mind had strayed long before his eyes had wearied.

It occurred to Reed to check with Elise and make certain she had all she needed for the ball. The idea of her company was enough to send him pushing out of his chair and trotting up the staircase. He was merely doing his duty as a host. Nothing more.

The door to her chamber was closed, so he tapped lightly. He didn't want to wake her in case she was sleeping. There was a faint sound of movement on the other side, and he became concerned when he heard the sound of strained, laborious breathing. Fear that she was perhaps ill had Reed shoving the door open and bursting into the room.

What he found made his blood run cold.

Elise lay on the floor, her hands behind her head and her knees bent. With each struggling breath she curled forward, only to drop back to the floor again. She rocked forward over and over again.

He was at her side in a heartbeat and had her face cupped in his hands to check for any signs of a fever.

"Elise! Elise, what's wrong? Where is the pain? Can you speak?"

Elise stopped rocking. Her shoulders hovered above the floor, her hands still behind her head. She quirked an eyebrow in Reed's direction.

"D'ya ever hear of knocking?" she asked, her tone and expression amused. He sat back on his heels, mystified now that the fear was gone. His right hand plowed through his chestnut hair while his heart slowed its beating.

"You nearly gave me apoplexy. If you are not in pain, then why . . . ?"

"I'm exercising," she explained with a smile. A dimple appeared in her right cheek. "After all, if I don't watch my figure, no one else will."

He was not sure which of those two statements shocked him more.

"Ex . . . er . . . ci . . . Good Heavens, Elise. I thought

you were having a relapse." The relief hit him with a rush, and he hugged her tight against his chest. His lips brushed back and forth across her hair. He inhaled the scent of gardenias—a scent that surrounded her like a halo. Tendrils of fire crept into his limbs and wound their way through his rib cage and along his spine.

He felt Elise's arms steal around his waist, and he opened his eyes to gaze down at her. Her eyes tightly closed, a furrow between her brows, she looked as if she were absorbing an exquisite pain. Even as he watched, she inhaled sharply, as if drawing the sensation deeper into her soul. It was then he realized with a jolt that she wore only her chemise and pantalettes.

It was like having fire and ice dumped in his lap at once. He jerked, then gently set her away from him and rose stiffly to his feet.

"I am terribly sorry, Elise. You must think me a monstrous cad. I cannot hope to excuse my behavior. I can only offer that I was so relieved you were not ill that my relief precluded good manners."

When he moved away from her, she looked up at him with hurt in her eyes. *Hurt because I no longer hold her? Or hurt because I treated her so shabbily?* He watched as she lowered her head with a look of defeat.

He stood there for several awkward seconds, then moved to the door.

"Reed?"

His hand froze on the doorknob.

"I don't think you're terrible. There isn't a man alive that I respect more."

She couldn't let him leave thinking he'd insulted her. The feel of him holding her, kissing her hair, the restrained love vibrating from him—she had only wanted to be engulfed by the moment. And the ecstasy of it had been painful because she didn't know when or if he would ever hold her like that again.

Damn his honor! And damn Angeline!

She was beginning to wonder, even if he did fall in love with her, would he break off his engagement to that little blond witch? These things were not taken lightly in Reed's time. People didn't jump in and out of engagements—even if there were very good reasons.

She heard him mumble a few unintelligible words, a look of regret stamped on his face, before he closed the door behind him. Was the regret from having to leave her or from ever coming through that door in the first place?

She sat on the floor for several minutes and stared into the distance. What should she do now? Everything she did was wrong.

She forced herself to shake off her doldrums and rise to her feet.

There was going to be a ball here tomorrow night, followed by a day of picnics and outings, and she had more important things to do than sit around feeling sorry for herself.

As a guest, she had little to do with the preparations, but she planned to check with Lil and Nell to see if there was anything she could do. And there was one last fitting for her gown.

Chapter 19

A REFRESHING BREEZE blew away the humidity on the morning of the ball. The scents of bougainvillea, honeysuckle and earth mingled with the smells of hundreds of fresh cut flowers, beeswax and baking bread.

Elise kicked the sheets from her and stretched her legs until they shook. She bounced from the bed and swept back the draperies, blinding herself momentarily, then reveled in the cool breeze and pure sunshine caressing her skin. The air in the twentieth century never smelled so good.

A day like this always made Elise feel invincible. There wasn't anything she couldn't do, and stopping this marriage was first on her list.

I can't believe my knees are shaking. I've flown Air Force missions and captained 727s, but my knees decide to give out on me over a dance.

She lowered herself to the chaise longue in disgust, giving her knees a break and marshaling her courage. There was no sense rushing downstairs now. She'd taken so long getting ready that there was no choice now but to make a grand entrance.

Several deep breaths and a few minutes of biofeedback stilled her racing heart. When her legs regained their strength, she rose from the chaise and picked up the fan of peach-colored feathers. A last-minute survey of her reflection in the pier glass bolstered her ego. Not bad. She'd seen herself looking worse. Actually, she looked darn good. She laughed at herself when she flicked open the fan and batted her eyelashes at an imaginary Reed. Thus fortified, she threw open the door and sashayed down the hallway.

At the top of the stairs she faltered for a moment, surprised by the crush of people mingling at the bottom. Her resolve returned, though, when Reed stepped into her view.

He was bending forward politely, his head cocked to better hear the comments of a fragile-looking, silver-haired lady. As if her gaze beckoned him, he looked up at Elise. His eyes did a double take, then seemed to absorb her as he straightened to his full six feet.

She curved her lips into a minuscule smile, trying to cloak herself with a serene aura.

Seconds dragged by as she stared at Reed. The crowd of people receded into a dark mist until just the two of them were left alone. A bolt of electricity joined them as surely as if they were touching.

Elise moistened her lips and fought the urge to run to him.

Reed's body moved ever so slightly toward the staircase, his gaze still looking upward, when a disembodied hand reached out to caress his cheek and force his attention away.

The dark mist vanished in an instant, and the crush of chattering, brightly dressed revelers stormed back into Elise's consciousness. Angeline was at Reed's side, her hand now moved from his cheek to his chest. At that moment Elise seriously considered asking Nell for a voodoo doll of Angeline. She would love to try her hand with a couple of well-placed pins.

The moment was over, but she was certain she had shared something special with Reed. A heady warmth lingered at the base of her neck as she made her way to him.

She tried her best to descend the stairs gracefully for a change and did a darn good job of it. Until she ran smack into Jeffrey.

"Miss Gerard. May I say how lovely you are tonight?" He bowed over her hand, brushing his lips against her knuckles without the slightest breach of etiquette.

Leave it to you to be on your best behavior, Jeff. You wouldn't do anything out of line with a whole houseful of people watching.

Elise recovered her hand and used both to hold her fan. She tucked her elbows close to her sides so he wouldn't feel invited to take her arm and lead her away.

"May I also say that your gown is by far the most fetching one here? What color would you say that is, precisely?"

"Peach."

"Hmmm, yes. A very becoming color on you."

"Thanks."

She hoped her monosyllable conversation would discourage him and he'd go away. Reed, however, saved her by appearing beside them, Angeline hanging on his arm as if superglued to it.

Reed shrugged free of Angeline's grip to take Elise's hand and kiss it lightly, as Jeffrey had. However, he held it for several seconds before releasing her fingers.

"Breathtaking, Miss Gerard." His husky voice sent a ripple traveling up her arm.

"Whoever did you have make your gown, Elise?" Angeline's eyes were wide, her look of sincerity spurious at best.

"Sukie made it. Exactly to my specifications."

Angeline's slow nod and quick scan of the gown was meant to be an insult. But Elise was confident the deep peach silk suited her. The off-the-shoulder neckline was draped with a diaphanous silk that rippled gracefully when she walked. The whole dress was cut for fluid movement, and Sukie had captured it to perfection. Best of all, there wasn't a ruffle or bow in sight.

"How very brave you are to wear a style so . . . unknown. And most women would be afraid to forgo their crinolines for fear of looking, well, limp."

"Thank you for noticing, Angeline. I've never been one to act like a sheep. You know, following the flock blindly no matter how outrageous their fashion statement is."

Elise almost laughed aloud watching Angeline try to decide whether or not she'd just been insulted. Her narrowed eyes made it clear the moment she'd decided she had been.

Reed interrupted before she could make a retort.

"Angeline, I feel I should take my houseguest around and introduce her to my friends. Will you excuse us for a moment?"

He slid Elise's arm under his and turned to enter the parlor, but Angeline grabbed her other arm and halted their progress.

"Oh no, sugar. You see to your other guests, and I'll

make sure Elise meets everyone. After all, in a sense she is my guest, too."

Reed's eyes flickered with irritation, but only for a second. Before he could respond, he was tapped on the shoulder by a rotund, florid-faced gentleman who asked his opinion on an investment. While Reed's attention was elsewhere, Angeline dragged her to a group of women and began making introductions.

"Mrs. Pembrooke, Mrs. Albright, Mrs. Cannon. May I introduce you to Reed's houseguest, Elise Gerard. Elise is suffering from memory loss, and Lilianna Dubose is staying here, looking after her. The poor dear does not even know what happened to her trunks or where she came from." Angeline's face was the picture of sympathy.

This procedure was repeated several times. Each time Elise tried to jerk away from Angeline's grasp, the grip would tighten as they moved to the next group.

All right, lady, I've had enough of your game. Elise dug in her heels and stopped in the center of the room.

"Angeline . . . sugar," she began in a loud, carrying voice, "I'm sure you don't realize this, but your nails are very sharp, and right now they are deeply embedded in my arm."

One final, ten-pointed jab squeezed her arm before Angeline bothered to remove her claws. Elise looked pointedly to the imprints, several half moons in the skin of her forearm, then raised her gaze back to Angeline.

"Why, thank you, sugar." Elise issued a veiled challenge with her forgiving smile.

The first notes of music drifted from the ballroom to filter throughout the house and into the gardens. The music hung in the humid air, mingling with scents of gardenia and frangipani. Drawn by the festive tune, pairs of exquisitely dressed couples wandered to the solid white ballroom.

Reed made slow progress himself, stopping every few feet to chat with well-wishers. Even though the announcement hadn't been made, everyone took for granted the reason for this party.

When he saw a break in the crowd he headed for it, knowing that his first duty was to find Angeline and begin the dancing. She nearly knocked him backward when she stormed through the parlor door.

If she had been an animal, her hackles would have been raised and her fangs bared.

She parted the waves of people like a prow of a ship. He stood, bemused, and watched her flounce up the staircase to disappear with a flip of her skirts into the room set aside for the ladies. Several eyebrows shot skyward. Her trip upstairs had been followed by dozens of eyes, all of which turned to Reed when she disappeared from view.

He knew without turning around who would be in the room Angeline had just left.

Elise stood in the center of several of his guests— mostly men casting admiring looks and comments. Reed felt a hackle or two of his own rise. When she saw him staring at her, she just smiled, shrugged, and crossed her eyes. The impish gesture was so unexpected he burst out laughing; then he wound his way through the crowd of people. He felt pulled to her like iron filings to a magnet. Her hand slipped into the crook of his arm, and she excused herself from her admirers. The movement was made without thought, as if they had been walking together for years, and it caused a dangerous coil of warmth to curl in Reed's chest.

They may as well have been alone for all the notice they gave others. When they entered the white, gilded double doors to the ballroom, a waltz had just begun. Reed released Elise's hand on his arm reluctantly. The pair stood together with an air of uncertainty. Several guests swayed or tapped their toes to the music in anticipation of dancing. No one was about to breach etiquette by dancing before the host officially opened the ball.

Reed cast his gaze around the room in search of Angeline, who was apparently still pouting upstairs. This called for a spur-of-the-moment decision. He bowed to Elise and said, "May I have the honor of this dance?"

Elise didn't answer with words. She simply looked up at him with sparkling eyes and slid into his arms.

They froze for a second, waiting for the beat, then stepped as one into the dance. Reed could not tell which beat he was dancing to—the music's or his heart's. His gaze locked with Elise's, and when he stared down into the mossy green depths of her eyes, he felt as if the dance they were dancing was spiritual rather than physical. He gave no thought to the steps. Elise moved as if she were an extension of his body.

So focused was his attention on her face, he didn't realize the only sound around them was the music. The chatter of his guests died down, and an uncomfortable silence fell over the crowd. He had chosen to dance the first dance, not with his betrothed, who was nowhere in sight, but with a houseguest who had just delivered a setdown to the absent woman.

The couple swirled around the dance floor, all eyes focused on them. Jeffrey stood back for several minutes, a silent observer, then turned to the woman beside him.

"I believe this ball is officially open, Mrs. Trahan. Would you do me the honor?"

The pretty, strawberry blond murmured, "I would be pleased, Mr. Vancoeur," and the pair swept onto the dance floor.

Others followed. Within seconds the floor was alive with a rainbow of swirling silks and satins.

Reed at last pulled his gaze from Elise and was surprised to see they were not alone. He was astounded then at his own behavior, at his breach of etiquette in not only beginning the dance with another woman, but at his total lack of attention to his guests. Elise had cast a spell over him, and he had rejoiced in it. He looked down at her again, and the facts struck him like a bolt of lightning.

I love her! Dear God, how I love her! And he knew without being told that she felt the same.

He fought the urge to pull her to his chest and had to glance away from her face to gather his wits.

Their reflection danced in the mirror in front of him. Peach silk swirled around their legs, and Elise's hair, worn loose around her shoulders, rippled in the breeze from the French doors.

Reed's breath caught, and he nearly stumbled when he watched their reflection dance by. For a brief moment he saw Elise with her hair up, in a loose sort of fashion, and her dress had glittering things dangling from it. And he was in his shirtsleeves, holding her so close their legs were touching.

He had never, to his knowledge, hallucinated, but now he considered it might be a worthwhile pastime. The feelings he experienced during that moment were very nearly overwhelming. He only hoped no one noticed how . . . overwhelmed he was.

Trying to recover from the effect she was having on him, he looked down at her and raised an eyebrow.

"Is it not amazing, Miss Gerard, what a few simple dance lessons can do for one's coordination? I must say you have improved immeasurably."

"Oh, Mr. Blackwell," Elise's voice nearly purred, "you ain't seen nothin' yet."

Elise's eyes crinkled with mischief, and he felt her, not surprisingly, take over the lead. She danced him away from the center of the room. Several huge, potted ferns stood on wide bases, and when Reed guessed that to be her destination, he followed her there with a flourish.

The two swirled behind the giant fronds. Elise held his gaze with a searing look and only the barest hint of a smile. The next step brought her against his chest, and he felt her thighs against his. Jolts of electricity shot through him at every point their bodies touched. Heat crept up his neck. The suggestive movements of her legs, her right knee between his, the rhythmic, ancient moves of her hips, sent flames licking through him. The heat of her stare told him she knew exactly what she was doing; this was no awkward misstep.

He returned her gaze with matching intensity and mirrored her movements. Her eyes fluttered closed and her head fell back. A sultry smile ignited a heat in him that threatened to engulf them both.

A ballet of emotions pirouetted through Elise's body as she felt the proof of Reed's desire. She knew the exact moment when he admitted to himself that he loved her, and her heart sang with joy. She no longer felt the dance floor beneath her feet. She was floating on air, and her love was the music she danced to.

She took her time opening her eyes, and when she did she encountered the penetrating heat of his. Their steps faltered, then stopped.

Her hands moved upward, and she lassoed his neck with her arms.

"Refresh my memory, Mr. Blackwell. Is it scandalous for a lady to kiss her dance partner?"

Reed's eyes glowed as he smiled down at her.

"It would be the ruin of her, Miss Gerard."

"Well then, darlin', isn't it wonderful I'm not a lady?"

His head bent forward ever so slowly when she came up on tiptoe to meet him. His lips felt like a butterfly against hers when he said, "I beg to differ." Her tongue darted out to entice him closer. He crushed her to him with a moan and kissed her deeply. So deeply it shuddered her soul.

An all-consuming fire of need swept through her. She pulled her arms from Reed's neck only to slip them under his coat and run her hands along the indentation of his spine. His shirt was damp, and the heat inside the jacket excited her all the more. Traces of starched linen, sandalwood and mint mixed with the scent that was his very own essence to create an aphrodisiac more powerful to Elise than any drug.

His hands came up to cup her face, and he placed gentle, deliberate kisses on her cheeks, her eyelashes, her nose. When his mouth returned to hers, he was no longer deliberate. The kiss had the urgency of being out of control.

With lips still touching he spoke, his breath caressing her mouth.

"I love you, little one."

Elise inhaled deeply of the sweet breath that carried those magical words. She pulled it into her lungs, and her heart, and into every cell of her body.

"Oh, Reed, I never thought I'd hear those words again." The last of her words were muffled as her lips covered his. Her legs turned to spaghetti when their tongues began playing hide-and-seek, and she realized the only thing holding her up was the steel band of Reed's arms.

He grinned down at her, a blue spark of jealousy flashing in his eyes.

"You never thought to hear those words again? Has someone else been telling you he loves you?"

Elise raised her eyes only far enough to peer at him through her lashes. Her gaze was torrid—meant to burn into his mind and brand his heart.

"Only you, darlin' . . . in my dreams."

He groaned and crushed her to him. She slid her hands to his neck. Mindless of the folds in his neckcloth, she shoved it aside and placed her lips to the pulse point of his throat.

Neither heard the *click click* of tiny, mincing steps until the intruder was upon them.

Aunt Lil rounded the wall of ferns several seconds before the distracted couple sprang apart, exchanging looks of shock.

Lil's bouncing gait and swaying skirts gave her the appearance of the Liberty Bell run amuck. Without ever once looking at the rumpled pair, she bustled by, singing, "Angeline is on her way downstairs. I'll be back in a moment to escort you out of here, my dear. Reed Blackwell, straighten your neckcloth" to a tune somewhat resembling "Yankee Doodle."

The white of Reed's teeth shone in a brilliant, indulgent smile against his rugged, tanned face, but Elise whirled and grabbed his coat sleeve.

"Angeline. Oh heavens, Reed, what about Angeline?"

His smile only faltered for a second.

"Let me take care of it, Elise. Angeline will probably be glad to be rid of me."

Elise couldn't stop her unladylike snort at that optimistic statement.

"You've got to be kidding. Good heavens, Reed, she chased you with the single-mindedness of a lion after its prey. She'll never let you . . ."

Lil chose that moment to reappear, less hurried but nevertheless a woman with a purpose. She bounced up and smoothed down several sections of Elise's mussed hair. Then she clicked her tongue and grumbled something about men's sweaty palms while she flicked the silk draping that fell from Elise's shoulders back into place. She then slipped her arm through Elise's and patted her with her free hand.

"Now, my dear, I must say I have thoroughly enjoyed our little stroll through the gardens. So refreshing."

Without looking back she sang again, "Neckcloth, Reed Blackwell."

The high-pitched shriek and crash of breaking glass were drowned out by a lively Virginia reel and the thick walls of the library. Reed sidestepped the brandy snifter with ease, but when the entire decanter hit the wall beside his head, droplets of the pungent liqueur sprinkled him liberally.

"Enough!" he roared when an ink holder found its way into Angeline's hands.

Angeline stood poised to hurl the ink in the direction of the decanter but must have thought better of it. She lowered her arm but held on to the ink.

"It's that Amazon trollop, isn't it? First she wormed her way into your home. You have even begun to speak in the same vulgar way she does. And now . . ."

"Angeline, you will mind your language." Reed marched over and snatched the ink from her hand. "Elise and I are in love. This was not something either of us planned, but what's done is done. I am willing to allow you to be the one to break it off. You can say you realized you don't love me or that I'm an insufferable cad. Whatever you want. Besides," he said, spreading his hands and gesturing to the ball going on outside the mahogany doors, "we never officially announced our betrothal. Give any excuse you like—I'll back up whatever you say. But," he nailed her with a glare, "leave Elise out of it."

Angeline returned Reed's glare as the music filtered into the library, making a mockery of the betrothal party. She stared with narrowed eyes until Reed was about to turn and leave the room. Suddenly she dropped onto the dark green velvet settee and buried her face in her hands. An occasional sob broke the monotony of the high-pitched whines emanating through her fingers.

Reed stood still, uncertain of how to proceed. Before he had time to formulate a plan, Angeline raised a blotchy, tear-stained face to him. Red eyes looked up at him. Her nose was pink, and crimson splotches dotted her face.

Now I see why she's never used this tactic on me before.

While he was berating himself for such a low thought, she spoke.

"You cannot marry her, Reed. Our baby is a Blackwell, and he will be born a Blackwell."

Reed's entire body jerked, then he stopped himself from laughing out loud.

"I beg you pardon, Angeline. I thought I heard you say 'our baby.' "

"That is exactly what I said, Reed. I did not think I would have to spell out that I am *enceinte*."

Reed did laugh at that.

"No, my dear, not under normal circumstances. But you see, one has to have been, shall we say . . . exposed . . . in order to achieve that delicate condition. And we have not been . . . exposed to each other in that manner."

"Oh no? What do you call what you did to me the night of your last ball?"

He froze. His heart began to hammer.

"What are you talking about?"

"I am talking about the night of your last ball, when you climbed into my bedroom window, foxed out of your head, and forced yourself on me!"

"You're lying!"

"You forced yourself on me, saying we would be married and you had no desire to wait. You had not even asked for my hand; yet you forced your attentions on me. Now you are going to be a father, and I will not stand aside and bear a bastard while you marry that trollop. I tried to get you to stop but you refused. You forced me, Reed Blackwell. And it was horrible!"

Her face was once again covered by her hands, but Reed took no notice. His heart thundered in his chest, and he fought to keep his stomach from turning.

The night of his last ball. Dear God, that was when he'd woke the next morning in a field by the river. He'd been wearing strange breeches and shoes but was naked from the waist up. He had no idea how he'd gotten there, where he'd been, or where those articles of clothing had come from. He still didn't know. And now Angeline was accusing him of . . . impossible.

"You had on strange clothes," she continued, as if reading his mind, "and when you staggered home, you were so drunk you left your shirt and coat behind. I was so furious with you, I threw them in the fire. The next day, when you came to Mon Coeur and proposed, I decided to forgive you."

Reed felt as though his thoughts were struggling through thick, black mud. Nothing made sense. He knew he hadn't been drunk that night. He very seldom drank at all, and when he did he held his liquor like a gentleman. Could he have had some type of seizure? Could he have been sleepwalking? Could he have been drugged?

Angeline was crying again, but now one hand lay protectively against her stomach.

Bile rose in his throat, and he swallowed it back. He took a step toward her and forced himself to speak, his voice not much more than a gravelly whisper.

"Make yourself presentable, Angeline. We have a betrothal to announce."

Elise alternately paced the floor or stared out the window of her bedroom, as she had been doing since Reed had gone into the library with Angeline. She couldn't fake an interest in the ball or the guests. Not until she knew the outcome of this meeting.

She saw a movement behind her in the mirrored blackness of the window and spun around, running to Reed when he stepped into the room. Something was wrong. She knew it. She stopped herself from flying into his arms, alarm bells going off in her head like a cockpit with an engine fire.

Hollow eyes stared out at her from a ghostly white face. His hair tumbled across his brow, the victim of repeated abuse from his fingers. As she watched he raked a handful of hair back into place, then clenched his fist as if to pull it out.

A pain started growing in the very center of her chest even before he spoke.

"I have to marry her, Elise."

His voice was hoarse and barely audible. She knew she couldn't have heard him right, even though her breathing had stopped and her lungs were beginning to burn.

"What?" Her own voice was nothing more than a whisper.

"Marry her. I have to marry her."

After what seemed like hours, she began to breathe again.

"What do you mean you have to marry her? Is she holding a gun to your head? You don't have to do anything. You're a grown man and no one can make you . . ."

Realization struck her like a kick to the stomach. All breathing stopped again, and she fumbled blindly for a chair. She had to sit down.

"She's pregnant. That's it, isn't it? She's pregnant."

Jealousy knifed through Elise with such force it staggered her. The thought of Reed sleeping with another woman caused a pain she could hardly bear. She raised hope-filled eyes, praying that he would deny it and say it was all a joke. His look of abject misery shattered her hope into sharp, jagged slivers that pierced her heart.

Elise stood with her fingernails digging into her palms, watching people all around toast the couple's happiness. It was sheer force of will and a good deal of self-inflicted pain that kept the tears from pooling in her eyes.

She would have preferred to stay in her room, locking the door and locking out the world and all its misery, but she learned long ago to face life with her chin up and her shoulders back. There was no way she would allow Angeline to see her upset.

The toasting mercifully ended when Obiah announced that dinner was served. Elise moved with forced nonchalance to the edge of the crowd. She didn't want to be herded too close to the "happy couple." Several more hours of this torture, and she could escape to her room and then . . . what? She didn't know if she could last that long.

A hand cupped her elbow and guided her toward the dining room. Jeff was grinning down at her with a sardonic look, and one sandy eyebrow raised when she glared at him.

"You did not think it would happen, did you?"

Elise stiffened at his words and removed her elbow

from his grasp with a yank. She tried to walk away from him, but he stayed close on her heels. Ignoring him didn't work, so she finally spoke over her shoulder.

"I have no idea what you're talking about. Now if you'll excuse me, I'm starved, and I see Lil waving for me."

Before she could make her escape, Jeff's hand shot out and grabbed her arm again.

"If you find yourself in need of consolation, my shoulder is yours for the taking." He was such a good actor, his sympathy sounded almost real.

Elise refused to dignify his comment. She simply jerked her arm free and wound her way through the crowd to Lil.

The magnificent array of food only caused her stomach to turn. She wasn't sure if she'd ever want to eat again, let alone eat any of the feast before her.

Her stomach lurched at the mountains of sliced ham, turkey and beef. Whole roasted chickens were surrounded by steamed, fried or raw vegetables. There were pickled watermelon rind, corn relish, potato salad, fluffy, pungent yeast rolls and baking powder biscuits. Dozens of raw fruits and vegetables were cut to look like flowers or birds. The dessert table held an array of confections, from airy meringues, custards and cookies to heavy cakes soaked in rum.

Any other time Elise would have plowed through a meal like this and sampled everything. But now she moved slowly through the line, allowing the occasional selection to be placed on her plate, not even aware of what was being given her.

Lil clucked in motherly fashion at the meager fare that Elise now held.

"My dear, I know a lady is not supposed to exhibit a great appetite, but one can carry things too far."

She bustled over to the French doors and stepped onto the veranda. Elise followed her in a trancelike state, not caring where she went.

They sat on a bench at a far corner of the porch in companionable silence. Lil did justice to her meal, managing to eat with gusto while at the same time maintaining her ladylike demeanor.

Elise rearranged the food on her plate. She sliced off a bit of ham and shoved it between her lips. She had always heard about food tasting like sawdust to a person who was very upset, and now she knew exactly what that meant. Every bite she forced herself to take had the taste and texture of sawdust. After just a few bites, she sat her plate aside and stared off into space.

Aunt Lil's pudgy, porcelain hand rested on her knee and patted.

"Now, now, my dear. These things have a way of working out. The deed isn't done yet."

Elise snorted for the second time that night and shook her head. If the deed hadn't already been done, she wouldn't be sitting here, feeling sorry for herself. But she stopped short of uttering the comment. It wouldn't help matters to broadcast Angeline's pregnancy. She also didn't deny what Lil was referring to. It was obvious Lil knew how she and Reed felt about each other.

"I wouldn't place any bets that this one's going to work out, Aunt Lil. The engagement has been announced. And I have a feeling that Angeline is not going to want a long engagement."

Lil didn't try to argue the point. She simply tsk tsked and muttered about impatient young people as she rose to her feet.

"Are you coming back in, my dear?"

"No. I think I'll stay out here for a while. Maybe the fresh air will do me good."

Elise watched Lil disappear back into the ballroom. She sat for several minutes, occasionally kneading her temples in an attempt to dispel the growing throb there. She decided distraction might work better. She rose from the bench and headed for the solitude of the gardens.

One circuit of the grounds proved to be peaceful enough, but her heart wrenched each time she heard a pair of lovers murmuring to each other in the darkness. Just as she was about to step back into the ballroom, a dark, staggering shape loomed ahead of her.

"So, what have we here? The little houseguest from nowhere."

Whiskey fumes and a noisome blast of bad breath forced Elise backward. With her head held sideways in a vain attempt to avoid a direct assault on her senses, she studied the intruder from the corner of her eye.

She had met him earlier in the evening. His name was Ballard Fetter, if she remembered correctly, and he was one of the many Angeline had given her "poor Elise" speech to. Even then he had been so drunk he could barely stand. His condition had gone downhill during the course of the evening.

Before she could finish sizing him up, he grabbed her wrist and dragged her into the ballroom.

"Had my eye on you all night," he slurred as he swung her into an unsteady waltz. "We'll dance awhile; then maybe you'll give me some of what you've been giving Blackwell."

Elise couldn't believe her ears. She tried to jerk free, but he held her by the wrist and had an iron grip around her waist.

His cravat was spattered with droplets of red wine, and an assortment of food clung to his beard. The front of his jacket was stained with unrecognizable grease spots. When he leered at her, his teeth were covered with yellow slime and dotted profusely with bits of green. Her stomach rolled.

"Mr. Fetter . . . it is Fetter, isn't it? I have no desire to dance with you nor to give you whatever it is you think I'm giving Mr. Blackwell. However, if you continue to breathe on me, I might be persuaded to vomit on you, but then that would be redundant, wouldn't it?"

Elise's smile was so sugary sweet, anyone watching would have guessed her to be enjoying herself.

It apparently took several seconds for the meaning of her words to wade through the alcohol in Fetter's mind. When he did manage to separate her facial expression from her words, his eyes widened in rage, and his grip tightened.

"I'll show you what you're going to give me," he said, "and if you don't want to make a scene, you'll follow me out this door real quiet."

Elise raised her eyebrows with feigned surprise.

"Why, Mr. Fetter, wherever did you get the idea that I don't want to cause a scene? Why, I have no qualms whatsoever of drawing attention to myself. After all, what would I have to gain by not doing so?"

Fetter stared at her blearily. Unaccustomed to women he couldn't intimidate, he made the mistake of calling her bluff.

His hand slid from around her waist to roughly squeeze her breast while he continued to clumsily dance and shove her toward the door.

Elise reacted without thinking. She stepped back with her right foot, then sent her knee crashing upward into his groin. She hit her target with brutal accuracy. Fetter rose several inches under the force of her knee. A blast of fetid breath swooshed over her in a muffled *Oooomph* that resounded throughout the room. The alcohol must have dulled his pain, because instead of falling to the floor in a fetal position, he held his crotch with one hand and lunged, bent over, in her direction.

Enough was enough. Elise stepped back, grabbed a handful of gown and hiked it above her knees, then spun around with a roundhouse kick. The outside of her right foot met with Fetter's forehead, knocking him backward onto the gleaming ballroom floor. When he hit, he slid for over two feet, stopping with his head halfway under Angeline's skirts before she squealed and ran away.

When the adrenaline stopped pumping, Elise became aware of a deafening silence. She raised her head to gaze at her surroundings. Hundreds of eyes stared at her, a considerable amount of white showing in all of them.

But the only pair that really mattered was Reed's, wide with shock and concern. She stood for several seconds, her chest heaving from exertion, before she remembered to drop her skirts. She smoothed a few imaginary wrinkles from the silk and flicked an invisible piece of lint. Retreat might be the better part of discretion right now.

With a shrug directed to Reed, she daintily lifted her skirts and stepped over the unconscious Fetter.

"He just wouldn't take 'no' for an answer," she said and held her head high as she walked out of the ballroom. She kept her regal bearing all the way down the hall and up the staircase, cringing when the ballroom erupted with the buzz of voices the minute she disappeared from view. She crumpled in a miserable heap only after shooting the bolt home on her bedroom door.

Chapter 20

He was having the dream again, but he couldn't control it. Elise was running through the house, calling his name, and when he found her, she pulled him into the library. Only this time he was the one to disappear. He watched, helpless, as she clawed the air, wearing a tiny, black shift that barely covered her, and screaming "Don't marry her."

He woke with a start. When he turned onto his back, beads of perspiration rolled downward from his forehead and trickled along his scalp. The bed linens were wound around his body, plastered to his sweat-drenched limbs, and they refused to loosen their tenacious grip on him. He took out his frustrations on the unfortunate sheet and kicked savagely. He felt an uncharacteristic satisfaction at the loud ripping sound his actions produced. Within seconds the sodden mass of linen lay in shreds on the floor and Reed was breathing hard, fighting the urge to put his fist through a wall.

Don't marry her. He could still hear Elise's words ricocheting through his mind. They were the last words she'd said to him last night as he walked out the door to announce his betrothal. He knew her whispered voice hadn't been meant for him to hear. Earlier she'd suggested that Angeline might be lying or that maybe the baby wasn't his. How could he tell her he'd forced himself on a woman? How could he explain that Angeline had known things she couldn't have known? She had seen the strange clothing. And now he knew he'd left behind the jacket and shirt in her room after . . . after . . .

He couldn't tell Elise, this strange and wonderful person who had appeared in his life, that he had raped a woman. Even if he could endure the shame of admitting it, he could never stand to see the revulsion on her face when she looked at him. The hurt in her eyes as he'd stood beside Angeline and announced their plans to marry had been a dull-bladed knife that had ripped into his heart. Choking out the words that he intended to marry Angeline was the hardest thing he'd ever done. And being toasted by the well-wishers, forcing a gaiety that he doubted he would ever feel again, was nothing more than an opportunity to numb his senses.

Unfortunately, it seemed to do the opposite. He was acutely aware of every man who came within two feet of Elise. And there had been many. She had insisted on returning to the ball, and it had looked as though she was trying her best to numb her own senses. She'd had quite a few glasses of champagne and danced several dances before the announcement was made. Reed knew. He knew exactly whom she'd danced with, how many times, and what type of dance.

It had been a slow and painful torture to watch her in

the arms of other men. With each of her new partners he'd had to speculate if that would be the man Elise would marry, now that he knew he would never be her husband. When Jeffrey, in particular, claimed her for a waltz, he had wanted to slam his fist into Vancouer's face. The thought of her spending her life with someone else, bearing another man's child, those warm, loving arms around someone else's neck and gazing up at him with those playful green eyes. Making love . . .

Once, he had brushed past her and their arms touched, and he'd reacted as violently as if she had wrapped her body around him.

He'd watched her follow Lilianna onto the veranda and forced himself to remain inside when Lil reported to him *sotto voce* that Elise needed some time alone.

He hadn't seen her return on the arm of Ballard Fetter. He'd only seen her smiling charmingly up at him while they stumbled through a waltz. It took him several seconds before he realized her smile was nothing more than a facade. And just as this knowledge dawned on him, he watched Elise slam her knee deep into Fetter's groin. It all happened so quickly that it was over before he'd had time to react.

He did react, however, when he'd had Big John escort Ballard out by the scruff of his neck. He'd excused himself from his guests and appeared outside the stables where Ballard was having difficulty finding the stirrup on his saddle.

Reed had proceeded to soundly pummel the man, all the while explaining that he meant for him to never step foot on Blackwell land again. In between each punishing blow he had calmly proclaimed that, even though Fetter was a cousin to Angeline, *smack,* he was forever persona non grata, *smack,* and if he ever touched Elise Gerard or showed his face on Oak Vista again, *smack,* he could expect the same hospitality he was receiving at the moment, *smack*. After having vigorously made his point clear, Reed had stepped over the once-again unconscious Fetter and retired to the kitchen to procure some ice for his knuckles.

He now flexed his fingers, working out the stiffness that had set in overnight. He still had the urge to slam his fist into the wall.

While he shaved, he focused his mind on the upcoming events of the day and tried to plan how to get through them. There was to be a picnic, croquet, a horse race, and *where in the name of God did she learn to do that?* His thoughts leaped back to the night before.

He'd never seen anyone move in such a fashion—certainly not a woman. And why had she not simply called for help? The ballroom had buzzed of nothing else the remainder of the evening, and he was amazed at the different attitudes taken. Some of the younger women had actually praised her actions, saying they'd wished many times that they'd had the courage and ability to fell Ballard. He apparently had garnered a slimy reputation among the ladies and was kept at a distance whenever possible.

Of course, most of the guests were aghast at Elise's unruly methods of deterring Fetter's attentions but held their tongues in front of Reed. Instead, they settled for walking around with pursed lips and raised eyebrows. He only hoped that if she chose to join the events of the day, she would not be cut dead.

Elise had been up for hours, after getting all of maybe fifteen minutes of sleep during the night. She brushed her hair mechanically and chastised herself for acting like someone in a bad Chinese movie the night before.

She closed her eyes and shook her bowed head, visualizing herself in a ballgown, kicking a drunk in the head.

Way to go, stupid.

A low, guttural moan crept out of her throat at the picture, and she wondered if she would ever be able to face all those people today. Even if she hadn't made a fool of herself last night, she wasn't sure if she could face Reed with Angeline and allow the woman to remain standing.

A decisive knock sounded at the door, and her spirits lifted slightly. Lil would have a positive outlook or an uplifting, if not weird, piece of advice.

But Lil was not the person who slithered through the door, closing it behind her with a *click*.

Angeline leaned against the solid wood, her ubiquitous ruffles today in shades of blue that matched her eyes. Those eyes were drilling holes of hate, but Elise refused to acknowledge her presence with more than a disinterested glance.

"I want you out of here," Angeline finally said, her voice starting out as a hiss and increasing in volume. "You have worn out your welcome, coming here uninvited and behaving like a trollop. You have tried to come between me and my betrothed, you have embarrassed us both, and you have ruined my betrothal party with your outlandish histrionics."

Angeline's chest began to heave. In the back of her mind Elise rather hoped that the scanty bodice would succumb to gravity and cause an embarrassing moment for the bitch.

"I want you gone before you can wreak more havoc. Pack your measly belongings and be out of here within the hour."

Elise sat casually in front of the cheval glass and continued to brush her hair during this monologue. Inwardly she longed to pounce on the little witch and yank her bald. Instead, she calmly laid aside the brush and fluffed her hair while studying her reflection. After a careful, deliberate smoothing of an eyebrow, she turned to Angeline.

"First of all . . . sugar . . . I haven't *tried* to come between you and Reed. I *have* come between you. As you were told last night and chose to ignore, Reed loves me, and I love him. Secondly, Oak Vista still belongs to Reed. I find it laughable that you march in here and order me out of someone else's home. Rather full of yourself, aren't you?

"Let me put this to you in a way you might understand, Angeline. You are no more to me than a pebble in my shoe, an irritant that is easily removed. And trust me . . . sugar . . . I will remove you, but in my own good time. Now, I believe I'll have some breakfast and join the others."

Elise rose, twitched the back of her skirt with one hand and enjoyed a final glance in the mirror.

When Angeline, visibly shaking, her face a contortion of rage, refused to move away from the door, Elise pulled it open with a heave, knocking her nemesis awkwardly into the middle of the room.

Elise swept through the portal, showing a bravura she didn't feel. She was well aware that she'd not only talked her way out of any reprieve from the day, but had issued a ridiculous threat that she had no hope of fulfilling.

Breakfast went better than she expected. Most of the guests were still asleep, and those awake had already eaten and moved on to other activities. She had the dining room to herself while she picked over the eggs, ham and sugar-sprinkled beignets Verda brought to her. The little maid was refilling her cup with steaming black cof-

fee when Jeffrey strolled into the room. When he saw
her, his eyes lit with amusement. He took a seat directly
across from her.

Elise scooted her chair out in preparation to leave,
hoping to escape and avoid having to even speak to him.

"I trust you slept well, Miss Gerard."

She wanted to slap the smarmy look right off his face.

"Like a baby, Mr. Vancoeur."

She rose to her feet then and slid the chair backward
with the back of her legs.

"I must say you displayed some very interesting dance
steps last evening with old Ballard. Wherever did you
learn such a thing?"

His wide-eyed look of innocent sincerity came close
to eliciting a few well-chosen curses from Elise. Instead
she held delicate fingers to her temples and batted helpless eyes at him.

"Why, I just can't remembah, suh. Where on earth
would a little ol' thing like me learn to do somethin' like
that to a big, strong man?"

Jeffrey laughed, but his mirth didn't quite reach his
eyes. He was studying her, and Elise felt like a deer
trapped in the headlights of an oncoming semi. Before
he had a chance to speak again, she tore her gaze from
his and forced herself to walk casually out the door.

Right into Reed.

She hadn't heard him coming. She would have chosen
another exit if she'd known he was there. His hands encircled her arms to steady her when she staggered backward. The heat of his hands burned a path from her arms
right into her soul. She longed to take his hands in hers
and drag him into the closest room, to have those hands
run over every aching inch of her body. Instead she
jerked her arms free and glared up at him.

He stood with his hands hovering inches from her

arms. Elise could almost feel him wanting to touch her again but knew he didn't dare.

His face was haggard, as if he'd not slept for days, and his bloodshot eyes were filled with misery. She knew her own pain so mirrored his it was as though she'd crawled right into his skin and been living his emotions. They stood so close his breath ghosted across her face. The smell of mint mingled with his scent, and she could almost taste it.

When his hands dropped to his sides the spell was broken. She snapped to attention and backed away.

"I have to go."

"Elise, please . . ."

She didn't look back as she rushed out the door. She didn't want to see his face if just hearing the anguish in his voice could tear so at her heart.

Chapter 21

CONFUSION PULLED HER in different directions. She needed to get as far away from the house as possible. She needed time to think. Emotions battled within her, and she wasn't sure which one would win—love or anger.

When the shock of his announcement had begun to wear off, the first seed of anger began to grow. Her anger at Reed was mixed with guilt. Elise knew he would never go into this marriage unless Angeline forced him. Nonetheless, she wanted him to defy the rules of society, damn his honor, and carry her off to some place that wouldn't care who they were or how strange she acted.

Bitterness and anger welled inside her. By God, she had honored his moral convictions, and then he turned around and got a woman pregnant. A woman with the morals of an alley cat, no doubt.

Elise's feet scuffed the ground in weary defeat as they carried her farther away from the house. She considered what would happen if she just kept on walking. At least she wouldn't have to face Reed again, with Angeline hanging on his arm like one of the twenty-dollar hookers on Bourbon Street. Then again, she supposed, there probably aren't any hookers on Bourbon Street, yet.

She grabbed at a handful of maple leaves on a low hanging branch and systematically shredded them while she continued her musings. She walked on, following a narrow path that took her away from Oak Vista and Reed. Too bad she couldn't escape her misery so easily.

Her thoughts were interrupted by the muffled sound of childlike crying. She forgot her own troubles for a moment while she searched for the source.

The path had thinned to nonexistence before she found what she was looking for.

Two little boys, each about ten years old, sat on a huge, fallen log that jutted out over a clear, sparkling stream. She had almost missed them, hidden as they were behind the thick drapery of a weeping willow. She watched for a moment and assessed the situation.

"It's not fair," the first little boy said between sobs, "we haven't done anything wrong."

"We ain't gots to do nothing wrong, Master Nicholas. We know'd we couldn't b . . . be f . . . friends forever."

Elise's heart ached for the two small boys who, she realized now, were being torn apart by racial barriers. While she watched, the little boys burst into tears again and comforted each other with a hesitant hug.

She took that moment to part the curtain of leaves and step into their little sanctuary. The nonchalant approach would probably be best.

"Hi, guys. What's the problem?"

The two friends jumped apart with terrified looks. The dark-skinned boy accidentally knocked his blond-headed friend sideways when they moved apart. He seemed to hang suspended for a moment, then tumbled head first into the stream.

"Oh, Sweet Jesus! Oh, my Lordy, ma'am. Save Master Nicholas, please!"

The little slave bounded back and forth along the log, the whites of his eyes glowing against the darkness of his face. His friend sputtered and thrashed below him.

Elise ran to the log and hitched up her skirts, then knelt to balance her knees on the crumbling bark until she could reach for the boy. Her first instinct was to dive in after him, but she knew the layers of clothes she wore would weigh her down and endanger them both. When one of Nicholas's hands waved wildly above the water, she clapped a firm grip on it and started to pull.

"Oh, thank Sweet Jesus, Missus. I help you pull him out."

She heard the voice and felt a tiny hand on her shoulder. Then her free hand was flailing to regain her precarious balance.

Panic seized her as she too fell headfirst into the water. She immediately started tearing at her clothes with one hand to rid herself of the extra weight, all the while holding tight to Nicholas.

She could have laughed out loud when her feet touched bottom, and she realized how shallow the water was.

She struggled for a moment to gain a firm footing on the slimy creek bottom and then straightened her legs. Her head broke the surface, and she rose until the water lapped just below her breasts. Why, the water wasn't more than four feet deep.

Nicholas must have felt her stand up because he stopped his thrashing and lowered his feet also. His chin floated just below the water, and when he stopped sputtering and coughing, he turned anxious eyes on her.

"Thank you, ma'am." His mouth filled with water when he spoke, and he shot it back out in a little arching stream. His previous expression of apology turned into one of horrified alarm at this latest behavior, and Elise knew he was scared to death of her reaction.

She dipped down to chin level with the water, looked him in the eye, and said, "You're welcome." Then she shot her own stream of water to land neatly in front of his face. She hadn't thought his eyes could have gotten any wider.

Her laughter danced across the water as she hugged him to her. The little arms tightening around her neck confirmed she had allayed Nicholas's fears.

She moved to hoist him back up onto the fallen log but stopped when she saw his little black friend.

The poor little guy had not moved from the bent-over position he was in when Elise had fallen. His eyes were bulging, tears dripped from his chin, and his little body shook from head to toe. He was chanting, "Sweet Jesus, I done it now, I done it now."

"Hey! It's okay. No harm done." Elise tried to reassure him, but he seemed to be in a trance. She waved her hands in front of his face a few times but got no reaction at all.

"What's your friend's name?" she asked Nicholas as she raked a handful of dripping hair off her cheeks.

"Cyprian, ma'am."

"Hey, Cyprian!" she shouted, loud enough to get his attention. He finally stopped chanting and focused terror-filled eyes on her.

"I done it, ma'am. I's sorry as I can be, and it be an accident, but I done it." He slowly shook his head back and forth in denial.

Elise stared at the quivering child, then cocked an eyebrow and sliced a sideways look at Nicholas before speaking again.

"Cyprian, give me your hand."

The small, pink-palmed hand stretched across the water to her, still shaking. When her fingers curled around it, she cast a devilish smile at him and yanked as she said, "Why don't you join us, Cyprian?"

His expression was priceless as he flew toward her and Nicholas. She held tight to his hand and didn't allow his head to go under.

Nicholas was screaming with laughter, which was cut off sporadically by copious mouthfuls of creek water.

Cyprian's legs churned, and he sputtered, clearly expecting his punishment to be death by drowning. Elise grabbed him under both arms and pulled him right in front of her.

"Cyprian, listen to me. You're not in any trouble. I'm not angry, okay? It was all an accident, and you're not going to be punished."

He looked at her with skepticism, but the shaking lessened. Nicholas removed any remaining doubt of his forgiveness by directing a stream of water to the center of Cyprian's forehead.

The brown eyes lit with delight and relief, and a spirited spewing contest ensued between the boys.

Elise released her hold on them after moving to shallower water. She grabbed up two handfuls of clinging fabric from her gown and dragged herself up onto shore.

The boys frolicked in the water while she tried to wring out her skirts on the creek bank. They arrived in a tangle of brown and white limbs to join her. She sat fanning her skirts around her when the boys approached in a tumble. Nicholas dropped to the grass beside her, but Cyprian remained standing.

"I know who you are. You're Miss Gerard, Mr. Black-well's guest."

Nicholas surprised Elise by knowing who she was. The mention of Reed brought back that sharp pain in her heart.

"Thank you, again, Miss Gerard. I'm terribly sorry we got you wet and ruined your frock."

"I think it would be all right if you call me Miss Elise. And don't worry about me. I won't melt, and this old dress will dry. So what were you boys so upset about earlier?"

She looked up at Cyprian and patted the ground on the other side of her. Cyprian looked behind him, as if expecting to see someone else standing there, then looked back at Elise with a confused glance. She reached out and pulled him down beside her, then scrunched both boys up in a tight cuddle. His little body stiffened beneath her arm, but it didn't take long before he started to relax.

"Okay, you're doomed to sit here all cuddled up and mushy with this old lady until you tell me what your problem is."

The boys gave a token resistance, which only created squishing noises from all the wet clothing. That turned into embarrassed giggles, but after several minutes Nicholas became serious.

"My parents say Cyprian and I cannot be friends any longer, Miss Elise. They say I am too old to have a darky for a playmate. But he is my best friend in the whole wide world."

Nicholas's voice quavered at the end of his little speech. Cyprian didn't look as if he could speak at all.

"Miss Elise, why do people look down on darkies? Cyprian looks just like me, only darker." Elise saw the resemblance now and mentally shook her head at society's double standards. "Why, his blood looks just like mine when we bleed. I know for a fact 'cause we're blood brothers."

She smiled at the pride in Nicholas's voice and wished she could do something to help.

"I know it's not right to choose friends by the color of their skin. Maybe it will make you feel better if I tell you that someday boys like you will be able to stay friends forever. They'll go to the same schools, live side by side as neighbors, work together. Why, when you boys are men, slavery will cease to exist."

Elise wondered if she hadn't gone a little too far with this last statement, but the obvious looks of disbelief on the youngsters' faces set her mind at ease.

"How will slavery go away, Miss Elise?"

"Nich-o-lassss." A lovely, dark-haired young woman in a yellow sprigged day gown stepped through the thick foliage. Elise offered up a silent thank-you for rescuing her from having to answer that question, before the soggy trio stood up.

"Nicholas, there you are! I have looked everywhere for you. And here you are with Cyprian. What did your father tell you about that?"

The young woman wore an accusing frown, but when she drew close enough to see the condition of Nicholas's clothes, she cried out and ran to him.

He squirmed under her motherly clucking and tried without success to get a word in edgewise.

Elise recognized the slender woman as one of the guests at the ball. She only hoped the woman had not been one of the witnesses to her impromptu entertainment last night.

"Excuse me. I'm Elise Gerard. Perhaps I can explain what happened."

The woman looked up as though she'd just noticed

her presence. The look of recognition destroyed Elise's hopes for anonymity, but she pressed on.

"You see, I was walking along the path and heard voices," Elise began, mentally editing the story as she told it. "They sounded upset, and by the time I reached the boys Nicholas was struggling to keep his head above water. Cyprian begged me to help, but I fell in, too." Here she pierced Cyprian with a "be quiet" look. "Cyprian tried his best to pull us both out, but we were too much for him and we pulled him in. Fortunately, we found shallow water before anything disastrous happened."

Elise felt like she should add "Yeah, yeah, that's the ticket" to the end of her speech. But, she consoled herself, there wasn't anything untrue about it. She'd just rearranged the sequence of events a bit.

"Why, I hate to think what might have occurred if Cyprian hadn't been close by." A thoughtful shaking of her head drove home the suggestion that Cyprian had, in all probability, prevented a catastrophe.

The young woman's face softened. She kept one hand on Nicholas but knelt in front of Cyprian to take his hand in her other.

"Cyprian, how brave of you. I cannot begin to thank you."

The little woolly head stayed bowed, his face hidden.

"I will talk to Nicholas's father and recommend he reconsider. Perhaps he will allow you boys to remain friends. How would you like that?"

Cyprian's head popped up. A smile broke across his face like a sunrise out of the darkness. Nicholas's expression mirrored his, and the two friends engaged in some vigorous head nodding.

The young lady rose and turned to Elise. She offered her hands when she spoke.

"I am Marisa Trahan, Nicholas's mother. I am so very grateful for your help."

Her two soft hands encased Elise's, and she patted them with genuine warmth. It was the first time Elise had felt completely comfortable with someone since she'd arrived here. It was a good feeling, one that she missed more than she'd realized.

"I really didn't do anything except complicate matters," Elise said with a grin. Then she wrinkled up her nose and shook her head. "I seem to be an expert at complicating things." A rerun of the previous night flashed through her mind.

As if reading her thoughts Marisa waved away her protests.

"Oh, fiddle. You only did what half the women at the ball would like to do. Very few of us have walked away from Ballard Fetter without his handprint on us somewhere." She giggled and her soft brown eyes lit with delight. "Why, I bet he thinks twice before he tries that again on a lady."

Elise couldn't help but laugh. Marisa's cheerfulness was contagious.

"Now, we need to get the three of you out of these wet clothes before you catch your deaths," Marisa said between giggles. Then, her voice laden with mischief, "Would you show me how you did that to Ballard?"

Shadows on the creek bank created a natural camouflage, and Reed realized he hadn't been seen when the group walked within a few feet of him on their trip back to the house. The chatter of the foursome faded as they moved farther away.

The stillness of the clearing, the moist, rich smell of earth mingling with a profusion of honeysuckle called to Reed. He found a patch of sunlight and stretched out in the warmth, staring up at a china blue sky and savoring the solitude.

When he reflected on all he'd witnessed in the last twenty minutes, a feeling of uneasy wonder tapped him on the shoulder.

He had followed Elise when she'd run from him in the foyer. His intent was to allow her to walk off some of her anger before he tried to approach her to talk.

Just as he had been about to catch up to her, he'd heard the boys and watched Elise cut through the trees to the creek. At first he hadn't wanted to interrupt. Then when they all took a dunk in the water, he was laughing too hard to help them. He knew how shallow the creek was there and how still the water. There had been no danger. He had, however, been ready to hit the water, clothes and all, if there had been any sign of trouble.

By the time Elise had climbed to shore, he was completely enchanted with her methods of reassuring the boys—not to mention the charming picture a thoroughly wet day gown created. He hadn't considered it eavesdropping when he'd watched to see what would happen next.

A blade of tall grass scratched at his fingers as he lay in the sun, thinking. He snapped it off and chewed on it in contemplation while he continued to study the sky and mull over what he'd heard.

He wasn't sure what it was that had made him so uneasy, but he'd felt chill bumps ripple up and down his arms when Elise told the boys about the end of slavery. It had not been a prediction. It had been a promise—one to which she had given a time period.

Dark tendrils of awareness had tickled the corners of his memory when Nicholas had asked how slavery would go away. Why would a child's innocent question cause such a flutter to his heart? It was almost as if he had known the answer.

A huge, white bank of clouds skidded across the cerulean sky. Like generous helpings of meringue, the flat-bottomed mounds climbed upward. Reed stared at the perfectly flat base of the clouds, and his mind drifted along with them.

An awareness, a knowledge began to filter into his consciousness.

He knew. Dear God, he knew.

A film of sweat erupted on his skin, and his breathing became shallow. He knew exactly what those clouds looked like from above. He could see the blinding reflection of the sun against their pristine whiteness. He had the desire to fall back into them—like a feather mattress. Just him and Elise.

The film became beads of perspiration. He sat up, plucked the long-forgotten blade of grass from tense lips. The bank of clouds tumbled out of view. Now he saw white lines of mist crisscrossing against the azure backdrop.

Contrails. *Good God, what are contrails?*

He jumped to his feet and scrubbed at his eyes with the palms of his hands. A perfectly blue, cloudless sky hung above him. There were no signs of crisscrossing lines, the likes of which he'd never seen before in his life.

He was going to throw up. The ratlike gnawing in his stomach grew worse with every word out of Angeline's mouth. The only possible end to this growing feeling was to throw up.

Maybe he could aim it toward Angeline. That would certainly shut her up—at least temporarily. Better yet, he could kill her, and then he wouldn't have this urge.

Guilt assailed him. He had no one to blame but himself for having to marry the woman. And he'd damned well better get used to her talking, without suffering any regurgitative or homicidal tendencies. His life was going to be enough of a hell.

"And we really must invite the Governor. Let's see, he and his family will bring the guest list up to . . . thirty-five, thirty-six . . . three hundred and thirty-six. Now. Have I left anyone out?"

He nearly sprayed a mouthful of brandy all over her precious, considerable guest list.

"You can't be serious, woman! What do you plan to do, invite the entire state of Louisiana?"

"Why, Reed, sugar, we cannot take a chance on slighting someone." Angeline laid her pen on the escritoire and flitted to the sofa. "Besides, Momma and Daddy are paying for the wedding, so why should you care how many people we invite?"

Reed's only answer was to slosh another finger of brandy into his glass.

"Now, I think London and a jaunt to the Continent is the perfect place for the honeymoon. We shall take a ship from New Orleans to . . ."

Her voice faded from his thoughts. The word "honeymoon" clanged around in his head like a ricocheting bullet. Honeymoon! He had not even considered that aspect of marriage. How in the world could he go off on a honeymoon with this woman? Why, he could no more bed her now than . . .

". . . and then return to London before coming home. It will be so wonderful. Just what I have always dreamed of."

"Angeline, there will be no honeymoon. It is out of the question."

Her eyes narrowed, and one perfect brow lifted in silent challenge.

"This is a very important season. I can't just go off and leave the fields in the hands of an overseer. I need to be here in case of an emergency. The . . . honeymoon . . . will have to wait until after the harvest." It would wait forever if he had his way.

Angeline's expression didn't waver. But her hand slowly slid from the necklace she'd been toying with downward to the still flat region below her waist. Reed's glance caught the gesture, and he read the meaning as clearly as if she'd spoken the words, "You owe it to me." Their eyes locked, and they stared each other down. His conscience battered away at his resolve, and when a tear collected and spilled onto her cheek, his resolve lost.

"Very well. But not abroad. Find somewhere over here for a . . . honeymoon." Lord, he could barely force the word from his lips.

She brightened at once and picked up a calendar; he knew, however, that the subject wasn't closed. He stifled a moan but didn't bother to suppress the curse he uttered under his breath.

Damn his memory. Damn himself for having that contemptible ball. Damn. Damn. Damn.

"We really do need to settle on a date for the wedding, sugar."

Oh, God.

"I believe the twenty-second of June is the best day. That gives me twenty days to plan and have a gown and trousseau made. I realize it is an obscenely short period of time, but . . . under the circumstances, we mustn't wait overly long."

Elise's birthday. He couldn't marry Angeline on Elise's birthday.

How do I know that? When did she tell me she was

born on June twenty-second? He couldn't remember the subject ever being discussed, but there was no doubt in his mind about the date.

"No!" He very nearly barked the word. "Not the twenty-second."

"But whyever not?" Angeline's whine at this latest obstacle pierced his eardrums. "The almanac says the weather will be perfect for an outdoor wedding. And with over three hundred guests it will have to be out of doors, so I . . ."

"Let's just say I have a personal aversion to getting married on the twenty-second of June, and leave it at that. If you want to wed on that day, find someone else with whom to do it." *Please!*

His vehement tone must have convinced her not to press the issue. She gave a little huff and flicked out a fold or two in her skirts before turning back to the calendar.

"Do you have any prejudices against the twenty-third? Or perhaps you should tell me what days you do not have aversions to."

Reed passed a weary hand over his eyes. He looked heavenward for strength.

"I have no preference, Angeline, other than what I have already stated. Consult your almanac. Plan the wedding for any day you wish, other than the twenty-second, and I will show up."

"Really, Reed. You act as though I am planning no more than a casual outing. This is your wedding, too, I will have you know. And under the circumstances . . . Reed! Where are you going? Reed Blackwell, you come back here!"

He slid the parlor doors closed and made it all the way to the foyer before the crash of breaking glass sounded against them. Probably the Waterford decanter. Nell would not be happy about that.

A freshening breeze swirled around him when he stepped onto the veranda. It blew away some of the miasma blanketing his brain and gave birth to a longing to plunge into the cool stream Elise had frolicked in earlier.

He pulled out the gold pocket watch left to him by his father and snapped the cover open. Two o'clock. Plenty of time for a swim before the horse race. Most of his guests were already lounging or napping in their rooms. The only ones braving the heat of the day were the younger folk, involved in a competitive game of croquet.

He discouraged any idle conversation seekers by striding purposefully away from the house. He didn't care if he looked like a man trying to escape something. He was deep in thought, and the farther he moved into the woods, the deeper his thoughts became.

Elise. Never had a woman so intrigued him. She invaded his waking and sleeping thoughts completely. How was he ever to find any happiness married to one woman and in love with another? Could he ever take Angeline to his bed? He doubted if it would be physically possible, if he were to remain in this frame of mind.

He only wished he had found it so impossible several weeks ago.

God, what a mess.

The stream appeared through the trees, and Reed followed the bank north to a section he knew was deep enough for his needs.

Overwhelmed with the need for the cool water to wash away his thoughts, he grabbed the back of his shirt and yanked it over his head. The boots and socks came off next, and his breeches ended up on top of the pile, inside-out. His fingers fumbled on the drawstring to his

smallclothes before he faltered. Best to leave those on
with all the extra people roaming the grounds.

He trotted to a flat rock protruding above the stream,
and without slowing hurled himself into the air. Muscles
knotted with tension as he slid into the water with barely
a splash.

A passerby would have feared for Reed's life, so long
was he under the water. The surface remained smooth
and undisturbed until he exploded from it, clear to his
waist, at least fifty feet upstream.

The water was cool enough to be refreshing and take
his mind from his problems. He blinked the water from
his eyes, then dove deep to reach the bed and stir up
murky clouds. He followed the slimy bottom until his
lungs began to burn, then surfaced to race upstream
again.

He didn't know or care how long he'd been swimming. He kept at it until his muscles ached and a welcome fatigue crept over him. The pile of clothing he'd
left on the bank was not far, so he submerged one last
time, then rose to fling his hair from his eyes and wade
to the sandy shore.

Waves of heat engulfed Elise's neck, then moved to
more disconcerting parts of her body. She could hear her
heart pounding in her ears over her shallow, ragged
breathing.

He looked like one of those perfect men in cologne
commercials, rising out of the water. But a Speedo never
looked as sexy as the clinging, transparent fabric hanging lopsided and precarious on Reed's hips.

In her mind, she could feel her hands trace the uniform ridges outlining his stomach. Her index finger
would draw a lazy, winding path from his chest to his
navel, and she would watch his muscles contract and

hear his indrawn breath when her finger slipped under the drawstring to flick it loose.

She inhaled sharply to avoid releasing a sob. Her eyes burned, then swelled with hot tears. The pain inside was a living thing, with claws that ripped and tore at her soul.

How can I stay here and watch him marry someone else? How can I leave and never see him again?

Reed flopped to the ground beside his pile of clothes. He lay back, one knee drawn up, his right arm draped over his eyes. He looked the picture of relaxation until his left hand balled into a fist and slammed onto the grass beside his hip.

He cursed, grabbed his pants from the pile and jumped to his feet, all in one movement. One leg rammed into a pant leg, then the other. He swore again and yanked them off, only to turn them right-side-out and repeat the process.

Elise ducked and started backing away. She hadn't expected to find him here; she'd thought he was in the parlor with the witch, planning their wedding. That's why she'd borrowed a horse from the stable and taken a long, hard ride. Now if she could just get to the tree where she'd tied the mare. The last thing she needed right now was to come face-to-face with Reed.

Her eyes stayed on him and the flurry of clothing while she backed away from the scene. That was her first mistake. Her second mistake was stepping into the front door of a ground squirrel's burrow. She only had time to grab for the spindly shrub branches before she crashed to the ground.

Chapter 22

Reed jerked his head up at the thrashing in the underbrush. His shirt hung from his fingers, forgotten. With eyes squinted, he peered into the shadows lining the woods and saw yellow flashes of movement. He finished pulling his sleeve right-side-out and slipped on his shirt before going to investigate.

His heart lurched with a mixture of pain and joy when he saw Elise yank the skirt of her gown from a bush. She looked up and stared at him.

They stood frozen for a second, then Elise said the word "No." It was more a sob than a word. She spun around and ran, the hem of her gown bunched high in her fists.

"Elise! Wait!"

Reed looked at his boots several yards away, then back to Elise. The woman was running with the speed of a man, and if he didn't catch her soon, he'd have no chance to talk to her. And they needed to talk.

The floor of the forest held all sorts of painful, sharp objects, and it seemed every rock, acorn and thorn gathered itself under his bare feet. After several seconds of hopping from one foot to another, he gritted his teeth and took off at a sprint.

Elise darted glances over her shoulder at him as she ran. Her speed increased when she saw him gaining on her. It wasn't until they burst into a small, grassy clearing that Reed was able to plant his feet firmly enough to catch up to her.

By the time he grabbed her shoulders and spun her around, she was crying too hard to put up much of a fight. She knocked his hands from her shoulders, then slapped them away when he tried to hold her.

"Just leave me alone! Leave me alone!" she cried, and shoved him backward before running away again.

He was not about to let her get away again. He caught up with her in seconds and threw both arms around her to pin her arms to her sides. The momentum of his body carried them both to the ground, and he threw himself under her to cushion her fall. They rolled for several feet over rocks and fallen twigs, and when they stopped they both lay there, catching their breaths and moaning in pain.

Elise was the first to move.

"Get off me, you big jerk." She shoved at his leg draped across her thighs. "Ow! OW! I think I pulled a muscle in my neck!"

She tried to sit up but fell back, her hand massaging her neck while she glared at him. Each movement caused a wince when she gingerly worked her head back and forth.

"Oh, God, I think you've broken my neck."

Reed struggled to his elbows and stifled a few winces of his own.

"Here, let me see." He leaned over her and tried to get a glimpse of her neck. Tugging at her hand only increased her anger.

"No! OW! Damn you, leave me alone!" She shoved at his chest, but he refused to be budged.

"Elise, stop being childish. If your neck is truly hurt, we need to know. This could be very serious."

She glared at him for an eternity, her green eyes vibrant behind unshed tears. Finally, she jerked her hand away and stared off into the distance.

Reed knelt before her on one knee and laid his fingers against the warm, ivory column of her neck. His fingers tenderly massaged her skin, evoking in him happier times when he'd been free to touch her. Reminding himself that she might be injured, he rotated her head a bit with both hands. The examination lasted several minutes before he leaned back and stared at her, allowing a serious frown to crease his brow.

"Show me exactly where it hurts the most."

Elise still refused to look at him but reached up and outlined the tendon running from her ear to her shoulder.

"Hmmmm. I see."

He leaned forward again, savoring the feel of her hair as he brushed away any remaining tendrils. He placed his hands on the grass by each side of her head.

"Tell me if this makes it feel better."

His breath stirred her hair a second before his lips touched her neck. She stiffened as a white-hot fire exploded through his body. His lips worked their way up the sensitive tendon to the hollow beneath her ear. He stopped to sample the sweet taste of her earlobe. A burning river of passion snaked through his body when she arched her neck toward him and drew up one knee in a sure sign of pleasure.

He followed the soft, heated path back down her neck, gently nibbling and tasting until he reached the outline of her collarbone. He could feel her pulse racing. Her sweet, salty taste lingered on his tongue.

"Do you hurt anywhere else?" he murmured while his lips still caressed her skin.

He felt, rather than saw, her head nod.

When he lifted his eyes, she was staring at him. She held his gaze while she raised her hand to unbutton her bodice and untie the ribbons of her chemise. She pulled the left side away and guided his head down to just above her heart. Her voice broke when she spoke.

"I hurt here."

A flash of pain and electricity coursed through him. He felt an unfamiliar burning behind his eyelids and a painfully familiar burning everywhere else.

He lowered his head and kissed the indicated area with infinite tenderness, forcing himself to be slow and gentle, no matter how torturous it was on him. His mouth lingered on the velvety swell until her shaking hands came up to drag the hindering fabric aside.

A ragged moan tore from his throat at her gesture. He was wracked with an exquisite, pulsing ache. It was all he could do to keep from ripping the fabric completely from her.

As he kissed away the pain as thoroughly as he knew how, soft, gentle hands cupped each side of his face and lifted his head. Her voice was so husky he barely recognized it.

"Let's see if I can find where *you* hurt."

She rolled to her side and pushed him onto his back. A little gasp escaped her when she saw his open shirt.

Angry, red scratches from the bushes he'd chased her through zigzagged across his chest.

She brought her hand up to caress the line of his jaw, and her eyes spoke an apology for running from him. Her gaze never left his as she lowered her head to his chest to find each scratch with her lips.

Her mouth traced the outline of every wound, and the heat of her tongue seared him like a branding iron. His fingers reached down to entangle themselves in her hair, the hair that fanned across his chest in an ever downward movement. He closed his eyes to keep them from rolling upward.

After kissing and paying homage to every scratch she could find, she moved her hands over his body in search of more injuries. He wasn't sure how much more he could take.

"Ohhh," she breathed in a whisper, "a massage might help you here."

His whole body jerked at her exploring touch, and his breath caught in his throat. He tried to swallow, but there was no moisture left in his mouth. The heat of her hand on him burned like a flame.

"Then again," she teased, "I think you'd be better off to soak it in something warm."

The thin thread of his self-control snapped with her words. A primal moan rumbled in his throat. He rolled atop her and yanked off his shirt.

Her eyes were alive with the heat of desire, her hands busy with the waistband of his trousers.

His gaze left hers only long enough to find her lacings. Elise worked as frantically as he, pulling and ripping at their clothing, desperate to remove all the barriers.

Finally! His hand found the silky smoothness he sought. He rolled to his side only long enough to rid himself of his trousers.

"Missss Elllissse! Helloooo! Misss Elllissse!"

They froze, two statues lying on the grass with bits and pieces of clothing scattered around them like colorful leaves from the trees.

"DAMN!" Reed roared. "Damndamndamndamndamn!" He slammed his fists into the earth, punctuating each and every curse.

Elise simply lay there, staring at the sky, a look of pained defeat etched solidly into her features, one lone tear sliding toward the ground.

It's just not meant to be, she thought. No, it was more than a thought. It was a feeling of certainty that dragged her down and held her pinned to the ground.

Her body still tingled, every nerve ending alive with the feel of Reed. Her mouth still tasted his. His scent still lingered in each uneven breath she took. Yet she felt as though someone had tossed cold water on her, then laid the world on top of her.

Reed brought what he could find of her clothing and laid the pile beside her. He knelt, ran the backs of his fingers along her cheek in a loving caress. Her eyes closed in a slow blink before she turned to him, expressionless.

"Stay here, little one. That's Big John. I'll go find out what he wants before he gets here." His eyes were apologetic beneath the tumbled waves of his hair, his voice husky with the passion he'd been unable to release.

She watched him walk away, his shirttail crammed haphazardly into his waistband. He had to stop every few feet to knock something off the bottom of his bare feet before he limped on.

His image blurred, then cleared when she blinked. Twin tears cut separate paths down her cheeks. Her heart felt like a balloon with a slow leak. She could feel it shriveling inside. Soon there would be nothing left.

I have to get away, she thought. I can't stay here and torture both of us.

She heard Big John's voice coming closer. Reed hadn't caught him soon enough.

"Well, Mistah Reed, Belle done come back to the stables without Miss Elise. She have a piece of tree branch still tied in her reins, so I knowed Miss Elise be all right. I was just afeared she be having a long walk back to the house."

She couldn't hear Reed's muffled reply. She knew though, that she couldn't go back to that house. It was time for her to leave, and now was as good a time as any.

With wearying effort she sat up and slipped on her bodice. The tiny buttons were a hassle to deal with now, when only minutes ago she hadn't even noticed them. She'd skipped one somewhere in her buttoning, but what difference did it make?

When she rose to fasten her waistband, a knifing pain shot through her ankle. She caught herself before she fell but sank to the ground when she tried a second time to put weight on her ankle.

"Damn."

This was definitely not her day.

"Nothing broken, little lady. Just a bit of a sprain. Why, with ankles that tiny, it would take very little to turn one." Doctor Freeport peered at her over his rectangular glasses, then raised his head and looked down through the lenses at the ankle in question.

She heard Angeline "hummph."

Elise didn't know what kind of story Reed had told them about what happened. And she didn't care. She'd already come back to the house once today looking like a drowned rat, her gown plastered to her body. Luckily Marisa had been with her to sing her praises.

This time she was carried in by a frantic Reed. Both of them had stains of grass and dirt all over them. *Oh, well. Let the gossips make of it what they will.*

A twinge of pain brought her attention back to her ankle.

"Should she not be in bed, Doctor Freeport?" Angeline's voice interrupted the examination. "Big John can carry the poor thing upstairs to her room, where she belongs."

"Nooo, noooo. Not necessary. No need for Miss Gerard to miss the festivities." He placed another cool cloth on the swollen limb. "Just keep it elevated and cool."

He turned his attention to Reed. "Have Tessa mix a lump of alum about the size of an English walnut with the whites of two eggs and stir that until it jellies. Then have her soak a cloth in it and apply that to her ankle. Just put a fresh one on when it starts to dry, and do that for at least two days."

His glasses crept down while he spoke until they were barely perched on the tip of his nose. He eyed Reed over them, then shoved them into place with his index finger. He shook his head and spoke to Reed in a low voice.

"And as for what ails you, son, I'd be a rich man if I could come up with a remedy for that."

Elise heard the comment, even though she was sure she wasn't meant to.

She glanced at Reed and saw that he was in worse shape than she was. Bits of dried grass and dirt clung to his hair and arms where his skin was sticky from chasing her. An occasional dot of red marred his shirt from the many scratches on his chest. At least his clothes were in order, thanks to Big John.

The huge black man had had no problem sizing up the

situation. He'd probably already known before he ever stepped into the clearing.

Reed had been so upset when he'd seen her ankle he would have carried her to the house then and there. But Big John's low voice had cut into Reed's plans.

"Now Mistah Reed, you knows you can't be walking into the big house, carrying a lady in the shape you in. Why, people get the wrong idea."

He'd had Reed's boots retrieved, the worst of the grass knocked off, and his shirt properly tucked in, in no time.

Too bad he couldn't have done something about Reed's face. If it had been haggard before, now he looked positively tormented.

Elise felt a little of the numbness begin to fall away from her heart and a warmth steal in when she looked at Reed. She struggled against the warmth. It was easier if she stayed numb.

"Yessir, just keep it elevated and use that poultice. I'll come around tomorrow for another look. No need for bed rest unless the little lady is tired." Doctor Freeport pumped Reed's hand and gave him a sympathetic pat on his shoulder before leaving.

Lil fussed with the cushions and pillows. She fluffed and pounded and rearranged them while she mumbled to herself. "If one is plump, one does not run. There are distinct advantages to being voluptuous."

Angeline glared at the doctor's back, then flicked a disgusted look toward Lil.

"What does he know? He's not much better than a horse doctor." She swung around to Reed after the doctor had left the room. "I still think you should have Big John take her upstairs."

Elise's voice stopped Angeline's whining.

"Oh, Angeline."

The woman turned to look at Elise.

"Butt out." Elise filled her face with as much sweetness as Angeline's was filled with hate.

"Why, you common little . . ."

Reed opened his mouth to cut off Angeline's outraged attack, but Nicholas came bounding into the room to effectively do the job.

"Miss Elise! Golly, look at your leg! It's so big. Does it hurt?"

Elise smiled at Nicholas's concerned little face and stifled the urge to wince.

"Only when I laugh, Nick." And she didn't expect to do a lot of that. When the throb grew worse, she fought a grimace. *What I wouldn't give for a handful of painkillers.*

Nicholas studied the swollen appendage with awe. A pudgy finger hovered in an apparent urge to touch it. He somehow managed not to. Instead he rammed his hands into his pockets and shook his head.

"It's too bad you are grown, Miss Elise. Or else someone could kiss it and make it better. At least that's what Momma does . . . used to do when I was small."

It was all she could do not to look at Reed. She willed her gaze to the floor and tried not to think about the last time—only hours ago—someone had kissed her hurts. Several seconds of uncomfortable silence passed. Just when she thought she was safe, her traitorous eyes glanced up at Reed and locked with his.

His discomfort was almost tangible. Every emotion played across his face, and Elise could read every one—guilt, love, lust, pain, guilt again. It finally ended with a look that said he would give anything to be able to do as Nicholas said.

"Do you suppose it would work on grown people, Miss Elise?"

Her gaze flew back to Nicholas with his innocent question. She blinked and looked back at Reed.

And then she lost control.

The first giggle sounded like a snort. She laughed out loud at the obnoxious noise. Before she knew it, she was so hysterically tickled she had tears running down her face and was holding her sides. She fought for control, only to lose it again when she looked at the four people, three of whom stared at her as though she were mad.

Angeline's eyes glittered with vengeance. She rounded on Reed, and Elise overheard the word "hospital." That did nothing to quiet her hysterical laughter.

Lil, on the other hand, patted Nick's head and smiled.

"Of course kissing a hurt away works on adults, dear boy. And I shall endeavor to find someone to do just that."

Jeffrey sauntered into the dimly lit parlor, the last of the guests to leave.

His arrival strengthened Elise's decision that it was time to go upstairs. If she listened to Angeline rub in one more wedding plan, she would go for her throat, sprained ankle or no sprained ankle.

She began to gather up the odds and ends within reach that had been left for her by the handful of the people who had not chosen to avoid her like the plague. She had invitations, calling cards, and a bird's nest scattered around her. The latter had been brought to her by Nicholas and Cyprian with the assumption that any type of gift would cheer her up.

Her eyes narrowed when Jeffrey bent to pick up a card that had fluttered out of her reach. Her expression didn't change when he went down on one knee, ignoring the fact that Reed and Angeline sat across from her. He took her hand.

"I've come to say good-bye. But before I go, I have been instructed by Lilianna and two dwarf dictators to come and kiss away the pain that has been inflicted upon you." He leaned toward her. His eyes trickled down her body to her ankle. "I assured them it would not be a hardship for me to do so."

A masculine choking sound came from behind Jeffrey. When Elise looked up, Angeline was staring daggers at Reed.

"Now, which one of your delightful ankles is giving you a problem?"

"Really, Vancoeur." Reed sprang out of his seat. "You can't mean to actually kiss . . . Lilianna didn't mean . . . well, it just isn't proper, man."

Jeffrey swiveled his body to face Reed and shrugged.

"Just an attempt to be accommodating, old man. But you're right. Kissing a lady's ankle could be viewed as ungentlemanly behavior. Might I settle for a hand?"

Before Elise could react, Jeffrey had his lips on her knuckles. They lingered there even though she was playing tug-of-war for her hand. Reed paced the length of the parlor.

Angeline grabbed Jeffrey's hand and pulled him away from Elise.

"So wonderful of you, Cousin Jeff, to plan to come all the way from Baton Rouge for the wedding. You must stay at Mon Coeur when you come."

Elise knew Angeline's actions were in no way an altruistic rescue from Jeffrey's attentions. It was just that the bitch couldn't stand for another woman to be on the receiving end of a man's regard while in her presence.

Before Jeffrey turned, he tipped an imaginary hat in farewell and winked.

Elise dragged her knuckles across her skirt to wipe away the feel of Jeff's lips. She could think of nothing to

say that wouldn't sound petty. One thing was certain—
Lilianna would be hearing about her unfortunate choice
of men.

"Reed, sugar, I really am exhausted. Could I persuade
you to abandon your . . . charming houseguest to see me
home?" Angeline fluttered her eyelashes so blatantly
Elise wanted to puke.

"No need for that, Cuz. I am on my way to Mon
Coeur as we speak. I can tether Zephyr to your carriage
and see you home myself. Save Blackwell the trip." Jeff
slid his hand under his cousin's elbow and guided her toward the door.

Angeline clearly wasn't expecting this, nor did she
like it. Elise didn't miss the veil of innocence she threw
over her calculating look.

"Oh. I had expected you to go into town and . . . do
whatever it is gentlemen do there."

Jeff's single bark of laughter was like a trumpet blast.

"No, Cuz. No plans for a night on the town. I believe I
will strive for respectability and see what that feels like."

"But there is no need to do so on my account." She
seemed to realize what she was saying before it was
completely said.

"Oh, but I wouldn't dream of turning respectable for a
cousin." Jeffrey laughed when he said it. "But I can assure you I have my reasons."

He gave Elise a smoky look and held it until it was
clear that Reed had seen it, too.

Elise took a deep breath.

There was that urge to puke again.

Elise didn't seem in quite as big a rush to go upstairs
once Angeline and Vancoeur were gone. Angeline had
made a few more feeble attempts to dispense with Jeffrey but gave up when Reed took the opportunity to

shake the man's hand and thank him for being so thoughtful.

Reed was glad to see them both go. He was beginning to wonder if this nightmare of a gathering would ever end.

And those looks Vancoeur had given Elise. Well, he had to keep reminding himself that Elise was not his.

Not his. Oh, God. The mere thought cut like a knife. He balled his hand into a fist and only barely kept himself from slamming it onto the desk.

Action was what he needed to keep from dwelling on the pain. But first he had to make sure Elise was as comfortable as possible. He poured a goblet of water for her and measured in a dose of laudanum left by Doctor Freeport.

"Reed, I'm ready to go to bed now."

Bed. He closed his eyes and swallowed hard.

"Dri . . . ahem . . . drink this. The doctor left it for you, for the pain."

Elise took a sip, then screwed up her face and shuddered.

"Yuk. What is this stuff, anyway?"

"Nasty, isn't it? It's laudanum."

"Whew. No wonder it gave people nightmares. Just the taste could do it to you." Elise took a deep breath and downed the rest without stopping.

Reed wondered at her choice of the word "gave." Perhaps it was best if he didn't question her right now. She'd had a trying day as it was. He ignored the niggling fingers of familiarity that scratched away at his memory. Just as he had ignored or excused all the other odd occurrences. His flashes of *déjà vu*, the sight of them dancing, the white streaks across the sky that weren't there—all those he attributed to distraction. Elise's strange words, her use of the past tense, and her unorthodox way of speaking he explained away by her illness or accident or whatever it was that had brought her to him.

Verda slipped into the room just about the time Elise finished her second round of shuddering. The little servant gave her a sympathetic pat on the shoulder and whisked a tea cake into Elise's hand.

"You try a bite of this, Miss 'Lise. It take away some of the bad taste."

Verda had been like a loyal puppy since the very first day of Elise's arrival. Indeed, all his servants seemed to love her. The house servants were never far away when she was inside. Even Nell, who was usually coolly efficient, treated Elise with the same warmth she had always reserved only for Reed.

"Verda, please ask Big John to come here," Reed said.

Before Verda could do as he bid, Elise spoke in a soft voice from her chair.

"Reed, could you carry me upstairs yourself? Please?"

He stood silent for several seconds while he rearranged the wine decanters on the tray.

"I don't think that would be wise, lit . . . Elise."

Her expression didn't change. "Please, darlin'?"

At her words and helpless look, Reed's heart felt like a shell that had cracked, and the contents of part pain, part melting heat oozed out in a slow trickle. It flowed through his veins and permeated every inch of his body.

He stared at her for a moment, then moved with swiftness before rational thought could return. She was in his arms in seconds, and he was striding toward the staircase.

Her arms went automatically around his neck, but he tried to ignore the sensation they caused. At the top of the stairs he turned left and almost charged to her bedroom. It wouldn't be wise to hold her much longer.

He kicked her door open, and it bounced against the doorstop and slammed behind him. He laid her on the bed as quickly as possible without actually tossing her there. His resolve was crumbling like a house of cards, and he knew he had to get away. He'd come too close this afternoon. If not for Big John . . . well, he was an honorable man, and Elise was no trollop.

"Darlin'?" Elise's eyes were all but closed. The black-fringed jade gazed up at him. "Could you help me with my dress? I'm so hot."

Frissons of heat shot through his limbs to gather in a most disconcerting way. God, how he was tempted.

"I'll call Verda."

A long sigh stirred the air. "Very well. But could you at least take off my shoe and throw another cloth on my ankle until she gets here?"

Hmmm, Reed conceded, no harm in that. But still, he was quick with the process and didn't focus on her ankles when they flashed before him.

"I'll make sure Verda brings a fresh poultice when she comes. And I'll hurry her along." Not that he would need to, where Elise was concerned. "I hope you have a restful night."

"I promise to sleep well if you kiss me good-night." He stopped in mid-turn. "Just this once." Her husky voice raked across his self-control.

Don't do it. It wouldn't be wise. The best thing for both of us is to walk right out that door.

Her lips were like feathers against his. He kept the light touch deliberate, almost brotherly. But there was nothing brotherly about what the kiss was doing to him.

Her arms twined around his neck; she buried her fingers in his hair. Scorching shivers raced to every nerve when her tongue drew a searing, languorous line between his lips.

An agonized moan tore from his throat. He fell across

her and rolled her to her side, barely mindful of her ankle. The buttons on her gown gave beneath his racing hands, and soon the whole thing was nothing more than a heap on the floor.

Her fingers fumbled, awkward with the few buttons his clothing presented. Impatient, he yanked the edges of his shirt apart. His buttons clattered off nearby surfaces.

The last barriers of fabric flew through the air to flutter to the floor unheeded. Her hands moved over him with excruciating slowness, and shivers wracked his body with each new touch. He tried to slow his own reactions to match her languid mood.

His hands had a life of their own. They slid across the satiny silhouette of her body. He had no control. His fingers somehow knew what to do, where to find her own special triggers.

He draped his leg across hers, and she turned ever so slowly to meet him.

"Reed?" She dragged out the word with her exhaled breath.

"Yes, little one. I'm here."

"Reed. My darlin' husband. I love you. I've loved you for a hundred and fifty years. But why . . ." her voice was slurred, "did you . . . give . . . me . . . that damned . . . laudanum?"

And then she was asleep.

Bloody hell! He'd knocked her out!

Knocked her out, damn it, and obviously caused some type of drug-induced delirium. How else could he explain her ramblings about one hundred and fifty years of love and that he was her husband? He attributed the icy fingers that grasped the back of his neck to his . . . heightened physical state. He refused to attribute them to anything else.

Bloody damned hell!

He lay there for what seemed an eternity, his arrested body in a state of shock, his breathing ragged. The profusion of whispered curses that drifted through the air would have made a hooker blush.

After he exhausted his vocabulary, he bounded from the bed and yanked on his trousers. He searched out his boots and balanced on one foot at a time while he rammed his feet into the soft leather. The rest of his clothes were gathered into a wad and flung into his rooms on his way to the stables.

A bruising ride through the night and a bracing swim in the stream . . . maybe it would help. Or maybe he'd just find a nice, secluded spot and howl at the moon.

Chapter 23

JEFF WAS CHASING her. She kept running but couldn't build any speed. Just enough to stay ahead of him. She hid behind stupid things like a glass door, or a lawn chair, and he didn't see her.

But he always came back.

She even flew—literally flew—without an airplane. Her body swam through the air, but not quite out of Jeff's reach.

Help! She tried to scream the word, but all she did was hiss. Just a low, sibilant, moaning hiss that no one could hear but Jeff. It seemed to amuse him.

He reached up in the air and grabbed her leg. She swam harder, but his pull was relentless. His hand curled into a fist, and he swung at her head. *Help! Reed, help me!* Her brain shrieked the words.

"Reed! Reeeeed!"

The scream finally came, and she shot up in bed. Her hair stuck to her cheeks, and she panted as if she'd really been running. Sweat trickled behind her ears and down her neck. She started to kick off the suffocating sheets, but nothing covered her. The sudden movement pierced her ankle with pain, and she cried out against it.

The door burst open and banged against the wall. She cringed and looked for an escape, forgetting her ankle. But it was Reed. Oh, thank God, it was Reed, framed in the doorway in a halo of light, like her guardian angel.

He was at her side, and she was in his arms in a heartbeat. She clung to him with a death grip, and he rocked her there on the side of the bed.

"There, there. It's all right. It's okay, little one. I'm here. I'm here."

His low, whispery voice reassured her. She could feel the vibrating hum of his words against her ear. He pressed the crystal goblet of brandy that had been sitting on her night table against her lips. She took a few sips when he tilted it back.

She shook with the memory of her nightmare, more vivid than any she'd ever had. He pulled her even closer and nuzzled her hair. His lips dropped what should have been calming kisses onto her tousled, sun-streaked mane. But the kisses were anything but calming.

Elise twisted in his arms until she lay across his lap. She lay there, just studying his face. He studied hers.

Vague memories of what had happened when he'd carried her to bed stirred in the recesses of her mind.

The laudanum. Damn the laudanum.

And damn his honor.

She turned her head and snuggled against his chest. Her face met warm, almost hot skin. A few softly curling hairs tickled her nose. Heavy brocade silk interrupted her wandering lips, and she silently cursed the loose dressing gown he'd slung on.

In no time, she had risen to her knees and shoved the robe from his shoulders. Her lips followed the same path they'd followed that afternoon. So did her hands. They traveled in different directions, until his raspy breath caught in his throat.

"Make love to me, Reed." She spoke the words into his mouth.

His groan rose from somewhere deep in his soul.

"Make love to me, darlin'. For old time's sake."

His groan intensified, and she had her answer.

He pulled her across his lap, and the two fell backward into the darkest shadows. He played her like a finely tuned instrument; played her over and over throughout the night. In return, she sent him above those clouds he'd watched today. And this time they fell together into the white, fluffy mist, into a spinning, dizzying vortex of blessed oblivion. No interruptions. No laudanum.

No turning back.

"I don't care what I have to do. I'll send you to Europe. I'll raise the child myself. Whatever it takes, I'll do it to get out of this betrothal."

The speech Reed had rehearsed was not at all like the one coming out of his mouth. He'd planned to be diplomatic, persuasive, but at Angeline's vehement refusal, he'd lost all thought of diplomacy.

"You don't love me, Angeline. And I don't love you. You can find someone you care for and still have a wonderful life. No one will ever know the child I'm raising is yours."

A sneer contorted Angeline's face, and Reed wondered what in the world he'd ever found attractive about the woman.

"I have given you my answer, Reed," her voice was almost a hiss. "You had best get used to the idea of our marriage. I am surprised your little tramp will still have you, considering you raped me. Does she not fear you would do the same to her? Then again, one cannot rape the willing, can one?"

He could feel the blood drain from his face, and Angeline stared with narrowed eyes. Her high-pitched laugh made an ugly rent in the air before she spoke.

"She does not know. Does she? Oh, how wonderful!" She rubbed her hands with obvious glee. "Yes, Reed, you will marry me, or Elise and everyone in New Orleans will know the truth."

If he didn't get out of here soon, he might give in to the urge to choke the life from this woman. He grabbed his hat from the settee and headed for the front door. He refused to say another word.

"Reed."

He kept walking.

"I want her gone from Oak Vista, Reed."

His hand turned the doorknob.

"I may be forced to tell her . . ."

He spun around on her, cutting off her words with a chopping motion.

"Breathe one word of this to Elise, and I will have no reason to marry you." He paused to let his words sink in. "Once you destroy my honor, you destroy any incentive I have to be honorable. You'd best remember that, woman."

Every window in the house rattled when he slammed the door behind him.

If she could only pace. Instead, her blasted ankle forced her to sit on the upper veranda while she waited for Reed's return. With her foot propped on an ottoman, she had to settle for some ferocious finger tapping instead, and that wasn't at all satisfying.

Not nearly as satisfying as last night. Her pulse quickened with just the thought of all they'd shared. Their spirits had joined, as well as their bodies, and it wouldn't have been surprising to her to find a part of Reed left behind, deep down in her soul.

Reed had told her when he rode away that he was determined to put a stop to Angeline's marriage plans. He'd vowed he would find a way for the two of them to marry, without Angeline's interference.

Elise wasn't so optimistic. She'd come up against women of Angeline's ilk in the twentieth century more times than she cared to remember. The personality was a familiar one. She knew Angeline would rather see Reed destroyed than see him choose another woman over her.

The wait wasn't long, and that was not a good sign.

She saw the cloud of dust rising in the air before she saw either horse or rider. Then with a thunder of hooves, a solitary horse burst onto the avenue of oaks and charged toward the house at breakneck speed. At first she thought it was riderless, but a closer look showed Reed bent low over the horse's neck, his body flowing with the straining muscles of his mount.

It looked as if he would charge right up onto the veranda, but at the last minute he yanked on the reins and flung himself from the stallion's back.

Elise placed her foot on the floor and hobbled to the railing, her heart in her throat.

Reed looked up at her, but he didn't seem to see her at all. She waited for him to say something—anything— but he continued to stare, his eyes focused on something inside himself.

The bubble of hope Elise had been harboring burst into a million pieces.

*   *   *

Now, more than ever, when he looked at this woman, his body came alive. This time though, the process was painful—almost too painful to bear.

"Did you really expect her to let you out of it, Reed? That self-centered little twit would rather see you in hell than let you out of her clutches."

The only sound in the room was that of Elise pacing the floor with a limping gait. He stood slumped against the mantel. His arms ached to hold her. But there was a question in his mind that had nothing to do with Angeline, and he had to get it off his chest.

"Elise," he shoved away from the mantel and poured himself a brandy, "there's something we need to talk about."

Her pacing stopped, but he continued to study the amber liquid in the cut glass snifter. He wasn't sure he could look her in the eye but forced himself to turn and face her.

She grimaced and shook her head. "Don't tell me there's more bad news."

"I'm not sure." He set the glass down without ever taking a drink. "Elise, last night when we . . . were together, well, you weren't . . . that is to say . . ." he turned and looked heavenward, trying to decide exactly how one goes about this conversation with a lady.

"Spit it out, Reed. I wasn't what?"

He spun around and nailed her with his gaze.

"I wasn't the first, Elise. That means you may already be married. What if you have a husband out there looking for you?" He tried but failed to keep the pain from his voice.

Elise stared at him, her expression unchanged except for the pallor that swept the color from her cheeks. She blinked, and her gaze fell to the floor as she sank slowly onto the love seat. She seemed to be searching for words. Reed took a seat across from her and waited for her to speak.

She sighed and closed her eyes. When she opened them again, she slid from the love seat to kneel at his feet. Her hands were icy in his.

"Darlin', look at me." He stared straight into her sea green eyes. "I have no one in my life but you. I can't tell you why I'm so sure of it, but I am. As for you not being the first, I know you're disappointed but . . ."

Reed cupped her chin with his index finger. "Little one, I could never be disappointed in you. I'm not concerned about that. It doesn't matter. What I'm concerned about is the possibility of a husband."

She rested her head on his knee and swallowed hard.

"You have to trust me on this, Reed. There's no one but you. Maybe someday I'll be able to have all the answers for you, but right now all I can say is you're the only man in my life."

She raised her head again and looked at him.

"Do you believe that?"

Her eyes were so clear and earnest, he could believe anything she said. He wanted to believe her. Surely she would remember if she had a husband. He was certain, if he ever found that perfect woman, that he would never forget his wife. Perhaps there was another reason why Elise . . .

"Let's not dwell on a problem that doesn't exist." Elise rose to her feet and began pacing again, ignoring the pain in her throbbing ankle. "The problem is Angeline and what to do about her."

Nothing could be done where Angeline was concerned. If he refused to marry her, she would make their lives miserable. He started to say as much when Elise spun around, her countenance drawn.

"Let's leave. We'll just pack up what we can carry and go start a life together somewhere else. Maybe we'll find my home and family. How would you like that?" Her voice sounded desperate, as if she were clinging to a last thread of hope.

She clenched and unclenched the skirt in her hand as she looked at him. Her eyes filled, and she quirked her mouth into a sad smile, as if she already knew what he would say.

"Elise, we can't run away and leave my child to be raised by Angeline. You've said yourself she's a vindictive witch. And you could never respect me if I did such a thing." He shook his head and stared at the floor. "No. We both know I could never walk away from this and leave it unresolved."

She looked up and stared him in the eye. Her voice broke when she spoke again.

"You're right. You'd end up hating me, hating us, and I could never live with that."

Reed turned and stared out the window. If she only knew how low his self-respect was now. If he could only explain why Angeline had him so cornered. But he'd rather marry the shrew than see the look on Elise's face when he told her he'd raped a woman that night after the ball. He could live with self-loathing. But he couldn't bear for Elise to know what he'd done.

She hurt all over. Her ankle throbbed, her stomach was in knots, and a pounding headache built in her temples. But that was all endurable compared to this sensation of having her still-beating heart ripped right out of her chest. She didn't even realize she had her hands pressed over her heart, as one would press near a pain to dull it.

She watched Reed kick, with increasing force, the toe of his boot against the andirons in the fireplace. It was obvious he struggled with some inner demon. Was he agonizing over Angeline or still worrying about the possibility of her having a husband? How ironic that he should be worried about himself.

The decorative brass andirons were beginning to show abuse.

"Mistah Reed! Mistah Reed!" a child's voice called from the back of the house. Before Reed could react, Big John's tiny son, Ambrose, burst into the room, Obiah close on his heels.

"Mistah Reed, Pappy done sent me to fetch you. The new mare be foalin'." He stopped for only a second to catch his breath. "Only nothin' happenin', and Pappy be afeared we gonna lose 'em both."

Reed squeezed his eyes shut and spoke through clenched teeth. "Thank you, Ambrose. Tell Big John I'm coming."

He stared back into the cold fireplace unseeingly for several seconds. A final, mighty kick sent the grate scraping sideways and scattered the stacked wood into a useless pile.

After a mumbled, "Please excuse me, Elise," he stomped through a set of French doors and headed to the stables, fists clenched and body rigid.

Left alone in the parlor, Elise sank to the love seat and bunched the skirt of her gown into her fists.

What she wouldn't give to have Jan here now. The need for her friend was almost tangible. It surprised her when she realized the only things she missed about the future were her friends. Jan's sympathetic ear and calm assessment of the situation was what she needed right now. No doubt her friend would have raised her spirits, if not given her a perfect idea for fighting back.

She could almost hear Jan now. "Elise, you're not trying hard enough to make this guy remember you.

Where's the woman who fought so hard to get into pilot training? Get off your butt and make this man remember you."

Elise argued with Jan in her mind. She made excuses for herself and for Reed, but Jan's voice relentlessly badgered her. She knew the conversation her friend's analytical mind would come up with. Jan always tackled a problem by asking "why" or "why not," then dealt with it according to the answers she came up with.

Yeah, she would probably say something like, "Okay, answer me this, Elise. Why is it Reed was so honor bound in the future that he married you, rather than have sex out of marriage? But yet he didn't appear to live by those same standards in the past, if Angeline is pregnant with his child."

Elise slapped her forehead with the palm of her hand. Lord, was she stupid.

That's what had been bothering her; the thing niggling at her brain the few times she'd allowed herself to think about Reed fathering Angeline's child. There had been a grating inconsistency with the whole scenario, but she had stubbornly refused to dwell on the image of Reed with Angeline. She had been an idiot to accept that bitch's word with no more than a token question.

But she still didn't know the story. What she needed to do now was somehow get Reed to tell her what had happened so she could blow holes in it. She needed to find out who else Angeline had been seeing and who could be the father of this child. Even if Reed felt honor bound not to kiss and tell what happened, she had to make him remember her. That would surely stop this wedding. After all, he was already married.

She jumped up and charged toward the foyer, but a shooting pain in her ankle stopped her dead. She glared at the offending appendage and struggled to overcome the urge to kick something.

"Verda. Just the person I wanted to see."

The little maid was passing the door with an armload of linens when Elise caught sight of her.

"What you need, Miss 'Lise? You shouldn't be on your feet. Here, I help you back to the—"

"No, no. What I need, Verda, is a strip of fabric, several feet long and about three inches wide. And ask Nell if I can have some ice."

Verda nodded her head so hard, her tignon went askew.

Once the items were brought to her, Elise soaked the strips in ice water and wrapped her ankle with them. This was more like it. The pain wasn't nearly as bad when she put her weight on it.

A flurry of concerned servants met her when she limped over the threshold to the kitchen. She waved away their coddling and ignored the curiosity her presence there caused.

The primitive kitchen conditions overwhelmed her for a moment, but she wasn't daunted for long.

"Tessa, I want you to pack a picnic for Reed and me, but I need to tell you what I want in it."

Much later, when Elise left the kitchen in search of one of the plantation carpenters, Tessa grumbled under her breath, shook her head in denial, and stared after Elise with a worldly-wise frown.

Luther, a young carpenter at Oak Vista, had a frown for her, too, but it was caused by confusion rather than wisdom.

"I knows what you wants, Miz Elise. At least I thinks I do. But that be a mighty tall order to build so quick."

"I know, Luther. Do your best, and if you don't get it finished, I'll understand."

Her next move was to send a message to Trahan Hall. Nicholas and Cyprian might be able to help her, if the timing was just right.

With the first wave of plans taken care of, all there was left to do was wait for Reed to return from the stables.

He was hungry enough to eat the horse he'd just helped foal. But more than food, he wanted a hot bath to cleanse his body of the slime of stable muck and birthing waters he'd been lying in. His arm ached from spending so much time in the birth canal of a horse. A horse whose contractions were strong enough to crush a man's arm into jelly. From the throb in his muscles, he wondered how in the world a foal managed to be born without broken bones. And in this case it happened to be twins.

He patted himself on the back for the safe delivery while he mounted the rear steps to the house. He'd hoped to avoid meeting anyone while in this aromatic condition, but Elise appeared in the doorway as soon as he stepped onto the back veranda.

"Better stay upwind of me unless you want to ruin your dinner." He stopped in his tracks and waited for her to retreat into the house.

Instead, she stepped onto the porch and headed toward him. When she got within sniffing distance, she backed away, screwed up her face and made a cross with her fingers.

"Phew! I see what you mean. You're really potent."

Reed widened his eyes in an "I told you so" look.

"Never mind. Go on up and get cleaned up for dinner. I have something special planned."

Reed's appetite sat up and took notice at her words. "What . . . ?"

But she simply waved her hands at him with a shoo-

ing motion. The next thing he knew she was halfway
across the yard to the kitchen.

He massaged his still-throbbing right arm on the way
to his rooms. Another surprise awaited him when he
found Luther coming out of his dressing room.

"Oh, Mistah Reed, I done finished. I hopes it be what
you want. I ain't never built nothing like that afore. I just
be gettin' ready to try it out and . . ."

Reed ignored Luther's anxious words and poked his
head around the dressing room door. His brows lowered
into a questioning frown at what he saw. He stepped into
the doorway and approached the odd-looking contraption.

There seemed to be a tall, slender tent erected over his
brass hip bath. A sheet of oilskin was tacked to a frame
built on wheels, and it hung down into the bath. Above
the oilskin was a small barrel on a platform.

He stared for several seconds, then spun around and
nailed the grinning servant with his gaze.

"Luther, what in the world is that thing?"

"Miss Elise call it a 'shower,' Mistah Reed. She done
tell me to build it for you. Did I do it wrong?" Luther's
initial look of pride began to dissolve into concern.
"'Cause if it ain't right I can fix it."

Reed turned back around to contemplate the thing.
What had possessed Elise to have this thing built for
him? Where in the world did she get her outlandish
ideas?

He realized he couldn't even think straight. Between
the events of the night before, his confrontations with
Angeline and Elise, and now the hours he'd just spent at
the wrong end of a horse, his mind was numb. He shook
his head to clear it. The movement stirred an unpleasant
draft that snapped him back to his priorities.

He began to peel away his muck-encrusted shirt.

"Okay, Luther, how does this thing work?" *Okay? Now I'm beginning to speak like her even when she's not around.*

Luther brightened immediately. His white teeth shone in his chocolate brown face. He bounded back into the dressing room, explaining how the thing worked and pointing out that the barrel had already been filled with hot water.

"You see here, Mistah Reed, when you is ready for the water, you just slide this here panel, and then the water'll come out these little holes I done drilled in the bottom. That panel stops up the holes 'til you is ready to get rained on."

Luther was so proud of his invention, Reed couldn't help but give him a slap on the back.

"Looks like a job well done, Luther. I'm anxious to try this thing out."

The young carpenter beamed and turned to leave when Reed started shucking the rest of his clothes.

"Oh, Luther."

"Yes, Mistah Reed?"

"Ask Miss Elise to join me in the parlor in about ten minutes."

"Yessir, Mistah Reed. I tells her. She sure one smart lady, ain't she?"

Reed nodded his agreement. "Extraordinarily so." Smarter than any woman he'd ever met. Or, at least she allowed it to show.

Once Reed had piled the stiffening layers of clothing into a heap, he stepped into the brass tub and pulled away the panel at the bottom of the barrel.

A wonderful shower of steaming water flowed over him. It felt as if he'd been caught in a hot downpour. The sensation felt so right.

He wondered again where Elise had come from that

she would know about such a device. It was all very strange, but what was strangest of all was that it all felt so right.

The warm water produced miracles in washing away his troubling thoughts, as well as the throb in his arm and the filth on his body. Even after all the soap had been rinsed away, he continued to stand under the downpour until the last drop of water had fallen.

It was well over ten minutes before he could dress and arrive at the parlor. He'd just have to apologize to Elise. The "shower" had felt so wonderful, he hadn't been able to hurry.

Elise was waiting for him on the love seat when he pulled the doors open. The late afternoon sun bathed her with its brilliance, and yellow gold streaks sparkled in her chestnut hair. Her thick mane had been pulled up and pinned at the sides, then left to tumble in big, wavy curls around her shoulders. No other woman he knew dressed, spoke, or wore her hair like Elise. No other woman he knew caused him to breathe faster just by looking at her.

He forgot to apologize for being late, or to even thank her for the shower. He just absorbed the sight of her.

She smiled when she rose, but the look in her eyes was so intense he felt as though he were being worshipped. The fierceness of her love for him emanated from her. They stood, staring at each other, a room and another woman separating them.

They both seemed to realize this at the same time. Their gaze broke, and they cleared their throats and cast about the room uncomfortably for something else to look at.

Reed noticed the basket on the love seat the same moment his nose detected a delicious aroma. He nodded his head toward the basket.

"What have we here? Is this the special dinner you have planned? It smells wonderful."

Elise nodded and scooped up the basket just a tad too quickly, then headed for the door without looking at Reed. When she finally turned to address him, her smile was much too bright.

"Well, come on, darlin', you've got a picnic dinner getting cold."

He hesitated only a second before taking the hamper and escorting Elise to the front door. Ambrose was waiting with the small carriage, and in minutes the two were on their way.

As they rode he remembered to thank her for the shower and told her how much he'd enjoyed it.

"Not like anything I've ever experienced," he said with a smile. "Do you suppose this is something you're accustomed to, where you're from? Where did you get the idea?"

Elise looked disappointed when she shook her head and said, "I don't know where I got the idea. It just popped into my head. Probably something I experienced before I lost my memory."

He decided her disappointment was from her failing memory.

"Dost thee have a destination in mind, milady?" He tried to keep his tone light and ignore the invisible fist that squeezed his heart every time he looked at her.

"The lady desires her knight errant to take her to the heights . . ." she hesitated, a wicked grin curved her lips as she looked at him from the corner of her eye. Her next words seemed not to be her first choice. " . . . where yon river bends, to enjoy the caress of the breeze, if nothing else."

Heat surged across the back of his neck and radiated downward. He nearly slapped the horse into a run.

Two live oaks stood sentinel on the promontory, and Spanish moss hung nearly to the ground in places. Bright patches of sunlight dotted the lush grass where the red checkered tablecloth fluttered to rest.

Elise settled her skirts around her legs and began pulling plates, napkins and wineglasses from the hamper. She swatted his hand away when he tried to help, so he gave up and made himself comfortable while he waited.

He was half-reclined, propped on one elbow, one booted foot planted beside his opposite knee. His muscles relaxed somewhat with the soothing sound of fish plopping in the water, the drone of a nearby bee, the gentle *clink* of china and crystal.

A warm breeze ruffled his hair and carried the delicious smells from the picnic basket.

The view of Elise's profile was occasionally enhanced when a breeze from the river billowed her hair off her shoulders and away from her face. He could tell by the way she held herself that she knew he was watching her.

It was as if they had agreed not to talk about the events of the last twenty-four hours. His body still tingled with heat from the intensity of last night. But the confrontation with Angeline had left him drained. He needed this time to remove those thoughts so that when he was alone again he could approach the dilemma with a clear head. It was hard to remove those thoughts, though, when he couldn't take his eyes off Elise.

She smiled when she reached into the hamper and pulled out a large covered platter. The mouth-watering smells intensified. This didn't smell like any fried chicken he'd ever had. He sat up and eyed the picnic basket with more interest.

She whisked the cover from the platter with a flourish and used it to fan the spicy fragrance toward him. His salivary glands came alive, but he couldn't for the life of him identify the questionable mass before him.

Elise tried not to look too anxious. She'd had to substitute several ingredients and make do with others. She wasn't sure if this was close enough to do the trick.

"It smells wonderful, Elise, but what in the world is it? Tessa's never fixed anything like this before." Reed stared suspiciously at the main course.

"It's called pizza. I, uh, I kept getting this craving, so I finally asked Tessa to fix it. It must be something I used to eat. I don't know any other reason why I would know what it is." She tried to act happy. "Who knows? What with the shower, and now the pizza, maybe my memory's returning."

He made no comment but continued to stare at the pizza. She rummaged around in the hamper and came up with a brown and white jug and a bowl covered with a checkered napkin.

Reed lifted a corner of the napkin and peeked in, then flicked it off and tossed it behind him. He quirked an eyebrow at her.

"Another craving?"

"They're called potato chips. All they are are thinly sliced potatoes that have been deep-fried. Here, try one."

These had been easier to convince Tessa to fix than the pizza. At least she hadn't grumbled as much. With each ingredient and step Elise had described in the making of the pizza, Tessa had mumbled or cried out "Oh, Lawdy!" She'd had to settle for goat cheese and plantation-made sausage, not to mention the lack or substitution of spices. And since Elise had never been the type to know her way around a kitchen, she hadn't even been sure of exactly what spices she did need.

She slid a wedge of pizza onto each of their plates and

handed one to Reed. He looked around, then rummaged through the wicker hamper.

"What are you looking for?"

"Tessa has forgotten to pack the silverware. That's not like her."

Elise's adrenaline began to surge.

"Oh! You don't use silverware. You eat it like this." She picked up the wedge. "Now, it's very important that you eat the pointed end first. It just doesn't taste the same if you don't."

She watched for his reaction, but all he did was raise one eyebrow and say, "Of course."

He bit into the pizza. His face lit with pleasant surprise, but he didn't show any sign of recognition. She took a bite herself, and her heart sank at the taste. It was very good, but it didn't taste like pizza.

Well, on to Plan B.

Reed uncorked the jug and poured the amber liquid into the two crystal goblets. He handed one to Elise and raised his glass in salute.

"Here's to a most extraordinary meal with a most extraordinary woman."

A melodic *ching* sounded when their glasses touched. Reed watched her over the rim of the crystal while he sipped his drink.

Elise almost faltered at his toast. Visions of their wedding night assailed her. She glanced into Reed's eyes and saw them widen in surprise but forced herself to put the glass to her lips and swallow.

Make it good, she thought.

She jumped up, coughing and sputtering, then shivered with a force that jolted her entire body. Reed leaped to his feet and hovered protectively.

"What in the world is this?" She held out the goblet

and turned it to stare at the liquid. "For God's sake, Reed, the stuff came out my nose!"

She watched him again for any sign of recognition, but he shook his head in surprise.

"This is whiskey, Elise. Why in the world would Tessa pack whiskey on a picnic lunch?"

"Actually, I packed it. But I thought it was cider. I must have picked up the wrong jug." *Yeah, sure.*

"I thought it was cider, too, when I poured it. I didn't realize what it was in time to warn you."

"Well," Elise shook the folds of her skirts and re-fluffed the puffy sleeves that hung from her shoulders, "no harm done. It seems I've just survived my first taste of whiskey."

They settled back onto the cloth and polished off the rest of the meal while they chatted. She avoided drinking any more whiskey but needed one more sip to wash down the last bite of pizza.

A glistening drop of amber clung to the rim of her glass. When she saw it she couldn't resist another attempt to jar his memory.

She watched the droplet hover on the edge, then start to slowly roll down the curved crystal. She allowed it to carve a lazy, moist path down the bowl of the goblet and halfway down the stem before she stopped its progress with a slender, tanned finger. She retraced the path of the droplet in an equally lazy manner. Her finger glided up the stem and caressed the moist bowl of the crystal. When her fingertip reached the top, she circled the rim and raised sultry eyes to Reed.

Without looking away, without blinking, she held his gaze and slowly—ever so slowly—parted her lips and touched the whiskey-laced finger to her tongue. Reed's eyes had taken on a glazed cast. He swallowed hard, almost gulping, when she closed her lips before leisurely withdrawing her finger.

She had definitely made an impression on him. One sweeping full-length glance confirmed that. But she could tell from his look that not one memory had been sparked from this whole fiasco.

With more dread than she expected to feel, she launched into Plan C.

"Reed," she said with a soft, coaxing voice as she leaned back into the grass and stared through the lacy green canopy above.

"Hmmm?" His voice was a velvety, fuzzy hum. He should be very accommodating. She tried to speak in a soft, understanding tone.

"When did Angeline become pregnant?"

Even to her own ears, the question sounded like a discordant note in the midst of a symphony. The only answering sound was the roar of blood pulsing in her ears. She turned her head, then rolled to her side to look him in the eye.

His lips were a thin, hard line, and he refused to meet her gaze.

"What's done is done, Elise. Talking about it won't change things."

"But Reed, sometimes talking about it can help clear the air. Sometimes it *can* make a difference."

He closed his eyes. A look of pain caused little crinkles to radiate from the corners. He shook his head in denial.

"I'm not proud of getting Angeline with child. It's not something I want to lay before me and dissect."

"But don't you find it strange that in the future . . ." she caught herself just in time. She took a few deep breaths to calm herself. "I mean, in the past you have never . . . for Pete's sake, Reed, you're not the type of

man to scr . . . have sex with a woman out of wedlock."
She was going to ruin everything. It seemed her mouth
had taken on a life of its own.

Reed's lips were a white line in his now-tormented
face. When he spoke, his voice sounded more defeated
than ever.

"How do you describe what occurred last night?" The
muscles in his face were tense, and his look was determined. "The subject is closed, Elise."

It was best not to push him. Somehow, she felt as if
she'd just nailed the final nail in her coffin. Last night he
had made love to his wife, but he didn't know that.

So much for Plan C.

And so much for a relaxing afternoon. It was clear
that the picnic was over. Elise made a few attempts to re-
capture a sense of lightheartedness, but a depressing pall
seemed to wrap around them, like an encroaching fog.

It took only a minute to pack up their belongings and
turn the carriage back to the house. The short trip was
made in uncomfortable silence. They turned onto the avenue of oaks and were halfway through the verdant,
green corridor when the wheels of another carriage
crunched behind them.

Reed didn't even turn around to see who it was. At the
sound of wheels, she felt him stiffen, and for the second
time ever, she heard him curse.

By the time Nicholas and Cyprian bounded from the
phaeton, Reed appeared to have come to terms with having to entertain visitors. He was believably cordial as he
handed Marisa down and told her driver to go to the
kitchen for a cool drink and something to eat.

Marisa greeted Elise with a hug. Unexpected tears
sprang to Elise's eyes at the welcome feeling of the feminine hug, and she held fast to her new friend long
enough to blink away the tears. Marisa studied Elise's

face when she pulled away, but Elise flashed her a smile and then turned to hug the boys.

The group noisily made their way into the parlor, and even Lilianna roused herself to join them. The dear lady had been making herself scarce by pleading a bad back and a need for rest.

"Elise, your ankle must be feeling better to allow you to move around as much as you have. I am so glad it wasn't serious." Marisa patted her hand with genuine warmth.

"It's much better, thanks. I just have a trace of a limp."

"Can we see if your ankle is as big as it was yesterday, Miss Elise?"

"Nicholas," Marisa admonished, "one does not ask a lady to expose her ankle. It does not matter how big it is. It only matters that she is feeling better."

Nicholas pursed his lips and squirmed in embarrassment. Elise caught his eye and smiled, then shrugged and crossed her eyes at him. He giggled and nudged Cyprian to make sure he, too, was a witness.

By the time Marisa and Lilianna turned to look, her face was the picture of sophistication, which only encouraged more boyish giggles. Reed, however, had watched the little scene, and now he wore a very thoughtful smile.

The impromptu party turned festive as tea was served and pungent spice cakes, still warm from the oven, were passed around. It was just too stifling to bear the thought of drinking hot tea, so Elise asked Verda to please bring glasses with a little ice in them.

Her request was met with inquisitive stares. She really didn't give it much thought. She just wanted to feel the cold liquid trace a path to her stomach on such a suffocating day.

When the glasses of ice chips arrived and she poured her lukewarm tea into one, Nicholas was on his feet again. He bounced questions off her like a racquetball against a wall.

"Miss Elise, don't you want your tea? Why did you pour it out into the ice? Don't you want your cake either? Can I have it if you don't want it?"

An indulgent grin curved her lips while she sprinkled in a couple spoonfuls of sugar and stirred the iced tea. Nicholas was still firing questions at her, his eyes coveting her cake, when she handed the glass to him.

"Taste."

At least that stopped the questions. But he was now looking at her as if she'd just handed him a glass of raw sewage and told him to drink it.

"Go ahead. Taste it. And, yes, I want my cake." She hid her smile at his horrified, then crestfallen face.

Nicholas shot an uneasy glance at Cyprian, who sat quietly apart from the others. Elise noticed the small, dark face looked relieved at not being asked to taste this toxic substance. Obviously Nick noticed it, too. He sauntered over to his friend and held the glass under his nose.

"Thirsty, Cyp?"

A violent shaking of the woolly little head answered Nick's question. Cyprian squirmed back in the seat a solid six inches farther away from the dreaded beverage.

"Oh, for Pete's sake," Elise said. She bounced from her seat and scooped the glass from Nick's pudgy fingers. "It's just cold tea. It's great."

She proved it by taking several sips—she had to remind herself it was unladylike to do otherwise. She unintentionally exploded with a breathy "Ahhhhh" afterward.

It really was funny. Such skeptical looks from her audience would have one believing she was Nell, mixing up one of her voodoo potions. She offered a glass to everyone in the room, and out of politeness they took it. Reed, she noticed, was the only one who drank with gusto. That fact buoyed her spirits somewhat; he had loved iced tea in the future.

But he was beginning to get that look men get when they want to escape. Any minute now he would remember a pressing problem and excuse himself to deal with it.

She was going to have to speed up Plan D.

At this rate, she would soon run through the entire alphabet.

Chapter 24

REED SEARCHED HIS mind for a polite excuse to leave. It had been a long, frustrating day, and he just didn't feel up to idle chitchat. He opened his mouth to announce an urgent need to check on the new foals. At that same moment a scuffle broke out in the shadows by the door.

"Nicholas. Cyprian." Marisa said firmly, "Stop that at once."

The two little boys broke their playful holds on each other and looked sheepish. Marisa continued to look at them with displeasure, but Reed could empathize with their restlessness.

"Hey, you guys come here, and I'll tell you a story," Elise said in the enigmatic vernacular she sometimes used.

Her gown billowed around her as she settled herself at the small desk in the corner. Her wiggling fingers indicated the boys should sit in front of her.

They scrambled to the floor around her feet with only a minimum of good-natured shoving. Their eyes held a glow of expectation.

She really was wonderful with children. It was wrenching to know she would never raise his babies; that it would be Angeline who . . .

"This is a story about a lady who lost her memory."

Cyprian and Nicholas exchanged wise, knowing looks.

"This lady just woke up one day and couldn't remember who she was or where she was from. And after a while it began to look like she never would remember. She became very forlorn."

The boys seemed a bit uncomfortable. They both wore sympathetic expressions that were as sad as Elise's. But the next instant Elise's face brightened.

"So the lady decided to make up an imaginary place. She decided it might as well be a wonderful, different place, with fascinating, magical inventions, and filled with people like no place else on earth.

"First, she decided to make it a place where lots and lots of diseases like smallpox, diphtheria, influenza and pneumonia could be cured or prevented.

"Next, she decided to make life a lot easier for all the people who lived there. She had hot and cold running water coming right into the homes. It poured into sinks and bathing tubs with just a turn of a knob. Why, it would even come right out of a pipe in the wall and shower down on a person, so you wouldn't even have to sit down to bathe. And then all the water would run right down a drain and out of the house."

Reed felt a hot tingle behind his ears.

"She also decided she wanted the people to get around faster and communicate easier. She imagined a magical box that allowed you to speak to anyone else who had one, anywhere else in the world.

"She decided there would be carriages with engines instead of horses, and they could travel faster and longer than any horse and buggy."

By this time the boys' eyes were wide, and they were spellbound by the story. Elise still sat at the desk, and now she began to fidget with something as she spoke.

"But best of all, this wonderful place she was from had a special way of getting people around. The people would climb inside a huge, metal bird, and then it would fly them through the air to wherever they wanted to go."

"No! Oh, Miss Elise, you are having fun with us." The boys were up on their knees now, enjoying every minute of the story. Marisa and Lil glanced at each other with indulgent smiles. Reed caught a movement from the corner of his eye. He turned to see Nell standing transfixed in the doorway, her eyes wide with amazement, as if she really believed the story. It surprised him. Nell wasn't usually the gullible type.

"No, it's true." Elise continued to fidget with something behind the desk. "The big, metal birds were all different sizes, and when they flew, they looked just like this."

Her hand appeared from behind the desk. With one fluid movement she flicked her wrist and sent a folded piece of paper sailing through the air.

All eyes followed the odd-shaped projectile as it glided across the silent room. It flew almost the entire length of the parlor, then slipped toward the floor to land perfectly, just like a bird.

"Wow! How'd you do that?"

"Would you learn us to fold paper like that?"

"Who taught you that?"

"Could you learn us now?"

The room exploded with little-boy questions. Elise

laughed and nodded while Nicholas scooped up the paper missile and began to systematically unfold it.

Reed's neck was tingling again.

He couldn't explain the cause for the sensation, but it was a deuced uncomfortable feeling. Perhaps he was coming down with something.

Nell finally stepped into the room and placed a fresh pot of tea on the serving tray. Her wide eyes were locked on Elise and filled with wonder. How unusual. Was it possible Nell knew something he didn't?

A white dart whizzing past his nose distracted him. He shook his head when Lil offered him more tea.

"Would you care for more tea, my dear?" Lilianna asked Marisa, then casually dodged another soaring paper bird as if she were accustomed to a constant barrage of them.

"Nicholas!" Marisa reprimanded in a stern voice. She turned back to Lil. "No, thank you, Mrs. Dubose. It is growing late and time I got Nicholas and Cyprian home."

The boys protested in unison, with Nicholas by far the loudest. The protests died at Marisa's quelling look, but a barely audible grumble rose again when her attention was diverted.

Reed, Elise and Lil walked the visitors to their carriage and waved them down the avenue of oaks. As soon as the front door was bolted for the night Lil excused herself with the announcement that her back had flared up again and that she needed a poultice.

Reed felt Elise's gaze on him while he walked her back to the parlor. In fact, she had been watching him all day, as if she expected him to sprout horns or grow another head or some such thing.

The entire day had been hellish. The confrontation with Angeline, breaking the news to Elise, and then spending hours at a difficult foaling. And on top of all that, Elise had started acting extremely odd—or, he should say, more odd.

First there was that shower contraption. Then the unusual food at a disconcerting picnic, followed by icing down everyone's tea. And to top it off, she told that outrageous story to the boys.

"Elise, is your memory returning?" His voice was hopeful, yet hesitant. It was followed by a stretch of silence before she answered.

"No. Is yours?" She almost snapped his head off with the words. She had never spoken to him in such a way. He stared at her in astonishment. Not only odd words but odd behavior. He was beginning to worry.

Her eyes closed, and her hand came up to sift through her hair as she dropped onto the love seat. The heel of her hand massaged the center of her forehead, and she released a long sigh. He expected her to speak, but she remained silent.

"I'm sorry, little one. It's been a long, exhausting day for both of us. It's just that you . . ." How could he put this? ". . . haven't quite been yourself this afternoon, and I thought perhaps you . . ."

She huffed with disgust and rolled her eyes toward the ceiling. She seemed to be contemplating a speech. It didn't take a genius to know she was upset with him. What he didn't know was why.

Her eyes suddenly filled with tears, and she jumped to her feet. None of the tears were allowed to fall.

"No, Reed. To answer your question, I don't remember anything more than I did the day I arrived here." Her voice held a telltale quiver. "My problem is, I'll have too much to remember the day I leave."

She lifted her skirts and started to run toward the foyer. Her swaying hoops caught between a table and the

love seat, and she struggled for a moment to free them.
She had yet to maneuver through there without the same
result. Her muttered "Damn" sounded more like a sob
than a curse, then she yanked the gown free and limped
through the door.

A healthy flash of ankle and calf was exposed during
this scene. Reed gawked at the sight of the white, ban-
daged ankle and foot. For just a split second it looked
like a low, bulky boot with pink lettering on the side and
bright pink lacings up the front. And for just a split second he saw the ugly thing on both of her feet. And the
vision seemed just as right as the thundering sound of
her ascending the stairs.

The early morning sun stole through a part in the
draperies and hit her straight in the eyes. She rolled over
and was immediately awake. Her first thought was of
Reed.

Good God, the man was dense. Was it possible she
hadn't stirred one single memory with all of her the-
atrics? He gave absolutely no indication of even a
shadow of remembrance.

She'd cried herself to sleep last night for the first time
since she'd come here. But before finally succumbing to
mental exhaustion, she'd made a decision.

It was just too hard to remain living here. Tension already vibrated in the air, and when Angeline showed up,
it would be unbearable.

Her own constant presence was making Reed more
and more uncomfortable. She could tell no matter how
much he tried to hide it. And as for herself, it was quite
possible she would drop-kick Angeline into the next
state if she had to put up with her again.

No, the decision was made. She would ask Marisa if
she could stay at Trahan Hall for a few days, under the

guise of getting out from underfoot of the wedding plans. Then, if Reed's memory of her didn't return, as much as she dreaded it, as much as it tore at her heart to think about it, she would ask Nell to send her home, to the future.

There was just no way she could stand by and watch Reed marry another woman. She would have to go back before the wedding, or else she might do something really stupid.

She couldn't claim she was his wife. The marriage license was a hundred fifty years in the future, not to mention the fact that Reed didn't have any black holes in his memory that would account for his acquiring a wife.

Anything she did publicly would make her look like a fool and embarrass Reed. Most of the small community of planters and their families already looked at her as though they'd just smelled something bad but were too polite to acknowledge it.

As painful as it was for her to admit, she was a prisoner who held her own key. She might never escape from the feelings she had for Reed, but she could escape this time period and go back to what she knew best. Besides, maybe when she traveled back, she would forget him, just as he had forgotten her. It would be a blessing if she did.

She didn't realize she'd been hugging the pillow tight against her chest until she flung it away to drag herself from the bed.

Cool water from the pitcher in the corner didn't do much for her puffy, red-veined eyes.

"Geez, Gerard, you look like hell," she mumbled to her reflection. Some elderflower gel and a tube of concealer would be a welcome discovery right now. Better yet, a hit man for Angeline would make her day and remove the need for the former.

She groaned at her own black humor. It wasn't in her nature to be vindictive, but she found she was beginning to wear the emotion like a comfortable old coat. Obviously, the last forty-eight hours had wrought havoc with her personality.

Well, nothing for it but to face the day and put her plans into action. They were a far cry from what she'd hoped to be doing, but at the moment she was fresh out of bright ideas.

She didn't clatter down the stairs this morning on her way to breakfast. The spring in her step was missing. On top of that, she had the unpleasant shock of finding Jeffrey seated across from Reed at the breakfast table. It was all she could do to force herself into the dining room.

Both men rose at her entrance. Obiah held her chair and nodded with a frown when she requested only coffee. Her appetite had been almost nonexistent to begin with, but Jeff's presence killed what little was left.

Actually, on reflection, he might make this morning go a little easier. It would certainly stifle any emotional scenes that were sure to arise when she broke the news to Reed.

Well, she thought, no time like the present.

"Reed, I plan to check with Marisa, but if it's all right with her I'll be leaving to stay at Trahan Hall as soon as I can get packed."

Reed's coffee cup rattled against its saucer, and he seemed to be having trouble swallowing his last sip. He took a moment to read her expression, probably to see if she was joking.

"There's no need for you to leave, lit . . ." he glanced at Jeffrey, ". . . Elise. You should stay until your memory returns. There must be a reason why you came to Oak

Vista. If you leave, you might lose your chance to find it."

Her eyes burned at those prophetic words.

"Yeah, no joke," she mumbled.

Obiah made a fortuitous appearance with her coffee. She busied herself with measuring an exact amount of cream and then studiously stirred it. Once she blinked the moisture from her eyes, she fixed her face with an artificial brightness and looked up.

"Oh, well, you don't need me around here in the way while the . . . uh . . . wedding is being planned." Lord, she nearly choked on the "W" word. A tight fist not only closed around her heart, but was closing around her throat as well.

Reed remained quiet. There was not much he could say in front of Jeffrey, but his eyes made a silent plea for her not to go.

The fist around her heart squeezed tighter. He looked as miserable as she felt. What could it hurt if she stayed?

It could hurt them both.

"And besides, I'm sure Aunt Lil would like to go home, and Angeline will be wanting to put a feminine touch on this bachelor . . . uh . . . home." Yeah, she'd probably even have the walls covered in ruffles and bows.

Just as she'd expected, Reed put up no further argument. But she wasn't prepared for the raw pain in his eyes. The two stared at each other across the table. His eyes pleaded with her not to go; hers pleaded with him not to marry Angeline.

Tendrils of steam from the coffee cup poised at her lips caused her eyes to tear up again. It snapped her out of her trance.

"Well," she said, placing her cup back on the saucer, "I have a million things to do. I'd better hit it."

She nodded a good-bye to Jeffrey out of politeness and saw that he had been taking great interest in the conversation and interaction between herself and Reed. He looked much too interested, and there was a sense of anger in his face.

When she reached the foyer, she overheard him say to Reed, "The lovely lady has an odd turn of words, does she not?"

"Why, I am offended that you should even ask. Of course you are welcome to stay here, for as long as you want." Marisa hugged Elise, then guided her to a satin brocade settee near the empty fireplace.

Elise was relieved at her welcome, even though she expected nothing less from Marisa.

"In fact, I could send Noah over for your things so you wouldn't have to make that hot, dusty trip back. Unless, of course you need to say good-bye to Reed."

"Oh, no. I told him good-bye this morning."

Actually, she had made a beeline to Nell, and then to the stables, after leaving Reed and Jeffrey. She wanted no opportunity for Reed to get her alone and talk to her. Her resolve would never stand up to even his slightest request that she stay. In fact, if she was only a little less of a woman, she'd be tempted to stay on as his mistress. Anything to keep from losing him. But she hadn't fallen that low—yet.

"I just felt like a fifth wheel there, what with all the wedding plans and all. Besides, I need to get on with my life, and it would be hard to do, living with the new . . . newlyweds." She turned the catch in her voice into a halfhearted cough, then ducked her head and rummaged in her reticule for a handkerchief long enough to blink the blasted tears away. She was going to dehydrate if she didn't get a grip on her emotions.

Her fingers closed around a small tin instead of a hanky, and she was forced to break into some serious coughing to account for the tears that spilled over onto her cheeks.

Marisa was beside her in an instant with a cool glass of water, patting her gently on the back. Elise took several sips, dabbed the hanky she finally found to the corners of her moist eyes, and shrugged when she laughed.

"There must be something in the air that I'm allergic to. I even noticed this morning that my eyes were all red and puffy."

She turned a bright, watery smile to Marisa. Her friend smiled back, but it was a knowing smile, filled with sympathy and compassion.

Chapter 25

"Ride with me, little one. Please. We need to talk."

Elise was torn between the urge to throw herself into Reed's arms and the urge to run away as fast and as far as she could. Instead, she found herself rubbing her thumbnail across a velvet stripe on the arm of the chair while she gathered her thoughts.

"Reed, you're getting married tomorrow. What could we possibly have to talk about?"

When her eyes met his, she felt as if a fist had punched her in the stomach. The pain in his eyes extended into his face and even the way he held himself. Fine lines were etched around his mouth and eyes, and dark circles gave him a haggard look.

She hadn't seen him up close since the day she'd left, at first because of circumstance and then because of choice. She'd ridden by the plantation every day with one lame excuse or another. But every single time she'd ridden by, there was evidence of Angeline's presence.

The last time she'd gone, she stopped at the edge of the woods just as the front door opened and Angeline stormed out.

Reed had strolled out behind her and propped himself against the door frame. Elise expected Angeline to continue her tantrum. Instead, she'd plastered herself against him and held his head while she forced a kiss on him.

Elise had almost gagged. She'd reined her horse around and headed home, trying desperately to rid her mind of the image of Angeline kissing Reed. If a kiss could devastate her so, what would she feel on their wedding night?

She hadn't gone far when the sound of thundering hooves gaining on her made her turn around and stop.

"Oh, hell," was all she managed to mutter before Angeline skidded her horse to a stop just inches away. Her smug smile begged to be slapped off, but Elise overcame the urge to accommodate her.

"Well, worshipping from afar, I see. I suppose I will allow it, as long as you maintain your distance." She narrowed her eyes and smiled with only one side of her mouth. "But don't be too upset if I decide to perform for you again."

Elise could only stare.

"Perform, Angeline? So you admit this is all an act. You don't give a damn for Reed."

"Of course I do, sugar. I give a big damn for his money and his position. I have invested years cultivating him for marriage. He is a much better catch than the pimply-faced boys still wet behind the ears. And who wants a smelly old man constantly pawing at them? Even if he were rich, it wouldn't be worth letting one touch me."

"So you're prepared to force Reed into marriage even though you know he loves me and not you, just so you don't have to be bothered with young boys and old men."

Angeline inspected the fingernails of her right hand.

"That about sums it up."

"I thought it was because you're pregnant with his child."

The nail inspection stopped. She dropped her hand and turned her head slowly until she stared Elise in the eye. She took her time answering, her voice filled with venom.

"That, too."

Elise threw her head back and stared at the sky.

"Angeline, you're so stupid. Don't you realize you'll both be miserable if you force him to live this lie? That baby is no more his than the pope's."

Angeline sucked in her breath with a hiss. "You don't know what you're talking about. Why, I have half a notion to give you a piece of my mind."

Elise laughed and patted the air in a frantic signal to stop. She'd just about had enough. Maybe it was time to take the gloves off.

"It makes sense that you only have half a notion. You don't have enough sense to formulate a complete one. And please, don't give me a piece of your mind. You have so little to spare as it is, I wouldn't want to be the one responsible for you rendering yourself into a vegetative state."

Angeline was furious, her body quivered, but she couldn't keep the hint of confusion from her face.

Elise laughed with disgust.

"Geez, Angeline. If a gnat dove into your well of intelligence, it would break its neck."

God, that felt good. Angeline's gasp at the insults was the icing on the cake, but Elise couldn't resist one parting shot from the nineties. As she wheeled her horse around to leave, she bestowed a sweet smile upon her adversary.

"If you followed me here for a battle of wits . . . sugar . . . you shouldn't have come unarmed."

Angeline's shriek had been sweet music to her ears.

Reed's voice snapped her back into the present—back into Marisa's parlor and the problem of having to face him the day before his marriage to that airhead.

"Elise, I feel I owe you an explanation. Maybe it's a selfish way of getting this off my chest, but I feel you have a right to know."

He'd been standing by the fireplace, running the brim of his planter's hat around and around through his hands. Now the hat was mangled almost beyond recognition.

The tiny bubble of hope she'd held floated away with his words. But at least she'd know the whole story now.

"All right, we can talk. But we'll talk here. Under the circumstances I don't think we should be any more alone than we are right now."

Reed glanced about, as if expecting the household to invade the parlor.

"Don't worry. Marisa's helping with a birth in the slave quarters, and the boys are with Nick's tutor." Elise assumed Marisa's husband, Jean Paul, was with the overseer. He was never here this time of day.

"What is it you have to tell me, Reed?"

He cleared his throat and abused his hat some more before finally attempting to speak.

"I raped Angeline."

Elise released an explosive "ha" before she realized he wasn't joking.

"You're serious." She flopped back in the chair and fought a wave of dizziness.

"I was drunk. I don't know how I got drunk. I don't

even remember getting drunk. But that isn't an excuse. I apparently decided to marry her during my intoxicated state and decided not to wait for the formalities to take place. I forced myself on her. Now I'm paying the consequences for a night I don't even remember."

A chill prickled up her neck and stood her hair on end.

"Exactly what night was it that you . . . got her pregnant?"

Reed's formerly brick-red face now faded to an ashen gray.

"In March I gave a ball with the hope of finding a lady who attracted me enough that I could consider marriage. People had expected Angeline and me to marry, but I found her . . . Anyway, when the ball was over, I went up to my rooms to sleep. The last thing I remember is lying down and teasing Nell by faking a snore after I drank her herbal tea. But I woke up the next morning out in a field, half-dressed and with no memory of how I got there."

I could tell you how you got there, Elise's mind screamed, *but you'd never believe me. You'd come closer to believing you got drunk and raped a woman.*

Her heart thundered in her chest, and her mind raced to find all the pieces to this puzzle. Her thought processes were hampered, though, by the excruciating memory of watching a half-dressed Reed disappear from her life.

Reed continued his monologue.

"I remember being plagued the next day with an overpowering sense of emptiness. It was almost as though a part of me had been amputated during the night. Looking back now, I realize it must have been guilt, not grief, that I felt."

Oh, dear God, darlin', it was grief of the worst kind.

"I decided that day to stop looking for the woman of my dreams and just marry someone who could give me a family. That's when I went to Angeline." He stopped for a moment and shook his bowed head. He muttered something under his breath, but the only words Elise caught were "consummate fool."

"I didn't remember anything when I saw her. In fact, that whole night is still blank. She said nothing at all about it, until the night of the betrothal ball, when I tried to break it off. That's when she told me, in painfully vivid description, what had happened. She'd been so upset she'd burned my shirt and coat, which I'd left behind after . . . She even mentioned how the clothes I was wearing were strange. They were like nothing I'd ever seen, and I still don't know how I came to be wearing them.

"Oh, God, Elise. Now do you see why I have to marry her? I owe it to her." He stopped his pacing and dropped to the love seat, his hat now a woven pile of straw. "Angeline isn't the nicest person in the world. In fact, she can be downright . . . but no woman deserves to be raped. And my child will be a product of that act."

That child is probably a product of a roll in the hay with a traveling salesman.

Couldn't he see that he wasn't the type of man to force himself on a woman, no matter what his condition? How could she convince him that he was not the father of this baby without telling him he was with her, in the future? He would never believe that. It would sound like the ravings of a woman willing to say anything to avoid losing her lover.

Should she tell him she was the woman he was with that night, and not Angeline? It would be her word against Angeline's. But how could she explain why they were together? As far as Reed was concerned, he'd never laid eyes on her before that morning she'd arrived in the past.

Her head began to throb, and she was sure her blood pressure was at stroke level. She shook her head to clear it, then cradled her forehead in the palms of her hands while she thought of a way out of this mess.

Reed obviously misread her actions. He stood, his head bowed, and tossed what was left of the ragged hat onto the seat he'd just vacated.

"I don't blame you. No one can feel more disgust at my actions than I do, myself."

Her head shot up at his words and the sense of misery he exuded. Her mouth took over and ignored any signals her brain might have sent.

"Reed, you didn't rape her. You were with me. Don't you see, it's not your baby. You were with me that night. We're married. You can't marry her because you're already married to me."

She'd taken his hands and now slid to her knees on the floor. He knelt beside her on one knee and pulled her to him. His tanned, work-roughened hand cradled the back of her head, and she nestled her face against his chest.

"Oh, little one, listen to what you're saying. I love you even more, if that's possible, for still wanting me after my dishonor. I don't deserve your love. I would live in fear of my actions coming back to haunt you and making your life miserable."

Elise raised her face and spoke in a voice choked with tears.

"Reed, think. Remember me. Right now I'm just a shadow in your memories, but I'm your wife. Your future."

His look was indulgent, pained, and she knew he thought she was rambling in desperation. With tender care, he lifted her and placed her gently on the love seat.

"I have to marry her, Elise. You don't deserve this pain, but I do. I deserve worse. I just wanted you to know the truth. I should have told you everything when all this started. It could have saved a lot of heartache."

He stared down at her for several seconds, his emotions clear in his eyes, then he turned and left the house.

Elise curled into a ball and buried her face in her knees as she sobbed uncontrollably.

"Oh, God, you're right. It could have saved so much heartache."

She wasn't sure how long she'd been curled up on the love seat when a gentle rap sounded on the door. Her cheeks felt taut from all the tears that had dried on them, but she didn't care. She didn't even bother to look up until she heard someone enter the room.

For once Aunt Lil wasn't bouncing. In fact, she approached Elise as she would a bereaved widow at a funeral.

"My dear, I should shame you for leaving Oak Vista and not telling me good-bye, but I understand. Truly I do. I don't know what Reed Blackwell is thinking of to let a girl like you go and marry that little puffed up, overindulged . . . well, I'd like to buy her for what she's worth and sell her for what she thinks she's worth."

Boy, did Lil hit the nail on the head with that one. It felt good to laugh, even if it was only a halfhearted chuckle. But the humor didn't last long.

"Don't blame Reed, Aunt Lil. He has his reasons."

"Oh, fiddlesticks. What possible reason could he have to marry that girl when he obviously loves you?"

What reason, indeed. Elise studied the pattern of the Aubusson carpet before finally looking Lil in the eye and shrugging.

The older woman's eyes narrowed for just a moment, then flicked to her reticule. She rummaged furiously for a second, then stopped. Both hands remained in the embroidered bag.

"Well, enough gloom. I understand this is your birthday."

Oh, good grief, she'd completely forgotten. What a hellish birthday.

"I brought you a gift. Just a token." Lil withdrew a tiny package and held it out to Elise. "Happy birthday, dear girl."

"Oh, Lil, how sweet of you. But how did you know? I didn't even remember, myself."

Lil wagged a pudgy finger at her. "I have my ways. I'm not as scatterbrained as people imagine."

Elise tried to formulate a response to that as she untied the ribbon and opened the little gift.

Her breath left her lungs in a broken sob. The tears flowed and dripped onto her lap, and still she sat, motionless.

"Elise! My dear girl! Oh, heavens! Marisa! Marisa, come quick! Something is wrong with Elise!"

Lil threw open the pocket doors and ran from the room.

Elise heard the clatter of shoes on the cypress floors, she felt someone shaking her shoulders and wiping her tears. She heard voices calling her name. But the only thing she saw was the gift in her hand—the gold filigree locket she'd worn the day she married Reed.

She stared at the cup of noxious tea and reflected that it would smell every bit as bad in a hundred and fifty years.

Not a lot of emotions penetrated her thoughts. It felt almost as if her heart and mind had been given generous doses of Novocain.

She was glad she'd made Nell give her the tin filled with tea before she left Oak Vista. It saved her a painful trip back to collect it.

Nell hadn't given it willingly when Elise told her she wanted the brew that would send her back to her own time. The kindly old woman had tried to convince her that everything would work out. Well, she'd been wrong, and now it was time to leave.

The wedding was scheduled for noon. High noon in the verdant, aromatic gardens of Oak Vista. The wedding at noon, to be followed by a gala reception with the whole countryside in attendance. Less than twelve hours away.

Her fingers brushed against the locket pinned over her heart. A sob escaped her throat, and she wondered where it had come from.

The house was quiet. Everyone had been in bed for at least a couple of hours when Elise tiptoed to the kitchen to brew her tea. She wanted to do this alone.

The rising steam began to lessen, and Elise picked up the cup and placed it to her lips. She'd discovered the first time she'd drunk it that the taste worsened as it cooled.

She held her breath and downed it. It didn't taste as bad as it smelled. That's right. Now she remembered.

She poured another cup and drained it and continued to do so until the teapot was empty.

All she could do now was wait.

Her movements were slow and methodical as she washed out the teapot and cup, dried them and put them away.

She climbed the stairs as if climbing the steps to her gallows, then closed the door to her room with a quiet *click*.

Her clothes all hung neatly in the armoire. To kill time she took each item out and folded it with meticulous care before placing it in the handsome, leather-bound trunk Reed had provided.

Each piece of clothing held its own memory. The mint green gown she'd had made to resemble the one she'd been wearing in the future when he'd appeared on her bed. The yellow skirt and bodice from the day she'd watched him swim, and he'd tackled her in the clearing. And, oh yes, the peach ballgown she'd worn the night Reed had danced with her and said, "I love you, little one."

As she lovingly smoothed the skirts, she noticed a dark stain on the fabric. Her brows knit in dismay when she found another one. Then yet another appeared, the dark peach splotch feathered across the silk. Confusion clouded her features when more stains appeared out of nowhere, until finally sensation began to replace the numbness, and she felt the hot tears burning rivers down her cheeks. Tears she wasn't even aware she'd shed. Tears that fell to the silken memory in her hands and branded it just as they branded her heart.

Oh, lord, it's going to be a long night.

Her eyes were still burning when she finished packing her belongings. She supposed they would be sent to Reed when it became apparent she was missing.

With that thought in mind, she sat down to compose a letter to Marisa. She needed to thank her for her kindness and friendship and tell her not to worry about her. It took her several hours and countless sheets of stationery before she finished one she was satisfied with.

She ended up telling Marisa that she'd suddenly regained her memory, that she was married, the mother of a small child and had been so anxious to see her family that she'd left immediately. She'd even mentioned that hopefully the "borrowed horse" would be returned before anyone even missed it.

The story would never win the Pulitzer, but her heart just wasn't in it.

She sealed the letter and placed it in the trunk.

By the time she collected the wadded balls of rejected prose and burned them in the fireplace, she could hear the servants beginning to move about downstairs.

With alarm, she yanked back the draperies and stared into the darkness. The diamond-studded night sky was already fading to dark gray. The stars were beginning to dim, and even as she watched, objects took form and became visible.

This wasn't good. She'd meant to be gone by now. The wedding was only hours away, and instead of disappearing she'd cried and reminisced.

If Nell gave her the wrong tea, she'd kill her!

Elise paced the floor for several minutes, stopping every now and then to see if she still reflected in the mirror.

How stupid! She wasn't a vampire.

She studied her hands and prayed they would become translucent and then disappear altogether.

A quiet rap on the door jarred her from her prayers.

Marisa cracked the door and peeped in, then stepped into the room.

"Oh, good. I thought I heard you . . . moving . . . around."

She stared at Elise, still dressed in her clothes from the day before, then glanced at the bed that hadn't been slept in.

She held the question in her eyes, but Elise just shook her head.

"Some nights I have trouble sleeping. Last night was one of them."

Marisa didn't look convinced, but she was too polite to pry.

"I'm so sorry. I stopped by to tell you we'll be leaving

for the wedding around ten thirty. Will you be rested enough to go?"

Elise caught the unexpected sob before it was fully born.

"No. I don't think I'd better go." Her voice cracked and tears burned her eyes. Damn. She hadn't thought she could cry anymore. She squeezed her eyes shut and turned her back to Marisa.

In the next instant she felt a motherly embrace encircle her shoulders. A hand smoothed her hair.

"Are you all right, Elise?"

Oh, no! Don't be nice to me! Don't be nice.

It was too late. The dam burst, and sobs wracked her entire body. They rose up from the very depths of her.

Marisa guided her to the edge of the bed and set her down. She gathered her into her arms and rocked her as she would Nicholas, patting her gently and crooning words of comfort.

"Oh, Marisa, I love him. I can't watch him marry someone else. I love him."

"I know, I know," Marisa murmured. "I wondered if you would ever admit it to me."

Elise raised her sodden face from where it'd been buried in Marisa's shoulder.

"You knew?"

Marisa gave a breathy laugh. "Even a blind man could see how the two of you feel about each other. What I don't understand is why he's marrying her."

The sobs had subsided, but the tears continued to flow. And along with them came the story.

The words tumbled out so fast she was barely making sense. A voice in her mind told her she was betraying a confidence, but she was past caring.

The only part she left out was the part about the future.

"He's convinced he f . . . f . . . forced her. She knew how he was dressed, and he's convinced the only way she would know is if it r . . . really happened. But he was with me." She struggled to stop snuffling like a baby. She couldn't possibly be making sense.

"Oh, for pity's sake. Leave it to a man to be so unbelievably obtuse. Of course, he was raised by the servants, so we can make a few allowances for that."

"What are you talking about? Make allowances for what?"

"Elise, anyone could know how Reed came home after that ball. Why, there are no secrets on the servants' grapevine. Even the most discreet homes have their dirty laundry aired on occasion.

"All the ladies of the households do their best to quell any gossip, but by the same token, they know just who to go to, to find out what's going on in other homes.

"But Reed, you see, was raised without a lady of the house. The servants were his family. One could certainly never place that cold uncle of his in that category. Anyway, just by having the nature of a man, he wasn't, shall we say, inquisitive enough to discover the wealth of information that flowed in and out of his home."

Good heavens, she'd been as dense as Reed. Her heart pounded, and she knew she had to get to Reed, to tell him.

She surged to her feet and was overcome with blinding dizziness.

"Oh, no! Not now! Not now!"

She dropped to her knees and scrambled to the chamber pot. Without hesitation she rammed her finger as far down her throat as she could. She retched again and again to empty her stomach of what little was in it.

Marisa was beside her, shaking her and pleading with her to tell her what was wrong.

The dizziness worsened. She was only barely aware of

Marisa dragging her onto the bed. A blanket of darkness settled over her.

"Not now," she whimpered. "Not now."

He knew what it felt like to walk to his own funeral. The walk to the minister standing under the arch of flowers was the longest walk he would ever take in his life.

He stood there now, next to Angeline, and tried to breathe despite the stifling humidity. With an evil sense of satisfaction, he noted that the plethora of nauseating ruffles on her gown were as wilted as her hair.

Angeline turned to look up at him and graced him with an angelic, loving smile for the benefit of the on-lookers. He didn't bother to respond.

The minister's voice began to drone.

As he stood there and stared, Angeline's face began to transform into Elise's. Reed blinked several times and even shook his head, but he could still see Elise. She had on a beautiful, white-beaded wedding gown with a matching veil. The gown belonged to Jan, who stood beside her.

Jan? Who is Jan?

Of course, Jan was married to Don, the man standing beside me.

Then it began. Memories tumbled over him like a cascading waterfall. They came so fast, one wasn't completed before another started.

Elise! She's my wife! My beautiful, wonderful, airplane-flying wife! And Angeline's baby isn't mine!

". . . reason these two should not be joined together in holy matrimony, speak now or forever hold your peace."

Reed's head jerked up, and he opened his mouth to speak.

A growing murmur of the crowd stopped him, and he spun around to see Jeffrey Vancoeur walking up the aisle. He stopped within inches of Reed.

"Terribly sorry, Blackwell, but I feel you might want to see me in private."

Reed glanced at Angeline, who was glaring at Jeffrey with murder in her eyes.

The two men excused themselves and entered the house from the rear. They both ignored the crescendo of voices as they walked away.

Reed listened in stunned silence as Jeffrey told him that Angeline was not pregnant and never had been. He summoned a terrified slave Reed recognized as Angeline's maid. She confirmed that she'd washed the rags from Angeline's "monthly curse" with clockwork regularity.

"You can thank Lilianna for ferreting out that tidbit of information. Not only did Angeline lie about being with child, Blackwell, but once she'd spun her story, she was trapped. She approached me in the hope I would help her out of her predicament by obliging to get her with child. She pointed out we were only second cousins. And, of course, by being a relative, I was honor bound to keep her little secret."

Reed breathed deeply in an effort to remain calm.

"How very enterprising of her. Tell me more."

"Not much more to tell, really. Of course, I wasn't accommodating."

"Of course."

"I threatened to expose her to you. She played her hysterics very well and promised not to go through with the wedding. She was very convincing. I left town believing the whole thing had been settled. Imagine my surprise when I stopped here at breakfast that day and found the wedding plans were in full swing. And she'd even managed to force out your charming houseguest. You know . . . the one you're in love with."

You're right, Reed thought, *and I'm going to shout it to the world.*

"I spoke with Angeline again, rather sternly I might add, and she tearfully swore to put an end to this charade. I'm afraid I can be very naive, and I woefully overestimated her character.

"I only just arrived back in the area today. Of course, I came straight here as soon as I was made aware of the day's festivities."

A beaming Reed held out his hand and clasped Jeffrey's as he clapped him on the back. He felt as if he'd just been given a pardon from purgatory.

"You're a good man, Vancoeur. I'll find a way to repay you."

"Repay me by marrying Elise Gerard. If any two people should be married, it is you two."

"It's a deal," Reed said with a laugh. "But before you leave, I have something I want you to witness."

He stuck his head out the study door and murmured to a passing servant. He turned back and smiled at Jeffrey. Amazing how his descendent was an exact duplicate in looks, but far more than a hundred and fifty years separated their personalities.

Within minutes the door crashed open, and Angeline and her ruffles stood in the doorway, vibrating with rage. The servant who brought her left at a run.

"What is the meaning of this?" she screamed as she stormed into the room.

Reed's voice was deceptively calm. In fact, she was forced to stop screeching and stand still in order to hear his quiet words.

"I believe you know what the meaning of this is, Angeline. I know everything. The wedding is off. In fact, the wedding was off when I remembered exactly what happened the night I supposedly raped you. I just hadn't had the chance to stop it."

Angeline took a breath to speak, but Reed held up his hand for silence.

"If you prefer, I can go out and explain to the guests what has transpired and reveal the content of my conversation with Jeffrey."

He nodded to Jeffrey. Jeffrey nodded back.

"I'm sure the guests are buzzing with conjecture as we speak. But I believe I am correct in assuming you don't wish certain facts to be known. Therefore, I am leaving you here to explain to our guests in your own words why we are not getting married.

"Bear in mind, however, that at this point I will not tolerate a blackening of my name, or Elise's, or Jeffrey's, for that matter." Again he nodded to Jeffrey, and again his nod was returned.

"Vancoeur, my good friend, might I impose upon you to remain here and insure that my instructions are carried out as requested?"

Jeffrey's face was comically solemn. "Wouldn't have it any other way, Blackwell."

"I leave her in your capable hands, then."

He flicked his gaze one last time over Angeline. She was trembling, but no longer from fury. It was the first time he'd ever seen her speechless. She might yet learn to exercise an economy with words.

He strode from the room, and as he passed into the hallway he heard Vancoeur's voice.

"Don't bother to swoon, Angeline. It won't get you out of this one. I'll simply dump this pitcher over your head and send you out there dripping wet."

Reed wasted no time in the stables. He slid a bridle onto his horse and jumped onto its bare back.

He had to saw on the reins to keep from running over Nell, who had darted in front of him, waving her arms.

"Mistah Reed! Mistah Reed! You remembers, don't you? You remembers Miz 'Lise."

"Yes, Nellie my love. I remember everything." It'd been so long since he'd smiled; this one hurt his face. "I'm on my way to get her now!"

"Oh, Lordy, Mistah Reed. Miz 'Lise done tell me to give her some of my potion to send her to her home."

Reed's breathing stopped.

"When did she ask for it, Nell?"

"The day she leave Oak Vista. She tell me she can't stay here and watch you marry someone else."

"Nooooo!" Reed's cry was that of a tortured animal. He yanked the reins and kicked his horse into a dead run. The cold that had gripped his empty soul since he was torn from Elise's arms now gripped him in a glacial bitterness.

"Mistah Reed! Wait! Mistah Reed!"

But she was talking to a cloud of dust.

She first became aware of the familiar, muffled ticking of the grandfather clock in the foyer. Her head felt muzzy, as if she'd been drugged, and she burrowed deeper into the covers and tried to go back to sleep.

Then realization dawned on her.

She was home! Oh, dear Lord, what had she done?

But wait! She sat up and stared ahead of her. This was her room in the past! She hadn't left! Dear, sweet Nell had switched the teas after all. She'd only given her something to knock her out.

Covers flew from the bed, and she grabbed the first gown she came to and began to struggle into it. She had to find Reed.

Could she convince him that Angeline had manufactured this story? Could he get an annulment?

She fumbled with the buttons at the back of her neck. How had she gotten here . . .

"Make one more move, and I'll hose you down with tear gas."

Elise froze with her elbows skyward, the buttons on her dress forgotten. She spun around to find the owner of the voice, his name a cry on her lips.

"Reed!"

And there he was—a work of art propped against the headboard, right beside where she'd been sleeping. The sheet was draped enticingly across his lap, his tanned, muscled chest exposed and begging for her fingertips to trace the many ridges. His fingers were laced behind his head, and the boyish grin belied the powerful man behind it.

She was on top of him in a heartbeat.

"Reed," she cried. "Tell me you didn't marry her. Let me hear you say it." Her words were distorted from the frantic kisses they each sought.

"No, little one. I didn't marry her." He peppered kisses along her neck. "How could I? I'm married to you."

Her head shot up, and she held his face between her hands. She studied his eyes—happy, blue eyes that sparkled up at her. Then she remembered his comment about the tear gas.

Her heart nearly burst.

"You remember?" It was part exclamation, part question.

He wasn't able to answer. He was buried in a cloud of cotton skirts and a flurry of kisses. When the kisses slowed and turned into long, languid expressions of love, Elise forgot she'd even asked.

She forgot everything but the moment. The rightness of how they fit together, the conflagration they both generated with a mere touch. There would be time for questions later. All the time in the world. But right now she joined Reed in wiping all coherent thoughts from her mind.

Many hours later, in the humidity of New Orleans in June, and under a light covering of sheets, Reed gathered Elise close. She felt his chest vibrate and heard his heart beat faster as he sighed. She snuggled even closer.

"What are you thinking, darlin'?"

He hesitated, as if collecting his thoughts.

"I'm thinking, little one, that I finally feel warm again."

ABOUT THE AUTHOR

Originally from West Virginia, Jenny has lived everywhere from Clark Air Base in the Philippines to Little Rock, Arkansas. She now makes her home in West Tennessee with her husband, son and daughter, and the world's sweetest dog. When she's not writing, she spends her time traveling, researching, taking fencing lessons and riding her Harley.

Jenny is also the author of *Lost Yesterday*, a February 1997 release from Jove, as well as *Waiting for Yesterday*, due out in August 1997.

You can write her at P.O. Box 382132, Germantown, TN 38183-2132.